FELL BEASTS AND FAIR

A NOBLEBRIGHT FANTASY ANTHOLOGY

ISBN 978-0-9891915-7-9

Published in the United Sates of America by Spring Song Press, LLC. www.springsongpress.com

Cover design by Kerry Hynds of Aero Gallerie.

FEATURING

LESLIE J. ANDERSON
C.A. BARRETT
TERRI BRUCE
AARON DAMOMMIO
M.C. DWYER
ANTHONY EICHENLAUB
FRANCESCA FORREST
CHLOE GARNER
W.R. GINGELL
LORA GRAY
KELLY A. HARMON
TOM HOWARD
ROLLIN JEWETT
TOM JOLLY
SAMUEL MARZIOLI
AMANDA NARGI
AIMEE OGDEN
BETH POWERS
DARRELL J. PURSIFUL
CHARLES D. SHELL
APRIL STEENBURGH
ALENA SULLIVAN
TROY TANG

AND EDITED BY

C. J. BRIGHTLEY
AND ROBERT MCCOWEN

CONTENTS

ACKNOWLEDGMENTS

Many thanks go to the talented authors who contributed to this anthology and to all authors who infuse their works with noblebright ideals.

Robert McCowen assisted with every phase of editing this anthology from story selection to copyediting. I'm immensely grateful for his insight and attention to detail.

And of course, the greatest thanks go to you, dear reader, for believing in noblebright fantasy.

C. J. Brightley
cjbrightley.com
springsongpress.com

FOREWORD

Noblebright fantasy offers hope in the darkest moments. In noblebright fantasy, flawed (yet realistic) characters can choose to be kind, honest, and principled even when it hurts. Redemption is possible, and good characters can make a difference.

Noblebright fantasy is fantasy for our time. It isn't utopian fantasy—we all know the world can be dark. Instead, noblebright fantasy offers glimpses of what it looks like to oppose that darkness with courage, integrity, love, and sacrifice, and how those choices can make the world a little brighter.

For more information, please visit Noblebright.org and SpringSongPress.com.

C. J. Brightley
Spring Song Press
SpringSongPress.com

P.S. - Please subscribe to the Spring Song Press newsletter!

Cloudy with a Chance of Dropbears

W.R. Gingell

They say Behind is dangerous and Between is chancy; that the human world alone, with its blind, bumbling occupants is a haven for the Fair Folk. Well, I'm not exactly one of the *fair* folk, and if Australia isn't as dangerous as the most feared parts of Behind, I'll eat my own wooden leg.

Properly speaking, there's Australia Behind and Australia Between, but when it comes to Behind and Between, it's nearly the same thing no matter where in the human world it joins up. Go anywhere Behind and it's the same Behind; all fae and vampires and selkies, that sort of thing. A few of us leprechauns, too. Behind is the place the human world doesn't know exists. Even Between isn't too different; it's just the way it looks that's different—depending on if you know *how* to look, if you get my drift.

It's not the same when it comes to travelling between places in the human world. I've been in civilized places like England and Canada, and it's a world away from the nightmare land of red heat and deadly animals they call Australia. They don't let you into Australia from Behind until you've passed your survival fitness exam, which should just tell you something.

I hadn't passed that exam. I didn't want to pass that exam. I would have gladly spent the rest of my life in a cubicle safely Behind the human world. And yet here I was, stuck headfirst in a tree on the human world side of Australia, with *my* behind exposed to the elements and the dull thud of dropbears hitting the ground around me.

Let me explain. I wasn't planning on going to Australia that day—that day or ever. I'm a leprechaun, the closest thing you can get to a living calculator, and until that day I was perfectly happy crunching numbers in my cubicle. For us, it's about the closest thing you can get to pure happiness unless you own your own private supply of gold coins to count every day. That rainbow with the promised gold at the end of it—that's what a cubicle and something to count means to a leprechaun.

I was ready for a big day. My wooden leg was hurting when I got up, and that means a day of either finding or losing huge amounts of money. And if you're going to tell me a wooden leg can't hurt, you can kick off out of here any time, because mine always hurts when there's going to be big money, so there. I just didn't know whether it was going to be a finding or losing day. Finding or losing doesn't matter to me—I just find out where the money's gone. Now, if it was my money it would matter a lot more, but it's not, is it?

I sat down in my chair at the office in an almost jovial frame of mind. I startled the coffee boy by grinning at him, scaring him so much that he spilled the coffee and had to go back for more. Serve him right, lanky-legged little lollygagger that he was. Grinning a bit wider, I logged onto my work portal and rubbed my hands together to see the first case waiting for me.

"Never failed me yet!" I declared, slapping my wooden leg. The first case that popped up on my portal was the one I'd been working off and on for the last few months; something from a group called Allied Traders. They were a group that worked across the Between border to trade with the human world, coffee and other stuff that the humans do better than Behind; and on paper, things almost looked kosher. *Almost.* Then you went a bit deeper and found that the things you should have found a bit deeper weren't there. Things like human resources—Allied Traders had warehouses on this side and the human side of Between for any resources from the human world—weren't in the warehouse they were meant to be in. Actually, there wasn't anything in the warehouses at all except a very sleepy fae guard once you got past the magical defences. Good thing leprechauns are so good at getting past anything magic, isn't it? That's what I thought, anyway, sitting there and grinning at my portal. I'd taken a trip yesterday, and last night I'd clued in my supervisor. If I did things right for the next twenty years or so, maybe I'd get promoted up the chain for this.

I went and got my own coffee before the coffee boy got back, eager to sniff out more payments that had a suspicious lack of product to go with them. I put it down on my desk and settled myself to sit down, but something sharp and hot seared my leg where my Behind Identify Card should be. I yelped and pinched it out of my pocket. Behind magic is the good stuff, but there's nothing that melts faster than an Identify Card, magic or no magic. Something about magic and the newer human manufactured substances doesn't blend well.

Now that I looked at the card, it was a lot blacker than it should be. Well, parts of it were blacker than they should be and it was still hot in my fingers, and now there was nothing burning in my pocket... I squinted down at it, irritated to find that my glasses weren't around my neck, and reached for the desk where the missing glasses should have been.

My desk wasn't there. Actually, the office wasn't there. No wonder the ground was so squishy beneath my peg—it was real grass, not the magic-fake they put in Behind offices.

Great. Someone had relocated the office without telling me. I'd send off a pretty well loaded message as soon as I found where those goons in Location had parked it this time. I'm as security conscious as the next leprechaun, but there was no way we'd been found so soon after the last move. I looked down at my Identify card again, and it looked a bit red in the middle. Red in the middle, and if I squinted at it just right, there were words making a black scrawl in the centre of the red bit.

Kill the kid and you can come back, it said.

I snuffled a dry laugh down at it. Somebody was having a laugh. It was a bit stupid, though; *kid* was the word used for human children, and who was going to find a kid Behind? I looked a bit closer, and a sticky breeze swept across my forearms, raising goosebumps in spite of its warmth. That wasn't just red behind the writing. It was Red. If somebody was having a laugh, *why was my Identify Card marked Red for Deport?* Deportation Red meant tried, executed, and deported. No return to Behind.

That was stupid. Someone *had* to be having a laugh. I was still Behind... wasn't I? But where in Behind was I? I looked around me, dazedly taking in the dark green foliage of trees and the playground, and the half tree that someone had turned into a house—wait. The *playground?* Fae don't have playgrounds. And why was the heat so heavy today? Where in Behind had access to this kind of muggy heat? Muggy... *muggy* heat? There's no muggy heat Behind; too many weather mages.

"No," I said numbly, sweat springing to my brow. "Because that means I'm—that means I'm in the *human* world."

Red for Deport. I was in the human world.

"What did *I* do?" I demanded of the hollowed-out tree house, my voice high and panicked. "I paid my taxes. *Found* taxes. Gave my leg for the Fae Corps in the Third War!"

I sat down in the grass and buried my head in my hands. This was bad. The worst. I couldn't survive in the human world. I wasn't trained. I wasn't ready. I didn't even have a job! Who would keep me in gold if I had no job? And the humans—

how was I supposed to communicate with them? I didn't even know if you *could* communicate with them; it was bad enough trying to communicate with the milk cows that were brought over from the human world when ours died out.

Something bit me beneath my trousers, and if the air around me was a muggy heat, this was a fiery heat. I yelled and shot to my feet, slapping at the spot, and pinched whatever the heck it was through the trousers and out into the open. It was an ant, squirming and dying, its broken legs flailing at me. With my Sight I could see the poison on its pincers, even if my normal sight wasn't good enough to properly make out the pincers, and when I looked back down at my leg, horrified, I could see the same poison beginning to course through my veins from the point of the bite.

But... but it was so *small*. How could it be so deadly?

I threw the ant away from me and slapped my hand back over the bite, drawing out the poison in the same way I'd drawn out the ant. It came out reluctantly, as fast-spreading as it had been in my blood. I didn't know if my legs were weak because of the poison, or the fact that I'd almost left it too late to treat comfortably. What was this place? What place had such tiny, deadly animals?

And why was it so skin-meltingly *hot*, for all that was gold?

I didn't dare to sit on the ground again. At home the grass was green and plump and cool, free from murderous insects and good for recharging; here, now, I could see that it was teeming with deadly life. Gold only knew what kind of other venomous insects were waiting to kill me. There was a nice, sunny spot on the metal play equipment; it was bright and sunny as well, painted in yellow and orange, and I felt that at least there was a shining spot to the day thus far.

I breathed out a sigh of relief, hopeful of soaking up a little energy from the sun, and sank down on the metal square.

It *burnt*.

For the second time in the last five minutes, I leaped to my feet with a howl, clutching my rear. Was it silver? Who makes human playgrounds out of silver? But there was no debilitating spread of *malaise*, no nausea; just a pained kind of after-burn that faded slowly but left me disinclined to sit down again right away.

It was just hot. So *gold-fired* hot from the sun that it had burned me to sit down on it.

I whimpered a bit. I didn't really care where I was anymore; I just wanted to go back home. I picked a spot in the shady brown instead of the sunny brown, and sat down—this time very carefully—on something wooden and duck-shaped that wobbled beneath me but didn't burn me. A sensation of coolness soothed my burnt backside, but I couldn't feel anything energetic in the grass beneath my feet.

I groaned into my hands. "Where can I even *recharge* in this place?"

"Athelas likes to use the waterfall in Snug," said a voice. "Zero prefers the sea. But if you want to use something nearby, there's always the Huon river."

I looked up wildly. It was a kid. Standing there in front of me with its hands in its pockets. I don't know if it was male or female—you can't tell with humans; they're all so ugly, and they don't smell of anything. At least with Behinders you can tell who's male and who's female by smell. I didn't know how long it had been there, either.

I stared at it while the sweat trickled down my temple and made a prickling line right to my collar.

Kill the kid and you can come back. That's what the writing on my card said. Well, this was the only kid in the area; long-legged and long-haired, it had a hopeful sort of expression to its face. I mean, it was still ugly, but it was ugly in a nice sort of way. It looked like you could pat it on the head without being bitten. Not that I could reach, but still.

"You appeared out of nowhere," it said to me. It sounded thoughtful but not surprised. "I don't know what kind you are."

I glared at it. It knew a bit too much for a human, didn't it? Or was it just confused? I said, "Kind? What do you mean?"

"You know—Behinder." It tilted its head. "I know you are one, just can't tell what kind. You're not tall enough for fae or pouty enough to be a vampire. Are you a troll?"

"Who do you think you're calling a troll!" I demanded, sitting up straight in outrage. The wooden duck wobbled and threatened to dump me in the brown, crackly grass.

"Oh, sorry," it said. "Didn't mean to offend you. I know a troll and she's really nice."

"That's because they're eager-to-please little nubkinses!" I snarled, clinging with both hands to the wobbling duck's wooden handles. "They should just accept that they're ugly and no one loves them."

"Oh," said the kid. It didn't try to say anything else; just sat there as if it was waiting for me to notice something.

I ignored it. "Red for Deport," I muttered to myself. "Who has that clout and who would do it? Who am I? Just a little government lep' looking for his next pay stream. No need to mark me Red for Deport, was there? Who's the sorry beetle that sent me off into the human world without a trial?"

"I don't know about that," said the kid, "but I don't think we're actually in the human world."

"'Course we are," I said, without paying too much attention. "Where else would we be? You're a human. The place *feels* human—gives me a nasty shiver."

"Ye-es," said the kid uneasily. "But—"

"And I'm a leprechaun. Don't go calling me a troll."

That distracted it. "Oh. There are leprechauns Behind! What's your name?"

"Five-Four-One."

The kid giggled. "Really?"

I scowled at it. "That's my batch number. What else would it be? Wipe that smirk off your face."

"Sorry," the kid said, but it was still grinning. "But around here there's a saying that goes *I'd rather have a number than a name like that*, and you've already got a number, so—!"

Maybe this one wasn't as intelligent as I'd thought it was. At least it wasn't as stupid as the human cows had been.

It was clever enough to notice my scowl growing. It managed to smother its grin a bit, and asked, "Why are you here, anyway?"

"Curious, aren't you?" I said sourly. I sneaked a peek at my card, but it was still red and black, the writing still jumping out at me. *Kill the kid and you can come back.* That was all well and good, but why should I? Who was this mysterious shanghai-er to tell me to kill someone for them? Even a human kid. That's the sort of thing I don't approve of.

But if I didn't, how would I get home? I couldn't live here. I needed my gold. I needed a place to recharge. Without those, I would die even sooner than a human in this human world.

I looked at the kid meditatively, which seemed to make it nervous. "What?" it asked.

"You," I said. "What are you doing here?"

"Same as you," it said, a bit more cheerfully.

"What?" Did it have a card, too? Death matches were illegal Behind, but the governing powers could be stretchy when it came to applying Behind laws to fae in the human world.

"I just appeared, like you," said the kid. "Well, I think so, anyway. Right in the middle of making dinner, too. They're gonna be annoyed—'s'pecially JinYeong. Stuff always happens when I'm cooking his choice."

"Cooking?" I glared at it. "What the everlasting gold are you chuntering about? Nobody cares about whether or not your dinner gets cooked."

"Yeah, but that's the thing," the kid argued. "JinYeong cares, and that means he's gonna be stroppy as all heck when he finds me."

"I don't care if JinYeong is stroppy as all heck!" I snapped. I didn't even know what *stroppy as all heck* meant. "What is this place, and why have you dragged me here? You've no business marking me Red for Deport!"

The kid looked indignant. "I just *said*! I didn't have anything to do with it; I was in the kitchen and then I was here. I mean, I think I know where I am, but when I tried to start walking home I couldn't get out."

"Out?"

"Yeah. It's weird; I can usually get in and out of Between without any problems, but whenever I try to walk past the picnic table to go home, I find myself walking back past the treehouse again."

"This isn't Between," I said, very slowly and loudly. "It's the human world." For all that was gold! It was a human! Why didn't it know its own world?

The kid looked like it was trying not to grin again. "Yeah," it said. "But you try walking out and see how you go."

I didn't like the way it was grinning, but I had to try now. I stumped toward the picnic table, my wooden leg sinking too deeply into the brown grass, and found myself walking past the treehouse instead.

"Flamin' weird, isn't it?" said the kid, in a chummy sort of way. "What d'you reckon's happened?"

I glared at it. Was it stupid or senseless? No one in their right mind should be that comfortable and trusting when they had been thrown into a closed circle with someone who, for all they knew, could have been ordered to kill them.

"Maybe we should see if we can get over it," the kid suggested. "I reckon its fae magic, and fae don't think about loopholes as much as I thought they would. Well, not when it comes to humans, anyway. They think we're as dumb as cows over here, so they don't usually make things too hard for us."

I coughed and tapped my wooden leg against the ground. "That right?"

The kid grinned again. "Yeah. Oi. If you give me a leg up, I reckon I can climb over the top of whatever spell they're using."

"A *leg up*?" Was that meant to be a joke?

"Or I'll give you one, but I think I might be lighter than you."

Oh. It wanted a *boost*. "I can get you to the first branch of that tree," I said. On the side that wasn't road and gravel, the trees surrounded the playground and overhung it; at least one of those branches should be caught in the same bubble as us.

And if the kid was right—who was I kidding? Of course it was right. There's nothing so snooty and self-confident as an intelligent fae. And they *all* think they're intelligent.

"Should I climb on your shoulders, or—"

"No!"

"Oh. Well, how am I going to—"

"Turn arou—" I snapped, slapping at the containment spell to see exactly where it was. And that was as far as I got. Something raw and strong and magical threw me across the playground the instant I touched fae magic. I hit the tree house, though it felt more like the tree house hit me, and for a very long, dusty, grassy time, I whimpered up at the sky.

There was the sound of running footsteps, and a voice yelled, "Five! Five, are you okay?"

I considered whimpering again, but the kid might have heard me. "No, I'm not okay!"

"Right," said the kid. Its face appeared above me, then wiry arms tugged at me until I could sit up. "Yeah. Um, can you stand up?"

"No!" I snarled, and stood up a bit hazily. I'd been winded, and that was as bad as it was, but there was no way I was going say that after the fuss I'd made. "If I've broken anything—!"

The kid was grinning again. Guess I'd underestimated how much it knew about injuries. "Look on the bright side," it said. "At least your peg leg isn't broken."

"With all this gold-perishing sunlight there's no other way to look at things," I grumbled.

"Yeah, the hole in the ozone layer is right above us," the kid said cheerfully. "Wanna try again?"

"No!" There was a pause before I said grudgingly, "Yes. But I have to pee first. Another impact like that and the grass'll think the rains have come to this gold-perishingly barren place."

There was a barely stifled laugh from the kid, but it said, "Wouldn't do that f'I were you."

"What? Why can't I pee?"

"It's not that you can't," the kid said, "but there was a redback on the toilet seat in the loo yesterday, and I don't know where it went."

"What's a redback?"

"Spider. Pretty deadly."

"Either it's deadly or it isn't."

The kid considered that. "Then I s'pose it depends on how quickly you get to the hospital, and if they have the stuff to treat it."

"I don't have to sit."

"I didn't say it lives under the loo seat; that's just where I saw it last. I was moving pretty quick then, so I didn't see where it went after that. And I think it got touched by Between a bit, so it might be bigger than usual."

"Is *everything* here trying to kill me?"

"Not everything," said the kid. Its eyes, which had been looking around curiously at something I hadn't seen, widened. "Oh. But *those* might be."

There were so many trees out there, all green and brown from the heat, that I didn't see them until the kid pointed them out. About four or five *very big* bears, their greyish pelts blending into the branches they clung to with long sharp claws, their eyes black and glittering in the shadowy foliage. They were each the size of a decently grown polar bear, surrounding the playground from every direction that contained trees, and now the tree branches began to shake as they made their way toward us.

"What are those? *What are those!?*" My voice cracked. I'm not proud of it, but that's what happened.

"I think they're dropbears," the kid said thoughtfully. "It's weird. They shouldn't exist."

"Dropbears?" I said feebly. "What are dropbears?" Whatever else they were, they were definitely Between creatures; chimeras made of possibility, magic, and malice.

"Kind of like really mean koalas," the kid said. It was looking less thoughtful and more alarmed as the dropbears shuddered closer through the trees. "They drop from trees and tear you to bloody pieces. They weren't—I mean, they don't exist. They're a thing that was made up for TV ads. They're not a thing that properly comes from Between."

I squeezed my eyes shut and hoped desperately that when I opened them, the dropbears would have disappeared. They didn't.

I said, "They do now."

But wait. We weren't Between—we were firmly in the human world. How in the woody green were Between-magicked dropbears approaching from *the human world*?

"How?" I panted, mopping more sweat from my brow than I'd thought possible for my body to contain in its entirety. "We're not Between! They shouldn't be here!"

"Yeah," said the kid. "That's what I thought. That's why I said we're Between, even though it doesn't feel quite the same. Zero isn't here, so I thought I'd wait and see what happened, but then you arrived so I s'pose we should try to do something about it."

"They been there all along!?"

"Mostly," the kid said. "They didn't start coming closer until you started flying around, though."

"*I wasn't flying around!* I was suffering blowback from your stupid—"

"I don't think you can really blame that on me," the kid said seriously. "It was the containment thingie. I'm not magical or anything."

"It's *Other*. You say you're *not Other*."

"Yeah. So you can't blame that on me, can you?"

"Well, it was your idea!" I said nastily. "I don't go around getting close to Other spells for no reason. I suppose you think I just threw myself in the air for the fun of it!"

"I thought it was pretty funny," the kid muttered, but when I snarled "*What?*" at it, it cleared its throat and tried to look innocent. "Nothing."

"See how funny you find it all when the dropbears get to us," I told it.

"Wait, though," said the kid uncertainly. "The spell should stop them too, shouldn't it?"

"Wouldn't count on it," I said sourly. Of all the ways to go! I'd survived the Third War, even if my right leg hadn't, and now I was about to be sent off by a pack of dropbears. Mind you, the dropbears were in the trees; they were still approaching, but it wasn't too much of a stretch to think they might not be clever enough to try and go over the spell.

Only they never did drop from the trees; they kept lumbering through the foliage in a storm of shaking until they were well past the tree we'd been trying to boost each other into.

"Oh," said the kid. "Reckon they figured out the spell, too."

"Yeah."

"We should try to get out again," said the kid.

It was clearer toward the front of the playground that faced the road, so we legged it toward that part. There was only one tree there, but before we got to its trunk the spell set us hurrying back toward the treehouse again.

"Reckon the treehouse is the centre of the spell," the kid panted, when we'd righted ourselves again. "Look, we can reach that branch, though. You ready to try again?"

I wasn't, but I said, "Yeah," anyway. What else could we do?

"Maybe I should try boosting you this time," the kid said.

"Yeah." I wouldn't have suggested it myself because I'm not a coward, but since it had suggested the idea itself... "That'll work."

And it worked. Oh boy, did it work. The idea had been to give me a gentle boost and circumvent whatever gold-perished magic some Other had put on the inside of the spell.

It gave me a boost, all right. We couldn't make sure exactly where the Other magic was without touching it, but it sure knew where we were. The kid boosted, I hit the Other magic, and with the Other magic behind it, that boost sent me sailing further into the air than the first jolt had done. I flew back over the playground, grass and trees a brown and green blur around me. There was a bigger blur of brown for just long enough for me to realise that I was going to hit the tree house headfirst this time, then I was stuck like a cork in a bottle.

And there I was, somewhere in Australia, human world side, head and shoulders in a tree with my rear exposed to the elements and the dropbears thudding to the grass all around me.

"Better wriggle!" yelled the kid. "They're in!"

I wriggled. I wriggled harder than I'd done since I was hatched, a crawling feeling running up and down the leg I didn't have any more, warning that my other leg was about to be bitten off. A scratching lower in the tree house made me stop short, unsure whether it was safer in or out, but then the kid popped up from a small hole in the floor and grabbed my arms.

There was another brief moment where I felt like a cork in a bottle before I exploded inward. The kid yelped as I head-butted its stomach but hauled me to my feet without retaliating.

"Couldn't wedge the door shut," it gasped. "It's too small for them to get in that way, anyway. Wouldn't count on the treehouse being strong enough to stop 'em if they really want us, though."

I poked my head out of the round window for another look at the dropbears. "They want us," I said grimly. All five of them were sniffing around the base of the treehouse. They didn't look too bright, but they didn't have to be to get us.

"I reckon it's a trap," the kid said. "They were out there, but they didn't get interested until you got here."

"It's not a trap," I said. "It's insurance."

"Insurance for what?"

"Mind your own business."

"It is my business! They want to eat me! Well, I suppose it's you they want to eat, actually, but I don't think they'll stop at you."

"No, it's you they want," I said, without thinking.

"I don't mean to be rude," said the kid, "but that doesn't make much sense. They only tried to come in after you got here."

"It can't be me they're after," I said. "I've been given a task to do and I can't do it if I'm dead."

"Then what am I here for?"

"To die," I said, and it wasn't wrong.

"I wonder if Zero and Athelas know about this?" the kid said.

It looked pretty comfortable for someone who was about to be eaten by dropbears. Was it expecting me to do something, or was it still waiting for that *Zero* it kept talking about? Trustful didn't even cover this kid.

"We came here a couple days ago because the locals have been hearing weird stuff and seeing lights at night; that sort of thing."

"So I'm not the first to arrive here," I said. I hadn't meant to say it aloud, but there was something about the kid's trustful face that made it easy to talk more than I should. "There have been other Behinders sent here."

"Yeah, that's what I reckon. And people have been disappearing."

"People disappearing?"

The kid nodded. "Yeah. A fair few of 'em, too. Locals, tourists, seasonal workers; doesn't seem to matter who. I reckon the dropbears must have been getting 'em, but why are there Between dropbears here?"

Humans disappearing in a particular spot? Now that was a pattern I was familiar with, and it was a pattern that didn't involve dropbears. The dropbears were part of something else altogether; *this*—this place was a human resources source. Not human-made or human-sourced resources like coffee; human resources. A stock supply of humans.

And that meant that Allied Traders was a human stock mill.

I grinned. "Now I'm getting somewhere!" I said, satisfaction thick in my voice. It's not like a human stock mill is *illegal,* so to speak. But there are some very specific rules about how the humans can be used, consent, and the safe disposal of them once they're through their indentures. Behind likes to stay a secret.

"What?" asked the kid, its voice quick and indignant. "What did you just figure out?"

"I know why your humans have been disappearing." Now, just how much could I tell it without it figuring out I'd been sent to kill it? "Someone Behind is stealing humans to sell."

"We'll see about that!" said the kid, with a martial light to its eyes. "Just *wait* until I tell Zero about this! Someone is going to be really sorry!"

"No one is going to be sorry," I snapped, "except us! They're going to get away scott free because we're going to die. There are still dropbears out there and we're still in here. They only have to wait. Or break the tree down."

The kid made a *piffle* kind of noise, which was annoying because this wasn't the situation where anyone should be making a *piffle* noise.

"We're properly Between now," it said. It was grinning; a tough, sideways sort of grin that was directly at odds with the usual trustful look to its face. "The dropbears brought it with them; can't you feel it?"

I scowled at it, because now that it had said so, I *could* sense it. "What's it to you whether we're Between, Behind, or human world?"

"That's the thing." It was still grinning. "Between likes me."

"It *likes*—Between doesn't like people."

"Yeah, well, I can do stuff here."

That settled it; the kid was wrong in the head. Humans couldn't access Between, and they certainly couldn't *do* things Between.

"Don't believe me?"

"Nope," I said, and looked out the window again. One of the dropbears slapped a paw against the tree house and the whole thing shuddered, us with it.

"Okay," said the kid, and pulled a sword out of thin air. No, it was an umbrella that looked like a sword. And now it looked like a sword again.

I blinked hard. It was a sword, but it hadn't always been a sword—no, in the human world it wasn't a sword. Behind, it had always been a sword. Between, depending on how you saw it, it could be a sword or it could be an umbrella.

I was definitely having trouble seeing. "Gold perish it!" I snarled. "Who taught you how to do that?"

"JinYeong," said the kid, admiring the sword. It looked pretty pleased with itself, and I didn't much blame it; pulling something out of Between is meant to be impossible for a human. Even for a Behinder, pulling a sword Between isn't the easiest thing in the world. "But Zero was the one who showed me how to see it properly. I've been practising pretty hard lately. Lucky, isn't it?"

"Yeah," I said, with a dry throat.

"Want something?"

"Yeah."

The kid looked around doubtfully. There wasn't a lot to choose from in the tree house; the umbrella was the biggest, sharpest thing in there. Apart from that, there were crumpled little canisters of what looked like thin metal, a few woolly bits of string, something whippy and wooden that could have been for supporting plants, and an assortment of sharp little things that were a mix of glass, metal, and wood.

The kid didn't look worried. "You have this one," it said, passing me the sword.

Kill the kid, said the words burned across my mind, *and you can come back.*

"I don't want it!" I snapped. "Gold perish it, do I look like my arms are long enough for that thing?"

"And there's your leg," the kid said. It was a bit pinker than it had been, though I wasn't sure why. "I didn't think about that. Sorry. How are you at archery?"

"All right," I said, hunching my shoulders. "And I'll thank you to remember that I can still cut a pretty pace with my peg leg!"

"Oh good!" the kid said, and picked up the whippy piece of wood and the longest piece of string. By the time the light of the window fell on them, they weren't plain wood and string any longer; they were a neat little recurve bow and bowstring. "Can you string it? I can't ever get them to bend back enough."

I took it and strung it in two seconds flat. I might have been trying to prove my mettle, but it was a good thing; the whole tree house shook again a moment after. The kid, who was reaching out to snap off old, dried twigs from the outside of the treehouse, nearly fell out the window. I grabbed it by the belt— why did I do that? I didn't have to do that—and after a furious bout of wriggling it came back in, brandishing six arrows at me.

"Enough?"

"Maybe," I said. That left me one bad shot, which in normal circumstances would be enough. This wasn't normal—but then, nothing in war was ever normal, either, and I'd survived that. "Not if they get in here first."

"Yeah, that's what I thought," said the kid. "You all right by yourself?"

"What?"

"Don't want to waste the sword."

"Do you know how to use it?"

"A bit," said the kid. "Ish. Zero hasn't finished my training yet."

"If you can't string a recurve, you can't hack down that lot with a sword," I said. It had been a while since I'd seen combat, but I still knew that much.

"Just as well you're gonna be up here shooting them, then; isn't it?"

"What?"

"Just make sure you shoot all of 'em so I don't have to do too much work." This time, it sounded like the kid was trying to be cheerful. "I mean, someone's gotta get 'em away from the base; it's not like you can shoot them at this angle. And maybe Zero will come soon. I don't *think* he'll leave me here."

"No use thinking about someone who isn't here," I said. "We're alone until we kill those bears and get over the spell."

"If I get 'em away from the base, reckon you've got a good shot?"

"Get 'em away from the base of the tree and I'll shoot every gold-perishing son of 'em," I said grimly. The kid was right: close range was good, but that angle was too tight.

"All right," said the kid, and vanished.

"Green and gold!" I swore. I hadn't expected it to go that quickly. I'd expected a bit more hesitation, a bit more whining—maybe a few tears.

I poked my head out the window just in time to see the kid streak from the door, right between two of the dropbears. It was howling at the top of its lungs, which surprised the dropbears so much that they just stood where they were for a moment before they lunged into the chase.

The kid was quick on its feet, I'll give it that. It wasn't even trying to fight, it was just running around yelling, waving its sword. I grinned a bit before I realised what I was doing and scowled instead. The dropbears lumbered after the kid, and I saw my shot clearing up. I edged the bow through the window, no longer afraid to have it knocked out of my hands by a high-swiping dropbear, and shuffled my upper body after it.

Just in time, too. They were in range, and at just the right angle. I lifted the bow—hesitated for a fraction of a second. *Kill the kid and you can come back.* The kid was still running in circles, but it couldn't do that for too long in this kind of heat. I didn't even have to kill it. All I had to do was wait, and the dropbears would do the job. It wasn't like the kid could make it back into the tree house now.

It was just a fraction of a second's hesitation, but in that time, one of them reached out faster than the kid could run and slapped it into the ground. I didn't hesitate again. My bow came up and I shot; twice at the one hanging over the kid, then at the next, then again, and again. The kid scrambled to its feet, bloody and staggering, and waved at me.

I nocked the last arrow and roared, *"Get down!"*

The kid dropped right to its stomach—who had trained it to do that?—and I snatched back the string on my last shot. I was too quick; my elbow hit the side of the tree house and the shot went wide. Flat on its stomach, the kid grimaced. It looked back at the dropbear and then over at its sword. There was no way it would make it to the sword before the dropbear got to it.

What else could I throw? What else was there to throw? The kid was going to die, and then I could go home, but what else was there to throw?

I furiously unscrewed my peg leg and hurled it at the kid. Stupid trustful little thing, it was still looking up at me. It caught the peg leg in its right hand and curled around in the same movement to flick it in the dropbear's face. The peg leg flickered, grew, shrank again—and hit the dropbear between the eyes. It bounced off, but before it hit the ground the kid was sprinting toward the treehouse.

What in the green and gold did that kid just do to my peg leg? And why didn't it hold?

"Shove over!" said the kid's voice.

I shoved over. It climbed through the hole in the floor, panting, and waved a crooked twig at me.

"Got another one!"

"What do you expect me to hit with this?" I grumbled. The stick had been crooked, and as an arrow, it was still crooked. "Clean your face up."

The kid swiped one hand below its nose, smearing blood. "It's not broken," it said cheerfully. "Reckon your leg is toast, though. Sorry about that. I tried to make it be something else, but it was *really* sure about being a peg leg."

"That was a good leg," I said glumly. The dropbear was out there gnawing on it, stupid beast. "You've got a black eye."

"I know. I can feel it swelling. What are we going to do about that last one? Can you shoot it through the window?"

"Help me down to the door at the bottom," I said. We were probably dead if I missed, anyway; at least out there we were closer to other sticks that might turn into better arrows. "I don't want to try shooting this thing out of the window."

"Yeah," said the kid, wriggling down through the hole in the floor first. It took the bow and arrow from me, then grabbed my whole leg as it came down and steadied my drop to the floor. A bit of training and this kid might make a good officer's boy. "We want to give you the best chance."

"Best chance, my eye!" I grumbled, steadying my half leg on the kid's bent knee. "Just get ready to run for another stick before the dropbear gets to us."

Then I took careful aim, steadied my wrist, and shot.

I missed, of course. The arrow was crooked, for all that's green and gold! But it hit the confinement spell across the playground, and where a straight arrow might have careened sideways due to the spell, this one turned sideways of its own accord for a bare instant before the spell pinged it back across the playground at twice the speed and a terrifying accuracy.

It went through the dropbear's head so fast that the bear probably never felt it. Something thunked into the treehouse with a bloody *smack!* and the bear collapsed into the brown grass, spilling blood.

"Flaming heck!" said the kid.

We stared at the dead bear in silence for a few minutes. I was ruminating on the certainty that I would never again in my life make a shot like that, whether or not there was a Fourth War. The kid must have been thinking of something else, because soon it said unexpectedly, "Oi. What happened to your pants?"

I clutched at the back of my trousers. "What do you mean, what happened to my pants?"

"Not there," it said. "The pocket."

My hand slapped the charred bit of cloth that should have been my pocket, and something black and rectangular came away in my hand, shedding tendrils of fabric that floated away on the hot air.

My card. My card was black as ink—black as hopeless death. Now it wasn't just Red for Deportment, it was No Return Whatsoever and Kill on Sight.

I looked down at it, and the kid looked down at it.

"What's that mean?" it asked. "That doesn't look good."

"Nothing," I said. I flicked the card away into the corpse-filled playground and it fluttered for a moment like black ash before it disintegrated. "Don't need it any more, that's all."

"Wait," the kid said. Its brow was furrowed. "Black... Athelas said something about black-carding a Behinder—wait! They're going to kill you?"

"D'like to see 'em try," I muttered. "I've still got one more leg."

"That thing you said you had to do," the kid said unexpectedly. "The errand—it was to kill me, wasn't it?"

"What?"

"You were meant to kill me, weren't you?"

"What—how did you know?"

"Makes sense," the kid said, shrugging. It wandered toward the most freshly dead dropbear and prodded it with one foot. "You remember I said people have been disappearing here and around Tassie?"

"I remember." I didn't look at the kid; for a ridiculous reason I couldn't pinpoint, I felt ashamed. Maybe it was because of how often I'd actually thought about killing it.

"Yeah, well some of 'em came back. Dead. None of the dead ones disappeared around here, but they all came back here, dead. And then I was pulled here, and there you were, and the dropbears... so... Do they always send you?"

"What?! No, they don't always send me! I'm just a pay-cheque lep'! I haven't drawn bow for twenty years, since the last war!"

"Oh." The kid seemed to accept that, which irritated me. Why was it still so trusting? "Then that was some flaming good shooting."

"Stop trusting people so quickly!" I snapped at it. "That's how you end up dying!"

"I've got good instincts about people," said the kid blithely. "So your card is black because you didn't kill me?"

I shrugged. "Never did learn to do what I was told. I found something I shouldn't have found, and someone sent me here because they wanted to make sure I didn't bring it up somewhere inconvenient."

"Oh," it said. Then, unexpectedly, "Want your leg back? It's a bit chewed up, but it'll still work."

It brandished the mutilated peg leg at me—when did it find that?—and a gobbet of dropbear spit smacked into brown dirt.

A rush of affection coursed through me. That was a good leg, that was. Lasted through the second half of a war and a dropbear attack. I'd polish up those bite marks nice and shiny and it'd be just as good as new.

"Go on, then," I said.

The kid cheerfully tried to screw my mutilated wooden leg back on—all right for *it* to be cheerful, *it* was only sporting a black eye and bloody nose; no one was going to kill it on sight—and promptly knocked me over again.

I glared at it and tried to get up, but something bigger sent me flying head-over-heels with one blow. When I managed to unscramble my limbs and my brains, there were three much larger figures in front of the kid. It wasn't until I was upright that I realized who they were, and then I wished I'd stayed on the ground.

I knew them all.

Massive, silver, and icily furious, that one in the centre was Lord Sero, heir to half the Behind world. Zero...the kid had said *Zero*. If the kid's *Zero* was Lord Sero, then—then that Athelas she'd spoken of—

My stomach dropped even further. At Lord Sero's left hand was Athelas, steward to Lord Sero; genteel, pleasant, and smiling politely. And if you don't know better than to trust that, there's no hope for you. On Lord Sero's right was *that vampire*. Not everyone knows about him; I guess I'm just lucky. I'd never met him before—though I'd seen his tracks—didn't want to meet him now. He was looking at me like he was curious about how long it would take to drain the blood from someone of my size as opposed to someone of a more average height.

All three of them. All three of them together.

I was going to die.

Great. Twice in one day. If it came right down to a choice between Lord Sero and dropbears, I would have picked the dropbears. At least they were stupid enough to go for a wooden leg.

I didn't even have time to blink before Lord Sero had me by the throat. I gaped up at him, completely out of words. What could I say? I didn't know what I'd done wrong. If he was angry at me for saving the kid, then why was he standing between me and it? If he was trying to protect it, why was he scruffing me?

So I just sort of choked at him for a moment or two until he said, in icy, fragmented words, "*What*. Are you doing. With. My. *Pet?*"

I choked at him again. This time, it could have sounded like, "*What?*"

"*Ah, baegopa!*" sighed the vampire, around Lord Sero's shoulder. I didn't know what he meant by the words, but the cold, sharp-edged grin he shot me was pretty clear. If Lord Sero didn't choke me to death, the vampire would drain me.

"Oi!" yelled a voice. I had the feeling it had been yelling for a while, but do excuse me if I was more concerned with the vampire and the fae. "Let go of him!"

Lord Sero turned, taking me with him. The vampire did too, still showing that half, tooth-edged, and utterly humourless grin, and we all stared at the kid. It stared right back at us, bloody, defiant, and ready to die. It looked so small and helpless.

Did that little human thing *really* just raise its voice at the Lord Sero?

"Let go of him!" it demanded again. This time it kicked him in the shin, too.

I winced and ducked my head, but Lord Sero only blinked. He looked down at the kid and said in an experimental sort of way, "Bad Pet!"

"He saved my life!" the kid yelled. "What did you hit him for?"

Athelas, alone of the four of them, looked amused. "We may have acted rashly," he said. "Zero, perhaps we should put our good friend the leprechaun down to recover. He seems anxious."

"*Ajig baegopa*," said the vampire, but he put his hands in his pockets and backed away leisurely as if that's what he'd been going to do anyway.

"We'll get you something else to eat," Athelas said to the vampire, as Lord Sero put me down on the ground very gently. "Pet will cook when we get home."

"I should put holy water in it," grumbled the kid.

The vampire looked startled. "*Ya! Petteu — noh —* "

"Holy water won't kill him," Lord Sero pointed out.

"No, but it makes him sneeze something flamin' good," said the kid vindictively.

"'S'cuse me," I said. "But if you've decided not to kill me, maybe I could just slip away sort of quietly—"

"What about your card?" the kid asked. "You can't get back Behind, can you?"

"I'll sort something out," I said hastily. "No need to worry yourself about me."

Athelas looked mildly amused. "What's this about his card?"

"He had one," the kid said. "Someone made it black, though. I think they did it because he wouldn't kill me."

The vampire's eyes went dark again, and he took a step forward. Lord Sero didn't move, but his voice was still cold when he asked, "So you *were* sent to kill Pet?"

"You've scared him again!" the kid said accusatorily. "Look, his wooden leg is drilling holes in the ground!"

I squeezed my eyes shut briefly and begged the kid, "*Please stop trying to help me!*" Every time it tried to help me, things got a little bit worse.

"Someone's sending people through Between," the kid said. It didn't listen real well, for someone with two ears still intact. "Far as I can tell, anyway. It's what they did to Five-Four-One. They're using normal Behind people to murder humans, we think. They kick them through without warning, tell them to kill someone, and if they don't their cards are blackened so they can never get back. But *he* didn't kill me. I think that's what the dropbears were for, to make sure."

"Who sent you?" Lord Sero asked. If I wasn't already feeling icy to my toes, I would have frozen.

"Can't know for certain, your lordship," I said stiffly, professional instinct taking over from personal. I must be crazy.

"*Ya,*" said the vampire silkily. "*Chugolae?*"

Even the kid looked worried. "He wants to kill you. Are you sure you really don't know?"

I cleared my throat. "Might have been a few odd quirks in the money trail of a company I've been following the last few months."

"What quirks?"

"Um." I glanced between Lord Sero and the vampire, unsure of which one I wanted to keep an eye on the most. "They're a group called Allied Traders; they trade with a few companies on this side of Between."

The kid blinked. "There are other humans who know about the Between and Behind?"

"You're not the only one, sunshine," I said, forgetting myself. I turned back to Lord Sero. "I mean, well, your lordship, um—well, they've been trading in what they call organic resources, but their holding sites are a front."

"No stock at any of them?"

"Not a sausage. I only caught onto them because they've been trying to be a bit clever with their taxes. Last night I told my supervisor about the investigation so I could take it up the chain."

"And this morning you find yourself thrown into the human world with orders to kill a certain human or risk never coming home," said Athelas. He was smiling. "A swift, decisive action."

"Got it in one," I said. My tone might have been a bit sour; I wasn't smiling about it all, but there was no way I was going to try and stop *him* from smiling. "And those empty warehouses—"

"Ohhh!" said the kid. It was angry again. "They've been— the *people* are the stock? I know you said they were *selling* them, but—!"

"Interesting." That was Athelas again. Trust him to find it interesting. "A two-pronged business; Behind, a human stock mill—"

"In the human world, a murder for hire set up," I nodded. "It's probably how they're paying for their human stock. Want to bet they're using all normal Behinders for it? If I'm righteous, I can't go home to tell about it; if I'm a killer, I'm home but in as deep as they are."

"*Munjae dulkae issoh,*" said the vampire silkily.

"Why *two* problems?" asked the kid. "We only need to find out who's been sending Behinders through to kill humans and stop them stealing other humans, don't we? They're the same problem."

"No, there are two problems," agreed Lord Sero.

"Perhaps three," murmured Athelas, and for what felt like the first time in ages, I grinned a bit.

Lord Sero shot him a frosty look.

"A visit to the human front of Allied Traders is in order, I think," said Athelas, ignoring both the frosty look from Lord Sero and a frowning one from the kid, who didn't understand the interaction but definitely saw it.

I grinned a bit more, because I wondered which one of them was going to tell their pet that the second problem was finding out who had hired someone to kill their pet through the intermediary of Allied Traders; or that the third problem was how that person knew this pet was cared for enough to merit being killed.

"You," Lord Sero said to me, "You're coming, too."

That wiped the grin from my face. It's probably part of why he said it. "Your lordship, they'll kill me if I go there!"

"They'll kill you if they catch you here, too," Athelas said mildly.

"Thanks," I said. "Got that idea myself."

There's a certain kind of calm to company buildings Behind. Some of that is because they're rooted in the surrounding greenery to keep their assorted Fae and Other employees as happy and productive as possible. Part of it is because Fae and Other are tricky folks who love to find tricky ways around business.

There was a kind of calm to the human offices of Allied Traders, too; but this calm felt like more of a smug calm. Something that got up my nose because it suggested no one could mess with them, and anyone messing with them was going to have a bad time.

It was a good feeling to break up a bit of that calm the moment I entered the building. It was a smallish two story building, unimpressive concrete on the outside but all white modernity on the inside, and I could feel the edge of Between that hung around it the minute I got in. They weren't expecting a leprechaun, and they weren't too happy to have one in there, either; all three of the secretaries in the lower level trotted after me, bleating, as I took the elevator up to the top floor.

One of them must have managed to warn the top floor, because when the doors dinged open, there was a meeting party. Well, a guy in a suit, anyway. There were a few sleek cubicles up here, with a few sleek humans pretending to work while they stole glances at me, but when they saw that I was a leprechaun, half of them rose to their feet to gawk shamelessly.

"Good evening, sirs and madams," I announced. "Please remain in your seats. Your company is being audited."

"On whose authority?" demanded the one in front of me. "Stay where you are, everyone. I'll handle this. Now, I don't know who you are, but—"

"You're the boss, are you?"

"I am the head of the board," said the human, drawing itself up. "Who are you, and what authority do you represent?"

"I'm with the BTA," I offered.

It smirked at me, which I found annoying. "Then you'd better sit down while I call your boss," it said. "I think you'll find your authority doesn't go for much around here."

"Then I suppose it's a good thing I'm not here under the authority of the BTA, isn't it?" That wiped the smug look from its face momentarily, which pleased me so much that I tapped my peg against the floor twice, smartly.

"But you said—"

"Didn't say I was here under the authority of the BTA, did I?" I reminded him.

"Then whose authority *are* you—"

"His," I said, as the elevator dinged again. I jerked my thumb behind me and cleared the way for Lord Sero, who was filling the elevator doorway behind me. The human swallowed and fell back; and as it did so Lord Sero stepped through the door, Athelas and the vampire flanking him. The human kid trotted in behind them, observing the scene with interest.

"Are you the head of the board?" Lord Sero's voice could have shaken the foundations of the building—or maybe it was just me that felt the trembling right to my bones.

"Yes." That was a definite tremor in his voice. I had the feeling he knew exactly who and what Lord Sero was. "Why do you want to know?"

"I want to know who you're working with Behind, who authorised a human mill start up, and who gave you the job of killing our pet."

"Your—your *pet*?"

The kid touched one finger to its eyebrow in a salute. "Hi."

"I'm not authorised to give you that information."

The vampire JinYeong laughed and said something softly.

"He says," said the kid, "that it'll be more fun finding out this way, anyway."

"Pet," said Athelas, "Show the head of the board into his office for us."

The kid shrugged and went and opened the door. The head of the board walked past it, his face almost as white as Lord Sero's and vanished within. The kid came back to stand next to me and hissed, "Won't he just call the Behind offices if we leave him alone in there?"

Athelas smiled faintly.

I said in an undertone, "That's what they're counting on."

"Doesn't make sense to me," the kid said. "Oi. I think that one's trying to sneak away."

That one was wearing a skirt, so I suppose it was female. She looked like she was trying to back away quietly, but when she bumped into JinYeong, who somehow managed to be behind her without a moment's notice, she sat down again very quickly.

One of the trousered ones in another cubicle asked, "Can we go? You've got our boss."

"You," said Lord Sero, "will stay. You will all stay."

"What did we do?" blustered the human. "We're employees! We're not responsible for what our company does!"

"Employees?" I laughed. I hadn't spent the last three weeks going over every inch of Allied Traders for nothing. "You're board members, every one of you!"

The female tilted her chin. "All right, what if we are? What we're doing isn't illegal, and we're making an unprecedented link between Human and Other kind."

"You tried to have me killed!" said the kid indignantly. "That's illegal over here!"

"We're not a human company," said the female. "We're a Behind company and we fall under Behind laws."

"And it's not like we've done anything but facilitate a thriving industry across borders," said another of the board members. "There's nothing you can do to us, legally!"

"Nothing according to human law," said Lord Sero, with a white, glittering smile that held no humour. "But we don't run by human law, either."

"We've done nothing against Behind law, either!"

"Between you and the dropbears," I said to the whites of all those self-righteous, terrified eyes, "I'd pick the dropbears every time. At least they only wanted to eat us; they wouldn't have tried to tell us to be grateful to help the ecosystem along."

"There's the little matter of coerced murder for hire and tampering with Identify Cards," Athelas said.

"You can't prove that!" said another of the suited ones.

The vampire laughed again.

"What an odd notion of our job you seem to have," said Athelas. "We, on the other hand, have a really very good idea of yours."

"Yeah," said the kid, scowling. "And we don't like it."

"You should go downstairs now, Pet," Athelas said pleasantly.

"What? They tried to kill me! I don't want to go!"

"Take her out," said Lord Sero to me.

Her? It was a she?

"It," said Athelas, in a reminding sort of way.

The kid said, "Oi!" at him.

"Yes, it!" Lord Sero snapped. "Take it out!"

I took the kid out. It protested the whole way down in the elevator, but since I was pretty sure I knew what was about to happen upstairs, I ignored the protests and dragged it out anyway. I knew that red look in Lord Sero's eyes; I'd seen it often enough in the war. Those board members, protesting and self-righteous and convinced of their own innocence, were staring death in the face.

The kid stopped complaining once we were downstairs— maybe it had expected to be kicked out at some stage. It boosted itself up on the secretary's desk and crossed its legs beneath it. "They always kick me out," it said glumly. "I mean, maybe I didn't want to be there, but if I'm part of the team I should have some of the responsibility, too."

"You're not part of the team," I said harshly. There was no way this kid should be present for what was going on upstairs. "You're the pet."

"I know they're going to kill the board members," the kid said, surprising me.

I wasn't sure if I was more surprised to know that the kid had seen through my harshness, or because it did actually know what was about to happen.

"Zero and them," it explained. "Athelas explained it to me once; their job is to investigate, judge, and apply the judgment."

"Doesn't bother you?"

"Yes," said the kid. "No. I don't know. But those board members—they're like animals. No, they're much worse than that. They think everyone else is an animal, and that they can do what they like with them. Over this side of Between, there's no other justice but Zero for humans when it comes to Other problems. Human prisons can't hold them, and there are too many people in Behind who turn a blind eye to that sort of thing to even try cases there. So when they start incorporating that sort of attitude and turning it into a business—"

"If it needs to be stamped out, there needs to be someone to stamp it out." I was a lot more certain than the kid; Lord Sero's unit might be irregular, but it was well within Behind laws. I had no problem with the way they were fixing the problem. "They're beasts, too; but they're beasts of another kind."

The kid frowned. "The *good* kind."

I thought about that for a minute. In the boardroom upstairs, three bloody emblems of death were tearing through human flesh to destroy every trace of evil from this part of the human world. And if I wasn't very much mistaken, they would soon go Behind to perform the same office there. Bloody beasts, but very necessary ones in the world of Behind.

"Yes," I said. "Beasts of a good kind."

ABOUT THE AUTHOR

W.R. Gingell is a Tasmanian author who lives in a house with a green door. She loves to rewrite fairytales with a twist or two--and a murder or three--and original fantasy where dragons, enchantresses, and other magical creatures abound. Occasionally she will also dip her toes into the waters of SciFi. W.R. spends her time reading, drinking an inordinate amount of tea, and slouching in front of the fire to write. Like Peter Pan, she never really grew up, and is still occasionally to be found climbing trees. Her website is WRGingell.com.

Don't Wake the Dragon

M.C. Dwyer

There is a game the children in my village used to play—perhaps they play it still; it's been too long since I left to say for certain—called "Don't wake the dragon." Like most childish games, it is fairly silly, and was likely started by an adult who was in need of a little peace and quiet. It goes like this: one child is the dragon. He stands in the middle of the chosen playing field with his eyes closed. One at a time, or in twos, the rest of the children creep by close enough to feel the warmth from his body. If the "dragon" hears their movement, or feels their presence, he can stretch out his arms and capture anyone in reach. These children are promptly "eaten" and have to sit out, and spend the rest of the game jeering and catcalling the dwindling number of survivors. The game lasts until either everyone has been eaten, or the last child is uncatchable.

I was a magnificent dragon. The others took to blindfolding me, accusing me of cracking an eye and cheating thereby. It wasn't true; I simply had an almost sixth sense as to where people were. I was nearly uncatchable, too: creeping silently on cat feet and holding my breath until I was past.

Both skills serve me well in my current profession. But they may have gotten me into my current spot of trouble.

It started innocently enough: I was passing off a purse I'd lifted from an unwary visitor to our fair city. It wasn't personal, and I didn't really need the money at the moment—I just liked to keep my fingers limber and lifting purses was good practice. I figured it served them right. If they were naïve enough to wear their money in plain sight, they were obviously in need of a little (expensive) reeducation. And since I usually passed off the spoils to the street kids, I salved my grumbling conscience with the reminder that I was helping to feed hungry bellies and hopefully prevent the creation of more thieves down the road.

Did I have to steal? Well, I hadn't started out as a thief. I'd left the village at sixteen when it was obvious no one was likely to marry the misbegotten daughter of a village priestess. Making my way to the big city, I'd had high hopes of finding decent work and a few friends. Little did I know there's only one line of work readily available to young girls with no protection. I stole food that first week when my stomach would not be quiet, and found—quite by accident—a dropped coinpurse. Returning it was obviously out of the question. If I'd gone to the guardsmen I would've been accused of stealing it (never mind the fact that if I had, returning it would be the last thing I'd do) and likely beaten for my trouble. I kept it, and used the bulk of it to rent a tiny room in a rundown but decent part of town. I steal just enough to retain the room and keep my belly full (the odd extra purse notwithstanding), and try to stay out of sight of the authorities. It has served me well for the past six years, anyway, though it's not the rosy future I had imagined.

I strolled down the street, glancing at the wares in shop windows and breathing deeply of the smells of candied pecans and pastries from the vendors' carts. I traded a coin for some of the cinnamon-glazed nuts, and walked down the street munching as I went. That's when I saw him.

He was tall, much taller than my own slight frame, with jet-black hair swept back into a tail, and his clothes had an air of subtle wealth—nothing too flashy, but well-tailored and expensive in cloth and design. He looked about him with the air of a tourist, gazing up at the shop signs and not paying much attention to what was happening near his feet.

It was too easy a mark to pass up.

I felt my fingers twitch in anticipation and brushed them free of sugar on my trousers as I angled my course to intercept his. I assumed a nonchalance I didn't feel as we approached, and at the last moment, pretended to stumble on a cobblestone, taking care to fall into him. That cobblestone almost did me in; it rocked under my foot, and my ankle gave a faint twinge of protest, but that didn't stop my fingers from sliding into his pocket and snagging the edge of the purse that peeped through the gap.

I gasped and apologized, sacrificing the last of my nuts in an attempted distraction, and tucked the purse into my pocket even as he righted me.

"I'm so sorry!" I gasped, using my now free hand to brush sugar and cinnamon from the sleeve of his tunic. Since my other hand was actively sprinkling him with what was left in the paper sleeve, this was an exercise in futility and he quickly pushed me away, preferring to finish the job himself.

"It's no trouble at all," he said, glancing up and offering me a grin that made my heart skip a beat. My, but he was handsome.

Sternly telling my heart to calm down, I offered an apologetic bow and quickly turned away. Which was when my pocket started wailing.

"Thief!" it cried in a high-pitched wail. "Thiiiiieeeeef!"

Spitting a curse directed at mages and mageborn alike, I took off down the street, yanking the purse from my pocket and flinging it away. Or, at least, trying to.

It stuck to my hand like spirit gum, clinging to my fingers and continuing to wail. Darn mages and their tricky spells.

I clenched the purse tightly in my fist and stuffed it inside my vest and under the other arm, hoping to stifle its cries. I put on another burst of speed, dodging the curious street vendors and passersby who looked at me strangely.

Rule number one of being chased is don't look back. It doesn't help, and only gives any pursuers that much of an edge.

Actually, I thought, rule number one should be don't get chased in the first place. If you're being chased, it's because you got sloppy. Or you missed the signs of magic and robbed a thrice-cursed mage of his thief-proofed purse. Tourist he may have been; naïve he apparently was not.

Several alleys and shortcuts later, I risked a look behind me. No one was actively following, and this part of town was unlikely to raise a fuss about a thief. I slowed and put a hand on my racing heart. The purse was still whimpering quietly to itself, and I began to look around for something to silence it. A bucket of water would help, drowning the spell and limiting its effectiveness till it dried; but fire would be a more permanent solution.

As I turned another corner, I spotted someone's pan of laundry bubbling over a fire. No one was in sight, so I quickly snagged a burning brand from the fire. Holding it awkwardly in my left hand, I brought my right hand with its clinging purse out and put it next the brand. This would be difficult to accomplish without burning myself, and I stuck my tongue out in concentration.

"I'd really rather you didn't do that," a voice said, and I nearly ran my hand through with the burning stick.

The purse stopped wailing and, when the man stepped forward and plucked it oh-so-easily from my fingers, positively purred.

I scowled, telling my heart that, good-looking or not, this man was about to make my life very difficult, so you may as well calm down, you stupid muscle.

I stepped back, brandishing my burning stick in a lame attempt to keep him away. If he had any more magical trinkets, hauling me off to prison would be a piece of cake.

"You're really quite good," he said, apparently deciding I wasn't going to speak. "I didn't even feel you take it. Though the distraction was a bit over the top. You didn't need to douse me in nuts. Having you throw yourself in my arms was quite distracting enough."

I felt a blush suffuse my cheeks and cursed my body for betraying me. I also dropped the stick, as I was in imminent danger of being burned.

"What are you going to do?" I managed to say, wondering if I had gotten my wind back enough to risk another attempt at flight.

He looked surprised. "Why, nothing. Nothing at all. You haven't stolen anything from me," he added, patting his pocket. "And, obviously, I merely followed you to make sure you didn't injure yourself when you fell against me." He glanced down at my ankle that was, come to think of it, throbbing faintly. It hadn't appreciated my flight through the back alleys of Etherwind.

"I'm fine, thank you," I managed, backing away another step.

"Don't go!" he said. "You might actually be able to help me. I'm new to town"—I couldn't contain a snort of derision—"and I'm a bit lost." He smiled at me again, a blinding smile that made me wonder if that was how snakes were said to hypnotize their meals into walking down their throats. I had a sudden sympathy for the meal.

Almost against my will, I found myself replying, "What are you looking for?"

"A tavern."

I silently pointed out the three that were in sight.

"No, a specific tavern." His smile was starting to irritate me, and my sixth sense was buzzing that something was a little off.

"Stop that!" I cried, kicking the burning coals from the brand I'd dropped in his direction.

His smile faltered, and he looked at me with sudden intensity. "You felt that?"

"Yes." I rubbed my arms. "It was creepy."

"Amazing!" he smiled again, and this one had a depth that had been lacking in his previous attempts. "My first day in Etherwind and I meet a null."

"A what?" I hadn't understood the word, but it didn't sound flattering.

"A null! You can sense spells in progress, even though you can't work magic. It can be a very useful talent."

I let out another snort. "If that were true, wouldn't I have felt your purse before I stole it?"

He waved away this objection. "You're untrained. That's only to be expected. Anyway. I'm looking for the Spotted Sow. Do you know it?"

I gave him a wary look. "Yes. You sure that's the one you want? I know several where you're less likely to get a knife in the back, and the cider is better, too."

"No, it must be the Spotted Sow." He smiled sunnily at me. "I'm meeting someone."

"Yeah, Lady Death," I muttered, but I turned away and motioned for him to follow.

We wended our way through the poorer districts of town and into what could only be called the slums. It was the sort of place the noblemen preferred to ignore the existence of, until they needed a particular sort of problem solved. And then they came to places like the Spotted Sow, to make deals in the dim taproom after which people "mysteriously" disappeared. I stayed away, though I could've been in on the take of a number of lucrative jobs that had use for a small, silent sort of person. I preferred to continue breathing.

I stopped across the street and nodded in the direction of the tavern. "There you go."

I turned to leave and felt his hand on my shoulder. It was uncomfortably warm and, I fancied, made my skin tingle.

"You should come with me. I think you'd be useful in the expedition I'm planning." He smiled warmly down into my eyes, and I felt my feet still without my willing them to.

Narrowing my eyes, I asked, "What sort of expedition?"

"It's a sort of treasure hunt," he said, still not removing his hand. I shrugged it off my shoulder, not sure I liked the sensation.

"The take will be more than enough for you to open up any sort of business you like," he went on. "It could be enough to buy you title and manor of your own, if that was something you wanted."

I allowed myself to be swept up in sudden dreams of wealth. I could picture myself mincing down the cobbled streets in those perilously high heels, with a parasol over my head and two or three lackeys carrying parcels trailing behind. I would be so blindingly wealthy that my background could be ignored as an eccentricity, and all of the young men would fall at my feet adoringly. I banished these pleasant dreams with a wave of my hand, but another idea crept in. I could, it suggested, set up a home for the street children. Rather than sending the occasional stolen purse their way, I could instead create a haven for them, and give them some hope. I waved this image away as well, but I couldn't deny that it was a temptation. It couldn't hurt to at least listen to his proposal, right?

"Fine," I said at last, but held up a forestalling hand. "I'm willing to listen. But no promises."

"Excellent!" he cried, and, taking my hand, pulled me across the street and into the Sow.

It was worse than I remembered. Even now, in the middle of the day, it was packed with ne'er-do-wells and idlers who gulped ale from dirty wooden tankards. Women of questionable morality brought refills, sat in laps, or dodged groping hands as their whim led them. I found myself shrinking against my still unnamed mark, preferring the dubious protection of his presence to the alternatives.

One drunken man reeled in front of us, careening into chairs in his attempt to accost my companion. There was a brief scuffle that left the man on the floor with a bloody arm and a suddenly sober look on his face. Jostling for position in the sudden chaos, I caught a glimpse of my protector's face, and drew back at the glittering smile. It was as hard and merciless as diamond, and I felt a wave of doubt at my decision. However, when he turned once more to me and offered his arm, my misgivings faded. We made our thereafter unassailed way to a table in the corner, where we sat, facing the room.

We had not even had time to catch a waitress' eye before two men placed themselves in front of our table.

"You Ariel?" One of them asked, a burly fellow with a bushy brown beard and a scar that ran across one white, sightless eye. The other eye looked over my companion and then me. "You're late."

"I'm Ariel," my companion affirmed, ignoring the comment, and both men sat down. The bearded fellow flipped his chair around and straddled it, making room for his sword and the buckler on his back. The other sat in his chair normally, but his eyes never stopped roving over the inhabitants of the room. He was clean-shaven, but I rather thought that was through lack of facial hair rather than any personal penchant towards cleanliness. His long, greasy hair was pulled back in a tail and his nails were dirty as he fidgeted with a sheathed knife.

"I am Ariel," he repeated, "but I'm not familiar with your names."

"Hendar," said the bearded one, and, "Ivis," said the other. All three turned expectantly to me.

"Lily," I said, returning their belligerent gazes as well as I was able. I'd heard things about Hendar, and they hadn't been nice things. I wasn't sure about Ivis, but if he was hanging out with Hendar, that wasn't a mark in his favor.

"Lightfingered Lily?" Hendar grunted. "I've heard of you. Just an ordinary street thief."

I shrugged, unwilling to return the compliment.

Ivis looked at Ariel. "Is she in on the take? I wasn't planning to split four ways."

Hendar pinned a gaze on him as well.

"Gentlemen," Ariel said, and I rather thought that was using the term generously, "if we are successful, one more split will not make a difference. And if we are not," he shrugged. "Well, if we are not, one more member might mean one of us survives to tell the tale."

Even more nervous now, but a bit intrigued, I leaned forward. "What is this job, exactly?"

Ariel beamed. "We're going to rob a dragon."

"No. Absolutely not." The voice cut through the bedlam of the tavern, causing a moment of silence. It wasn't until Ariel pulled me back down into my chair that I realized the voice had been mine.

"Shut up, you fool," Hendar whispered. "You want the whole city to know?"

I gave him my most derisive snort. "Know what? That you're a pack of fools?" I'd abandoned caution at some point, and didn't exactly regret it.

Ariel raised placating hands. "It's not such a fool's errand as you think. I have a few… trinkets"—he patted his pockets and winked at me—"that should allow us safe passage into the dragon's cave. After that it's merely a matter of sneaking past without waking him up. The treasure is in the cave beyond."

"Oh, is that all? I needn't have worried." I rolled my eyes. "Where did you get this inside information?"

"I had an… associate who went with me before. He was able to get past the dragon and reported what he found." His smile slipped slightly. "Unfortunately, he didn't make it back out."

"How did he report if he didn't survive?" That was Ivis, as skeptical as I.

"Communication stones." Ariel flourished the ring on his hand. "If we all wear these, we can stay in constant contact."

"I've already said I'm in," Hendar growled. "I don't need your baubles."

Ivis had gone back to darting glances around the bar, but said, "If the take's what you said it is, I'm in."

"Excellent," Ariel beamed. He turned to me.

I was still undecided. While fabulous wealth was a definite draw, I kept reminding myself that we were stealing from a dragon. A *dragon*. You know: sharp teeth, breathes fire? Stop gazing into his beautiful blue eyes, you ninny!

Ariel placed a hand on top of mine. "We need you."

I thought I heard Hendar snort, but I was drowning in blue and couldn't be bothered to care.

"Fine," I said. "I'm in."

"Good." He smiled at me, a warm, personal smile that made something flip over in my stomach. He removed his hand and turned back to the others, and I felt suddenly bereft.

Easy does it, I cautioned myself. You don't even know him. Caution warned me to slow down and consider what I'd just agreed to; a reckless urge fed by my flip-flopping stomach said, why not? It'll be fun.

Travel plans had been made while I wrestled with myself, and next thing I knew, I was promising to meet them all at the north gate at dawn in two days' time.

The next morning, I woke up and stared at my watermarked ceiling for a very long time. Had I been ill yesterday? A brief fever that turned off my brain? What had I been thinking, agreeing to this sort of expedition? I rolled over with a groan. Stupid, stupid. There was nothing for it; I'd have to hunt down Ariel and tell him I'd changed my mind. I'd look like a fool, but at least I'd be a live fool.

To that end, my first stop for the day was going to be the Spotted Sow. I didn't know where Ariel was staying, and the Sow had a couple of rooms they occasionally let to customers. It was as good a place to start as any.

I stood across the street, staring at the entrance to the tavern and rethinking my plan. While it was fairly quiet, relatively speaking, I didn't really want to go in the front door without even the dubious protection of Ariel. I'd heard too many stories, and my experience of yesterday was fresh in my mind. I didn't even own a knife; I'd be totally defenseless.

All right, problem-solve: I could stand here and hope he came out. I laughed at myself for this one. I could peer in the door and see if he was in the taproom. Possible, but I could still get drawn into an altercation that I'd rather avoid. I could ask the kitchen. They'd know if anyone was staying over, as they'd be the ones waiting on him. Done.

I wound through a couple of noxious alleys, giving a wide berth to the sleeping humans mixed in with the refuse, and eventually found the backside of the Sow. It was about as attractive as it sounds. The door stood open, and when I peered in, I could see one very large woman stirring a pot over the fire. It smelled of burned porridge, and my nose wrinkled in distaste.

"Mistress," I called, standing in the doorway.

She glanced up at the sound, and waved me away. "Shoo. No handouts. Get out of here."

Stifling the urge to tell her I wouldn't eat her swill anyway, I put on a polite smile and said, "I'm just inquiring about your current guests. I'm looking for a man—tall, black hair? Is he staying here?"

She advanced toward me, brandishing her porridgy spoon. "No, no, no one is staying here like that. Now get out."

I retreated quickly, disappointed. Short of knocking on the door of every inn and posting-house in the city, I had no way of finding Ariel except by chance. With this vague notion in mind, I made my way back to the wealthier parts of town.

Wandering the streets that grew more crowded as the day progressed, I saw no tall, dark haired forms that could be Ariel. I did lift a couple of purses out of habit, and nearly gave myself away when the unexpected weight of one caught me off-guard.

Heart racing, I ducked my head and hurried around several corners so I'd be out of sight when the man I'd lifted it from inevitably noticed its loss. Slipping into a shadowy doorway, I opened the drawstring and gasped. It was almost entirely gold. I quickly closed the purse and tucked into an inner pocket. And then I stood and thought.

While not enough money to set me up in a trade of my choosing, there was definitely plenty to make me think seriously about my life. I didn't want to be a thief forever; the risk of getting caught and ending up on a ship to a prison colony would only increase as I got older. And I would, eventually, get caught. I nearly had yesterday. It had only been Ariel's strange whim that led him to hire me instead of handing me over to the city guards. Speaking of Ariel's strange whims, a percentage of a dragon's hoard would definitely be enough to change my life. And with a little bit of preparation, I might actually survive the attempt.

I set out again, but headed now for the mage quarter. I had enough cash to make some specific purchases, and the first one was accomplished at a weapons dealer at the edge of the mage quarter. A few minutes in the shop left me lighter in the purse but with a serviceable dagger at my belt. There was a green stone in the hilt that tingled when I rubbed a hand over it, which hopefully meant the shopkeeper hadn't lied.

My next stop was a bookseller, but I had no luck at the first three I tried. The fourth one was owned by a tiny old man whose face was a mass of wrinkles, but he was extremely knowledgeable and picked out two books for me. One was called *Meditations on Magic* and the other had no title at all, but was bound in dark, supple leather that held together an assortment of hand-written notes that contained—or so the shopkeeper promised—exactly what I was looking for. Since I hadn't been able to tell him what I was looking for, I had to take his word on that.

Feeling slightly better about the fool's errand I'd agreed to, I spent the rest of the afternoon purchasing improvements to my wardrobe, along with a leather pack and a map of the northern lands. I wasn't entirely certain where the dragon's cave was, but rumor had always placed it somewhere in the northern mountains. I added thick, woolen socks and fur-lined pants to my pack, and laid in a supply of jerked meat and dried fruit. While I assumed Ariel would be providing food, it didn't hurt to be prepared.

Between the books and my new, warm clothes, the pack was nearly full, but I only had one more stop to make. One of my last purchases was going to be a cloak. I would have loved to be able to afford a wyvern-skin cloak; they were practically indestructible, even to dragon fire. But since that would have taken five or six bags of gold, I was going to have to opt for what my last few golden coins could purchase—a simple woolen cloak imbued with fire-proofing spells. The clerk could make no guarantees about dragon fire, but swore I could sit in a furnace for at least an hour before the spells would burn away. It would have to do.

I walked home, self-conscious in my newly acquired wealth. I avoided the seedier parts of town, not wanting to lose any of it, and reached my rented room with a sigh of relief. Dinner was easily obtained from one of the taverns on my road, and then I went to bed early, anxious for dawn.

Sleep eluded me for a while. I'd never owned anything bespelled before, and the cloak and dagger's presence buzzed at the edge of my mind in an unfamiliar fashion. Fully conscious that I'd be traveling most of the morrow, I sternly banished the sensation and shut my eyes. Eventually, I slept.

Dawn found me at the north gate, stickily eating a fruit pastry as I awaited my companions. Ivis appeared first, scuttling into sight sideways, darting glances everywhere. I rolled my eyes. If he continued to act like that, he'd attract the attention of everyone from here to the dragon. Studied nonchalance, that was the key. I wandered over to a water trough and rinsed my fingers clean. As I was topping off my water flask, another recent purchase, I noticed Hendar lurking in an alley and couldn't repress a shiver. *That* man knew how to lurk properly. That was three of us; where was Ariel?

At the sound of approaching hoofbeats, I looked up, expecting guardsmen or the like. Instead, I saw a magnificent black stallion, and I had a sinking feeling in my chest as I looked up to see its rider. Ariel. Of course.

He was leading three others, already saddled and ready to ride. Hendar and Ivis approached, and each chose a mount without hesitation. That left one for me, but I made no move to take the reins.

"Lily?" Ariel said, and I looked up into his eyes. A day apart had done nothing to lessen the force of his presence; if anything, it intensified it.

I gulped. "I don't know how to ride," I whispered, ashamed.

"I should have thought of that," Ariel said, and smiled warmly. I felt a tingle all the way down to my toes, and curled them inside my new boots.

Swinging a leg over the stallion's neck, he dropped easily to the ground. Working quickly, he transferred the pack from behind his saddle to the other horse. He held out a hand for my pack as well, which I gave up reluctantly. It made me nervous to put my belongings out of reach. He attached the reins to his horse in some fashion I didn't see, and then laid out a piece of fur behind his horse's saddle.

I watched all this skeptically, not sure I liked where it was leading, but I didn't see that I had much choice. Ivis and Hendar were already mounted, packs in place and turned toward the gate.

Ariel remounted as smoothly as he'd dismounted, then extended a hand to me. I took it uncertainly, then gasped as I was pulled suddenly into his lap.

"Here," he said, "put your foot on mine and then swing around behind me."

I was no doubt beet red, but I did as he instructed and in short order found myself perched behind him.

"All set?" he asked, smiling over his shoulder.

Confronted with the vast expanse of his back, I looked in vain for a handhold that wasn't extremely personal and eventually settled for clutching his jacket at the sides.

"Yes," I managed to say, and we started off with a suddenness that made me squeak in fear and clutch at his waist.

He chuckled and patted my arm, and we headed out.

I repositioned my hands and tried to forget the feel of firm muscles under my fingers.

He's not for you, I told myself, but I didn't want to listen.

The day was an exercise in patience as my nerves were rubbed raw by his proximity and the rain that started to fall midmorning. I huddled under my cloak, wishing I'd added waterproofing spells as well. Ariel steamed gently, and I suspected he had some sort of water-repellent spell in progress. My hands itched occasionally as I clutched his coat, adding one more discomfort to my misery.

We called it quits early, stopping at an inn midway through the afternoon. As the only girl, I got a room to myself and huddled in front of the small fire with a cup of tea. Eventually I warmed up, and pulled out my books to read until suppertime.

They were not what I expected.

The first one, *Meditations on Magic*, was a series of essays about what magic is—and is not. It was interesting, but not particularly helpful as I had very little background in magic to draw on. I gave up reading and started flipping through the pages, pausing when a word or phrase caught my eye. About midway through the book, a title caught my eye: "Nulls and other Nonsense." I read eagerly.

It has been posited by some, it began, *that there are in existence so-called 'nulls'—people who can sense magic being worked, but cannot touch it themselves. This is, of course, balderdash, as anyone who can sense magic can work it—at least to some degree. The author has never met any such person, and finds it doubtful that there is in existence a person who possesses the magical sensing ability but is unable to use it to touch magic. It would be like expecting a person who can sing to be unable to speak. The abilities are intertwined, and though they may vary in degrees of training and talent, one never finds one without expecting the other.*

I turned the page, eager to learn more, but the author began talking about soulstones, whatever those were, and unless I wanted to know the easiest (and most commonly overlooked, in the eyes of the author) way to free a captive—break the stone—the essayist was not particularly helpful. I read to the end of the essay in the vain hope he'd return to the topic of nulls, but eventually closed the book in frustration.

At this point, my stomach growled, reminding me I needed supper, so I made my way downstairs to the dubious companionship of my fellow travelers.

The days repeated in a similar fashion as we worked our way further north. Every morning I woke up, frequently with a groan from an uncomfortable pallet or—on the worst nights—a bed of grasses or ferns, and cursed whatever crazy notion had gotten me out on the road and into this adventure. By the time breakfast rolled around, I started to feel more at peace with the world, which may have had something to do with the scenery. I cursed myself for a fool, but found my eyes pulled back like a needle to true north. Ariel's shapely form held my gaze, and I watched him like a moonstruck teenager with her first crush.

After about a week of this, I decided enough was enough, and asked him to show me how to mount the horse and hold the reins. This put some distance between us, and made me more comfortable. So much more so, that I put a hand on the hilt of my dagger and rubbed my thumb across the stone. It prickled at my touch, and I dropped back to the end of our train so I could draw it unnoticed.

Looping the reins around one arm and hoping the horse wouldn't take it into his head to bolt, I drew the dagger and held it in my right hand. With my left, I drew a finger across the flat of the blade, trying to remember what the swordsmith had said. Yellow for spells of healing and growth, blue for spells of confusion or misdirection, red for emotions, and black for harm or death. The dagger turned slightly purple under my finger's path, and I scowled. Still, it was better to know. I sheathed the dagger, picked up the reins again, and tried to convince the horse I wanted him to speed up. I had only marginal success, which was about what I had in my attempt to look at something other than Ariel's back. I gave up with a shrug, and decided to simply admire the view.

We camped out that night, being unable to reach another village before nightfall. We were passing through an area that was mostly grassland dotted with herds of sheep and the occasional copse of trees. It was near one of these we stopped, built a fire in the remains of previous travelers' ashes, and cooked a simple stew. I say we; it was Ivis who did the actual cooking. He was a surprisingly good cook, and we generally deferred the cooking duties to him when we camped out. He'd settled down a fair bit once we'd left town, and no longer let his gaze rove suspiciously about. I offered what help I could, preferring, at this point, his company to either Hendar or Ariel's. I fetched water, gathered firewood, and gathered bowls at his grunted directions.

After dinner, I took the bowls down to the stream that ran through the trees and scrubbed them out with sand, then sat with my feet in the water and watched the sunset. The water was cool, and I wondered how much colder it would get before we reached our destination. It was early September, and the rains were already cold. The further north we went, the colder it would get. Would we finish our quest before winter closed in in earnest? I didn't know, and I didn't want to ask. I sighed, wondering not for the first time if it was too late to turn around and go home. Except—I would go back empty-handed, and there was nothing much waiting for me in Etherwind. I sighed again. For better or worse, I was committed to this adventure.

I returned to camp to find the three men laying out their blankets.

"You have first watch," Ariel said, softening the blow with a warm smile.

I felt myself responding to the smile even as I sighed a third time. I'd forgotten it was my turn for first watch. On nights we camped out, we took watch in turn, three hours at a time and three people per night. That meant at least one night I'd get an uninterrupted night of sleep, and the others I'd get enough to survive on. I threw a couple of sticks on the fire to keep it alive, then turned my back on it to gaze out over the grasslands and towards the road. After about an hour I began to get drowsy, and stood up and walked the perimeter of the camp for a while. I checked the horses, watched the stars move across the sky, then went and stood by the fire to banish the chill that had crept over me. Another hour crept by, and it was nearing time for me to wake up Hendar, the next one on duty.

As I waited, the hairs on the back of my neck raised as though I was being watched. I looked at each of the men in turn, but they were all obviously asleep. The feeling grew, along with the sense of general wrongness I get sometimes when someone is doing magic. I glanced again at Ariel, but he was deeply asleep, moving restlessly in the grip of some dream. The sense of pressure increased until I wanted to scream, but I could see nothing wrong. I spun around, but saw nothing. There was no moon tonight, only the vast expanse of stars and the smoldering coals of our cook fire.

Feeling like a fool but unable to take it anymore, I crouched by Ariel and touched his arm. He roused instantly, drawing a knife and putting it at my throat before I could even squeak in protest.

"Lily," he said, removing the knife but not smiling his customary smile. It made his face unusually harsh in the dim light.

"Something's wrong," I managed to whisper once my heart had slowed. "I can't see anything, but there's something just— wrong." I couldn't explain it any better than that.

Ariel looked around for a moment, and then breathed deeply of the night air.

Scrambling out of his blanket, he swore loudly and impressively. "Up, up, you fools!" he shouted to the other men. "Up or die in your beds!"

I sat in the dust where Ariel had knocked me, shocked and unsure what to do. Figuring that more light couldn't hurt, I threw a few more sticks on the fire. Hendar and Ivis were up and moving, throwing aside blankets and drawing weapons. As the branches caught, providing more light, I saw Ariel by the horses. He had his stallion saddled and bridled already, and tossed his pack over the back, strapping it down with a few quick moves. I gathered my own pack, still intact, and slung it on my back. If we were going to make a quick getaway, I wanted to be prepared.

There was still nothing in sight, but the feeling of being watched was still there, as well as the itchy feeling of magic in progress. Hendar and Ivis were circling the fire, staring out into the night. Ariel rode back through camp, and paused to reach a hand down to me. I took it unthinkingly, and found myself in his lap again.

"Hold on," he murmured, and I wrapped my arms around his chest. Wheeling his horse, he said over his shoulder, "Don't look it in the eyes."

"What is it?" Hendar grunted.

"Basilisk," Ariel said, and jabbed his heels into his horse's flanks.

Hendar started screaming profanities and cursing Ariel as we galloped away. Looking back towards the fire, I saw a large, thick shape rise up. It was like a snake, if a snake could be as thick as a man was tall. Its head had a frilled crest and a mouth full of teeth that glistened in the firelight. Hendar and Ivis stood immobilized before it, and then we were too far away for me to see clearly.

We galloped at first, then slowed to a canter, then alternated between a canter and a trot for some time. The moon finally rose, a thin crescent that illuminated the lighter track of the road, and we finally slowed to a walk. The horse's sides were heaving and flecked with foam, and I patted its neck in sympathy, trying not to think of the events of the night and failing.

Ariel had abandoned them. He'd saved me, and abandoned them. Was I sorry for their deaths? Not really, but they had been companions, and Ariel had left them behind without a moment's thought. What did that mean? And more specifically, should I be worried?

For the moment I cherished the illusion of safety, tucked in his arms, but while my body rested my mind worked faster than ever.

"Are you all right?" Ariel murmured, the first words either of us had spoken in a while.

"Hmm?" I asked, startled from my thoughts. "I'm fine."

"Do you feel the basilisk anymore?"

I shook my head, but couldn't suppress a shudder.

"It's all right," he said, giving me a one-armed hug. My arm pressed against my dagger, which tingled against my skin, and I felt tears start to my eyes. I turned my face into his chest and cried while he held me.

Eventually, we stopped for what little was left of the night, and I fell asleep, too exhausted to care whether Ariel was keeping watch or not. The next morning, we came across a walled city, which was most likely Tressa if I was reading my map correctly. They had a substantial garrison, where we stopped first to report the basilisk. The commander seemed a bit skeptical at first, but Ariel's word as a mage was persuasive.

"You should be able to catch up to it today," he said. "After a meal of that size it won't be going anywhere for a while."

My face blanched with remembered horror, but I found myself nodding in agreement. Three horses and two men would gorge even so large a creature as the basilisk.

"You were lucky to escape," the commander said.

Ariel smiled faintly. "I was lucky to have been awake to sense its approach. It's not like they make a lot of noise."

I frowned a bit at this, but bit my tongue in confusion when Ariel glanced down at me with a conspiratorial wink.

And then we were out of the garrison and down the road before I could think. I followed behind Ariel, rubbing my prickling dagger hilt thoughtfully.

We spent the rest of that day in Tressa, resting at an inn and taking the opportunity to bathe and launder our travel-worn selves. I spent the day curled up with the second of my two books, which turned out to be a series of journal entries by a mage in training as he navigated the various pitfalls of magic and school. It was comedic and serious by turns, and by the end of its pages I felt like I had a much clearer sense of what magic was, and what I might someday be able to do with it. I also felt able to set the horror of yesterday at a distance, and slept that night untroubled by dreams.

We were back on the road early the next morning, Ariel having found a new horse for me, and we fell into a new routine fairly quickly. Another week of travel brought us to foothills, and two days after that we were in the mountains proper. It was cold at night, and I was grateful for my new clothes. I sent a mental thank you and apology to the man who'd inadvertently blessed me with them.

I also took some time each day to practice sensing spells. This was the first thing the unnamed journal writer had learned, and he offered several tips in the course of his entries—things he'd tried, things that didn't work, and so forth. After a few days I was much more in tune with the magic going on around me, and could feel the difference between the simple spells in my cloak and the more elaborate one at work in my dagger. I also started isolating the various bits of magic I felt from Ariel, and was both amazed and shocked at the sheer amount of magic he used in the course of a day. There was magic in his jacket, which felt a bit like the spell on my coat, so I assumed it was some sort of weatherproofing. There was magic in at least one of his rings, and in the jewel I hadn't even noticed in one of his ears. There was magic in his horse's saddle, and magic in Ariel's smile whenever it was turned towards me. That one, at least, I could gauge using my dagger, but I grew more adept at spotting it when it happened, which helped lessen its effect. He used magic to start the campfire; he used magic to hobble the horses at night. I'm pretty sure he used magic to convince the various innkeepers to give us a discount when we stayed in a village.

It was still easiest to sense the magic by touching the object in question, though even with that I got to the point where I could reliably sense a spell simply by being in close proximity. I practiced this with my dagger as we rode, trusting my horse to stay close to Ariel's with minimal guidance from me, and pulled my hand back in tiny increments to see at what point I lost the sense of the dagger, then starting over.

I think Ariel had some idea of what I was doing; at least, I found myself at the receiving end of his smile more and more the closer to the dragon's cave we approached. Since I couldn't contain the blush that this produced, I used it, smiling in confusion whenever it happened. He also started touching me casually at every opportunity—on the shoulder, on the head, at the waist, and each contact tingled with magic. I began to feel like a rabbit who sees a fox in every bush. No, worse—a fox who claims to want to be friends.

It was in this state of persecution that we arrived in the dragon's valley. His cave, so Ariel informed me, was at the far end of the valley and partway up the mountain. We would need to hide at night and approach during the day, when the dragon was more likely to be sleeping.

"*More* likely?" I asked. I wasn't having second thoughts—by this time they were more like twentieth or thirtieth thoughts. "You mean you don't know for sure?"

Ariel shrugged. "Dragons hunt at night. It only makes sense that they'd sleep during the day." He smiled, and I still wasn't proof against it.

"Fine," I said. This was why I'd come, after all. It seemed silly to back out now after coming this far.

Ariel grinned, a much more genuine expression. "We'll cross partway across the valley today, and camp until tomorrow. No fire, I'm afraid; that'd be a dead giveaway."

I nodded tersely, and followed him down into the valley. We set up camp in a pile of boulders, and from the signs of previous use I guessed he'd used this spot before. That evening, at his suggestion, I went down to the creek and scrubbed all over with a strongly pine scented soap. It made my skin tingle, though not from magic this time, and by the end of it I smelled more like a mountain forest and less, I hoped, like a tasty human.

Dinner was a simple affair of dried meat and a bit of bread from the last town we'd passed through, and I retired to the top of a rock to catch the last sunlight and see if my magic book had anything to say about dragons. It didn't, at least that I could find, and I reread the essay on nulls for the hope it gave me. If the author was right, I could learn to do magic, and my life would never be the same again. Assuming I survived the dragon, of course, I could attend the mage school and have my pick of jobs. Nobody cared if a mage was of humble birth; magic covered that ill, too.

Get through tomorrow first, I cautioned myself. Then make plans for the future.

We started at dawn, leaving the horses hobbled among some pines and leaving most of our supplies behind. I carried my water flask and a handful of jerky. Ariel had a small satchel slung over one shoulder and nothing else.

The climb was steep, and several times I needed Ariel's assistance scrambling up rocks his long limbs had taken in stride. His hand was warm in mine, and for once did not tingle with magic. I braved a glance at his face, and found it as warmly smiling as always, though again, without the prickle of magic. I felt a wave of vertigo that had nothing to do with the distance down to the rocks below, and let him catch me close for a moment.

"Are you alright?" he asked in concern.

"Just a little dizzy," I said breathlessly.

"It's probably the elevation," he said, and helped me sit down. "Rest for a moment and have a drink. We can slow down, too."

After a while the dizziness passed, leaving me a little lightheaded and a bit confused.

We finished the climb shortly before noon, and found ourselves on a protruding lip of rock that marked the entrance to a long, dark slash in the face of the mountain.

"This is it," Ariel said quietly. He pulled several things out of his satchel. One was a ring that he slipped onto my finger. "Communication stone. Speak into it and I'll hear you." He slid a pendant over my head. "This one is a light. Once I activate it, it will stay on, so tuck it under your shirt if you don't need it." It started glowing as he spoke, and I slipped it under my collar. The last thing he offered was a velvet sack, which he put into my hands and then held.

"This last one is the most important," he said, looking into my eyes. "Once you get past the dragon, you'll pass into another cavern that's full of treasure. Don't touch any of it— some of it is bespelled, and touching it could wake the dragon. Somewhere in there is a large, polished stone about as long as my hand. It will be quartz, and may be slightly greenish in tint. Put the sack over it and pick it up, then bring it out to me." He squeezed my hands. "It's very important you do this first. Once I have the stone, I can keep the dragon asleep, and then we can collect as much treasure as we want. Understand?"

My heart was pounding and I rather thought my hands would be trembling if they weren't being held so tightly, but I nodded. "Don't touch anything, get the polished stone, bring it to you first. I understand."

"Good." He smiled, searched my face for a moment, and then kissed me very gently. It was a sweet kiss, full of promise, and made my heart race for an entirely new reason. "Go," he said, pushing me towards the entrance. "Be safe."

I stumbled away in a daze and had to pause in the entrance to shake myself firmly. I still had to sneak past a sleeping dragon and retrieve a stone before we were home free.

Slowly easing one foot forward at a time, I crept through the long, narrow entranceway, wondering how the dragon fit through, or if he could, catlike, fit through anywhere his head could pass. The light from the entrance faded, but I hesitated to pull out the pendant that glowed faintly beneath the cloth of my shirt. I had to pass the dragon first, and I didn't want a blinding light to give me away before I'd even started.

I had a sense of the walls on either side retreating, and felt that I'd entered a large chamber. The air was cooler here, and I could hear the drip of water echoing from a long way off. I paused there for a moment, and had a sudden memory of playing "Don't wake the dragon" with the village children at home. There was, I thought, a large, warm mass somewhere ahead and to the left. I angled my slow, cautious steps towards the right, and found a wall to follow. The floor was smooth and free of stones, and I stepped out a little more confidently. My awareness of the dragon grew until I imagined I could see him. His head would be turned away from me, resting on his front claws, and his tail would be wrapped around him like a cat's. He was beautiful in my imagining, and I stopped and silently scolded myself for feeling guilty towards a product of my imagination.

Under my hand, the wall took an abrupt turn, and I guessed that this was the passage to the second cavern. I walked slowly for another minute, and then decided I could risk a little light. Clenching the pendant in one hand, I removed a finger at a time until I simply removed it and held it aloft like a lantern, staring around me in wonder. The cavern glittered everywhere. Every surface, every wall was covered in gold and jewel-studded finery. I wanted to run my fingers through it just to feel the sensation, but jerked my hand back when I remembered Ariel's warning. Remembering his words prompted me to look for the stone. I found it easily enough, standing on a pedestal in the center of the cavern. I approached it slowly, sensing the power pulsing from it. I held a hand next to it, and wondered if I was imagining the warmth that seemed to be emanating from it. Putting the pendant back around my neck, I pulled out the velvet sack and prepared to pick it up. A careless finger brushed the stone, and sudden power pulsed through the cave, bathing it in greenish light.

Mageborn, a voice whispered.

Who, me? I wondered, and the voice concurred.

What is it you wish of me?

I had no answer to this, and stared at stone for a moment. "Who are you?"

I am the dragon tied to this stone. If you possess the stone, you possess me.

Without quite knowing why, I pulled the ring from my finger and dropped it into my water flask. When that was done, I said, "I didn't know that. Why are you tied to the stone?"

Because a mage wished to possess my power. The voice had turned curious, and the light from the stone took on a swirled pattern. *It is strange. You have no wish to possess me.*

"Not particularly."

Yet you are here. Have you given your will away? You are entangled in magic.

"Entangled?"

The light pulsed again, and I could see sticky, cobwebby threads of power trailing from me back outside.

"Yuck," I said, and swept them away with my hands. Surprisingly, they dispersed as soon as I touched them. I shook my head, shocked at how clear it felt. A lot of the events of the past few weeks took on new clarity, and I grimaced.

Who is it whose bidding you obey?

I didn't like the wording, but couldn't argue with it. "His name is Ariel. He offered me gold if I would bring the stone out to him."

The power pulsed angrily, and the light spun crazily, making my head spin. I shut my eyes.

I would rather be bound to you than this 'Ariel.' I can reward you greatly.

I stood there a moment longer, thinking, hand unconsciously on my dagger. For the first time since I'd purchased it, I felt not a trace of reaction when I touched the jewel. I drew it, and ran a finger down the blade. It stayed cold and inert under my touch, and I sighed.

Picking up the stone, I slid the velvet pouch over it, but kept a hand underneath. The cavern was plunged once more into near darkness, lit only by my pendant. Retracing my steps, I quickly passed the still sleeping dragon and emerged, blinking in the sunlight. My silent approach allowed me to surprise what may have been the first honest expression I'd seen on Ariel's face. It was a smirk, and a self-satisfied one at that. He was tossing his ring in the air and catching it, chuckling quietly to himself all the while. He was, I thought, not so handsome as when he smiled.

"Was any of it real?" I asked.

He dropped the ring, but fixed his expression so quickly I could have believed I'd imagined it, if it weren't for the sticky trails of magic that were already creeping toward me. I brushed them away impatiently, and had the satisfaction of seeing his smile falter.

"Lily?" he said, attempting to recover. "Did you get the stone?"

I sighed. "Have you said one real thing to me? Ever? Or was everything a lie?"

Ariel didn't respond, which was answer enough.

"Do you want to wake up?" I asked, and Ariel's eyes widened.

Oh, YES.

In one smooth motion, I removed the velvet bag and tipped the stone out of my hand. It shattered spectacularly, and the mountain shook with the dragon's mighty roar. I'd done it. I woke the dragon.

I owe you a great debt, small one, the dragon said. He was as beautiful as I'd imagined, especially under the light of the sun. Here on the valley floor, his scales went from dark emerald to pale green, with tints of purple on his wings and claws.

"I owe you one, too," I responded. "I'd like to think I wouldn't have given the soulstone to Ariel, but I don't know if I could've broken free without your help." I blushed. I'd felt bad for Ariel to the last, but my regrets were mostly for myself. I'd wanted it to be real, but suspected all along that it wasn't. I was ashamed and glad and sad all at once.

Regardless, should you ever need help, you know where to find me. He held up a claw and dropped a small velvet bag in front of me. It spilled gold coins and an amethyst ring set in silver across the ground. I scooped these up, and felt the tingle of magic from the ring.

"What's this?" I asked, picking it up.

There was hint of a laugh in his voice. *Should I ever need you, I will find you, as well.*

I smiled and slipped the ring onto my finger. "Deal."

With that, the dragon launched himself into the air and vanished from sight. I saddled Ariel's black and headed out, leaving the valley behind me.

ABOUT THE AUTHOR

M.C. Dwyer grew up in a small town in Nebraska, has circumnavigated the globe at least once, and ended up back in Nebraska. She has been a student, a librarian, a store clerk, a teacher, a student again, and an occasional world traveler. Some day she might figure out what she wants to be when she grows up, but she isn't holding her breath. She enjoys binge-watching kdrama, learning new languages, and creating new fantasy worlds to escape into. M.C. is the author of the short story "Of Grief and Griffins" published in the anthology Still Waters, *as well as the forthcoming novel* Bleddynwood.

BLANCHE, BEAR-WIFE

ALENA SULLIVAN

The café sits on the corner of the town square, its back to the woods and its face to the other shops around the town. The windows are stained glass, a hodgepodge of color and shadow, not really depicting anything, just rioting shades of light spilling their reflections onto the sidewalk. There's no real sign, no name, just a square wooden shingle, anachronistic, hung above the door, reading CAFÉ in letters that are just a little lopsided, maybe. My Grampa carved that sign with his own hands, back before the War, before they started to shake.

It's during the ice storm in February that the bear first comes by.

"I hate to be a bother, but it's mighty cold out," he rumbles apologetically, hugging his ice-crusted coat tight around his shoulders as he ducks through the doorway.

"It is, that," I admit, smiling a little crookedly and pouring a hot mug of apple cider. I reckon that's the sort of thing a bear could drink—it's something warm, at any rate. I set it on the counter as the bear lumbers up and takes a seat on the stool across from me, gingerly testing it against his weight before he settles properly.

Rosie nudges me, elbow bordering on painful against my ribs. "He's a *bear*," she grits out through clenched teeth.

I lift a shoulder in a shrug. "It's cold out there." My Gramma, who raised me, is a little old lady who believes in real Southern hospitality, in making everybody welcome and looking after them all the same. When she opened this place, it was the only joint on the street that didn't have a sign in the window that said *whites only*, and she never looked twice at anybody, not for their color or their war wounds or their piercings or tattoos. She doesn't like *my* tattoos much, but she loves me, with or without them, and I'm not gonna shame her by turning anybody away in this weather.

"A freaking *bear*," Rosie repeats, a little louder, a little shrill, and I can feel my mouth go tight around a cringe. The bear flinches.

"That's no call to be *impolite*," I say, trying not to be rude in my own turn. Smiling, I ignore the now actively painful elbow in my side and turn to the bear, putting a hand over his shaggy paw. "This one's on the house, sir." His fur is clouded with little ice crystals that crunch and melt a little under my palm.

He makes a face that might be a smile, but is mostly a baring of teeth and a huff of breath. "Mighty kind of you," he says, nodding his head in acknowledgement. He has manners—real manners, ingrained, like my Grampa—you can see it in everything, in the way he holds himself straight and sits like somebody's paying attention. To be fair, people are; the smattering of folks that came out in weather or were too dumb to leave before the ice really started coming down are all pretending not to stare and doing a thoroughly poor job of it. The bear is ignoring it with more dignity than I know I'd manage. Gramma would say he's a real Southern gentleman.

He drains the cider and asks for another, polite as you please, and I tell Rosie to go look after the folks at the tables, that I've got this one. She makes a noise that might be annoyance that I'm serving the bear or might be relief that I'm not making her stick around and do it with me. Knowing her, it's a little bit of both. I don't know how she's got so little of Gramma's lessons stuck to her bones, but she's always been a little prickly, a little wild. She'll talk your ear off, she'll drag you on all kinds of craziness, but heaven forbid the craziness comes from somewhere other than her. She just wants to go her own way, Grampa always says, if only she could be bothered to find it. It's hard to rebel, though, in a family like ours, where they'll love you no matter what kind of crap you pull. Rosie's always given it a college try, though, that's for sure. I've always been too shy for that kind of thing—or not even shy, I guess, but maybe just a little strange. It's quieter in me, I think, than it is inside other folks.

I serve up the cider, stirring in a spoonful of honey for good measure. That earns me another smile and a grateful nod, and I get a little warm feeling in the middle of my chest the way I always do when I do a little something to make somebody smile.

"Much obliged for the hospitality, ma'am," the bear says, closing his eyes and taking a deep breath of the steam coming up from the cider.

"Blanche," I say, "and it's no trouble, really." I give the counter a quick wipe down and start rearranging the muffins on their stand, filling in the gaps from where people have picked from the middle.

"Blanche," the bear repeats, the _ch_ sound sticking to his teeth a little, like butterscotch. I kind of like the way it sounds, coming from him. "Well, Miss Blanche, trouble or not, you've been very kind. I'll get out of your way now, let your customers get back to their meals in peace." He hasn't glanced round the café even once, but his words make all the nosy folks in the room jerk their rubbernecks around and pretend to pay attention to their own business again. I laugh a little without meaning to, reaching up to cover it before he thinks I'm laughing at him.

His eyes are crinkled up too, though, warm even through the glossy black, like he thinks their busybody shenanigans are silly instead of troubling. I appreciate folk who can laugh at their own situations—like Gramma says, it don't matter how serious you take life, it's over eventually anyways. "They can mind their own business," I tell him, a little belatedly. My cheeks go a little warm.

He huffs out an amused noise, a little chuffing of warm air, and says, "I don't know about you, Miss Blanche, but I find that most folk think everything's their business." He slides off the stool, standing up on his hind paws, and slides a twenty across the counter to me. God knows where he pulled it out from, he's not wearing a stitch that isn't fur or melting snow, but I'm not about to shame him by turning it away. "For your kindness," he says, ducking his head like a man tipping his hat, and he starts for the door.

"I don't let folks pay me for that," I say, half teasing, half serious. "If you do that, you start losing track of when you mean it."

"Fair enough. Call it an advance on my tab, then," the bear says, and just like that, he's out the door and into the ice, dropping to all fours as he goes. The door catches the wind and bangs shut behind him, hitting the bell and making it jingle like an omen.

"What on earth is even going on in that head of yours?" Rosie asks, flicking me with her hand towel as she comes by for a coffee refill. "*A bear!*"

I duck my head so she doesn't see me smile. "He's quite a gentleman," I tell her, as prim as I can, sounding as much like Gramma as I can manage.

"He's quite a mess, is what he is," Rosie says, rolling her eyes at the puddles of melted ice and snow under the counter. "I don't know how you got like this."

"Like what?" I ask, not really paying attention to her as I go round to the front of the counter and start in on the puddles with the mop. There's always something soothing in cleaning, a kind of power over the environment that makes me feel safe. Grounded, kind of, like I can feel my roots again.

"I don't even know," she says, scrubbing a palm over her face. "You're just weird. You just—he was a *bear*, Blanche! What were you even thinking, letting him sit in here?"

"Hmm," I say, completely disregarding the question in favor of savoring the faint, lingering smell of dark earth and wild things, of trees and honey and rain in the evening.

"I love you, you know," Rosie says, sighing a little, "but you're just impossible."

His name is Red Paw. He shows me why—one shaggy brown paw is stained reddish, like old blood, and the claws are cut short, ragged little blackish stubs.

"What happened?" I ask, serving up his usual cider with honey. I slide an apple cinnamon fritter on the saucer without being asked. I know everybody's order, every time. Gramma calls it a gift. Rosie calls it being a weirdo, but then, Rosie has a tattoo of her own name and a bunch of roses (real original) in an impolite place to talk about, so I try not to listen when she gets too judgmental. She's got her own troubles to work through, I think. Red Paw nods his thanks and takes a nibble, more delicate than you'd expect.

"I had a pack of difficulties with a little man who liked to take things that weren't his," Red Paw says slowly, like it was maybe a little more violent than that and he's trying to spare my sensibilities. Part of me doesn't like it when folk try to do that, to clean things up just because I'm a lady, but on him, I can kind of understand why he's worried about scaring me. After all, his teeth are pretty big, and his other claws sure are sharp. He's real careful with them, though—he hasn't torn or broken anything yet, not even a napkin. He's gentler than most men I've met, really.

"What'd he take?" I ask, prying despite myself. I know it's bad manners, but I can't help it. He's got this air about him, like he's been places far away, like he's seen things that maybe other folks can't see at all. He's got this look like Grampa gets when he talks about the War, like whatever he's thinking about hurts him in ways that don't show up when you go looking for scars.

Red Paw makes a face that might be a grimace, rubbing a paw across his muzzle contemplatively. "I don't rightly remember, actually," he admits. "It was a long, long time ago, somewhere else. I know he took my grandmama's wedding ring off me, but there was—" he stops, rubbing the place between his eyes like his head hurts. "I think there was something else, something important, that I can't quite wrap my head around, but it's gone now, either way."

My heart hurts for him a little. Losing something is bad enough, but losing something and not even having the memory of it to hold onto? That feels like a whole other kind of stealing, a whole other kind of losing.

I put a hand on his red paw, running a thumb over the rough edge of a sawed-off claw. It pulls at the skin of my finger a little, like rough sandpaper or the edge of a log. "Does it hurt?" I ask, turning the paw over and looking at the thin white scar that runs down the pad on it.

"Not exactly," Red Paw says, paw curling up around my hand. "More like an old bruise or a sore tooth. It's a bother, up in my head, but it doesn't hurt in the flesh."

"Like when I know I've got something to do, but can't remember what it is, or when I'm avoiding chores and know it'll be more work tomorrow," I say, fighting not to smile and losing. "But more, probably."

He huffs out one of his little bear laughs. "Something like that. I was different, before, I think, but it's been so long that I don't recall what sort of different I even could've been."

Grampa says the same thing about the War, that hurting people, even for good reasons, that it changes you. It shows, now, in the way his hands shake all the time, even when he's calm, but the shakes are just the parts of it I can see—Gramma used to say there was an earthquake in him, one he was holding tightly onto, and that having to hold that tight to something that big changes a man. I think maybe it changes a bear, too.

"You must have other people to be attending to, Miss Blanche," Red Paw says, ducking his head and pulling his paw back all of a sudden, like he's just remembered we're not the only folks here. To be honest, I'd almost forgotten about the other customers myself. There's something about him that just pulls you in.

"Rosie's mostly got it," I say, but I'm already moving around the counter to go do a quick check of the tables. "Everybody knows she's the personable one, anyways." She is, too, to everyone but the family. I think she just talks to people because she thinks one of them will give her a way out of here, out of the mountains and out of Georgia. She thinks she's some kind of cosmopolitan. I think there's something chasing her in her own chest, and she just wants to run from it instead of turning to look at it face-on. Everybody's got some kind of wolf in them, I think, looking to keep them scared of the things that are good for them, that are all wrapped up in destiny. Rosie's is just maybe bigger than others, or she's just more inclined to run. Either way, it's her wolf, not mine.

"You seem plenty personable to me," Red Paw says, raising his mug in a sort of salute to me.

I can feel my cheeks go hot. "Not hardly. I don't know why Gramma put me in charge—I can hardly talk to folks if I don't know them."

Red Paw cocks his head, looks at me like I'm some kind of strangeness he's never seen before. "You talk to me just fine, and everyone else is scared to even look me in the eye."

"Just cause TV is easier to watch than reading a book doesn't mean it's a better way to spend your time," I tell him, another set of words straight from Gramma. She's coming out of my mouth more and more these days—I can't say I mind, but it's still a little odd to hear her words in my voice.

He's bear-smiling again, eyes crinkled up, and I have to turn away so he doesn't see me go red again. "You're a complicated lady, Miss Blanche."

"I'm not," I say, pushing my hair out of my face and behind my ear. It's too dark, makes my face look waxy and paler than it is. I'd like hair the color of his, a warm brown, but there's no dyeing it unless I want to pay to keep it up every other week, and I don't have the money and I can't stand the smell. "I'm all kinds of uncomplicated, really." It's true—there's not much to me, as Rosie reminds me all the time. I don't do anything, don't go anywhere—I live in the kitchen and between pages of books, and there's not much complicated about that. People are complicated—that's why I mostly don't talk to them. I get this kind of fluttery panic in my chest around them, really; I can handle the little stuff, the *what can I get you today?* and the *how're you doing, how's your wife?* But when it comes to the real stuff, the *social* aspect, as Rosie puts it, well, I'm not much use.

Red Paw is different, but he doesn't feel complicated. Strange, and maybe a little dented up inside, but not complicated. He's too regal for normal-people-complicated things, for the kind of petty and nitpicky most folks are. It's a royal sort of thing, the kind of majesty that all the wild things have, the kind of grace you can't really touch, can't really imitate. It makes me feel safe, somehow, like I'm alone, but he's *there*, still, and that's—well, it's just plain nice, is what it is, and I like it.

"You've got to be a little complicated, to talk to me like you do," he says, and there's a little bit of Rosie in the way he says it, that same self-consciousness she gets when boys tell her she's pretty and she doesn't quite believe it.

I shake my head, putting a hand on his shoulder and squeezing. There's still some flakes of snow caught in his fur—it's flurrying a little outside, but nothing heavy. March is nearly here, and the snow is on its way to turning into rainstorms. "That's what I mean," I say, as gently as I can, like when Grampa has one of his fits and Gramma sits him down and reminds him who he is, where he sleeps now. "Folks make life *too* complicated. Be kind to the people who're kind to you, and be kind to the rest, too, when you can manage it. Everybody's got some kind of troubles, even if they don't show. It's that simple."

I go, then, before he says anything else—sometimes I can't bear when people talk to me, especially if I've said too much. I make the rounds of the tables, refilling coffees and clearing places where people have already left, and by the time I make my way back around to the counter, Red Paw has cleared out, leaving a neatly folded twenty under the edge of his mug.

I catch the corner of the bill with two fingers, edging it out from under the cup without tearing it, my other hand full, and slide it into the pocket of my apron with my other tips. There's not a lot else in there, but winter is always slow.

I don't mind the slow so much, with him for company.

Lou Woodcross is a sour little man who leaves bad tips and stares at me and Rosie's chests when we take his order. He's the sort of man who tells you to smile even if you're already smiling, like he has some kind of right to your feelings or like maybe you're not smart enough to be allowed to be anything but thrilled by his scraggly, leering face. He's a turkey hunter with a nasty beard and a nastier attitude, and even Gramma only puts up with him when she's feeling especially kindly.

I do my best to be nice to him, even though he's all kinds of ungrateful—he's got a bad shoulder and a bad leg from some kind of accident, and I think maybe it's the pain that makes him mean. Either way, everyone deserves a decent cup of coffee and something sweet now and then, even if they're terrible.

He's right in the middle of telling me that his coffee's too cold and the muffins are dry when the door opens, the little bell jangling, and Red Paw ambles in, covered in snow and dry leaves, and takes a seat at the counter.

Woodcross goes stiff, eye twitching a little, and he says, "You let that kind of thing in here, girl?" like he has some kind of problem with bears in general and maybe Red Paw in particular. He's a crotchety old racist in any case, and even I can't quite be patient all the time.

"Drink it or don't, Woodcross," I tell him, refilling his coffee and not much caring if I slosh a little on the table in the process. He jerks his hand back from the hot coffee as it hits the wood and splashes, and I see he's got a ring on his finger that I've never noticed before. It's a lady's ring, thin silver with a red stone, and it catches the light in a way that makes me stare.

He harrumphs and ducks low, pulling his cap over his face and ignoring me in favor of the newspaper. "Backtalkin' *and* staring. You used to be polite, Blanche," he says, all petulant. "Hangin' around the wrong sorts'll change you, it will."

"That what happened to you, Woodcross?" Rosie asks sweetly, hip-checking me out of the way and taking over. "You spend too much time with hillbillies up in the woods, getting all sexist and backwards?" Rosie is always better at dealing with people's nastiness than I am. She's got just enough of a sharp edge in her that she gets a little bit of vicious joy, I think, in turning people's crap back on them.

Grateful for the rescue, I meet Red Paw at the bar and pour him his cider. He comes in near about every day now, and I can't pretend that I don't look forward to it. "And how're you today?" I ask him, shaking off the weird, uncomfortable smile I use for Woodcross and feeling a real smile tuck up the corners of my mouth. Already I feel better, like going home at the end of the day—I can stretch when he's there; not my back and my arms and such, but whatever makes me up as a person, it gets to come out and shake all its soreness out and take a deep breath or two. It's the sort of comfortable you don't much get as a grownup, the kind I mostly only had as a kid, when I'd get to curl up in Grampa's arms and cry when I skinned my knee, or when I'd fall asleep while Gramma read me stories, or when I'd tell Rosie all the things I thought, uncensored, when we were too young to understand secrets or boundaries or things like *supposed to* or *ladylike* or *proper*. It's so nice that I feel greedy and maybe a little selfish, talking to him, like I'm taking something from him, but he seems to like talking to me, too, so I figure he must not mind too much.

"I'm doing just fine, Miss Blanche," he says. He takes a sip of his cider—not a sip, really, exactly, but the way cats drink water, his tongue reaching out and scooping some up. It doesn't seem rude, though, or particularly beastly—it's somehow elegant, actually, like the way rich folks eat with their forks upside down. "And how are you?"

The smile on my face is probably too wide to be ladylike when I say, "Well, I'm doing better now." I don't feel embarrassed, though; I don't imagine he'll judge me overmuch for one reckless smile or too much affection. He doesn't seem like the type of man who expects ladies to portion out their affection in some kind of Victorian sense of propriety. He seems like he could maybe use to have people give him more real smiles, anyways.

He cocks his head in that way he has, like he's studying me, and he says, "Somebody giving you a hard time about having me in here again?"

"Rosie gives me a hard time about everything," I say, still mostly smiling. "That's what sisters are for." I can't help but glance at Woodcross, though. He's still hunched in his seat, taking sips of coffee that are somehow antagonistic. I don't know how anybody can manage to try to pick a fight by sipping coffee, but if anybody could, it's that man.

He cocks his head a little further, then follows my gaze to the seating area and Woodcross. The hairs on the back of my neck stand up, and it takes me a second to realize he's growling.

"What's wrong?" I ask, putting a hand over his scarred paw, making him jerk back around, like he'd just remembered I was there.

He clears his throat a little and shakes his head, like he's shaking water off. "I don't—I don't rightly know, Miss Blanche. I do apologize."

It's alright, then, and we chat for another while as he drinks his cider and makes his way through an apple fritter and a blackberry tartlet and a piece of blueberry cheesecake. He eats a lot, but he's not messy about it—it's just like suddenly the food is gone, and he's licking a claw clean.

"Ahem," someone says, fake-clearing their throat.

I look up from talking to Red Paw, and Woodcross is standing at the register, looking torn between being twitchy nervous and just plain hateful as he glares at Red Paw. Red Paw is very still, like a dog that catches a scent. I pat his arm absently, crossing over to the register myself.

"What do I owe you?" Woodcross asks stiffly.

"Four ninety," I say promptly. Woodcross always gets the same thing. I don't know how he doesn't know his own total by now, but I guess some folks just don't pay attention to things. He's too busy ogling the ladies to pay attention to math, most likely.

Woodcross is fishing it out of his battered wallet when the lady's ring on his finger catches the light and flashes.

"Pretty," I say, so I'm not just staring at it like a freak again. "Where'd you get it?"

Woodcross clears his throat again, this time for real, and shifts a little, uneasy, glancing fast at Red Paw and away. He thrusts a five over the counter at me, crumpling it up in my hand, says, "Keep the change," and makes for the door like a rabbit.

Red Paw makes a low, dangerous noise in his throat and says, "Excuse me, Miss Blanche," polite as you please, before he tucks a bill under his mug and follows Woodcross out.

My chest hurts, all of a sudden, like when you watch a sad movie and something heartbreaking happens and you want to cry but you feel stupid about it. I don't know what's wrong, exactly, but something is, so I go around the counter and push open the door. The bell jangles, too loud.

It goes like slow motion, or like funky jump-cut editing or something. My chest aches the whole way through.

Red Paw is standing there, teeth wrapped around Woodcross's left hand, the one wearing the ring. Woodcross has his other hand up, and his fingers are sparkling with something red and green at the same time, shimmering like an oil slick and crackling like electricity. He makes a grab for Red Paw's scarred paw with that hand, and I smell burning hair and flesh and hear an almighty crack all at once, and just like that, Red Paw is gone.

Woodcross is laying on the ground, clutching his arm where his hand used to be, and Red Paw, or what used to be Red Paw, is standing there, stark naked, holding the red and silver ring in his hand.

I'm pretty sure I scream—that must be what makes him turn to me, ring dropping out of his fingers and hitting the snow like another drop of blood. He crosses over to me, suddenly-human face aghast at frightening me, at the violence.

Looking up into his human face, I can't judge Rosie for wanting to run from the wolf in her chest—mine is right here, is staring me down, and it's *terrifying*. Not because of Woodcross or the blood, but because he's not *him*, all of a sudden, he's—he's just *somebody*, and I can't handle this kind of thing from just *somebody*. I can't handle people hardly at all, let alone—let alone *this*.

"Are you alright?" he asks, cupping my face in his hand, thumb running across my cheekbone. "Miss Blanche, what's wrong? Did I frighten you? Talk to me."

I bite my lip hard, feel it wobble, and I squeeze my eyes shut so the tears don't fall out. Hard as I try, I can't get any words to come up out of my throat—they're all just stuck in the back of it, a hard knot of horrible that I can't spit out. He's not Red Paw anymore, he's not—he's not *mine*, he's all of a sudden *people*. He's a complicated thing, he's company, and the smell of dark earth and silence is gone. I could talk to him, maybe, if he was just ordering up a coffee or a slice of pie, but *talk* to him?

"I can't," I say, raw and ragged like my mouth is bleeding. I think of all those stories, things like *The Frog Prince* and *Beauty and the Beast*, and I wonder if those girls felt the same—if they could talk to the forest creatures but not the men, because men are—you're supposed to *be* something for men, supposed to have the right words and the right little gestures and all those sorts of things, but before they're men, they're pieces of forest, of solitude and quiet observation. It feels like a betrayal, somehow, and I know that isn't fair of me, it's not, because Red Paw—but he must have another name, a man's name, now, or even always—wasn't really a bear, was cursed to wear that shaggy coat, and he must feel *free* now. I should be happy for him, I know I should, and I'd be properly polite and tell him so, I would, but I can't get my mouth to open again. This is the other thing, the thing Woodcross stole, however long ago—his humanity—and it's as jarring and out of place on him as the ring was on Woodcross.

He's still looking at me, brow furrowed, mouth half-open in confusion, when Rosie takes my hand and pulls me away, out of the doorway and down the street.

I don't even manage to say anything until Rosie has us halfway to the creek down below the churchyard, her hand tight around mine. Even then, all I manage to get out is, "What?"

She just shakes her head and keeps towing me along until we get to the rocks by the creek, the big ones that stick out across the water like some kind of pier made by giants. She pulls me out across the biggest one, the one we used to play on as kids, and she tugs me down at the edge of it, sitting us down side by side with our legs dangling out over the water.

We're silent for a minute, me frozen and her thoughtful. When she does talk, she makes a couple false starts, clearing her throat like a smoker before she manages to say things properly.

"It's how happy endings are supposed to go," she says, smiling a little lopsidedly and looking out over the water. "You know, true love and beasts turning into men and everything."

"I—" I start to say, but my throat catches again and she puts a quelling hand on my knee. My apron, coffee-stained and ancient, rumples under her hand, dingy white against the bright red paint on her nails.

"But you're weird, you know?" she goes on. She doesn't say it unkindly—more like saying *you've got black hair* than some sort of judgment. "You're—you're all quiet, inside."

It startles me a little, because I don't know that I've ever caught Rosie paying that much attention to things outside her own self.

"Me, I'm like—like out here, how the creek never really shuts up, never stops going? It's like that in my head, all the time, you know? But you're like a rock, you know, like you're solid all the way through, and the edges of you maybe get warm when the sun comes out, but never the middle. There's always something in you that's secret, kind of, that's curled up and quiet." She stops, gnawing on her lip, and I watch with a sort of distant fascination as she chews half her lipstick off. "But around him—and don't get me wrong, I still think it's plumb crazy that you talked to him in the first place, let alone let him stick around and keep chatting you up, alright, but— around him, it's like whatever that thing is, that quietness? It's like maybe it stuck its nose out into the light for a minute. Like I could finally see you, you know?"

I do know. That's why it hurts so much, why the hazel of his eyes is so spooky, because I'm used to the black. It's like how now, if Rosie weren't here, I'd be alone, even if there are frogs and squirrels and fish and deer and things—they're not judging me on the standards that human folks do, they've got their own little rituals and things, and they're *uncomplicated*. There's something beautiful and quiet in that, and in the way he was—the kind of simple grace that people never have. It's not quite the same as the quiet that I've got in me, but it makes me feel like maybe my quiet could be safe next to his. And looking at him, seeing that *gone*—

"I think," I say, my throat scratching horribly with the tears I haven't let go yet, "I think maybe my heart's broken."

Rosie rests her head on my shoulder, her fat auburn curls tumbling down my arm and getting in my face a little. "I want to say that you're an idiot, but it also kind of makes sense, so I don't think I can blame you for it." She kicks her feet a little, idly, and we both watch them swing.

I think about saying something else, about trying to explain to her the whole of what's going on in my head, like I would when we were kids, but she's too human for that now. Children are wild things in a way that people who have to move in the real world can't be, and there's too much in between us now, too many crushes on boys and rides in cars and lessons about manners and Sundays in church and mornings spent doing hair and makeup and evenings spent watching TV or reading books.

I think the silence works, too, though. Rosie kicks my ankle now and then, and I kick back, and we sit on the big rock, feet dangling, and we don't say another word.

Somehow, it helps, just a little, knowing that even Rosie has this much quiet in her, even under all those thorns.

He's waiting when I come in for my shift the day after the ruckus. I take a minute to look over him, on the other side of the glass door, before I open it and the bell rings and he notices me. Now, just for a moment, it's still quiet, inside me and around me, and I can really look.

He's got a scruffy beard that almost looks like his old coat, shaggy and brown, and his hair curls down over his ears and his forehead in rough little tangles. His shirt hugs his shoulders like some kind of plaid skin, and it pouches out a little with his round stomach. He still looks a little like a bear, if I squint—it's in the way he holds himself, the way he's curled around his mug and the counter. He still holds the mug carefully, like he's minding his claws, and his right hand is still strange—there's a white scar running across it, all the way up under his shirtsleeve, and the tips of two fingers are missing, and all the skin on the right side of his hand is reddish and patchy, like it's been burnt. Woodcross's magic, I suppose, but it looks stranger on human flesh than it did on his paw.

He cocks his head, then, and the gesture is so familiar my breath catches in my chest. He turns to the door like maybe he heard me, or smelled me, or something, and, caught out, I push it open. The bell jangles faintly, like it's ashamed to interrupt.

"Miss Blanche," he says, ducking his head and rubbing a bashful hand over the back of his neck.

I swallow and open my mouth, but no words come out. I don't even know what to call him anymore—there's no way I'm supposed to keep on calling him *Red Paw*; he doesn't even *have* paws. I can feel the shuddery panic I get when I try to talk to people for too long start up in my chest, something way past butterflies, and I feel bad again for passing any kind of judgment on Rosie for wanting to run from the wolf in hers. Some things are just terrifying.

He smiles tentatively, a crooked hitch of his lips, and his eyes crinkle in the way they always have. In the low light, they could maybe be black instead of that strange hazel, and the shine in them is the same. "Could I trouble you for a cup of cider, maybe?" he asks, low and soft, like *I'm* a wild animal, skittish and ready to bolt. Maybe I am. I nearly choke on the hysterical laughter that bubbles up under my breastbone.

I move on autopilot to the counter, taking up my apron and tying it around my waist like I have nearly every day of my life. I gather all my hair up in my hands and tie it back with Grampa's old bandana, and then, well, I'm out of ways to stall, so I pull out a mug and pour the cider.

My hand shakes when I hand it to him, and I think about Grampa's hands, about his earthquake, and about men changing. He takes the mug from me, wrapping his scarred hand around mine and holding on for just a second or two longer than he really needs to. It makes my chest hurt. I wonder, looking at my shaking hand, if maybe any kind of war changes you, if maybe I could be a different woman if I fought the panic people bring out in me.

I think Grampa would probably want me to try. He'd never tell me so, would never put that kind of thing on me, but—but there was something so nice about getting to spend time with another somebody without being scared the whole way through, and that makes me think that maybe it'd be worth trying.

Swallowing hard against the tremble that's hovering in my throat, I say, more awkward and stilted than usual, "And how're—how're you today, sir?"

His face cracks open on a smile, eyes crinkling up until I can barely see them. "It's Joe," he says, stretching out his hand across the counter. He puts his gnarled fingers on the back of my hand, waiting, and it takes me a minute, but I manage to turn my hand over, just enough to let him take it. "And I'm doing better now." His hand squeezes mine, strong but careful, and my eyes drop shut. Like that, I can almost relax enough to like it, like holding his hand—with my eyes shut, I can forget he's a person and remember that he's *him*. I open my eyes, because that feels too cheap to stomach, and he says, gentle as can be, "And how're you, Miss Blanche?"

I choke a little on the panicked laugh that comes out of me then, but I manage to say, "I could be better," without throwing up or running for the hills, so I give myself a little mental pat on the back. Learning to read wasn't easy, either, but it was worth it for the books. Red Paw—Joe—he's maybe worth a little of that, too.

"You really couldn't be," he says, squeezing my hand a little again and smiling right into my eyes.

Rosie whistles as she comes round the counter, tray on her shoulder. "You're mighty smooth for somebody as didn't have thumbs or eyebrows yesterday," she says, raising her eyebrows at him and patting my hip as she goes by. It's somehow reassuring, in that weird way that folks acting like themselves somehow always is.

Joe laughs, and it's the same little huff of air that he laughed when he was a bear. "Sorry." He looks at me again, more serious, and he says, "Miss Blanche, I know I had no right to go upsetting you like I did, but—" he clears his throat a little, ducking his head, "—but I hope you'll let me make it up to you."

A proper gentleman, Gramma would call him. And rightly, too. I feel like a heel, treating him like he's just *somebody*, after all the days he's made nice just by being around, after how kind he is, even when I'm this much of a gibbering idiot.

"I, um," I say, tugging my hand back to cover the red I can feel rising on my cheeks. "I think I'd—I think I'd maybe like that." It comes out quiet, barely a whisper, but Joe catches it anyways, and the width of his smile tugs a little one out of me in response.

"Well, then," he says, standing up and sliding a neatly folded bill under the edge of his cup, "I guess I'll be seeing you tomorrow, Miss Blanche." Still beaming at me, he nods that precise little nod, like he's tipping a hat he doesn't have, and then he's out the door, the bell jingling in his wake.

My hands are still shaking and my chest still hurts, but there's something nice in it now, too, a kind of cool sunshine-y feeling, like the creek in summer or a really good apple. The air smells, familiarly, wonderfully, like dark earth and trees.

"There you are," Rosie says, soft and satisfied, from behind me. Her hand squeezes my shoulder, once, briefly.

I smile, too widely for it to be pretty or polite, and it feels good. "Here I am," I agree. I let the quiet places in me stretch, just a little, let them be *more* than quiet. Shaky hands or not, it's worth it.

ABOUT THE AUTHOR

Alena Sullivan is a graduate student in the Stonecoast MFA program for Creative Writing. Her speculative fiction has appeared in Strange Horizons, Urban Fantasy, Expanded Horizons, *and elsewhere. One of her stories is in Rich Horton's* Year's Best Science Fiction and Fantasy 2017, *published by Prime Books. Her speculative poetry has been included in* Goblin Fruit, Star*Line, Illumen, *and elsewhere. Her website is alenasullivan.wordpress.com.*

A MIDSUMMER NIGHT'S BEDTIME STORY

CHARLES D. SHELL

L ong Tom slept in a ball at Eliza's feet, burrowed into the comforter covered in pastel cartoon characters. The big tomcat rarely left the seven-year-old's side except for the occasional foray outside. The only sound in the room was the quiet hum of the air conditioning.

At thirteen minutes past midnight, a sound woke the feline. He looked over at the crack in the baseboard near the corner. A scent reached his nostrils. His fur rose and a hiss escaped his jaws as an ancient, instinctive hatred filled him. He jumped off the bed and stalked to the corner without a sound. He sniffed at the small hole in the wall, his tail huge with alarm.

When the attack came, it was too fast for even the nimble cat to escape. He let out a caterwaul of pain that nearly woke Eliza... then quiet returned to the room.

The trio had trouble holding a conversation over Eliza's wails and Dale's angry shouting into the telephone.

"I toldja it was the Unseelie! Toldja!" Thornspur said over and over as they sat inside the kitchen cabinet.

"Yah. Poor kit got pointy-stuck," Mudlick said. "Stuck."

Featherpetal rolled her eyes. "Whose fault is that, addlebrain?" She pointed at Mudlick.

Mudlick's big, toad-like mouth turned down in a frown. He pulled his threadbare cap over his eyes.

"He's gonna cry again, Petal!" Thornspur said.

"I don't care." She crossed her arms as sobbing came from beneath the cap. Her stern expression softened and she patted Mudlick on his back. "It's all right, Mudlick. We'll fix it."

Mudlick pulled up his cap as plump tears rolled down his oversized cheeks. He gave her a soulful look. "Fix?"

"Yes, we'll fix it," she said.

"How we gonna do that, Petal?" Thornspur asked.

"Umm… I'm working on it," she said. "First, we have to make sure that book is safely out of mortal hands."

Eliza looked over at Long Tom's bed and felt the tears coming again. It was mixed with a dull anger towards whoever had done such an evil thing to her beloved cat. Her father still talked with the police over the phone as he tried to comfort her.

"I'm telling you that some hooligan was in my house, officer!" Dale said into the receiver. "The cat was inside last night and I found it hanging from a tree this morning!"

Eliza started wailing again.

"I'm sorry, honey," Dale said as he silently berated himself. "I'll get you a new cat."

"I don't wanna new cat! I want Long Tom!" she screamed.

Dale's ex-wife Anna had picked a wonderful time to be out of town. He tried explaining the situation to another unsympathetic policeman before taking Eliza to his sister's house and rushing into work.

"Okey doke! They're all gone!" Thornspur said, squinting out the window into the painful sunlight.

"Gone," Mudlick said as he sucked on his toes.

"Let's get to searching. We know the Chronicle's here somewhere and there's no glamour on it. We'll be thorough and it shouldn't take long."

"Thurra," Mudlick said as he walked along the carpet. "Fuzzy."

Featherpetal sighed. She flew out of the air duct and hovered in front of the bookshelf. None of the books looked familiar, despite a large number of Gaelic words. This mortal had a lot of books. Thornspur hovered next to her.

"Where should we start?" Thornspur asked.

"Grab a book and start reading."

"And Mudlick?" Thornspur pointed at the floor where the plump spriggan bumped into a trashcan, spilling its contents over the floor.

"Try to keep him from setting the house on fire."

"That's it, then," Featherpetal said, shoving the last book back into the case. She looked around at the ransacked chaos of the father's den. Mudlick's legs stuck out from underneath a couch cushion. "It's not here."

"It's gotta be, Petal!" Thornspur said. "We didn't get drawn here by accident! Someone spoke our true names!"

"So where...?" Featherpetal looked over at a painting of a sunflower. One side of the painting rattled from the air blasting it from a nearby vent. She flew over and pulled the side open, revealing a hidden safe.

"Iron!" Thornspur shouted.

"Irrun!" Mudlick yelled from underneath the cushion.

"Calm down. It's only a safe," she said—but kept a discreet distance.

"They've warded it against us!"

Mudlick yelled incoherently.

"Will you two shut up? Mortals use iron all the time. It doesn't hurt them, remember?" She landed on top of the desk and looked up at the formidable obstacle. "The father must have recognized the book as valuable and put it in there."

"What do we do?" Thornspur asked. "We can't go through iron!"

"Irrun!"

"We don't have to, addlebrains. He'll open it eventually. Once it's out, we can take it back," Featherpetal said, "before he can call forth any more of the Unseelie." She looked around at the wrecked room. "Now we have to fix this den back the way we found it."

"What? I'm a Pixie Knight! Not a Brownie!" Thornspur shouted.

"Bwownie!"

"You'll do what I say. We can't alarm the mortals any more or he might never take the book back out."

"But...!"

"Start cleaning."

Eliza sniffed and rubbed at her reddened eyes as she looked down at the spot where Long Tom slept the night before. She felt like crying again, but she was emotionally spent.

Her father ransacked the house trying to find out how someone had gotten inside. Finding nothing, he resorted to changing the locks. The locksmith assured him that the locks he removed hadn't been tampered with.

After spending an hour double-checking every window, Dale sat up with his daughter as she read some old storybooks. Dale used to read to Eliza but she was now a voracious reader who disdained help unless it was a very big word. Eliza eventually succumbed to sleep.

"Why are we watching this mortal girl?" Thornspur asked as they looked down from the ceiling vent.

"She pretty," Mudlick said with a grin.

"Because whatever Unseelie is lurking below might come back tonight. And it might not be satisfied with killing a cat," Featherpetal said.

"So?" Thornspur said.

Featherpetal pointed at Eliza. "She could be harmed or killed."

"So?"

Featherpetal sighed. "If the covenant with the mortal world is broken—even if it's done by a minor Unseelie—we might get the blame. Especially after Mudlick was the one who lost the Chronicle."

Mudlick frowned and started to cry again.

"Will you stop that? I said we'll fix it!"

"What does one mortal life matter, more or less?" Thornspur asked.

Featherpetal raised an eyebrow. "Maybe you'd like to take that up with Queen Titania or King Oberon?"

Thornspur's eyes widened.

"Break the covenant—or allow it to be broken—and they will find out. And neither one will be happy."

"'Beron!" Mudlick cringed in fear.

"I guess we can watch the mortal brat for a few nights."

"That's what I thought you'd say."

Mudlick looked down at Eliza and a grin split his broad face. "She pretty one. We guard."

A half-asleep Eliza touched the indentation where Long Tom had once lain. She felt tears coming again when she heard the sound: an unhealthy skittering from the baseboard in the corner. She bit her lip in fear and tried to see through the gloom.

At first she thought it was a rat. She wanted to scream but her breath froze in her lungs. The dark shape slouched forth from the crack and stood on two legs. Two red sparks on its face glared at her.

Eliza found her voice and screamed.

"Daddy!"

A guttural laugh came from the misshapen form.

"No one hear you, mortal meat."

She screamed louder, which caused more laughter. The small, humped form crawled up onto her bed. Frost rolled off its back.

"I give you reason to scream, meat."

Eliza fumbled with her lamp. If she could turn on the light, she'd wake from the nightmare. Her fingertips touched the switch and light spilled over the bed. Instead of vanishing, the creature merely flinched from the light and Eliza got a good look. The thing had dark skin, a huge head with oversized jaws and was dressed in scraps of fur.

Eliza wanted to scream again, but she couldn't find the breath as the creature scrambled up the covers towards her. It left a trail of luminescent drool in its wake. It chuckled with every step, drinking in her fear.

Its chuckling stopped when another small figure landed in front of it. It was a tiny, winged man a few inches tall, dressed in garish blue silk and wielding a rapier. The miniature man was unnaturally slender and moved like lightning.

"Hold, boggart! This mortal child is under the protection of Thornspur the Pixie Knight!" Thornspur said, moving his rapier with blurring speed.

The boggart froze in surprise for a moment.

"Begone! Get lost, you Unseelie ruffian!" Thornspur danced around in an elaborate series of fencing moves.

The boggart's eyes narrowed. "My mortal meat."

"No, she's not!" Thornspur said.

The boggart lashed out with one of its long arms and knocked Thornspur the length of the bed. He skidded to a stop, his head spinning and rapier imbedded in a teddy bear.

"Haw!" the boggart said and advanced towards Eliza again, setting off renewed terror. A second winged figure landed next to the first. This one was a miniature woman in a shimmering, feather-fringed dress.

"You acorn-brain! Next time stab first and threaten later!" Featherpetal said.

"He cheated!" Thornspur said, getting to his feet.

The boggart was nearly to Eliza's feet when another small figure dropped in front of the boggart. This figure had no wings and its arms were nearly as thick as its stout body.

"You no hurt pretty mortal!"

The boggart's eyes widened in fear. "Spriggan!"

"Yah!" Mudlick said as his oversized fist propelled the boggart across the room to imbed into the wall. As mighty as the blow was, the boggart wouldn't have been killed except that chance interceded. A steel stud poked out of the baseboard just inside of the drywall, impaling the boggart. The boggart let out a gurgling moan of pain and smoke poured from its mouth. It twitched a few more times and then dissolved into a foul cloud of gas.

"Go poof!" Mudlick said with a satisfied nod.

The three faeries had a moment of silence. It was a solemn thing when one of the sidhe perished—even one of the Unseelie Court. Eliza stared at the three tiny humanoids with a combination of wonder and fear.

Featherpetal, Thornspur and Mudlick stood in front of Eliza. Mudlick, being a bit top-heavy, fell over and looked up at Eliza with an upside-down grin.

Eliza giggled despite her fear.

"You pretty," Mudlick said.

"She can see us! I mean *really* see us!" Thornspur said.

"She has the sight," Featherpetal said. "A human child with elf-sight. I didn't think there were any left."

"A-are you gonna hurt me?" Eliza asked in a small voice, clutching her comforter to her face.

"No, child," Featherpetal said. "We're here to protect you."

"Purtect!" Mudlick said, righting himself.

"Okay," Eliza said, as if that made perfect sense. She pointed at the hole in her wall. "What was that?"

"Boggart." Thornspur sneered. "Foul minion of the Unseelie Court!"

"The Un... what?"

"Unseelie Court," Thornspur said. "The dark children of the Sidhe."

"Children of the she?" Eliza's forehead crinkled up in confusion. "She who?"

"Not 'she'—*sidhe*."

"That's what I said—she." Eliza folded her arms defiantly.

"No, no!" Thornspur jumped up and down, fists pumping in frustration.

"Leave it be, Thornspur," Featherpetal said, stifling a grin. "She doesn't understand."

Thornspur scowled.

"We are of the light faerie folk," Featherpetal said, picking her words carefully. She pointed at the hole in the wall. "That was one of the dark faerie folk."

Eliza's face brightened. "You're good fairies!"

"Close enough," Featherpetal said. "My name is Featherpetal and I'm a sprite. My friend with the sword is Thornspur, a Pixie Knight."

Thornspur bowed with a flourish of his cap, evincing another giggle from Eliza.

"And this is Mudlick... a Spriggan," Featherpetal said with a sigh.

Mudlick grinned and hugged Eliza's leg. Eliza squeaked in surprise when the pressure on her thigh became painful.

"Careful, Mudlick," Featherpetal said. "Sometimes you don't know your own strength."

The grip released.

"You're *strong!*" Eliza said with wonder.

"Yah. Spriggan strong." Mudlick smacked a fist into his palm with a crack.

"Wow."

"You pretty," Mudlick said.

Eliza smiled. "You hit him good."

"Yah. Boggart go poof."

"Boggart?"

"That was a boggart, child. A lesser Unseelie... I mean a lesser dark faerie. We think he slew your pet."

Eliza's face scrunched up and she started crying.

"Why is she doing that?" Thornspur asked.

"Her pet died, emptyhead!" Featherpetal said.

"Poor kit!" Mudlick started crying in time with Eliza's sobs.

"Now they're *both* doing it!" Thornspur said. "Stop it!"

They both cried louder.

Thornspur opened his mouth to yell again but Featherpetal slapped her hand over it.

"Hush! That's not helping." Before Thornspur could pull her hand away, Featherpetal started singing. Her voice was honeysuckle-sweet and her words spoke of elfin meadows and streams of liquid moonlight. Eliza's crying trickled off and her eyelids grew heavy. Her head drooped over the pillow and after a moment she was asleep. Mudlick's crying stopped.

"That's better," Featherpetal said. "We'll guard her until sunrise and then visit her again tomorrow night. You!" She pointed at Thornspur. "Fix the hole in the wall."

"I'm no Brownie!"

She glared at him until he complied.

"Daddy said I had a nightmare," Eliza told her visitors the following night. "He didn't believe me."

"He may not see us anyway," Featherpetal said, "if he doesn't have the sight."

"The sight?"

"Elf-sight. You can see through our glamours."

"Glamour? Like supermodels?"

Now it was Featherpetal's turn to be confused. "I... don't think so. It... it's an image. An illusion that mortals have trouble seeing through."

"You mean it's not real."

"Yes."

"'Kay."

"What's your name, child?"

"Eliza."

"That's a fine name," Featherpetal said.

"Pretty," Mudlick said. Thornspur had no comment.

"How come bad fairies are tryin' to hurt me? Why'd they kill poor Long Tom?"

"Long Tom?"

"My cat."

"Oh. Well, dark faeries rarely need a reason to harm mortal creatures, but they and the cat folk have an old enmity," Featherpetal said.

"Nimmity?"

"They're enemies."

"Oh. But that boggey thing was gonna hurt me."

"Boggarts delight in pain and fear. After your cat was gone he thought it was safe to harm you."

"Boggart go poof!" Mudlick said.

"Yes, Mudlick—Boggart go poof," Featherpetal said.

"Will you stop saying that?" Thornspur said.

"Where'd it come from?"

Featherpetal pointed towards the crack in the baseboard. "It emerged from the depths of your house through there."

"Is it dead?"

"Quite dead."

"How come it came *here?*" Eliza asked. "And how come you're here?"

"Your father has a book that is dangerous for mortals to possess. It has a portion of the Chronicles of Faerie. Several *true* names of the Seelie and Unseelie are contained within its pages. To speak names draws attention of faerie folk. Much as we three were drawn here."

"I don't unnerstand."

"True names have power in the Courts," Thornspur said, "if spoken properly and completely."

"Oh," Eliza said.

"Your father must have read portions of the Chronicle aloud. It was only good fortune that we were drawn as well as the boggart. The Chronicle has names of many potent faeries," Featherpetal said.

"Potent?"

"Powerful."

"Oh."

"And we need to retrieve the book from your father's safe before he can draw in more Unseelie—dark faeries. Until we do your household is in deadly peril," Featherpetal said. "Can you help us get inside his safe?"

Eliza shook her head. "Daddy told me to never go near the safe. That's where he keeps his guns."

"Guns?" Featherpetal asked.

"Mortal weapons," Thornspur said.

"Oh yes, now I remember. Loud, smoky things."

"Make boom," Mudlick said.

"We don't want your father's guns, we want the book," Featherpetal said. "Before it's too late. Will you help us?"

"I dunno. Dad'll be awful mad."

"We can't do it without you, child. The safe contains far too much iron for us to bypass."

"Iron?"

"Yes, iron. It's deadly to all faerie folk except the dwarves. The purer it is, the more deadly. We can't even touch pure iron without burning."

"Like silver to a werewolf?" Eliza asked, wide-eyed.

"Yes child, something like that."

Thornspur rolled his eyes.

"How come my daddy has your book?"

"It was lost a short time ago. Your family and mine have some history. It ended up with your clan back in Ireland during one of our family squabbles."

"Ireland? My great-great-sumthin' grandpaw lived in Ireland, I think."

Featherpetal frowned. "That's a long time for mortals?"

"Well, yeah!"

Featherpetal shrugged. "Time is different for my folk. Mudlick lost the book to your kin right before they had some sort of famine. Then we lost track of it until a few nights ago. We didn't even know it was on this continent. You mortals move very fast."

"Enough chit-chat!" Thornspur said, his wings buzzing like an angered bumblebee. "We need to get into that safe!"

"I dunno...." Eliza bit her lip.

"Pplleaase...?" Mudlick said as he hugged her leg. "Mudlick lost book. Me sorry."

Eliza smiled. "'Kay."

"Good," Featherpetal said. "Until we do, we'll have to remain on guard at night. The boggart may not have been the only Unseelie drawn in."

Eliza looked around the dark room in trepidation. "There might be more bad fairies?"

"Have no fear, child. We'll make sure you're safe if there are. Now sleep."

Featherpetal sang her to sleep again. Mudlick curled up at her feet in Long Tom's vacant spot.

"Mrs. Gable's cat just had a bunch of kittens," Dale said at breakfast the next morning. "Did you want to maybe pick a kitten?"

Eliza's face momentarily brightened and then sunk again. The pain of losing Long Tom was still too fresh. She shook her head.

"Okay, but if you change your mind let me know. It'll be a few days before she's given them all away."

"'Kay, daddy."

"Sylvia is going to watch you this afternoon. Please don't give her a hard time."

Eliza beamed and nodded. Sylvia had a habit of chatting on the internet for long periods. During her chats she was oblivious to Eliza's activities.

Eliza closed the door to her father's den. Featherpetal and Thornspur flew down from the ceiling. Mudlick sat on top of the oaken desk.

"Well?" Thornspur asked.

"She's on the internet talking about boys. She wouldn't notice me jumping out the window."

"Internet?" Featherpetal blinked.

"Yeah. Computer stuff."

"Computer?" Thornspur asked.

"Yeah. It's a thinking machine. Kinda." Eliza began to get frustrated.

"Never mind," Featherpetal said. "If I remember correctly, if you turn the dial on a safe in the right directions, it opens."

Thornspur opened the false painting.

"I don't see a dial," Thornspur said. "Just a bunch of black squares with numbers."

"It's got a keypad," Eliza said.

"A what?"

"You push the buttons in the right order and the safe opens."

"Oh. What order?" Featherpetal asked.

"I dunno. But I think Dad's got it written down somewhere in here."

"Where?"

Eliza shrugged. "Maybe in the desk."

The quartet discovered that Eliza's father wasn't the most organized fellow. The antique oaken writing desk was crammed with papers in every drawer as well as stacks on top. Eliza, Featherpetal and Thornspur dug through the reams of paperwork. Mudlick tried to help but kept forgetting what he was doing.

"What's a '1040 form'," Featherpetal asked, squinting at the tiny print.

"I dunno. The box said 'taxes'," Eliza said.

"Taxes?" Thornspur asked.

"Tribute," Featherpetal said.

Thornspur glared at the piles of paper. "How is this tribute? Where are the jewels or moonlight wine?"

Nobody had an answer.

"This is boring," Eliza said at the forty-minute mark. "I'm tired."

"She's right. This is worse than spinning straw into gold," Thornspur said, tossing several receipts into the air.

Mudlick snored from the bottom desk drawer.

Featherpetal bit her lip in frustration. Her eyes swam from the dozens of pages she'd read through. "How many numbers does the 'keypad' need?"

Eliza shrugged. "I dunno."

Featherpetal rolled her eyes. "Does he open the safe a lot?"

"Not too much. He takes the guns out to shoot at the range or to clean 'em. I think that's all."

"Then he'd probably keep the numbers someplace easy to find." Featherpetal pulled the top drawer open. It was difficult to open entirely due to notepads, loose papers and manila envelopes stuffed inside. Thornspur and Featherpetal crawled through the debris.

"I found it!" Thornspur yelled with triumph.

"So did I," Featherpetal said, holding up another note with 'Safe #' scrawled across it. After going through the notes, over a dozen different numbers were found.

"Which one is it?" Thornspur asked, flitting around in frustration. "Why is there more than one?"

"I guess daddy changed the combination. He's real careful."

"So which one is the last one?" Featherpetal rifled through the notes, trying to discern the latest.

"I dunno. We can just try 'em all, can't we?"

"I suppose."

After the third wrong number, a light next to the keypad glowed red and the LCD display said: *Too many incorrect entries.*

"What's that mean?" Thornspur asked.

After trying to enter more combinations and discovering that the keypad was unresponsive, they gave up. Eliza looked around at the debris and started stuffing papers back into the drawers and boxes.

"Will daddy notice that we messed things up?" Eliza asked.

"Child, did we really mess things up more than they were already messed up?"

Eliza giggled. She slipped back into her room without Sylvia even looking up from the computer's monitor.

"I can geas him," Featherpetal said that night.

"Geese?" Eliza frowned. "You're gonna turn my daddy into a goose?"

"No, no!" Featherpetal said. "I said *geas*."

Eliza blinked in incomprehension.

"Enchantment."

"Huh?"

Featherpetal thought carefully. "A magic charm."

Eliza's face brightened. "Oh!"

"He will believe that he needs to get his gun for some reason and will go and open the safe. Once he does, we'll go in and get the Chronicle."

"That's not bad," Thornspur said. "When?"

"Once he's asleep. It's easier to do when he's asleep, especially if he has elf-sight."

Eliza lost interest when Mudlick started tickling her. The powerful spriggan was surprisingly gentle with the girl and his smile illuminated the room. It took several tries to get the attention of the two.

"Do I need to do anything?" Eliza asked between laughs.

"I don't think so. Once the safe is open we should be able to safely retrieve the Chronicle as long as we don't touch the iron."

"Okay," Eliza said, losing interest. She went back to playing with Mudlick.

"You stay here and keep an eye out," Featherpetal said to Thornspur.

"What? Why?"

Featherpetal's voice went down to a whisper. "There may be another Unseelie in the house. Someone has to guard her and I may need Mudlick's strength to retrieve the book."

Thornspur puffed up with pride and fondled the hilt of his rapier. "I'll keep her safe."

"I never had any doubt."

It was nearly midnight when Dale slipped into a troubled sleep. He'd spent all evening paying bills online and reviewing the state of his finances—after checking all the doors and windows again. Once his breathing steadied, Featherpetal began her haunting song of charm. Dale's mind was wrapped in a potent geas that urged him into quasi-wakefulness. He stumbled into his den in a quest for his 9mm pistol. His sleepy fingers botched the combination once, but the second time the safe came open. He pulled out the pistol and staggered off in search of an imaginary burglar. Once he departed, Featherpetal flew Mudlick up to the safe.

"Careful, Mudlick. Don't touch the sides with bare skin."

"Yah," Mudlick said, walking over the steel safe's bottom wearing Eliza's bunny slippers. He looked through the piles of paperwork contained within the small cubicle, tossing out folders of financial records. After a minute his face poked back out.

"Well?"

"Not here," Mudlick said.

"What?"

"Nuffin' here."

The two of them looked through the safe three times before giving up.

"But… but where else would he keep it?"

Mudlick shrugged. "Maybe he not have it."

"*Some*body spoke the names. If it wasn't him…" Featherpetal's eyes widened.

"What matter?"

"Eliza! That boggart didn't seek out her father, he sought *her* out! *She* must have spoken the names!" Featherpetal smacked her forehead. "Curse me for a Nixie! I should have realized it earlier! I'll bet only a human with elf-sight can read the names properly! He was captured too easily by my geas to have it, so..."

Gunshots and Eliza's screams echoed through the house.

When the dark shape emerged from the crack in the baseboard, Thornspur unsheathed his bronze rapier and flew over to confront it. Part of him wanted to call out to his two friends for help, but pride—combined with a realization that they probably wouldn't hear him—stayed his tongue. He landed on the hardwood floor in an en garde position. Then he realized what kind of Unseelie he faced.

A goblin.

A trickle of fear penetrated his heart. It was the most fearsome of the lesser Unseelie. It was devilishly clever, strong and ruthless. He didn't know if all three of them could beat such a foe, forget doing it alone.

"Ahh... Pixie Knight," the goblin said with a voice like a strangling infant. "Tiny Pixie Knight. You wish to fight me?" Its dark, warty form was twice Thornspur's size, even hunchbacked as it was.

Thornspur swallowed.

The goblin laughed. "If you step aside and let me have the mortal morsel, I will let you live."

For an instant Thornspur considered the offer. The goblin was more powerful than he was, but Thornspur was quicker. If he wanted to escape, he could. He caught a glimpse of Eliza's sleeping face illuminated in the moonlight. If he fled, the goblin would kill her and eat her heart. Even without considering how angry King Oberon would be to allow the death of a mortal at faerie hands, she was... nice. He steeled his courage and faced the goblin.

"If you retreat now, I'll let *you* live, goblin!"

The goblin's yellow-glowing eyes narrowed with anger.

"I'm going to pull off those wings, Pixie."

The goblin attacked and Thornspur flew to meet him.

Dale held the pistol in his hands as he staggered drunkenly through the darkened house. There was a burglar out there—that much he knew—but he was a bit fuzzy on the other details. In fact, everything was fuzzy and he'd run into the kitchen wall a few times before he realized it wouldn't get out of his way. A distant part of him thought that he should be a bit more alarmed about an intruder, but couldn't quite fathom why.

After navigating the kitchen and the hall, he came to his daughter's bedroom and fumbled with the doorknob.

Thornspur's duel with the goblin was silent except for the goblin's laughs. Thornspur's tactics were simple: he flew at the goblin, sliced its face or shoulders with his blade and then flew back before the goblin's powerful claws could rend him apart. With a slower Unseelie it would have been easy, but a goblin was only slightly slower than a Pixie. He'd already received several superficial scratches from the goblin's claws. The wounds his blade made to the goblin didn't slow it in the slightest. It licked at the dark blood seeping from the scratches as if it was nectar.

It was a magnificent display of Seelie swordsmanship, but the end was never in doubt. The goblin's claws tore into Thornspur's side and wing, spinning him around and smashing him into the distant bookcase. His blade went flying and was lost underneath a small avalanche of books.

The sound woke Eliza. When she caught sight of the goblin, she screamed. The goblin smiled and stalked towards her, slavering in anticipation. Thornspur struggled to escape the pile of books but was pinned by a weighty tome.

"Face me, goblin!" Thornspur shouted in challenge.

"Snack first." The goblin smiled. "Girl heart. Nummy."

Eliza's bedroom door opened and her father stood there with a pistol. In Dale's groggy perceptions there was an intruder in the same room as his daughter—although he couldn't *see* it exactly. The pistol rang out, putting several rounds into the goblin's chest. What would have been fatal to a human intruder merely stung the goblin. The Unseelie whirled and lunged at Dale, who was too dazed to evade the attack. He would have died except a pair of small-but-powerful arms propelled him the length of the hall into the living room couch. He spiraled down into unconsciousness.

"Eliza-daddy *run!*" Mudlick said as he threw Dale from the goblin's path. Deprived of its primary target, it lashed out at the spriggan, sending Mudlick flying into the kitchen with droplets of faerie blood splashing the wall.

"*Mudlick!*" Featherpetal screamed as she flew over the goblin's head, interposing her winsome body between the goblin and Eliza. Thornspur had squirmed free from the books and recovered his rapier. His wings damaged, he climbed on top of Eliza's bed for his last stand.

"I'm scared, Thornspur," Eliza said.

"We won't let him hurt you," Thornspur said, trying to project confidence he didn't feel.

"Sprite and pixie. Pixie and sprite. In my belly for a midsummer delight. Hur!" the goblin said as it walked forward. It took its time, savoring the hunt.

"Not only are you revolting, but so is your poetry," Featherpetal said. Taking a deep breath, she sang. It wasn't a quiet, relaxing melody. This was a single, powerful note that rattled teeth, set every dog barking within a square mile and cracked most of the glass in the house. It was directed at the goblin and he smacked his misshaped hands over his pointed ears. Grimacing, he moved forward against the force of the sonic assault. Step by step, he closed the distance.

Mudlick pulled his body out of the side of the kitchen cabinet. Three deep claw wounds trailed down the side of his torso but the hardy spriggan didn't notice.

"Goblin bad," Mudlick said. He looked around the darkened kitchen until his eyes fell onto the pegs where oven mitts hung. Then an object sitting on top of the stove caught his eye. A rare spark of inspiration shot through his under-utilized brain.

Featherpetal watched her death approaching, but she wouldn't yield. Thornspur urged Eliza towards the window, but her father had secured it too well. The single note wavered and started to fail. The goblin's sadistic grin widened as it smashed Featherpetal to the ground, putting an abrupt end to her song. Thornspur leapt to the attack but was slapped aside with contempt. The goblin grabbed Featherpetal in a grip of steel and covered her mouth. Its fingers gripped one of her delicate wings.

"Sprite wing," the goblin said. "Like paper."

Featherpetal writhed in agony as the goblin pulled harder on her wing. His sadistic smile outshone his yellow eyes.

"Pain taste good."

The goblin recoiled in agony as the iron frying pan came down on top of its head with all the force Mudlick could muster. He wore the clumsy, oversized oven mitts on his hands as he swung the pan.

"Goblin bad!" Mudlick said as he swung again. Smoke poured from the goblin's head at every blow. The goblin dropped Featherpetal and tried to escape the deadly assault. The iron pan rose and fell like an executioner's axe. The goblin let out a hideous shriek as Mudlick drove it into the floorboards like a nail. Foul-smelling vapors poured out from underneath the pan after Mudlick's final blow. A charred outline was all that remained of the goblin.

Mudlick grinned, satisfied. "Goblin go poof!"

"I can't believe she had the Chronicle the whole time!" Thornspur said as Featherpetal examined his healing wounds. The yellowed Chronicle sat next to them, covered with crayon stains. It had been one of the books that had pinned him, covered with a different book jacket. "Why didn't she tell us?"

"She's only a child, Thornspur," Featherpetal said. Mudlick and Eliza played with dolls on the floor. Eliza dressed Mudlick in one of her doll's dresses and they were having tea together. Mudlick was oblivious to how ridiculous he looked. "She thought it was a story book and our true names sounded like gibberish to her."

"Well she nearly got us killed—and she slept through my epic duel!" He folded his arms and jutted his chin out. "She thinks Mudlick's a great hero but... aww, never mind."

Featherpetal grasped Thornspur by his chin and looked into his eyes.

"I know what you did, Pixie Knight Thornspur. You saved her life by facing a goblin in single combat. You're the bravest Pixie I've ever known." She kissed him on the lips.

Thornspur's cheeks turned cherry-red as he swelled with pride. For once he was at a loss for words.

"There's no more presence of the Unseelie here. The crack into the Unseelie Courts has closed." She pointed at the corner where the baseboard was now whole. "I've sung new memories into her father's mind. He'll forget all of this in a day. There's no reason for us to stay. Now comes the hard part."

"Hard part?"

"Parting those two." Featherpetal pointed at Mudlick and Eliza.

"But I want you to *stay!*" Eliza said, tears rolling down her cheeks.

"Mudlick want to *stay!*" Mudlick cried in time to Eliza's sobs.

"To stay in the mortal world would violate the Changeling Accord! Do you want to risk the wrath of King Oberon?" Featherpetal said.

"Don't care!" Mudlick hugged Eliza's leg. "Wanna stay with Eliza!"

Eliza hugged him back. "Stay!"

"Oh, by the Weird Sisters! You *can't!*"

"Why?" Eliza and Mudlick asked.

"I just told you...!"

Thornspur took her by the shoulder and shook his head, smiling.

"You can't out-stubborn a spriggan, Petal," he said.

Featherpetal opened her mouth to disagree but the sight of Eliza and Mudlick hugging melted her resolve.

"All right, but you've got to maintain a glamour whenever you're around other humans."

Mudlick nodded vigorously. "What Mudlick look like?"

"Kitty!" Eliza said.

"I'm telling you, Anna, that cat is weird," Dale said to his cell phone as he sat on the porch watching Eliza play along the sidewalk. The plump, black-and-white cat she'd named *Mudlick*—he had no idea where *that* name came from— followed wherever Eliza went. The two of them chased lightning bugs in the deepening evening.

"Weird how?" Anna asked over the phone.

Dale squirmed. "Well, for one thing I don't know where the devil it came from. It looks pretty healthy for a stray."

"But you got it shots and everything, right?"

"Oh yeah. The vet said it was—and I quote—'the healthiest cat I ever saw.'"

"So what's the problem?"

"It... looks at me like it understands what I'm saying."

There was a moment of silence on the line.

"Yeah, I know what that sounds like, Anna."

"I'm glad."

Dale was momentarily distracted when a local dog moved in Eliza's direction. Their neighbors did a poor job of controlling the huge German Shepherd, and Dale constantly worried about the aggressive beast harming his daughter.

Repeated requests had little impact on the neighbors. He relaxed when it moved away.

"And… have you ever seen a cat smile before, Anna?"

"That's just a snarl."

"No, I mean *smile*. Like the Cheshire Cat from *Alice in Wonderland*."

Another pause. "Have you been drinking, Dale?"

Dale sighed. "I knew it was a mistake saying anything."

"I'm sorry, Dale, but how did you expect me to react?"

"I was hoping…" Dale trailed off when the German Shepherd reappeared and ran towards Eliza. He dropped the cellphone and bolted towards his daughter. That's when he saw the German Shepherd retreating at high speed. He froze in the middle of the lawn and his eye twitched a little. He walked to the back yard and picked up the cellphone.

"Dale? Dale? Are you all right?"

"I… I haven't been drinking. But I intend to start as soon as I hang up."

"What?"

"Anna, I think I just saw…"

"Yes?"

"I could swear—*swear*—I just saw our daughter's cat chasing away the neighbor's dog with a baseball bat in its paws…"

ABOUT THE AUTHOR

Charles D. Shell is a native of southwestern Virginia. His story "Boneyard Prophet" was recently published in Threads: A NeoVerse Anthology.

LOVE AND ROOM FOR MONSTERS

AMANDA NARGI

J ames Custer Rook was one of the most valuable chess pieces on a board that had been set nearly a millennium before he was born, inside the tightly woven web of conflict that had always existed between mortal kind and the Gifted. He had cased thousands of undercover operations during his active work as one of Mab's Black Cats. He was familiar with the tradecraft of nearly every human intelligence agency in the world, knew when to use it, when to exploit it. He likewise knew the snakes' secrets of the few intelligence organizations that operated solely out of Shadowood. To his knowledge he was the only Faen to ever successfully plant a double agent inside The Order. And he had done it twice. But nothing he had ever accomplished or failed at in his many years in service to Mab and the security and freedom of his people had prepared him for this.

He was standing inside the cafe of The Wellspring, the little bookstore where Wil was supposed to meet his friend Maggie to study. He was there to pick Wil up, to take him home. But Wil wasn't there.

He forced himself to listen as Maggie's mother, the charming and empathic Amelia, told him that Wil wasn't in the bookstore. That he never had been. She assumed his football practice had run over.

"Jack?" she quested, lowering her voice. Her hand ghosted over his arm, fingers tightening almost imperceptibly in the folds of his worn leather jacket. He had the absurd thought that with her uncanny intuition and her natural discretion, she would be a potentially valuable recruitment opportunity.

"Is everything alright?" She pressed, when it took him too long to focus on her face.

Be calm, he told himself, even as his vision began tunneling. He smiled, and it was easy, convincing even. But Amelia was not a human civilian. He knew she was reading the colors of his aura, could taste the mounting panic in the air around him. He could see it in her eyes.

"Yes," he said. Confident. Casual. "I'll give his coach a call. The homecoming game is coming up—I'm sure it was just an extended practice."

In his mind, Jack was screaming around corners, checking for repeat faces in the crowds he had passed while walking through the plaza to the quaint little bookstore, the license plates of a dozen unmarked cars in the parking lot, cataloguing the exit and entry points of the small open-air shopping center and its handful of boutiques. Nothing had seemed out of the ordinary. He had been sure for months that their relocation to Rochester had gone unnoticed. They were in the dark. He would have known.

He would have known.

Amelia knew nothing of the nature of Jack's real work, but she had seen the way his eyes collected the details of a room with frightening speed. Knew instinctively the knowledge and skill that lurked behind those eyes. She had read it in the colors of his aura the first day she had met him, drank in the deep blue instinct that drove Jack to protect, to serve, grappling with the stain of black blood on his hands that clouded the purples of loyalty and patience and understanding. She knew he could be trusted, and that he was a vault of secrets, well-guarded as dragon's gold.

"Let me know when you reach him?" She said, letting her hand fall from his arm.

Jack heard the offer in her polite words. An attempt at casual, but edging on worry now.

He turned and waved, gave Maggie a smile when she leaned over the counter of the coffee bar to catch his eye.

"Thanks," he said. "I'll tell Wil to give Maggie a call in the morning. I'm sure he'll want to reschedule."

Amelia said nothing as he swept out of her bookstore, her daughter oblivious to the fear that had coated the room like the trails of a thick, yellow slug.

Jack hit the sidewalk outside and for ten seconds, he was firing on all cylinders before the machine came to a grinding halt. He stared out into the street at the end of the sidewalk, unaware that he had stopped moving for a few precious seconds. He had no idea where to start. He felt like he had the first time he had been operational on his own, well trained but inexperienced, coming to the fast conclusion that the bullet points in his apprenticeship were only a foundation to begin building on. He needed to act, but there was no clear directive. He dialed Wil's cell phone number. It went straight to voicemail. He checked the app that would allow him to track Wil's phone. Nothing. His cell was off, or it was dead.

He resisted the urge to crush his own cell phone in the palms of his hands.

Wil had been at school today; he knew that much. If he hadn't been, Wil's homeroom teacher would have had the office call him on his personal phone. If he hadn't made it to football practice, Jack would have gotten a call from Wil's coach.

Jack had been against the idea of extracurriculars from the start. Especially one so intimately physical as football. Wil was ten times stronger than any average human teenager. One misstep and he could accidentally kill one of the other boys on the football field. Varza and Illinca argued that Wil needed an outlet for his strength, his natural aggression. Kade told him that football would allow him to exercise his anger without the fear of a real threat to test his control. In the end Jack had relented. But he had never stopped waiting for the other shoe to drop.

Wil had come a long way but he was still suffering, still unsure of himself and his place in the world. He was angry and scared and in too many ways still the mute, feral boy Jack had pulled from a dog crate in a burning building what seemed like a lifetime ago. At sixteen, Wil was physically maturing into an adolescent who had to be concerned with the emotional challenge of relearning how to be human, with the power of one of the Infernals suffused in his veins. It made him unstable. Jack had seen that particular pot boil over more than once in the two years he had spent trying to protect this innocent, bright, intelligent boy—to give him a measure of peace in a world that had already chewed him up and spit him out before he had learned to speak his first words.

It had been the most difficult decision he had ever made, letting Wil attend a public school. When he'd first decided to let Wil stay with him, he thought it would be easy to send him to school, to let him explore his newfound freedom. He was wrong. It seemed like neither of them had slept a full night in two years. Countless nightmares, the anger, the sheer uncontrollable anger that built up in a flash and spilled over at a moment's notice in the boy. It was broken dishes on the floor and blood in the sink from his constant nervous scratching at the skin beneath his ribcage, the curve of his shoulder, his hip. His absolute refusal to let anyone near him with a pair of scissors to cut his hair. It was the animal sound from the back of his throat, as if he'd been kicked, if Jack forgot in the first few days not to close any doors in the rooms where Wil was hiding. Endless hours of silence. The stealing; food, mostly. It had taken him half a year to convince Wil that he could eat when he wanted to. He just had to say something.

He was at the end of his rope. He'd never had children, he was losing his mind, and for the first time in his considerable lives, James Rook asked for help. Two years in Boston; two years of combat training and surveillance exercises on the street and a thousand, thousand puzzles solved on the rug in the evening and Wil was making progress. Tannis and Kade had likely saved them both.

So when Wil asked him if he could go to school, his cheek on one of his knees as he set the pieces in the jigsaw puzzle across the floor from Tannis, Jack was proud of the kid, and absolutely terrified. Jack compromised that they would consider it when they were back in Rochester. He had been doing well in his lessons with Arges and she agreed that Wil could be ready for a basic high school curriculum in a matter of months. She would prepare the documents and arrange the tests. All Jack had to do was choose a school.

He had vetted the facility himself. Identified no internal or external threats. Broke into the school for three consecutive weeks with Wil until he was satisfied that the kid had committed the entire floorplan to memory and knew the most direct route to each exit. He called Arges once a week to confirm that she thought he was ready. She told him it was okay to admit that he was the one who wasn't ready. He stopped calling after that.

Jack scrubbed at his face, the phone still gripped in his hand. Willed himself to clear his head. He wasn't thinking about the problem at hand, he was wasting time and Wil was still missing. What if this was a false alarm, if Wil had simply forgotten to mention a change of plans to him (Jack had to remind himself that it was possible, Wil was a teenager, a highly trained teenager but a teenager nonetheless), and even Amelia hadn't been immediately concerned. But Wil wasn't an average teenager, and Jack had his fair share of enemies, and they had planned for this, so why couldn't he think straight?

He would start at the school and work outward from there. The coach would have called him if Wil had skipped practice.

The school had a very strict attendance policy; it was one of the reasons Jack had picked it for Wil.

He stepped into an alley, looking for a shadow that would give him access to one of the black paths—the hidden roads only traversed by the dead, which would get him to Wil's high school in the shortest amount of time possible. He opened his phone one more time and dialed Varza, dimly aware that his legs were shaking.

Varza picked up on the first ring. Spoke before Jack could get a word out.

"He's here."

Jack stopped walking, stared at the greying red brick walls of the alley without seeing them. He was not relieved. Varza's usually calm, supple manner of speaking had come to him tightened. A vibrating tightrope about to snap.

"What happened?" He tried to make it a soft inquiry, but it came out clipped and dark. Varza spoke very carefully, and that more than anything sent the blood rushing into Jack's ears, the pressure of his own heartbeat in his head physically jolting him an involuntary step forward.

"He's safe. Come by with your car. Take the long way. He needs some time."

He didn't say, 'He needs some time to calm down', but that's what Varza had meant. Wil was in the room with him, and he was upset.

"What happened?" Jack said again.

Silence. Jack imagined the tightrope beginning to fray. He spoke again, quietly this time, closing his eyes.

"Please, prieten vechi." *Old friend.* "What happened?"

Varza had started breathing again. This time when he answered, Jack felt the weight of his fears slide like molten lead to his stomach, dropping it to the floor.

"I don't know," he said.

Varza lowered the phone from his ear with deliberate, over-emphasized movements. Wil was sitting on the floor of his office, back to the wall, head in his hands. Varza noticed that Wil had chosen the one spot in the spacious office where the office door created a blind spot for anyone entering the room. He could see everything, but remain unseen himself until the door was closed again. At least, he would if his head wasn't bowed. Still, Varza was impressed.

"Wil?"

No response.

Varza let the silence in the room hang. Took a moment to observe while he decided what to do next.

He glanced at the door, which had closed, mostly, in its cracked frame. Wil hadn't broken in, not exactly. But he'd thrown his shoulder at it, pounding on the ironwood frantically until Varza had opened it for him. He didn't think Wil was even aware that he'd damaged it in his panic.

The hair on Varza's arms stood on end when Wil exploded through his door. He was dressed in a pair of grey sweatpants and nothing else. His arms were bruised and torn up, and there were the remnants of what looked like duct tape on his wrists. His back and shoulders were covered in red welted abrasions, each of them two and a half inches wide, some of them beaded with tiny droplets of dried blood. There was a bruise on his cheek. Varza recognized the difference between an open palmed strike and a closed fist. Someone had slapped him, hard. More than once.

Wil crashed into the wall and slid down it like he was afraid someone was coming after him. He was hysterical. Varza checked the hall, closed the door and managed to get the iron deadbolt in place despite the damage to the frame. He closed his eyes, checked the halls. The perimeter of his building. The streets in a five-block radius. Nothing.

When he'd flipped out his phone, Wil spoke, his voice a choked off rasp that scared Varza more than the bruise on his pale cheek.

"Don't call Jack," he said. Varza's head came up so fast Wil flinched.

"I'm not calling him," the blonde vampire said calmly. "You are."

Wil let out an inhuman noise and laced his hands across the back of his neck, bowing his head between bent knees. His knuckles were bruised.

"Wil, he's going to be worried. You need to tell him you're safe."

Varza held out the phone, but Wil didn't look up.

"He's going to be so mad," Wil mourned quietly at the floor. "I did everything wrong. I just want to go home."

"Then call your father," Varza tried again. Gently.

"I can't," he sobbed. "I ruined everything."

Varza crouched down, keeping always a little over an arm's length away. He didn't know if Wil wanted to be touched. It was better to stay in his line of sight, outside of any threat radius.

"Wil, you remember what we discussed, if anything were to happen? Anywhere, anytime?"

The redhead nodded, his long hair framing his face.

"What are you supposed to do?"

Wil answered quietly. Efficient and precise.

"Get out. Whatever it takes. Get in contact if there's an opportunity, but it's more important to stay in the dark. Meet here, or at the safe-house. Tell Varza..."

He trailed off. His fingers tightened on the back of his neck.

"Go on, frățioare." *Little brother.* "That's exactly right."

Momentum was key. He had to keep Wil talking, or he was certain the boy would simply stop and not speak again. This had happened before. In the beginning, when Wil was still afraid of closed doors.

Wil took a deep breath, and kept going.

"Tell Varza, green for no action taken—clean exit. Yellow for action taken, no witnesses. Clean exit."

Wil struggled with the next color.

"What is... cum ar fi fructul? Portocaliu? Right?"

"That's right," Varza said, lowering himself to sit on the floor. "Orange."

"Orange for action taken, possible witnesses. Clean up required. Red for action taken, witnesses confirmed. Casualties. Damage control required."

Varza was about to prompt him to continue, when his phone rang. He put it to his ear, holding Wil's gaze. Hazel eyes under a curtain of wild red hair.

"He's here."

When he hung up, Wil had gone silent, dropped his eyes to the carpet under his feet.

"Wil?" Varza tried again, unable to completely cover the frustration rising in his chest. "I need a color."

The boy was caving in on himself. His shoulders collapsing under the strain.

"Wil. Give me a color."

"Orange," Wil said.

Jack thought he had prepared himself for the day he would receive a message containing only one word—a single color.

After he'd hung up with Varza, he'd taken one of the black paths to his apartment to pick up the car. While he was fighting with the old lift door on his garage—the thing was older than he was, he was sure of it—he'd called Amelia to assure her that Wil was safe. He'd gone to see a family friend, and Jack was on his way to pick him up.

She was glad, and her gifts did not travel well over the receiver of a phone, so she believed the calm relief he projected over the strain in his voice.

"Teenagers," she laughed. "If I had a nickel for every time Maggie forgot to text me something, I'd be a rich woman."

Jack laughed, but it started to sound hollow and he cut it off abruptly. She was silent for moment and he waited, finally getting the garage door all the way up.

"It's okay to worry, you know."

He wasn't sure he could answer, so he didn't.

"Maggie asked me if you would tell Wil she's free this weekend. She'd like him to stop by to work on their project."

"Yes," Jack said, clearing his throat. "Yeah, I'll tell him."

"Have a good night, Jack."

He hung up the phone without answering her.

Jack slammed the door of the Camry, slammed the key into the ignition and was about to slam the car into reverse, when his phone blinked on. He flicked open the screen and read the message from Varza.

Orange

For a second, Jack did nothing. He stared at the word, uncomprehending, and then, for the first time since he had gone to The Wellspring, the world came into focus. He dialed Varza as he floored the car back out of his driveway, leaving black rubber on the pavement behind him.

"Put him on," Jack said when Varza answered. It wasn't a request.

To Jack's utter astonishment and mounting fury, Varza hesitated.

"He's been very quiet since he gave the color, Jack."

"I know. It's alright, put him on."

He did know. The reason he didn't have a set of coordinates or a place name could only be because Wil had stopped talking. It happened sometimes when he was startled or outright afraid. Switching to Romanian sometimes helped. Sometimes not.

There was a soft sound on the other end of the phone as it changed hands. The first thing Jack noticed was how unsteady Wil's breathing was. It sounded like he'd been crying.

Jack felt his boot flatten to the floor over the gas pedal. He forced himself to ease off the accelerator.

"Hey, Marigold," Jack said without preamble. "Maggie missed you today."

A whine. It was an animal noise, and Jack felt his heart in his throat.

"It's okay," Jack said softly. "You're okay."

A shift. Maybe the phone moving from one ear to the other. Still no words. Jack kept going.

"Do you want to meet me there, or do you want me to pick you up?"

He had no idea where *there* was, and he needed Wil to focus. To tell him.

He let that question hang for sixty seconds before he tried again.

"Wil, this is important. Anything over a yellow and we have to make sure that there's no traceable evidence at the scene."

He had to force himself to say *at the scene* with a steady voice.

"What was your color, Wil?"

Finally, a very small response.

"Orange."

Jack tried not to let out his breath audibly.

"Where?"

"Where the showers are," he said. Jack was about to ask him what in the world that meant, when he heard Wil give a frustrated huff on the other end of the phone. He waited.

Varza was murmuring something in the background.

"Nu..." Wil began again, half to him. Half to Varza. "I don't... În vestiar?"

"The locker room?" Jack confirmed. "At your school?"

"Yeah."

"Okay. Thank you, Wil. I need to talk to Varza."

Easy, achievable action. That's what Tannis had said. Give him reachable goals, something to occupy his mind.

Varza came back on the line wordlessly.

"Mundane or Gifted," Jack said. "Can you see anything?"

Varza was silent and Jack gave him time to walk through the locker room in Wil's school while he tamped down the urge to blow through the next three red lights he came up on.

Varza spoke then, but it wasn't to him. "Wil, go into my closet and find a coat. There's boots in there that should fit you."

Jack tightened his grip on the steering wheel. He listened to the sound of Wil moving away.

"Mundane," Varza said, voice pitched very low. "There's no trace of Faen energy besides Wil's. But there is significant damage to the locker room. And Wil is injured."

Jack had to remember he was driving. Varza continued, anticipating him.

"Bruises. Abrasions. Nothing serious."

"Meet me there in ten minutes," Jack said through clenched teeth.

The line went dead.

Varza was glad to be able to confirm that whatever had happened in the locker room was mundane. If it had been Gifted the protocol would have changed drastically, their timeline moved up. But Wil had been injured, and the locker room... He helped Wil into a hooded sweatshirt with a zipper down the front. Some of the abrasions were starting to mottle with bruises. Dried blood flaked off his pale shoulders when he shrugged into the offered clothing. One stripe across Wil's pale collarbone was weeping a clear fluid, the skin torn in places. It would need a bandage.

Wil stepped into the boots and didn't bother lacing them fully before letting Varza help him into a coat. Before they left the office, Varza opened a sterile white package and began kneading a square of clear plastic filled with an electric blue gel in his long, elegant hands. Wil watched him with interest. When the packet began to cool against his palm, Varza stepped closer to Wil. He reached out his free hand, looking for any signs of uncertainty from the boy. Giving him the chance to step back. Then he took Wil's uninjured cheek in his hand, and pressed the ice pack to the other.

"Hold this here, like that. I'm going to walk in front of you. I go first, just like you practiced with Kade."

Wil nodded, held the ice pack against his face and waited for Varza to put on his coat. Wil moved with him when he turned and walked to the door. It was an uncanny, liquid motion, as though he could anticipate movement before it became decisive action.

In the glass window over the door, Varza caught a glimpse of Wil, hovering over his shoulder, ice pack pressed to his face. Hair in his eyes. One hand on the door latch, Varza pulled an elastic from his wrist with his teeth, and handed it back to Wil. Then he pulled the deadbolt free, checked his watch, and they were gone.

Jack had circled the building twice, avoiding the security cameras. The only thing he had found out of the ordinary was the disturbed gravel outside one of the double-doors that lead into the basketball court. As if someone had fallen, and scrambled to get back to their feet in a hurry.

It didn't take Jack long to lose patience after that. He was now the only one who didn't have any idea of what they would find on the other side of those doors. It was driving him mad. His only comfort was that if it were The Order, or one of his own personal enemies, Varza would have known.

It couldn't have been the Faen traffickers who had taken Wil and sold him to the necromongers in the first place. Jack had seen to that. Personally.

But mundane didn't mean harmless, just potentially more manageable. Possibly not as serious as it could be. If Wil had transformed in front of someone, killed someone...

He pressed his fingers into his eyes. The color had been orange. No casualties.

When he saw Wil, he thought he would be furious. He had braced himself, reminded himself that this was the first time something like this had ever happened. Wil had remembered what to do in maddening fragments, but he'd remembered. This wasn't the place for his anger, even anger fueled by worry. He was surprised to find that when Varza walked Wil across the football field to meet him, Jack only had one thing on his mind.

As soon as Wil was within arm's reach, Jack pulled him into a hug. The kid huffed in surprise, before he closed his long arms around Jack's shoulders.

"I'm sorry, Rook," Wil said, muffled by the fabric of Jack's shirt. "It's all ruined."

"It's okay," Jack said, glancing at Varza. The blonde vampire shook his head. Wil still hadn't actually said what happened. "We'll fix it, kiddo. I'm just glad you're safe."

It was Varza, bless him, who kept the conversation moving. Jack suddenly just wanted to take Wil home. But they had a job to do.

"Tell us what happened, Wil."

The redhead stepped back from Jack, scrubbed at his face with the heels of his hands. Jack didn't miss the cuts and white scrapes there. He glanced back in the direction of the basketball court, then again to Wil.

He marked the set of Wil's jaw, the stiffness there, the way he ran his hands through his hair to rub at the shell of his ear. His right cheek was bruised. Knuckles raw and starting to purple. A few of his fingernails were cracked.

Jack made himself wait. Counted the seconds. Willed himself not to push. Wil put his hands in his jacket pockets, squared his shoulders and began to speak.

Practice had ended late that afternoon, and Wil had been agitated on the field. They weren't allowed to have their phones on them during practice and on a normal day that made him nervous. His phone was his safety net. But he was supposed to meet Maggie at The Wellspring, and he would be upset with himself if Jack showed up early and he wasn't where he said he would be.

He'd gotten off the field first, barely hearing his coach announce that he would be leaving early, and to lock up the equipment before they left. He was in the middle of typing a text to Rook, already planning the one he would write to Maggie in his head, when two of his teammates crowded him from behind.

"Hey, Scarlet, the team is going to Cassidy's place tonight. His parents are out of town. You coming?"

"Sorry," Wil said, taking a step back as though he were planning to close his locker door, forcing the other boys off his shoulders. "I can't."

He heard Kade in his head: *If you're in too close, create space. There's a radius for everything. Calculate the length of your opponent's arms. Their legs. Outside of those distances, they can do whatever they want, but they'll never touch you.*

"Don't have daddy's permission?"

Wil ignored the question. He was still unsure of the reasoning behind making true statements in a nasty tone, as if he should be ashamed that he listened to Rook. The two boys stepped back.

They were still too close, by combat standards. Inside the threat radius for a solid kick to the small of his back or the soft side of his knee. But Wil was mostly satisfied. He didn't bother turning to see which one of his teammates it was. He didn't know them all by name yet. Numbers were easier, and everyone seemed to have a nickname—or most of them did, like when Rook called him Marigold. He was still working out the details. But he did know these two by name. Rickey, the team captain, and Seager, his best friend, one of the cornerbacks.

"It's team building, Scarlet, you have to come," Rickey said.

In fact, Wil didn't *have* to do anything. He'd had enough of that for a lifetime. The words alone got his hackles up.

"I can't tonight," Wil muttered. He wasn't good at typing and talking at the same time. "Sorry."

He'd barely finished his message, about to press send, when Seager reached around him and tried to pluck the phone from his hand.

"Calling daddy already?" He snorted, too close. "Couldn't wait?"

Wil's hand shot out, his fingers closing around the other boy's wrist easily, and the next steps were in his head; hours and days and months that bled into two years of the same motions happened in a matter of seconds before he ever realized he was doing it.

Wil pulled Seager forward, jamming his arm up to the elbow into his open locker. Stepping back, he calmly kicked the door closed on Seager's arm.

The metal door bounced with a solid crack on Seager's bent elbow and his teammate yelped at the pain of it. At the last second Wil had pulled the strength of his kick, and he knew that the most Seager would suffer was a painful bruise. But he had done something far worse, something he understood from a time before Rook, an instinct that made the hair on the back of his neck stand in end. He had presented a challenge for dominance. He had two choices now. He could grovel and spend his life exposing his belly for these other boys. Or he could fight.

The odds were not in his favor. Rickey owned this team. They had only known Wil for a matter of weeks, and none of them particularly liked him. He didn't speak much to them. Went straight home after practice. They knew he had no siblings, that he was the child of a single parent home and that he much preferred to eat lunch with Maggie than with them.

They thought he was slow because he was still learning the nuances of speaking English, of the social order among vanilla mortals. But he'd had them pegged the moment he'd tried out for the team. They operated like a pack, but Wil had been in a real pack once. The kind with teeth and claws—and he wasn't afraid of these boys.

The problem was, there were 58 members on the team roster, and most of them were in this room with him.

"What is wrong with you?" Seager shouted, pulling his arm free of the locker. He rubbed at his elbow, and Wil was momentarily relieved that his assessment of the kick was correct—no permanent damage. He knew from experience that sometimes he underestimated his own strength. He was still working on that.

He opened his mouth to apologize, hearing Tannis in his head this time: *giving ground is not always a retreat*. And he was sorry. None of these boys knew what had been done to him, none of them would ever understand that his reactions were a product of nightmares and the slow patience of Rook, guiding him back to a place of control. Over himself, his own body. His circumstances.

He didn't know exactly what he would say to explain to them why he had done what he'd done. But he was willing to try. The slap caught him off guard.

Wil registered the movement a second too late. Focused almost entirely on Seager, he hadn't seen Rickey move. The blow took him full across his right cheek, whipping his head to the side. He was too close to the sitting bench in front of the stand of lockers, and when he widened his stance to keep himself upright, his shin hit the bench with an audible crack. He stumbled, his hip thudding painfully off the metal surface of it, and he tumbled over the other side onto the floor. His phone skittered across the cement.

They were on top of him after that.

It seemed like all of them, but his rational mind was still calculating and he knew that for the space available it was probably six at most. When someone produced a roll of duct tape, it occurred to Wil that they had planned for this, and he had simply provided the opening.

Rickey slapped him again, one of his cleats grinding into his sternum, and Wil couldn't help the muted cry he pressed to the inside of his teeth. Wildly, he remembered Kade's explanation: *pressing down on the sternum is exceptionally painful, but relatively harmless unless too much force is applied.* And it really was. He gasped out a breath when Rickey stepped off him, but it was only to let the others get to work.

Someone pulled one of his arms underneath the bench, his other was dragged over it. They duct taped his wrists together so that he was hugging the bench, several boys sitting or standing on his right hip and both his legs. They were overzealous with the tape, and wound it in messy crisscross patterns around the bench and his forearms up to the elbow before tearing the length off the roll. Wil could already feel his fingers going numb. He scrambled as best he could, trying to get his legs out from underneath the crushing weight of the boys, but it wasn't any good. There were too many bodies, and a white-hot pain in his elbow froze him up for a second. Seager pulled back to kick him again, but Rickey stopped him. Wil stared at his bound arms. For a second, everyone was still. And then Rickey picked Wil's phone off the floor.

"We were just trying to do you a favor," Rickey said, tapping the phone against his thigh.

For a second, Wil thought he misunderstood the definition of the word.

"Favor?" He blurted. "An act of kindness?"

"Are you stupid?" Rickey snapped back. "That's what I said."

Wil stared hard at his team captain. He was pretty sure he understood kindness as a word, but language was entirely contextual. He might be thinking of a different word.

Rickey was still tapping his phone lightly, an unbroken chain of rhythms.

"We wanted you to loosen up, be a part of the team."

"Guess your texts to daddy were more important," Seager cut in. Some of the boys jeered.

Wil gave it some more thought. Came to a conclusion.

"I don't think the word 'favor' means what you think it means," he said, his voice trembling only a little.

Rickey's face darkened. The tapping had stopped. And Wil watched him lob his cell carelessly into the shower room, where the water was still running. Heard it shatter when it hit the tile. Wil looked on wordlessly as the roll of industrial duct tape was passed around to each team member. Not all of them accepted it. But the ones who did tore pieces of varying length off it before handing it to someone else. The ones who didn't quietly gathered their things, and left. And on, and on.

Wil had stopped hearing them when the phone was destroyed in the shower. His whole world narrowed to a point, greying around the edges. He was dimly aware of the shouted obscenities, the taunts and someone aggressively ruffling his hair, making it hurt.

He was back in a too small cage of first-forged iron, hands crushing his chin inside sweaty palms, leaving fingerprints on his jaw, checking his teeth and the color of his eyes and the stock of his muscles.

The first searing tear of the duct tape being pressed against his back and ripped suddenly free, snapped him out of the memories. He was grateful. It was important that he didn't change in front of these boys. It was important for him to stay in control. Rook believed he could do it. He held onto that, pressed his lips together and just held on, because it couldn't last. None of these boys knew what real pain was; they would get tired or bored if he did nothing, said nothing. It was just duct tape. Only words.

They kept doing it, one for each of them, gently smoothing the creases out of the grey material before ripping it off. They cheered the first time they drew blood. Wil could feel his skin growing hot, and he drew his shoulders in close to his chest even though he knew it wouldn't help. He tried to think of Rook, who gave him a name that meant something to both of them, who stayed up with him with the lights on in the kitchen when he couldn't sleep, who didn't get angry when he broke half the dishes in the house because he needed to hear something breaking to get the screaming out of his head. Rook thought he could do it. He wasn't going to change in front of these boys. Someone pulled his head back by his hair and pressed a strip of duct tape to his collar bone, patting him hard on the cheek several times before tearing it free.

It startled a scream from him. The skin was thin there, and tore free in places, and Wil Scarlet lost his mind.

It was his own scream that brought him back to that place. It was always the screaming. The too many hands touching his skin reminding him of the man who eventually took him, cage and all, from the dark, oil lamp-lit labyrinth of the underground market. The dolls' black eyes in the pitted, hollow sockets, and the scarecrow grin that split wide at the seams when he'd put a collar on Wil and told him what a good dog he was going to be.

Rook told him he would never go back to that place. He promised.

He thrashed wildly, felt the familiar tightening of his skin and the bunching of muscle. They laughed until he got one of his legs free. He didn't know whom he struck, or where, only that he was certain this time he had broken something. He kept his head down, because his eyes were always the first to change, and he was half way there, just barely hanging on to his shape in his mind. He strained wildly against the bench and the duct tape, felt the bolts in the concrete beginning to pop free. He rocked it, hysterical, the aluminum bending under the flexed muscle of his bound arms. They were beginning to back off now, not because of the injuries a handful of them had sustained—some serious, some glancing, now that he had his legs free. They scattered because he was still screaming and the bench was coming free of the floor, and he didn't care what they saw. He just wanted to go home.

They were gone when he started kicking savagely at one of the bench legs until the metal caved under his heel. The room was empty, only the sound of water running, and why couldn't he stop screaming? His chest felt tight and his cheeks were wet and he could taste blood in the air. His blood.

He got his feet under him in a flat-footed crouch and ripped the bench free of the concrete, sending spider web cracks across the floor. The sudden release of tension sent him backwards into another row of lockers, his body meeting the hollow metal with a sound that detonated like a thunderclap. He pressed his feet into the bench on either side of his bound arms, and pushed against the flat silver surface even as he thrashed and pulled, finally, finally tearing his arms free from the surface of the bench.

His panic mounted when he realized that he couldn't separate his wrists. He had no leverage with the mangled bench between his arms, and his screams turned into hoarse sobs as he continued twisting and pulling against that tape. But he was stuck, it was too much, and he just wanted to go home.

He flinched violently when one of the boys from his team stepped gingerly out of the shower room, the hems of his jeans wet from the water and his bare feet leaving dark grey tracks on the floor. He approached Wil with his hands up, like Wil had a gun on him.

Wil bared his teeth, his chest heaving, and the boy stopped. Kept his hands up, palms out. Met Wil's eyes and held them.

"I'll get it off," he said. "That's all."

Wil felt the growl rising in his throat and had just enough clarity left to swallow it down. To shut his lips over his teeth. He stared hard at the other boy, assessing. His mind started to clear, with something tangible to focus on.

He recognized the sandy blonde as Number 44. He could picture the surname on his jersey but couldn't remember what it said. Wil flicked a glance at the shower room. The water was off now, but there was still steam hovering over the tiles. He looked back in time to see Number 44's face fall, the bloom of shame in his brown eyes. He had been there the whole time.

"It's just me," the boy said quietly. "I'm sorry."

Wil let him take a few steps closer. Satisfied that Wil wasn't planning to kick him, Number 44 lowered himself to a crouch in front of the new kid and carefully began unwinding the tape from his wrists. It was hard at first; Number 44 was nervous, and his hands shook as he tried to free the end of the tape from the bloody, twisted mess around Wil's wrists. It came free after a few tries, and though by that time they were both trembling, Number 44 took his time, peeling the tape off with care, flattening his thumb against Wil's wrist and the back of his hand to dull the pain of it coming free of his bare skin.

They didn't speak. Wil watched his face, and Number 44 studiously avoided his eyes until it was done. He glanced up and then quickly backed off, standing to grab his bag, his shoes.

Wil pulled his arm out from under the bench, and sat with his hands in his lap, uncertain what to do. Then he heard Number 44 at the door hesitate, and then speak.

"Don't quit," he said. "That's what they want you to do." Then he was gone.

With a scream of frustration, Wil kicked the battered bench so hard at the lockers some of the locks snapped free, clattering to the floor. He threw his elbow at the locker stand behind him until he felt the metal beginning to cave, feeling his skin tighten across his shoulders and this time he let it happen.

Wil was Gifted, and he was unlike anything the world had seen since the shifters of Dun Luna escaped into the sea and were never seen again. Tannis told him he was a miracle. The necromancer who bought him turned him into a science experiment. He had the essence of an Infernal spirit in his blood now, an exiled God, a son of one of the I'enna. Wil still wasn't entirely clear about what any of that meant, but he knew what he could do.

His form bled into black and took the shape of a monstrous canine, sleek fur the color of octopus ink and dripping a tar-like substance that dissipated into wisps of ash and smoke when they hit the concrete around him. His paws left craters in the floor when he flexed his claws. He bristled, rolling his shoulders and feeling the familiar heat under his skin. All four of his eyes were the molten swirl of amber and liquid gold when he opened them. He felt the skin over his muzzle bunch and fold as he pulled his lips back over his long teeth, letting the growl build in his chest to a full-throated roar that shook the room around him.

He slammed into the locker stands, riding them to the ground like living prey, pulling out sections of fragmented metal with his teeth, his claws sinking into the cement and steel.

He put his shoulders down and ripped the other benches free of the floor, shaking his head violently, sending the pieces flying in all directions. Wil paced through the carnage as his fur began to turn from ash to embers and then to burn, his long tail cutting shadows through the flames. The wash of heat turned the metal and tile black. He found Rickey's locker and tore it to shreds, along with everything inside it. This set of lockers was bolted to the wall, and he unhinged his maw, his ancillary jaws opening horizontally from his back set of teeth, black muscle fanning like flower petals, a rolling staccato purr that sounded more like a shriek filling his chest and his throat as he crushed the locker stand between all four jaws and tore it free from the drywall.

He could smell them. All of them. He shouldered his way into the shower room, knocking tiles free, the heat rolling off him creating curling clouds of steam as it boiled the water. He opened his jaws, ready to tear each shower fixture from the wall one by one, when the crunch of broken glass under one of his forepaws brought him up short.

His tall pointed ears flattened slowly. He stepped back and whined at the sight of his cell phone. He touched it with his nose, pawed at it gently, his tail smoldering dimly before going out. Wil looked around, his four eyes picking up not only the carnage, the chaos, but the rage and fear that he had painted across the walls.

He stumbled out of the shower room, his sweatpants damp from the steam, tripping over his own feet as he made his way into the gym and on to the basketball court.

It was dark.

Rook and Maggie were waiting for him, and he didn't have a phone, and it was dark outside, and what had he been thinking?

He threw himself at the double doors that lead to the football field, tripped and sprawled in the gravel, cutting the heels of his hands. Wil stayed there on his hands and knees for a few precious seconds, his legs shaking, duct tape still somehow clinging to his skin in places.

Varza was closer. He bolted.

Jack and Varza were staring at the locker room, unable to speak for the time being. Wil had explained it. But the words paled in comparison to the utter destruction in the room. The redhead was standing behind them, his hand fisted in the fabric of Jack's coat, murmuring apologies into the silence over and over in Romanian, in English. A Frankenstein version of both.

Finally, Jack reached back to put a hand on Wil's head to quiet him. Tawny hazel eyes looked at him, lips parted like he was going to start apologizing again.

"This isn't your fault, Marigold," Jack said. "You weren't the animal in this room."

Varza looked at them both. Turned again to the room.

"I will take care of this," he said in low tones. "The two of you go home. I'll keep you updated."

Jack hesitated.

Varza nodded at Wil. "He's injured. I'll deal with this."

"Call me if you need anything," Jack told him, and he meant it. "Thank you, prieten vechi."

Varza smiled softly, reached up and slid his glasses off his aristocratic nose. He folded them up and tucked them into the pocket of his vest.

"Cu plăcere."

Jack and Wil started to turn, Wil's pale, bruised fist still holding on to Jack's coat, when Varza stopped them momentarily.

"Wil, take this for now. Until I can replace your old one."

Wil caught the burner phone with one hand, seemed to struggle with the idea of letting go of Jack, and wanting to go to Varza. The blonde vampire waved him off, affectionately.

"I know," he said. "I know. Go home now. Get some rest."

Wil let Jack walk him back to the car, punching in the only five numbers he kept memorized for emergencies (plus Maggie), and set the speed dials with one hand. It was very quiet. The crunch of gravel under their boots sounded like machine gun fire. They said nothing on the ride home; Wil only letting go of Jack's coat once they were both inside the car. When they were back inside the apartment, the stairs creaking and the hardwood cold under their bare feet, neither of them were ready to speak again. They went wordlessly into the bathroom, and Wil sat down on the tub so that Jack could clean his arms off and the abrasions on his collar bone and the ones across his back and shoulders. Jack stepped out once he was satisfied that Wil's injuries were all bandaged properly, and found himself suddenly lost without something to do.

He stared at the kitchen, the little balcony off the living room with the folding table. Wil emerged in the doorway, face clean and hair tied back, hovering near to his shoulder, but Jack didn't mind.

"Hey kiddo," Jack said, careful to keep his voice pitched low. "Let's sit outside for a while."

He could feel Wil visibly relax behind him. It was getting colder at night now, early October and there was the threat of rain in the air, so they both bundled back into their coats before going out onto the balcony. Jack set his phone to a Romanian Top 40s radio channel coming out of Constanta, and set it in the speaker before sitting down at the table. There was a puzzle laying half-finished on the cracked, weatherproofed surface, but neither of them moved to start working on it. Wil drew his knees up to his chest and they listened for a while as the radio droned on, alternatively playing eighties rock, current Romanian pop hits, and for some inexplicable reason, a song by Atomic Kitten.

"Marigold?"

Wil turned to look at him.

"I wanted you to know that I'm really proud of you," he said, the words sneaking up on him in the dark. Wil shrugged, turning back to watch the fairy lights hanging in the yard.

"I didn't do anything," he said. "I changed at school, I ruined the locker room. I got angry."

"Hey, listen to me. Someone assaulted you today, and no one expects you to do nothing when you're threatened. You could have hurt those boys. You may have even wanted to, but you didn't. You didn't change in front of anyone. No one saw you and you didn't hurt anyone. I don't care about the locker room, and neither should you."

Wil ran his finger down his nose, a tell that he was trying hard not to cry. Jack pretended not to notice. When Wil spoke, his words were thick and he couldn't look Jack in the eye.

"I just get... so angry," he said, and to Jack it sounded like grieving. "I'm angry all the time, and I don't know what to do with it all."

"It's okay to be angry, no one's telling you there's anything wrong with that. Unless... someone *has* told you that it isn't okay for you to be angry," Jack said taking a risk. "Then I'd like to know who, and an estimate of their current coordinates."

Wil snorted, a wet laugh escaping him and catching in his eyes, holding there for a heartbeat or three. Jack leaned forward in his chair, his own smile relaxing as he continued.

"It's okay to be angry. It's what you do about your anger, about any of your emotions, that defines you. The things that were broken today, Wil? Were just things. They can be replaced. You didn't hurt anyone, that's the important part."

"Am vrut să." *I wanted to.*

Jack did not say, *I'm a little sorry you didn't,* but it was a near thing. He considered Wil, who was stealing glances out of the corner of his eyes at Jack, waiting.

"Are you worried that the next time you want to, you'll do something about it?"

Wil didn't answer right away. His shoulders were stiff—the question had caught him off guard. This was the hardest thing for Wil, to admit when he was worried about something. Jack could see it in his eyes every time they had occasion to address it, which was not often. Not often enough. Wil admitted to him recently after a brief, frustrated argument about communication, that if he gave his fears a voice then somewhere, someone would remember them; locked away in the recollection of the person he'd confided in, and they would never die. Jack could understand that, at least. So he gave Wil time to answer the question while he leaned back in his chair. It took Wil longer than usual to respond, and he picked his words carefully when he did.

"I'm not worried about hurting anyone. I just don't want to be so angry anymore. I don't want to break things, or yell. Dar..." he trailed off. Struggled for a second longer. "Sometimes I'm angry and I don't even know why. People talking makes me angry, the sound of chewing food, that guy who is always having a conversation with his neighbor in the middle of the street for no reason?" Wil finally looked at him, to confirm Jack knew what he was talking about.

"And then he pretends like he doesn't see you when you're driving down the road?"

"Yes!" Wil said, throwing up his hands. "Why would he do that?"

Jack was trying very hard not to laugh, because Wil was being serious, but he couldn't quite hold it in, and then Wil was laughing too and Jack couldn't remember the two of them ever laughing so much together. His vision blurred, the fairy lights making the edges soft, because Wil was laughing, it had been such a terrible day, which was the biggest understatement since NASA described the Challenger explosion as a "malfunction", but Wil was laughing and it was the best sound Jack had ever heard.

It took them a while to settle down. They didn't stop until the neighbor who shared their driveway came out into the backyard to tell them to keep it down. Jack apologized through some residual laughter, which their neighbor did not appreciate. Wil had to hold his breath to keep from laughing any more.

When they had finally quieted, Jack tapped the table with his knuckle to get Wil's attention one last time.

"I know what it's like, to be angry all the time. I can't promise you that it won't happen again, but maybe we can make it more manageable. Okay?"

Wil was looking up at him, cheek resting in the crook of his folded arms, his hands bunched in the cuffs of his sweatshirt, hood drawn up over his ears. He nodded.

It was getting late and even Jack was starting to feel the cold. He was about to suggest they go inside, when Wil spoke up.

"Rook?"

"What's up?"

"Are you hungry?"

Jack stood up from his chair his chest swelling a little, proud of the kid, and nodded to the balcony doors. Wil stood gingerly, following him into the house.

"I could eat," Jack said, shutting the doors behind them. "You?"

"Yeah," Wil said. "I could eat."

About the Author

Amanda Nargi is a graduate of the Creative Writing program at the State University of New York at Oswego. Her short fiction has appeared in the Great Lake Review. *In 2010 her flash fiction was recorded for release on NPR. Amanda is a member of Publishers Marketplace. She currently lives in Rochester, NY.*

Inheritance of Nightmares

Beth Powers

The dragons dropped me off just before the foothills to the mountains. Much as they wanted to be rid of me, they said they daren't go closer to the territory of the darric fieron. I did not turn to watch them fly away or wish them well. Nor did they return to their human forms to offer me words of parting. But I understood. They had given me—a lone woman running for her life—sanctuary, and I had brought destruction to their peaceful community. We did not part ways as friends.

With my feet firmly planted on the ground once more, I took a deep breath—pine and wildflower—and sighed. This place smelled of home, and the air was crisp, rather than heavy with moisture and salt like that which rolled off the south sea. I had been away for many years, but my feet would never forget the path they had run in the other direction, fleeing the nightmare beast that had become my permanent shadow.

I had no doubt that it was chasing me still.

Before I'd walked more than a few hours, the wind shifted, and I knew it would snow before the day was out. My mother was a powerful windshaper, and I had only inherited a small amount of her skill—I knew when the weather would change, and I could make minor alterations to the courses of winds that swirled near me. Since I was almost always on the road, predicting the weather had been useful on more than one occasion.

But I could not change its mood. For that, I was glad that the dragons had insisted on giving me a heavy fur-lined cloak for the chilly journey through the air. I had shed my own when I fled to the south—no, I would not think on that brief, happy time.

The first flakes didn't begin to fall until I was well into the scraggly pines that clung to the hills. It took me longer than it should have to realize that the raised hairs on the back of my neck weren't just paranoia at being back in these hills. Someone—or something—was watching me. I suspected I knew what it was, but I hadn't thought the beastie would be able to outfly a dragon. Besides, I didn't smell anything out of the ordinary—maybe a hint of copper but the scent wasn't right for the monster that haunted my nightmares.

Even without heightened senses, I would have likely noticed the boy before long. He was doing a poor job of trailing me. Pivoting, I plucked him from his hiding place and pressed him against the nearest pine with my hand on his throat. Closer now, I could smell wood shavings and grain interlaced with the fear. He smelled like valleyfolk. "Why are you following me?" I demanded.

Before he could answer, I realized that he wasn't the only one I smelled. There were at least four others, and the scent of copper had grown stronger. Magic. In addition to the minor windshaping abilities, I had a bit of leeching magic, which, in theory, allowed me to steal power from others, but it also meant I could smell magic. It had saved my life more than once because I usually smelled the beast before it arrived.

Shifting, I let the hood of my cloak fall, but kept my face profiled to the boy and the others who still believed themselves to be concealed. I tightened my grip on the boy's throat, so he would know not to move and addressed the rest, growling darkly, "Move against me and he dies." I had no intention of strangling a child, but I'd lied enough that I knew they wouldn't hear it in my voice.

The skritch of a drawn blade interrupted the silence. Before its owner could use it, a woman stepped out from the tree line. She wore leather armor and carried a sword, but hers was not drawn. The scar that split her forehead from hairline to eye made her seem older than she probably was, but her voice held the confidence of command as she ordered the others, "Hold."

"But she's—" a whiny voice protested from somewhere behind and to my right.

"I said *hold*," snapped the woman before turning. She held her palms away from her sides. "The boy is inept, but we mean you no harm, traveler. Your path simply crossed our patrol."

After giving her another assessing look, I shifted my grip from the boy's throat to his leather jerkin and shoved him in her direction. She seemed sincere, but then, so had I. I'd just as soon part ways with them quickly.

But I forgot that I had lowered my hood, and by turning, I now faced her. She saw my mismatched eyes and hissed, "Cursed Witch." I heard several more blades being drawn. I started to wonder if I had been gone from these hills so long that the valleyfolk had forgotten the stories.

I rocked forward onto my toes, ready to move, but I waited.

Instead of attacking, the woman simply gave the boy a hand up and bowed formally. She said, "We offer you no sanctuary, Witch." *Smart woman.* "But we will not hinder your path."

When the beastie first came after me, I'd stuck to the hills. I knew them, and I could circle back home every few months. After about a year, the usually hospitable hillfolk became suspicious, and some even turned me away to sleep on the dangerous hillside alone. That's when I started hearing stories about a young woman traveling the hills. She seemed pleasant enough when invited into your home, but when she left, destruction rained your village. Some said she wasn't human at all, but a wild dog or a great beast that took to the skies at night. It wasn't long before they started calling her the Cursed Witch. And then, I realized the woman was me.

Several of the valleyfolk began talking at once. "But, Patrol Leader, if she's the Cursed Witch—I've heard the stories—we'll all be destroyed—our homes—we can't—"

"Silence!" the leader snapped, sparing one sweeping glance at her patrol. She turned back to me and repeated firmly, "We have no quarrel with you."

I simply stared at her. It was true; I had been gone for a long time. But were the valleyfolk's memories so short that they had forgotten the danger? She knew not to offer me sanctuary, but still, the fact that she also did not threaten violence meant a great deal to me. It was stupid, but kind.

The collection of unfamiliar smells from the valleyfolk almost caused me to miss the rot of the beastie. The patrol leader had offered me kindness, so I returned it with advice. "When the monster arrives, do not fight it. Run." Believing that they had no cause to do otherwise, I turned and threw myself off the path, shifting into my hound form as I did so. I was faster on four feet than two, and I hit the snow-dusted dirt running. The heavy cloak drifted to the ground behind me— usually my clothes and possessions changed with me, but sometimes the magic chose not to take something. I hoped I didn't regret the loss later.

Behind me, a crash allowed me to think, *Good, they took my advice*, before the patrol leader shouted, "Stand your ground, Patrol! We stand between the creature and our homes."

Idiots. But I couldn't judge them too harshly. It was their duty to defend the valley from monsters. Still, if they stood against the beastie, it would deal with them before continuing the chase. I'd used the delay to escape before—and only later heard the tales of what the beast had done. But recently, I'd had the misfortune of experiencing the aftermath of the beast's destruction. I wasn't fool enough not to run, but I could choose the direction.

Circling the nearest tree, I doubled back. It only needed to catch my scent, and it would give chase. It always had.

The sounds of fighting increased as I reached the clearing, and I had to dodge to narrowly avoid missing one of the patrolmen tumbling through the air. Most of them were on the ground—the beastie made short work of those it had no use for. Similarities to another scene almost made me hesitate. But the beastie had sunk its teeth into the patrol leader's leg. Still, she fought, stabbing it repeatedly with a small sharp blade to no effect. The smell of rotting copper was almost overwhelming—it must have fixated on her because she was the source of copper-scented magic.

Although it could be distracted by other magic, the beastie craved mine. I angled my path to take me into the beastie's field of vision but never leave the relative safety offered by the trees. The wolf-like head did not acknowledge my presence or give any indication that it was willing to relinquish its prize. The patrol leader's movements had weakened. Rot was slowly replacing the scent of copper in the clearing and I wondered what kind of magic the beastie used.

I altered my course once more, gathering my leg muscles to spring. Leaping straight for my nightmare, I cleared its head with the intention of springing off the leathery patch on its back between the wings and away. It would have to notice me.

But I miscalculated. Impossibly fast, the beastie dropped the patrol leader and whipped its wolf head around, clamping jaws onto my flank. My side exploded as its razor teeth sunk through fur into flesh. Instinctively, I tried to wriggle free, but it only tightened its grip until I could barely breathe. Winds swirled around me, as it took to the sky wings beating the air.

It had never caught me before, but I had always assumed it simply wanted to kill me, not to carry me off. As the pine trees faded into the pelting snow and we left the scent of copper behind, I resolved not to learn its intentions. I shifted back to human, hoping that the change would loosen its grip, but the powerful jaws held fast. Gray patches drifted in between the falling snow, and I thought I was passing out from the pain. Then, I realized the beastie was leeching my magic. My magic, in its various forms, was a part of me. If the beastie leeched it all, I would die.

Taking a deep breath to calm the panic rising in my mind, I told myself I just needed it to open its jaws. I'd outsmarted it before. It had dropped the patrol leader because I'd given it better prey. Maybe I could do that again.

Closing my eyes, I poured the remainder of my magic into the winds that buffeted our flight. I had no power left to direct them, but I hoped one found its way to the beastie.

With my eyes closed, I didn't notice a change until the smell of rotting things dropped away. Opening my eyes, I found myself falling, rather than flying. Up and down the world was white—either the snow had increased or we had flown higher in the hills.

Mustering shreds of power, I pulled a scrap of wind beneath me, and when I hit the ground, it only felt like I'd been kicked by a horse, rather than buried by a landslide. As I struggled to get my feet under me—I couldn't afford to stop running, even now—I vowed never to go back for anyone who was stupid enough to stand between the beastie and me again.

It ended in nothing good.

Spinning in a slow circle, I surveyed the whiteness. Not a pine in sight. I was lost.

I shivered without the cloak, but after a few tries, I decided I didn't have enough power to shift back to hound. I pressed one gloved hand to my side, stumbling forward in the deep snow. My body bore the scars of years' worth of dodging the beastie—I'd been running since I was a girl—but this was the first time it had ever gotten ahold of me.

I decided to head uphill so I didn't backtrack. The incline seemed steeper—perhaps we had flown all the way to the mountains? With my free hand out to prevent unexpected encounters hidden by the sheet of snow, I pressed on. Another step sunk me waist deep, and I lost my balance, pitching forward. My outstretched hand connected with something soft but solid. Instead of waiting for the stench of the beastie's magic to hit me, I pushed away from the fur beneath my gloved fingers and lurched to the side.

The snow under my feet vanished, and I fell with the snowflakes into empty air. A scream tore from my throat, already raw from the biting cold. My flailing hand caught, cutting the sound short and sending a jolt down my body. Pain seared up from my midsection as the motion pulled the wound, threatening to tear me in half.

Blinking upward against the black spots that began to overwhelm the falling snow, I saw another larger hand engulfing my own. My mind couldn't make sense of that—the beastie had claws, not hands, and besides that, it could fly. I couldn't see beyond the hand to determine to what manner of creature it belonged.

It hauled me back onto solid ground, where I lay gasping in snowflakes as they spiraled down from the sky. I couldn't feel my wound anymore. In fact, I couldn't feel much of anything. The outline of a shadowy figure started to become visible in the surrounding white. It looked vaguely human-shaped, but perhaps the beastie had only folded its wings. Then again, these mountains were home to many a strange creature, and looking human didn't always mean you were.

As the figure moved toward me, I closed my eyes, comforted by the fact that I didn't smell the sharp rotten scent, which marked the beastie's magic. I only caught a faint trace of woodsmoke, making my nose itch like a trapped sneeze, so perhaps my ability to sense magic simply wasn't functioning properly. Whatever this creature was, it would eat me in truth, and I wouldn't suffer having my life drained away slowly. Satisfied, I surrendered to the cold beyond pain as the creature lifted me from the ground and carried me away.

My eyes snapped open to relative darkness, so different from the white of the blizzard. I was shivering hot and shaking uncontrollably, although evidently not yet eaten. I could feel the bone-deep cold having it out with the knots of burning pain that raged on the left side of my body. Near my head, fire crackled. In the dim light, I saw a shape crouched over my feet. It appeared human, if on the large side. Pain stabbed through my toes. I panicked. If it ate my feet, I couldn't run, and running was the only thing that kept others safe. Sometimes.

I heard a snap like a dry branch above my head. I could almost feel the beastie breathing down my neck with its oversized wolf's jaws, stretching out claws, covered, much like the rest of it, in alternating patches of scales and fur. I tried to shift to hound, forgetting the beastie had drained my magic. Human, I remained.

I couldn't run. I couldn't fight. I'd proven on more than one occasion that I was no match for the beastie. Something wrapped itself around me, and I willed myself not to struggle in the embrace. But, still, no rotting things assaulted my nose. Instead, I was overwhelmed with sharp woodsmoke-drenched power, like a forest fire raging around me. Exhaustion pulled me down before I could sneeze.

The burning pain and bone chilling cold had melted into a nice pleasant warmth, and I wondered briefly if I was dead. Then I tried to move. Muscles screamed, informing me that I was very much alive. Puzzled, I opened my eyes. Rough rock arched over my head, and I could see the snow still coming down beyond the mouth of the cave. Someone obviously lived here, judging from the trunks, crates, and firewood stacked along one wall. A fire roared beyond the pile of furs and blankets wrapped around me. I imagined both combined to supply the warmth.

When I lifted my head to look around, the world tilted dangerously.

"Here." The gruff sound originating behind me was little more than a grunt, not unlike the noises the beastie made.

Reflexes kicked in, and I scrambled across the dirt floor, putting the fire between me and it as I pulled up the blankets for the little protection they offered. My side began to throb in time with my pounding heart, but I had moved quickly enough to see the outstretched hand (no claws) pull back and the wingless shoulders slump. A resigned look crossed the rather human face of the man who had approached me from behind.

I breathed carefully, trying to slow my heart without aggravating my wounded side as I studied him. Even crouched down, I could tell he was a big man, built like a bear. His skin was as rough as his voice, from the harsh mountain weather or old scars, I couldn't tell. He appeared to shave rarely, and this wasn't one of those occasions. Dressed in furs with haunted eyes, he looked like someone who could survive a lonely life in a mountain cave. My mind was slow to connect the pieces—the form in the snow—the creature crouched over my feet—

He'd saved me from a chilly dive to my death, but I still asked softly, "Are you going to eat me?" After all, some predators liked to play with their food.

Murky black eyes narrowed, and I thought I saw a flicker of bluish light across his forehead, but in the dim cave, I couldn't be sure. Anger flashed across those too dark eyes and was left to smolder as he straightened and turned, taking a few steps away.

Hoping his answer wasn't complicated enough to require contemplation, I asked with concern, "Can you talk?"

"Yeh." He didn't turn and it could have been another grunt. I couldn't be sure.

If he was playing games with his food, he wasn't very good at it. He seemed more offended than anything, so I took a deep breath and started over, telling him, "I'm sorry. You startled me. I'm Sian." It wasn't like I could stop him from eating me.

He half turned back, but the angry resignation had not left his face. After giving me a long look, he finally responded, "I'm called Dagr." His voice was deep and gruff, but this time, I could understand the words.

"Well met, Dagr." With only a fraction of an instant of hesitation, I held out my hand and hoped he thought my fingers shook from the cold.

Turning the rest of the way, Dagr regarded me warily and didn't move.

I did not withdraw my shaking hand, and finally, he approached me—cautiously, like a deer about to bolt. Only he was much too big to resemble a deer. As he shook my hand, I watched something between confusion and astonishment edge out the anger in the dark pools of his eyes.

The introduction ritual complete, he backed off a few steps and sat on his haunches. I made myself lean against the cave wall to appear relaxed. It was a mistake. My breath hissed through my teeth as cloth pressed into unhealed wound.

The sound did not escape unnoticed. "The thing that sunk its teeth in you had awful big jaws—what was it?" Dagr asked, watching me intently.

Shifting restlessly, I tried and failed to find a comfortable position. I realized he must be responsible for the bandages wrapped tightly around my middle because how else would he know the size and nature of the wound?

"A curse from my father—those who feared him fear me and send the beastie hunting." I shuttered. I'd never encountered those responsible for the hunt, but my mother had told me stories of them and of my father and how I came to possess such a strange mixture of magic.

Dagr frowned before asking skeptically, "What is there to fear about you?"

I knew I was on the small side in human form, even for a hillwoman. The only thing distinct about me was my mismatched eyes—one soft brown and the other ice blue. But even so, with my unimpressive light brown hair and unremarkable features, I could imagine the difficulty Dagr was having in picturing me as dangerous, especially when I was in a shaking huddle on the ground. "You should know better than to believe everything you see," I told him stubbornly. I hadn't figured him out yet, but I had smelled magic in the cave. I wasn't the only one who wasn't what I appeared.

At my words, his face drained of color, and I could make out the rune-ish symbols standing out starkly on his forehead. If they were runes, each was ruined by a jagged, slightly raised scar running through it. When I didn't press the advantage (because I didn't know what I had said to make him react like that), he asked, perhaps attempting to lighten the mood, "Are you telling me I invited the Cursed Witch into my home?"

It was my turn to feel like I had been punched in the gut. I hadn't expected the stories to reach this lonely place, but I could have kicked myself for forgetting, even for a moment, the danger that followed me. I could not undo the aid he had already rendered, but he deserved to know what kind of a monster he had brought into his home.

Instead of answering his question—I could hardly tell him the answer was 'yes'—I decided to show him. I wasn't sure I had the strength, but some of my magic had replenished. "I'm hunted for this," I said as I shifted, replacing the small woman with an oversized hound that filled a good portion of the cave. In this form, I was even bigger than the wolves that roamed these mountains, standing high enough to look the still-crouching Dagr in the face without tilting my head. My distinct salt-and-pepper coat and floppy ears further distinguished me from my four-footed kin. But if you plucked off the wings and filled in the patches of scale with fur, the beastie that hunted me would closely resemble my hound form. After all, it was designed to hunt my father's bloodline.

When a widening around the eyes was the only reaction Dagr presented, I wagged my tail and shifted back. I liked him for not running in terror when he met my hound form, especially when he must have confirmed my connection to the Cursed Witch by now, and I liked him even more for steadying me when my two feet decided not to support my weight right away. Close proximity allowed me to rest my fingers lightly on his arm as I said quietly, "And this."

This close, I knew the sharp woodsmoke smell originated with him. Feeling for the hum just under my skin, I used it to tug at the power I could sense buried deep in him.

My pull on his magic spurred more of a reaction than my shifting. He couldn't get away fast enough. Jerking backward as though he'd been burned, he stumbled and nearly landed in the fire. I took a step forward to help him, and he fended me off, whispering harshly, "Don't come near me, leech." That time, I clearly saw green spark through the vein in his temple.

I retreated, hot tears of fury blurring my vision. "You're just like the hillfolk—" An old arrow wound in my leg ached in time with the new one on my side as I continued, "—and the people who cursed my father, afraid of what you don't understand." I surged to my feet, wrapping the blanket around me and clutching it with white-knuckled hands. "Thank you for your hospitality." I half-bowed in his direction before spinning on bare heels and stomping toward the exit. I was prepared to march out into a blizzard half-clothed with the confidence that my rage would keep me warm.

Suddenly, Dagr filled the cave mouth and effectively blocked my way. "You're not going anywhere," he growled, towering over me.

His sudden hostility reawakened my ingrained fear of the beastie—just remove the wings—and it was too much. I backpedaled, tangling my feet in the blanket. I fell hard on my backside, causing involuntary tears to spring to my eyes as I yelped in pain.

Dagr looked as though I'd slapped him and remained rooted to the spot. His shoulders slumped and he mumbled something unintelligible before retreating to the other side of the cave.

"What did you say?" I asked shakily, unable to decipher the grunts.

He didn't look at me, just stared into the crackling fire between us, but he did repeat his words. "I said, I understand more than you know." His voice was laced with the heavy weight of experience. "I'm sorry for frightening you." This last sounded tired and defeated, like my reaction fell in line with the rest of the world.

I knew why I was afraid of him, but most people weren't cursed to be hunted by a magical beastie before they were old enough to fight back. My skittishness resulted from my situation; it didn't explain why the rest of the world would feel the same. Unless they had cause—as with the Cursed Witch—people didn't usually fear magic users, even this far into the northlands. Curious, I asked, "Why do *you* expect me to be terrified?"

"Does it matter? You clearly are," he bit out bitterly.

I waved his evasion away while agreeing, "Yes, yes, you're big and scary," that earned a wry twist of the lips from him. "I get that, I can be big and scary too. Big and scary tried to take a chomp out of me recently, which explains me. But you expected that, which means it's happened before. I don't see why anyone besides me would fear you—unless you do eat people." I kept my face straight, even though I was joking with that last.

He finally raised his eyes to meet mine. His were hard, black, and unfathomable. "They have reason to fear me, just as I have reason to fear leeching magic." His eyes unfocused, drifting to memory. "It's been used ill on me too many times." His focus snapped back before he explained carefully, "I'm not exactly human."

I gave him a good look up and down before replying, "You look like a man to me."

Dagr shook his head, but not before a small smile tugged at the corners of his mouth. "I'm not." He watched intently for a reaction as he said, "I'm daemae."

I examined now visible lightning sparking through his veins, illuminating his face. My people were neighbors with the darric fieron. Of course we had heard of daemae, beings formed of magical energy and bred by leeches as power sources since full-blooded leeches didn't possess power of their own. But I'd always thought daemae stories were spun to frighten children. "Daemae are pure magic," I insisted before repeating, "You look like a man to me."

His eyes narrowed as he retorted, "You look like hillfolk, and yet you walk in their nightmares." I flinched at that. "Well, so do I. You wield leeching magic and yet you don't understand daemae. You change shape, but you don't expect others to do the same?"

I frowned. "First, I haunt their nightmares because they've met mine. Second, I have leeching magic, but I'm not a leech, not in the sense you mean. Third, my shapes are both solid, and so are you. I felt it. I have trouble believing magical energy can take the form of a man." My words reminded me I had felt something else too. I closed my mismatched eyes and breathed deeply. Woodsmoke. Without other distractions, the smell was overpowering. I sneezed, twice. "Okay, I believe you." I opened my eyes to find him looking surprised. "What?" I asked. "If you know leeches, you know the magic allows us to sense other power. I can smell yours, but most people can't, so why should they fear you?"

He looked at me as though the answer was obvious. "If you are from the hills, you must know of the leeches' allies."

I raised an eyebrow and asked, "So you're telling me that your darric fieron master has been waiting in the shadows this whole time to jump out and command you to eat me?" Darric fieron were generally a bad bunch, but then so were leeches. Together, they and their experiments were the source of all manner of legends and nightmares in these hills, including my own personal one.

Most of my unusual mix of magic originated with my shapeshifter father. The darric fieron had tried to rip his power from him and give it to a leech, hoping to bind the two so the leech could shift *and* steal the magic of others. Only the spell had backfired, reversing to give the leeching magic to my father instead. It also gave him the edge he needed to escape, which earned him the beastie on his trail. I'd never met him, but I assumed it had eaten him and moved on to me because I had inherited his natural and unnatural powers. I figured the beastie was the darric fieron's way of cleaning up their mess. "And daemae serve the leeches, right? So you can't be here because once they have you, there's no way to break a leech's hold."

He grinned, showing teeth. "Not quite 'no way,' but it's certainly not easy." My eyes caught on the broken runes etched across his face, and I wondered what he'd had to do to escape.

I nodded. "Okay, so no darric fieron in the shadows?" I had no desire to meet those who commanded the beastie. "If you wield power yourself, why do you fear mine?"

He answered quietly, "Because it matches that which was used to control me. And I cannot use mine. It would act as a beacon to those I escaped, and they would find me again."

I sucked in another deep breath, filtering out the scent of Dagr's power. Running through the wash of woodsmoke was a faint trace of mud. I'd smelled something similar woven with beastie's rotting scent. The same people hunted us both. Only the beastie would find me—it always did—and lead them straight to Dagr. Using the cave wall for support, I pushed myself shakily to my feet. I grimaced as my stiffened wound protested, but I remained standing.

"Where are you going now?" Dagr asked mildly. His eyes were sad, but his voice betrayed no surprise, as though he knew the answer all too well. He made no move to stop me this time as I took a lurching step.

"My presence puts you in danger," I informed him, taking another determined step. "I cannot allow that."

"*Me*? In danger? How?" He sounded incredulous. Apparently he had anticipated the reaction but not the explanation. He probably thought I had come to my senses and decided to be scared of *him*.

I halted my slow progress. "That magic beastie that's after me? It's still coming. And it answers to the darric fieron." I turned toward him and explained, "I'll continue on to my hillfolk kin." No need to tell him that they were unlikely to welcome me. "Thank you for all you've done for me." I gave the open-mouthed Dagr another half-bow that threatened to topple me, and resumed my exit, ignoring my barefooted semi-clothed state once again.

I heard a rustle behind me as though he had started in my direction. He probably remembered my last reaction because the noise stopped. Instead, he cleared his throat and matched my polite tone. "I would appreciate it if you didn't leave."

I paused to ask, "Didn't you hear what I just said?" I'd seen the terror in his eyes when he felt my leeching magic. He didn't live by himself on the side of a mountain because he was eager to face off with the darric fieron.

"Yes, but if you go out like that, I'll just have to carry you back frozen again." He had a point there. "I've fought the creations of the darric fieron before. Whatever is after you won't hurt you here." His voice was so determined that I almost believed him. But he hadn't met my beastie. And I knew what it sounded like when you tried to convince yourself.

Still, there was the matter of clothes. I could see the snow falling again—or still falling—in thick heavy flakes. I remembered running, not knowing when the beastie would emerge through the sheet of white. My heart thudded in my chest and my legs folded beneath me, severely limiting my options.

Strong arms prevented me from a painful meeting with the floor as I collapsed. This time, I didn't flinch.

"You can leave as soon as you're on your feet again," Dagr murmured soothingly as he scooped me up. "When you come to your senses, you'll be running anyway," he added in an even quieter tone.

"Are you sure you don't eat people?" I asked Dagr as he shook the snow off and bent down with an armload of firewood. It had been several days since I'd tried to leave, and I was finally able to walk around without suddenly sprawling on the cave floor. Since it hadn't shown its distorted face, I could only conclude that the beastie was having difficulty tracking me through the blizzard, which continued without abating. It let up enough this morning that Dagr ventured outside for more wood.

Before going out, Dagr had pointed me toward a wooden trunk, and I had abandoned the blankets for actual clothes while he was gone. My own garments had not survived my wounds and my trek up the mountain. The clothing options were limited by what fit, and I ended up in an emerald green dress finer than anything I had ever owned. I didn't have any luck with the shoes, so my feet remained bare. Most of the other clothes didn't look like Dagr's either, hence my question.

Dagr's back was to me when I spoke, and I saw the muscles in his neck tense. His expression remained stony and tight as lightning forked toward his jaw. Then, he glanced back and saw that I was joking. He gave me a tentative half-smile in return and explained, "Sometimes, I help travelers stuck in the snow. Most don't stick around to pack their nice things."

He turned back to stack the wood, and the stench hit me—rotten and slimy with a hint of mud. I stumbled back, but beastie must not have reached the cave because the snow outside was unblemished.

At my sudden movement, Dagr turned, and when he saw my sheet-white face, he asked, "What is it, Sian?"

I swallowed hard, "It's here." I met his eyes and told him seriously, "You should leave."

He gave me what was probably meant to be a reassuring pat on the shoulder and said, "I'm big and scary, remember? I'll persuade it not to eat you." He turned toward the cave mouth.

I reached a shaking hand to catch his arm. "I already owe you my life. I won't be responsible for your death."

He gently removed my fingers, "That thing doesn't want me. If you stay hidden it won't know you're here."

I should have explained it didn't work like that. I should have started running then and there, but my feet remained rooted to the spot. I let him walk outside to face my nightmare.

By the time Dagr waded into the snow piled outside the cave, I could see the beastie. It had paused, wings folded, sniffing the air. Dagr addressed it in a conversational tone. "I think you and I should talk, especially since you probably don't like those holding your leash any more than I do."

The beastie tilted its head and flared its nostrils at Dagr. I'd never tried to talk to it—until this last time, I'd never even been close—maybe it really was considering his offer.

Without warning, one massive claw lashed out and slammed into Dagr's side, tossing him out of my field of vision. Unfazed, the beastie sniffed the air again. I remained frozen, afraid to move, even though I now knew it hunted by smell.

A dark form erupted from the snow, and I realized it must be Dagr as he collided with the beastie's back legs, toppling them both. I found I could breathe again when the beastie turned its attention away from me to focus on Dagr. I dropped to my knees on the cave floor, partially concealed by empty crates.

A few seconds too late, my sluggish mind processed what the distraction might cost him. The beastie thrashed, sinking its claws in Dagr's chest as it stood, pinning him to the snow-covered ground.

I remained frozen. I didn't know what to do. I had tried running. I had tried letting dragons fight on my behalf and they had been no match for the beastie. Now I was hiding. Each time, the outcome had been the same. Others paid for my choices.

Expecting the beastie to subdue the threat and continue the hunt, I was surprised when it paused, flexing its claws to anchor them more firmly. Dagr's scream was drowned out by the beastie's howl. The snow dampened the sound, but it echoed through the cave. The beastie flapped its wings, and I wondered if it had found new prey to hunt.

Wind gusted around my hiding place in the cave. I couldn't bring myself to fight the beastie, not after it had caught me, but maybe I could use the wind to my advantage again. My magic had completely recovered from the last attack, and I gathered it all to my hands. Raising my arms over my head, I let the wind waft through my fingertips and take my magic. These gusts were strong, and I did not have the power to move them from their chaotic path around the cave, but I needed only to nudge them in the right direction to send them hurtling back toward the beastie. It stood on the flat area between the cave and the sheer cliff of the mountain.

My plan might not work. It wasn't as though the beastie was standing on the edge, but the beastie had its wings stretched open like sails, and I hoped that they would function the same way.

The magic-laden winds slammed into the beastie and drove it backward slowly but steadily. It howled in frustration, but didn't relinquish its grasp on Dagr. Under its claws, he slid across the snow toward the edge of the cliff.

I had to decide between one heartbeat and the next. If I did nothing, I could probably slip away and the beastie would lose my trail for a time. But it would take Dagr with it. I didn't know if the daemae could survive the drop, but I doubted he could fly.

I moved, dashing out of the cave to slide barefoot across the snow. I reached them as they teetered on the edge. The beastie was almost over with Dagr's body anchoring it to solid ground. Dropping to my knees, I tried to dislodge the beastie, but my fingers scrambled ineffectively where the shiny claws dug into Dagr's fur cloak.

I had only moments before it would realize its true prize was under its snout, and the push of the wind gusts would not last much longer. In desperation, I poured the last of my magic into my right hand and reached up. The beastie's head darted, trying to grab me like before, but I was ready for it, and this time, I wasn't dodging. I managed to get my hand over its nostrils and released my magic. At the same time, I pushed, as though my human strength could do anything to move it.

At first, I didn't think it worked, but then the beastie's nostrils flared and it snapped at the air. Tangling my fingers in Dagr's fur cloak, I leaned my whole weight across his shoulders, trying to stop him from being dislodged by the beastie's sudden movements. It lifted first one claw and then the other to swipe at prey that wasn't there. Free of Dagr, nothing anchored it to the ledge and it tumbled backward, spiraling down into the nothingness of the falling snow and taking its smell of rotting things with it.

"Dagr?" I asked, but his face was still. Lightning sparked weakly—purple and teal—across his throat, so he was alive. Not knowing how long my trick would keep the beastie away, I didn't want to be out in the open when it returned. Using my grip on the furs, I attempted to drag Dagr backward toward the relative safety of the cave. He slid a few inches, but I heard stitches pop as I fell over backward. The ground was uneven and he was dead weight. I just didn't have the mass to move him in this form.

But I had given my magic to the winds, and I didn't think I had enough remaining to shift to hound. Reaching a hand over the edge of the cliff, I collected the residue of my magic from the winds that swirled up from the chasm. It took a few tries and I had to close my eyes to concentrate, but I finally managed to switch forms.

Trying not to cause more damage, I gathered a mouthful of the fur near the neck of Dagr's heavy cloak and leaned the weight of the hound into dragging him backward. Once I had him moving, we made good progress over the snow, and I didn't stop until we reached the fire that still crackled pleasantly.

I knew I should leave him and run—the beastie could be back any minute—but what good would my leading it away do if he bled to death here on the floor of the cave? I needed human hands to examine the wound, so I shifted. The emerald dress was wet and cold against my legs, but I ignored it as I carefully peeled back the fur cloak and the fabric of Dagr's shirt.

I almost panicked as the scent of rot hit me, but it wasn't strong. The wounds from the beastie's claws oozed dark sludge. I leaned closer and confirmed that to be the source of the smell. Rotten woodsmoke. I didn't even know where to begin. I'd never been much of a healer—my sister said I didn't have the temperament—and these wounds already looked like they were infected. The cuts from the beastie's claws were deep, and looked dangerous even without the ooze. I needed magic. It wasn't the most efficient, but if you overloaded a wound with it, the body would figure out the rest. It was a bit of a bludgeoning method of healing, but it usually worked.

Only one problem—most of my power was riding the winds down the side of the mountain.

I curled my fists in frustration. There had to be another way. Closing my eyes, I took a deep breath—I couldn't afford to let my guard down. If the beastie returned, I needed to know. Wounds or no wounds, Dagr would be better off without me if it returned. I only smelled the rotten ooze—and woodsmoke.

Dagr shouldn't need my power to heal his wounds when he had more than enough of his own. With my eyes still closed, I studied him with my leech sense. The woodsmoke swirled lazily in a fixed pattern, never increasing or decreasing. Dagr had said that he couldn't use his power or those who hunted him would know his location. Apparently, that resolution extended to using his magic to heal himself.

I frowned and opened my eyes. The lightning was fading with each flicker. If I didn't do something soon, Dagr was going to die. But I wouldn't condemn him to a life of being chased. No one deserved that.

I had a pretty good handle on the thread of magic that smelled like mud and must belong to the leech or the darric fieron that he feared. It was the only magical scent that drifted beyond Dagr. Reaching out, I used a shred of my own magic to encase the mud. I rolled it between my fingers until I could barely smell the other magic. That should keep anyone on the other end from feeling what I was about to do.

Returning to Dagr, I removed one of his heavy gloves. "I'm sorry," I said as I gripped his hand in both of mine because I was about to become his nightmare.

As soon as I reached for his magic, Dagr's eyes flew open, but seemed unable to focus. He started to struggle weakly and gasped, "Stop. Please." But I put one hand on his chest between the claw marks and held him in place so that he couldn't injure himself further. Closing my eyes, I worked my way past his magical defenses. They were formidable, and if he had been fully conscious, I'm not sure I would have succeeded.

When I began to move the woodsmoke-scented power toward our joined hands, he stopped fighting me, but his hand trembled beneath mine. I pushed down any second thoughts about bringing his fears to life before tightening my grip and taking as much power as I dared.

Opening my eyes, I patted Dagr's hand and laid it gently by his side. Pain and panic warred in his voice as he rumbled haltingly, "You—ruined—it—all." Tears leaked from the corners of his now-closed eyes and tracked down the side of his face to mingle with a flash of green lightning.

I didn't tell him I had no intention of letting his enemies track him. When I leeched power, I converted it into my own magic. I just needed a little time to make sure the power used to heal him wouldn't register as his. But I didn't tell him any of that because I didn't think he would trust an answer coming from me.

Instead, I stood and retrieved the basin of water we had set to melt that morning. Fetching a clean cloth, I washed Dagr's wounds. I didn't think that water would fight against the ooze, but it couldn't hurt. His breath hissed out through his teeth when I touched the cool cloth to his skin, but I didn't stop when he flinched or cried out. As I worked, the scent of woodsmoke diminished to be replaced by more familiar smells of hound and fresh hill country air.

By the time I'd removed as much of the ooze as I could, Dagr had stopped reacting to the pressure of the cloth on his wounds. His breathing was shallower and I couldn't see any sparks in his veins. I'd run out of time.

Taking a deep breath, I couldn't smell woodsmoke coming from anywhere besides Dagr. Tossing aside the cloth, I placed a hand over each set of claw marks on Dagr's chest. I poured power scented with hound and the hills into his wounds. I hoped his body would know what to do with it and that daemae weren't *that* different from humans. I hoped I hadn't waited too long.

I didn't stick around to see if it worked—I didn't want to put him in more danger if—when—the beastie returned. Before I left, I rolled a spare blanket into a cushion to put under his head and pulled another over him. "Please be okay," I whispered to his unmoving form as I shifted to hound and slipped out.

It would make the sense to put as much distance between myself and Dagr as quickly as possible. But I couldn't smell the beastie yet, and I wanted to make sure Dagr survived his wounds. I resolved to watch the cave from an outcropping of rocks located slightly uphill. I would stay until I saw Dagr moving under his own power, and I would leave at the first sign of trouble.

Finding a space between two boulders that offered some shelter from wind and snow, I lay down with my head on my paws to wait. It had been a long day, and with nothing to fight or save, I drifted off to sleep.

"Sian?" It was impossible to tell how much time had passed, but it was still daylight when I awoke to Dagr calling my name. Had I been in human form, I might have answered before I remembered that we were no longer in the cave pretending to be safe from our nightmares. It was snowing again, and a thin layer covered my fur.

Dagr leaned heavily against the cave entrance. Even at this distance, I could see the wounds on his chest—I couldn't tell if they were healing, but at least they didn't look to be covered in sludge. After waiting another moment, Dagr frowned and turned to shuffle back into the cave.

I stood and shook the snow from my fur. That was it. I needed to put distance between me and the beastie. If Dagr collapsed after this, he was on his own. I glanced wistfully at the cave. It had been nice, but this was the last time I would put someone in danger. Even if I thought I'd outrun the beastie, even if they offered me sanctuary, even if I wanted to pretend that I could be safe, I wouldn't let anyone else get hurt just because my nightmare had wings and haunted me like a whirlwind of destruction. No more.

Before I could vanish into the snow, Dagr reappeared, and I froze. My mottled coat would probably blend in with the snow-covered rocks, but I thought any movement was likely to catch his attention. He held a dish in each hand, and he balanced them carefully as he sat down at the mouth of the cave. Placing one dish by his side, he took out a utensil and began to eat the other. He didn't say anything, just stared out into the falling snow.

When he finished, he returned to the cave, leaving the other dish where he had placed it. I didn't know if it was a peace offering or bait, but I almost went back.

Almost, but I didn't. I turned and worked my way through the rocks. The wind wasn't blowing in my favor, so I heard the beastie before I smelled it. Something clicked and scrambled against the stone, and I looked back. The beastie clamored over the edge of the cliff like a monster from the abyss. Its wings appeared functional, but maybe the winds around the mountain were too strong for it to fly.

Expecting it to charge in my direction, I gathered myself to run, regardless of the hazards of slippery rocks. But instead, it flicked its tail and lumbered toward the cave. I paused, confused. It had never not chased me.

I took a deep breath as it approached the cave mouth, but the only magic I could smell was my own.

It wanted my magic.

The strongest source of my magic at the moment was the power I had drained from Dagr and converted to heal his wounds. Power he now carried. It was after him.

This time, I didn't hesitate. I ran.

A wave of rotten hill air, hound, and woodsmoke hit me as I rounded the entrance to the cave. The beastie's back was to me, but I saw it had already chomped down on Dagr's shoulder. He struggled ineffectually to free himself. His movements were jerky and desperate. I couldn't separate the scents of magic in the room. It had already started to feed on his power. Only, Dagr was all power. If it drained him, he would die.

I growled and launched myself at the beastie's back.

It spun faster than I'd thought possible without releasing Dagr, and swatted with one claw. I dodged, but a faint throb from the wound in my side reminded me what would happen if I was too slow. I twisted in mid-air and narrowly avoided landing in the fire.

I snarled at the beastie and inched closer to Dagr, who was no longer moving. I could smell a faint hint of woodsmoke intertwined with the more mundane smells of furs and man, so I knew he was alive, but I didn't know for how much longer.

Even with his eyes closed, I could see the terror etched on his face. I shifted my attention to the beastie. A growl started deep in my throat as I realized he'd probably looked like that when I leeched him too. No one deserved to have their nightmares come to life.

The beastie flapped its wings to maneuver in the confined space. Power wafted on the air, making the hair on the back of my neck stand on end. Woodsmoke, hound, rot, hill, and mud. Maybe it was our initial conversation about the nature of magic and man, maybe it was the fact that I could still smell Dagr *and* his magic, but it hit me. With the beastie, there was nothing *under* that smell, and there never had been. I could smell Dagr's power because I was a leech but I could also smell *him* because he was human, or close enough. Not so with the beastie.

It shook its head, releasing Dagr and tossing him into the cave wall. It turned its attention toward me. For the first time in my life, I wasn't scared of that leather-fur nightmare face or the rows of sharp teeth.

Because I'd realized it was a spell.

And for all that mattered, I was a leech.

It launched itself in my direction, and I dove under its attack. In the past, I'd thought it a flesh-and-blood creature, and I'd run. This time, I hoped my nose hadn't failed me as I jumped on its back. Not having hands in hound form and unable to get purchase with my paws, I bit down on a leathery patch just above the wing. The beastie squirmed to dislodge me, and it nearly succeeded when it knocked me in the wounded side with its tail.

Pushing the throbbing pain from my mind, I took in a deep breath through my nose and traced the pattern in the layers of rot and mud. Closing my eyes, I directed my leeching magic to pull at the weak spots. I felt the spell give. As it began to unravel, rotten insubstantial slime buzzed in my mouth. It made me want to vomit, but I held on until I tumbled through the beastie that faded beneath me to slam into the ground. I didn't stop leeching until I could no longer smell the beastie's magic.

Afraid that if I spit it out, it would reform and hunt me again, I swallowed hard against the rotten taste and lay where I had fallen, concentrating on converting the spell into my own mixture of power.

I heard a crash from across the cave and hoped it was Dagr. I waited until my stomach stopped churning before opening my eyes. Shifting back to human, I approached where Dagr had fallen amid a pile of smashed crates. I had led the thing here. I hadn't run when I should have. And I had become his nightmare incarnate by leeching his power.

Then, I'd let the beastie do the same.

The emerald dress, already ripped and stained, caught on one of the half-broken crates, and I heard the hem of the skirt tear as I dropped to my knees beside Dagr. The fine garment was beyond repair anyway. I couldn't look at Dagr. I didn't want to see the expression on his face or the fear in his eyes.

I reached out to touch the hand curled by his side, to see if his heart beat, but I pulled it back before my fingertips brushed his skin.

"Sian?" his voice shook, and I cringed, not knowing what was worse—him hating me now or him hating me more when I used magic again to heal these new wounds. He coughed. It sounded painful, but I couldn't bring myself to move. I didn't want to be more of a monster to him. "You could have told me you were the one who was likely to eat someone," he chided.

I glanced up sharply, searching his pain-lined face, because it almost sounded like...yes, there was laughter dancing in those bottomless eyes and a smile ghosted across his pale lips.

For once, I couldn't match his humor. "Now you know why people fear the Cursed Witch," my voice came out hoarse with the smell of rot simmering in my throat, "Oh, Dagr, I'm so sorry."

"What for?" he asked nonchalantly, but he tensed as my magic brimming hands rested on his wounded shoulder.

"This." Once again, I poured converted power from my fingers. A small gasp escaped Dagr when the magic hit him and his face scrunched in remembered pain before he turned away from me. I felt hot tears track down my own face, but I didn't stop.

When most of the spell that used to be the beastie but now smelled of hound was gone, Dagr captured both of my hands in his larger ones and said, "Enough," without opening his eyes. I stopped feeding him power, and looked down at the torn fabric of the emerald dress. He struggled to sit up and lean against the wall of the cave while I waited for him to run—or tell me to get out of his home. Instead, he reached up to brush a tear from my face. "You've no cause to be sorry, Sian. I'm a mite jumpy around magic, but you're not them. You faced your nightmare to save me from mine."

I frowned. I'd brought the nightmare to his home in the first place. It was because of me that he'd been forced to relive his worst fears time and again today. "I can't guarantee they won't hunt you for what I did," I pointed out softly, even though I could still smell a hint of hound and hills choking out the mud that connected him to his nightmares.

"I know." He tilted my chin so I would look at him. I could see power once again sparking through his veins, and I didn't think he was lying to himself when he said, "but I can't run forever."

Finally, it sunk in that I couldn't see fear lurking in his too dark eyes. A smile tugged at the corner of my mouth as I cleared a space to sit beside him and said, "Well, if you decide you'd rather have someone eat your nightmares for you, let me know."

ABOUT THE AUTHOR

Beth Powers writes science fiction and fantasy stories, researches old pirate tales, and lives in Indiana with her cats. Her work has appeared in Daily Science Fiction, Deep Magic, Aurealis, *and other magazines. Visit her on the web at bethpowers.com.*

ANGUS MCCARN AND THE TALE OF TWO TALES

ROLLIN JEWETT

Angus McCarn woke up early that Sunday morn. He knew that the fish in the stream outside Ballybunion where he lived would not wait for him should he sleep late. He had fished the stream every Sunday for fifty-two years and wasn't about to let the fish think that he was getting too old to catch them.

Yes, he was getting on in years, but that didn't keep him from doing the things he truly enjoyed. Like fishing, singing the old songs, smoking his clay pipe, and telling stories. He was the best storyteller in all of southern Ireland. At least, that's what the townsfolk said of him. He walked into town every Saturday night and sat in the Redwolf Tavern at his usual table, and as soon as someone bought him an ale, he'd begin to tell a story. Oh, he would sometimes be challenged by a stranger from another county who thought he could tell a better story, but usually everyone just wanted to listen to Angus and went home after that. They knew he was the best.

It wasn't just the stories he told, it was the way he told them—his eyes ignited by the fire of his imagination, he would gesture broadly and his voice would whisper or shout with dramatic intensity. And no one dared question the authenticity of his tales, for he told them with such spirit that they all had to be true.

He told tales about when he was a young man growing up, and of his adventures with the fairies, spirits, and leprechauns that inhabited the grassy knolls surrounding Ballybunion.

He had told a particularly good tale the night before, and though he had stayed out to the wee hours to tell it, he was ready this morning to cast his hook into the stream near his cottage and wrestle with a big trout if luck should have it.

He donned his leather coat and placed his pipe and tobacco in the left pocket. Then he placed a potato, a hard roll, and some cheese in his pouch, took up his pole and was off. It was a beautiful spring morning into which he walked, and he delighted in it and began to hum a tune that his mother had sung to him as a child.

"Oh, yes, the man is lucky who can call the world his home. And yes, the man is lucky if his house is all his own. And if the man is lucky, then the fairies shine their light, and love the man who's lucky every day and every night."

Yes, Angus was a lucky man. He had all the friends he needed and all the time in the world. True, his cottage was about to fall in on him and he had no one around to keep up the grounds. But what was a small thing like that compared to all that he did have? He was in good health for a man past his prime, and he certainly had enough to eat and enough to keep him busy.

As he walked along the path that led to the stream, he was filled with happiness and love for the life that he led. He was not rich in money and land, but he was rich in heart.

As he neared the stream where he fished, he heard a small voice crying as though in trouble. Angus hurried toward the spot from where the voice seemed to come, and to his astonishment he saw a tiny, red-bearded man standing on a rock in the middle of the fast-flowing stream. Wonder of wonder, it wasn't a rock—it was a turtle! And it was swimming against the current, unaware of the tiny figure on its back. The little man was cursing at the turtle and jumping up and down on its back, waving his tiny arms.

Angus, though he had told many stories about them, had never seen an actual leprechaun before. And though he was very surprised, he could not help laughing loud and hearty at the sight of the wee bearded man surfing on the back of the turtle. The little man spotted Angus and yelled, "Don't just stand there laughing like a fool! Help me before he goes underwater! I can't swim!" Angus winked at the leprechaun and said, "I'm wise to your ways, little man. My grandfather once helped one of your kin and before he could get so much as a 'thank you, sir,' the little devil had vanished."

"I'll thank you right now if that's your only concern. Just get me out of here. I see he's taking a deep breath!" cried the little man. Angus was neither foolish nor heartless enough to watch the little man drown. He said, "Hold onto your beard, I'll get you out of this mess." He unwrapped a little of the string he had on his pole and cast his hook and line out to where the little man and the turtle were.

"Grab onto the line and I'll pull you in," Angus told him, "only don't try anything funny, or I'll let loose the line." The leprechaun was in no position to try anything funny even if he wanted to.

Just as the turtle dove beneath the water, Angus hauled the leprechaun in. He caught the little man in his hand and held him tight, but not too tight—for he was only as large as a finger.

"Well, I went fishin' for a trout and caught myself a wish instead, eh?" said Angus to the leprechaun.

"Not so fast," said the leprechaun, "I'm not that kind of leprechaun. I can't just fulfill a wish just like that. I have to see proof that you are worthy of a wish before I can grant you one."

"None of your double-talk! I saved your little life, didn't I?" said Angus, "Doesn't that make me worthy of a wish?" And he drew back his arm as though to throw the little man back into the water.

"Alright, alright," said the leprechaun, "don't get hasty. First, set me down and tell me your name."

But Angus knew better than to turn a leprechaun loose once you had him in your hand. He would be gone like a flash and laughing all the way. Angus took his hook off his line, put the little man in the crook of it, and stuck the barbed end into a tree so that the leprechaun could not escape. Then he bowed and said, "Angus McCarn's my name, and who might you be?"

"I be Chris Tinker," said the little man, "of the Shannon Leprechaun Order. I've heard of you and your storytellin'. Your grandfather and his grandfather had the same gift. I also know that you've never seen a fairy or sprite in your life, yet you persist in telling the townfolk stories about us and our ways. I'll admit, you do seem to know a lot about us." He gave Angus a sly look. Angus laughed. All the stories he had told had been passed on to him by his forefathers. He was happy to know that they had mostly been true.

"Yes," said Angus, "I also know that I have a wish comin' to me, isn't that so?"

"Well," said Chris Tinker, "I suppose you do. But I was just wonderin' if you're a gamblin' man or not?" He gave Angus a wink and waited for an answer.

Gambling was against the church, thought Angus, but this was different. Yes, this was very different indeed. Besides, most of the men in town gambled anyway, as long as Father O'Dell wasn't around to see it.

Angus knew that this was probably a trick of some sort and that he should just get his wish and have done with it, but he was curious about the leprechaun's question.

"Well, I might gamble a bit now and then, but what has that to do with a wish?" asked Angus.

"I'll tell you," said Chris Tinker, "Do you know how I came to be on that turtle's back when you found me?"

"No," said Angus. "How should I know?"

"Well, here's where the gamblin' comes in. Now, I know your love of tellin' stories that aren't entirely true. I've been called the best leprechaun storyteller in all Shannon, and you've been called similar things. I say we each tell a story about how I ended up on the back of that turtle. My story will be true and you can make yours up. And after, if we decide that your story is better than mine, I'll grant you two wishes instead of one. But if we decide that mine is the better of the two, you get no wishes and you have to let me go. Now, are you a gamblin' man or aren't you?" asked Chris Tinker.

Angus thought for a moment. Well, if it is a trick, he hadn't really lost anything, had he? And if the leprechaun's story was good, Angus could retell it in the tavern that night. And if Angus's own story was better, then he'd have two wishes instead of one; no matter how you look at it, he'd come away with something.

"I'll do it!" cried Angus, and so it was. "Who shall go first?" asked Angus, who already had a story brewing in his mind.

"Well seeing as I already know my story, it being true, why don't I tell mine first. That way, you'll have time to think of yours," said Chris Tinker.

"So be it," agreed Angus, "but let me light my pipe and find a decent stone to sit on. Would you care for a smoke?"

"I would, thank you," said the leprechaun, as he reached for his own tiny hare bone pipe. Angus poured a little of his own tobacco into the small pipe, spilling most of it, then lit the two pipes. At last, they were ready.

"Well, it started this morning, before the dew sprite had even made her rounds," Chris Tinker began, "I was safe at home, sleeping like a pup, when I heard a loud noise outside my window in the hollow tree where I live. I looked outside, and what do you think I saw?"

Angus shrugged and took a draw on his pipe.

"I saw a shadowy figure crouched outside my tree, making a sound that would stop your whiskers from growing. I thought it might be a banshee or some other such evil thing so I stayed hidden, not making a sound. Well, it didn't go away, so I thought that perhaps I should investigate. I slowly walked around to the front door of my tree and opened it. I looked at where the thing should have been and it was gone. So, as I turned to go back inside, what do you think I see starin' me right in the face—but what looks to be the angel of death himself, a-screamin' and howlin' to knock the breath right out of you!

"I nearly jumped out of my beard, I can tell you. Now, leprechauns have magic, but not enough when it comes to dealin' with the devil himself. My only thought was to get away from this demon and hope that it might pass me by if I stalled it long enough. It wore an evil-looking shroud which covered its face and body, and though it wasn't much taller than a tree stump, it hissed and moved like a serpent on fire!"

"Now, now," said Angus, a bit unbelieving but enthralled at the same time.

"Now, now, yourself, man! I mean to tell you that in all my years of seeing and encountering evil fairies and such, this was the diller of them all. I could barely move, I was so scared. When he came for me, I felt my heart in my feet and started running toward the stream as fast as I could. I knew that if I could make it to the water, I might be safe, since evil spirits can't stand water, and there are more places to hide, too. Well, he chased right after me, growling and tearing up the ground as he went. I leaped to the right and to the left, hoping to lose him, but he followed just as close as ever. I was about out of breath by the time I reached the water, but once my legs get started, there's no stopping them. The thing was just behind me and gaining, when I reached the stream. I was out of time, and I knew I had to think fast. In the moonlight I saw a group of large stones in the stream, leading across, and jumped on the closest one, with the idea of crossing the stream and escaping. I was hoping that the raging devil-creature would not be quite so eager to keep after me since I was heading into the stream, seeing as it was too big to cross on the stones. I was in luck. It stopped at the edge of the stream and let out a terrible yell. I was still crossing on the stones, when one of the stones began moving. It was the turtle, and he began to swim downstream."

"So that's how you ended up on his back, eh?" Angus laughed, "but what about the thing that was chasing you?"

"Well, be patient and I'll tell you," said Chris Tinker. "I was glad to be away from that thing, and even though I was not completely out of danger, since I can't swim and I was on the back of a turtle in the middle of a stream, at least the thing had stopped chasing me. As I sat on the back of the turtle, I could still hear it. It was moving along the side of the stream and I hoped the turtle would not decide to return to shore. Though it had been very dark, sunlight began creeping into view, and soon it was bright as day. I could still hear the demon wailing and running alongside the stream, and finally it burst from the wood and I could see it clearly!"

"Yes, yes!" said Angus, anxious to hear what the devil-creature looked like.

"It was a large grey fox that a hunter had bagged. It must've gotten away and couldn't get out of the bag completely. Poor thing, it was frightened and howling so. It had simply come to me for help. Many of the animals around here do. Anyway, it wasn't a devil-creature or anything of the like. Just an ordinary grey fox!" With that, Chris Tinker burst out laughing and slapped his knee so hard, he dropped his pipe.

Angus had to laugh at the story. Imagine, a leprechaun thinking a grey fox was the devil-incarnate.

"Not a bad story, at that," said Angus, filling his and the leprechaun's pipes, "I'll have a time out-doing you on that one." Angus then took out his potato, roll, and cheese and offered some to the little man, who did not refuse it.

"After we eat, I'll give it a whirl," Angus said. They ate and enjoyed the meal and each other's company, and admired the afternoon. Angus loosened the hook from around the leprechaun's waist, but did not take it out completely. He knew that even though they had a bargain, leprechauns were not completely trustworthy, and Chris Tinker would probably run away if given the chance.

"Alright, I think I got one," said Angus after their pipes were filled and lit a third time. He was rather enjoying this and whether he got his wishes or not, he had a story or two to tell at the Redwolf tonight.

"This is the way I see it," he began. His mind always had a story there, whether it was one he'd heard or one he was in the process of making up. They all seemed real to him, even the ones he created, as though it had perhaps happened in another life. And he truly believed what he was saying, which was why most people believed that his stories were true.

"You know as well as I that the best time to catch the fish, minnows in your case, is early, early in the mornin'. Before, as you said, the dew sprite makes her rounds. Well, the way I see it is that being that a leprechaun is as good a fisherman as the next man, perhaps you had it in your mind to go fishin' in the early hours, when the fish are just wakin' and fancy a bit of breakfast. Well, let's just say that you got your little reed pole and a hook of thorn and set out to catch your own breakfast. Now, if you're like me, you probably do this every Sunday, rain or shine, and you take some gratification in the fact that you never come home empty-handed, even if it only be a small one or two."

"I must say that you're fairly close to the truth on several counts, except that my fishin' day is Tuesday. But continue," said Chris Tinker.

"Alright. Now, maybe you made your way down here to the stream, put a crumb on your hook and cast your line near the edge of the water where the tiny carp hide. Then you sat down on a mossy rock, lit your pipe and waited for a hit. Now, supposin' you got comfortable and hadn't had a bite. It bein' early, you might just fall asleep, now wouldn't you?"

"Not with my blamed hook in the water, I wouldn't!" exclaimed Chris Tinker.

"Well, let's just say you did," continued Angus, "So, there you are, sound asleep with a baited hook, and holdin' on to the pole in your sleep. Now, you know as well as I that the trout in this stream get rather hefty this time of season, and they'll go for just about anything big enough to swallow. Now, suppose a little lazy minnow was to bite that crumb you had on your hook and not make enough fuss to wake you up..."

"I'd feel 'em in my sleep, I would!" said Chris Tinker.

"Not if you'd had a bit of whiskey and not enough sleep last night, you wouldn't!" countered Angus. "A trout would be tickled to find a minnow for breakfast, especially one that couldn't seem to get away from him, for reasons unknown to him. He wouldn't think twice about swallowing that minnow, not knowin' that there was a little hook there as well. So, he might take the hook and, well," laughed Angus, "take you along with it!" Angus roared at the thought of Chris Tinker being pulled through the water by a large trout.

"That's not funny!" cried the leprechaun, "it's almost happened once or twice. I've lost several of my best poles that way, not to mention some fairly good-sized breakfast minnows!"

Angus was still chuckling, but knew he should get on with the story. He regained his composure and continued, "Well, you'd probably have woken up by then, and found yourself slidin' through the water like a snake. You'd be afraid to let go the pole since you can't swim and you'd sink like a bucket in a well. Oh, you might call out, but who'd hear? So, you'd be holdin' on for dear life, hopin' that the trout might pass by a rock or tree limb and you might get out with your skin. But, the trout thinks he's hooked and he wants to give it a fight, so you're in trouble."

"Yes," said Chris Tinker, acknowledging the seeming hopelessness of the situation.

"A trout in trouble," continued Angus, "is like a beacon to other, larger fish. Remember, they're all hungry in the mornin' and they'll go for anything that moves. So, there you are, defenseless and wet, holding on with both hands while the trout pulls you through the stream. You might look like a tasty treat to another trout who's followin', lookin' for an easy meal."

"That I might," said Chris Tinker, with a pained expression on his face. "But what's to come of me, eh?"

"Now, don't look that way, all isn't lost," said Angus. "True, you might be swallowed by an even larger trout, but you're in luck; because he doesn't chew you, you go straight to his stomach. And there you sit, wonderin' what to do now."

"In the trout's belly!" shouted Chris Tinker, "that's a wonder!" He couldn't help but chuckle. "What then?" He was enjoying this tale immensely, partly because it was so absurdly amazing, and partly because it was his own hide that Angus was speaking of. He could hardly wait to hear what happened to him next.

"Luckily for you," said Angus, "you still had your hare bone pipe in your mouth and believe it or not, it was still lit. This set you to thinkin' and you didn't waste much time puttin' the lit end of your pipe to the tongue o' that trout, and begorra! If a fish could yell, then that one sure enough did! He spit you up and out, and you went sailin' through the air like a shootin' star, and got caught in the leafy branches of an old oak. Well, you thought you were safe and sound, didn't you?"

"Faith," sighed Chris Tinker, wiping his brow, "what more can happen to me?"

"Well, I'll tell you," continued Angus, "unfortunately, you landed very near a mother owl's nest and she was spyin' you, thinkin' you'd make for a tasty meal for her chicks. Not only that, but she wouldn't have to travel far to catch you. You'd gathered yourself up and seen her the same time she'd seen you, so you knew you'd have to think fast."

"I'll say," said the leprechaun, "Life isn't easy for a man my size. It's certainly not all fun and games like people think. But don't leave me hangin' there in the tree! What's next?"

"You inched out on the limb, bit by bit, as the owl inched out after you. The stream was below you and the owl was beside you—what would you do?" asked Angus.

"That's some predicament you put me in, blast you!" cursed Chris Tinker, "but I'd rather drown than be lunch to an owl's brats!"

"You jumped, alright," chuckled Angus, "You held your nose, said a prayer and hopped off the limb just as the owl reached out her claws to grab you!"

Chris Tinker put his hands over his eyes, not wanting to hear what was next.

"And you landed right smack on top o' that turtle, who was so startled, he almost swam out of his shell."

Chris Tinker opened one eye and said, "You mean, I didn't drown?" he asked, fearing the worst.

Angus roared with laughter. "Of course not, you silly fool, or you wouldn't be listenin' to this story!"

"Darned if you didn't have me almost believin' it was true!" said Chris Tinker, opening both eyes and taking a deep breath. "Well, I guess you get your wishes since your story was by far the better of the two. What'll you have?" he said, resignedly, "A pot o' gold and a high seat in the county? A pretty wife and servants to work your land? Riches and fame? What'll it be?"

Angus laughed to himself. "How do you like that?" he said, "All the years I've been telling stories about you folk, now I'm here, talking to you, man to, er, elf, with wishes to boot. Doesn't that take it?"

"Your forefathers could hardly believe it either when they stumbled upon me. I mean that literally," said Chris Tinker with a comical grin.

"I wish I knew all the stories that they had told," said Angus, reflectively, "I'll bet they had some amazin' ones to tell."

"Leapin' lightnin'! You are a gamblin' man and you just made your first wish!" howled Chris Tinker with delight. That took care of one wish and it was an easy one. Angus laughed, too. He shook his finger at the leprechaun.

"You tricked me!" he said, "But, actually, I could certainly have made a much lesser wish. Now that I think of it," he continued, rubbing his chin, "I don't think I could have thought of a better wish had I been trying!"

"And I personally shall see that it's granted," said Chris Tinker, solemnly. "Every Sunday, as usual, you shall come to this place, fish, and listen, while I expound to you the stories that I once told your ancestors. Stories about my people and the other strange fairies, elves and such, that abound in these hills and knolls. The ones that have been all but forgotten. And you shall retell them in the Redwolf and thereby keep them alive!" Angus stared at the little bearded man for a moment.

"You mean to say that you were the one who passed those stories on to my father's fathers?" he said. Chris Tinker nodded and winked. "Now, how else could they have known so much about us and our ways?" he asked, chuckling. "Someone had to tell 'em. And now," he said, pointing a crooked little finger at Angus, "I'll be tellin' you!" It dawned on Angus that he'd been used, and very artfully at that.

"You planned this whole thing, now didn't you?" he said in a playfully accusing tone.

"Like I told you," said Chris 'Tinker, "I had to find out if you were worthy. I see now that you are, and I'm glad for it. I've got stories that'll set your ears and them at the Redwolf's burnin', I do."

"Well, flamin' clover!" shouted Angus. He could not believe it. "So we both got a wish, then, eh?"

"Ah, but you still got one comin' to you. Have you made up your mind yet what you'll have? I must be gettin' back to my tree," said Chris Tinker.

"Well," said Angus, knowing already what he wanted. "I would like my place fixed up a bit. I'm too old to do it myself and there's no one to do it for me. Could you grant me that?"

Chris Tinker yawned and blinked. All of a sudden, he was unhooked and out of the tree and standing on Angus's shoulder. "Go home," he said, "You've got what you asked for. Not much of a wish, if you ask me, but if you're satisfied…"

"You could've gotten away at any time, you rascal!" cried Angus. "Every thing my family ever said about you folk is true.

You are a devious people, indeed!" Angus and the leprechaun both laughed, and then said goodbye until the next Sunday, when they would meet again.

On his way home, Angus thought about everything that had happened that day. Very strange, he thought, that the leprechaun could have planned everything so cleverly. The whole day had been contrived from the beginning. Even the leprechaun's story had probably been untrue. He thought about how surprised his ancestors must have been, and how surprised he had been to meet Chris Tinker. The townspeople would never believe this tale, but it didn't matter. Angus believed it, and would tell the story tonight at the Redwolf. And next week he would meet the leprechaun again, and he would have more incredible stories to tell. And so it would go for a long, long time, for he was to live a great many years, always telling stories. He didn't know then, as he walked back to his newly renovated cottage, how the legend and fame of his story-telling was to grow in his part of the world. Even so, he knew it was a very special day, and he sang softly to himself:

"Oh, yes, the man is lucky who can call the world his home, and yes, the man is lucky if his house is all his own. And if the man is lucky, then the fairies shine their light, and love the man who's lucky every day and every night."

ABOUT THE AUTHOR

Rollin Jewett is an award winning playwright, screenwriter, poet, actor, singer/songwriter...etc. Mr. Jewett's feature film credits include "Laws of Deception" and "American Vampire." His poems have been seen (lately) in The Gathering Storm Magazine, Red Weather Literary Magazine, The Write Launch, Weasel Press *and others. A short story "The Girl in the Forest" was recently published as part of* Ghost Stories: An Anthology *by Zimbell House Publishing. His plays have won several awards and have been produced all over the world. Mr. Jewett lives in Holly Springs, NC, with his wife and son. His website is http://rollinjewett.com/.*

Everything Mimsy

Samuel Marzioli

When Nico was a boy, his mother told him about a world beyond our own, tucked into the seams of reality like a spiderweb in the corner of a room. She draped herself across his mattress at bedtime, pressed her bulk into his side, her eyes fixed on the business of her knitting.

"It's unique," she said, deft fingers making both yarn and needles dance. "A place that welcomes people like you and me because we're unique too."

"What makes us unique?" Nico asked.

"Something in our genes? Our Filipino blood, perhaps?" She smiled, as if doubtful but amused by her own suggestion. "Or maybe a promise to an ancestor by *Bathala* Himself, who sustains the worlds and binds them all together."

"*Bathala?*"

"That's a longer story than we have time for now, and in the end, it doesn't really matter. What matters is that we are."

Nico grimaced, leaning up on his elbows to better see his mother. He was a skeptical child, especially where extra-ordinary claims were concerned. Ever since the veil of Santa Claus and the Easter Bunny had been snatched away, there was little room inside him left for silly things like magic.

"Then why haven't I gone there yet?" he said, more a challenge than a question.

"It only lets us visit when we're ready."

"I'm ready now!"

She wrapped the beginnings of a scarf around his neck, a watermelon pattern with fringe the color of its rind. "Maybe you are, my sweet. And maybe you and I will both go there together." She smiled again, the skin of her cheeks sliding into dimples. "Only time will tell."

Nico's mother died soon after. The doctor said she had a weak heart, but Nico didn't think that could be true. The way she'd always made him feel so loved, her heart was the strongest thing about her.

His remaining family shuffled him from house to house for years, because they couldn't stand the burden or expense of having him around. At 12, he moved in with his father's third cousin, twice removed, a stern old man who radiated ambivalence from every liver spot and wrinkle. By 17, he graduated high school and moved into his own apartment. At 21, he married his best friend Cathy.

He didn't love Cathy enough to promise her forever, but he'd gotten her pregnant and had no intention of abandoning her the way his father had abandoned him and his mother. Once the child was born, he had no time or money left for college, so he took a job working as a mail handler in a US Postal Service facility. It was a ramshackle building where industrial machines hummed and whirred, and the wheels of passing forklifts kicked up dust from the corroded concrete flooring. His workstation consisted of aluminum containers filled with newspapers and magazines, and it was his job to clear them out before his shift ended.

You Live, You Work, You Die, someone had scrawled across the wall in the men's locker room one night. Nico's co-workers chuckled when they saw it, but Nico only frowned. He much preferred his own prescription, "Abandon hope anyone who dreams of happiness." Because while ten-hour shifts made for a dire experience, work was just one wall in the prison of his life.

When Nico arrived home, he found Cathy reclining on the couch in her pajamas. Their son Dominique was mashed against her breast, a curtain of her hair resting on his head like a greasy, black toupee. Nico might have been amused by the sight of it had they not been in that same appalling state that morning.

"Busy day?" he asked, taking in the clutter, the reek of rotting food wafting from the sink and trash can in the kitchen.

Cathy shrugged. She edged forward, struggling through the weight and roundness of her belly, and mumbled something about making dinner.

"Don't bother," he said. "You've rested this long. Why quit now?"

She held up a limp middle finger before easing back onto the couch. "Jerk," she whispered, and he knew he deserved it.

Dominique began to cry. Cathy shushed and rocked him while Nico made spaghetti. Sauce from a can, meatballs from a bag, precooked noodles from a Tupperware container left for who-knows-how-long in the refrigerator. It took fifteen minutes to prepare the meal, and that was the best he could pull from that ragged frame of his, running on the dregs of a microwaved breakfast and a fast-food lunch.

Cathy ate her dinner on the couch while Nico sat at the dining room table. He took a few bites, dumped the rest into the sink and slipped upstairs, unnoticed. As he changed into pajamas, he thought about how insubstantial he had become.

Like a poltergeist, flustering the residents of his house, but accomplishing little else.

Something had to change. He knew it, Cathy knew it, and—the way Dominique always cried whenever Nico was home—maybe the baby knew it too. The only problem was, he didn't have the faintest clue about how or where to start.

Nico woke in the dark of early morning. Something had roused him from his sleep, but as he drifted into consciousness the memory dimmed and he could remember nothing but the specter of a presence. Had someone called his name? He couldn't decide so he sat up, casting anxious looks around to probe the edges of his room.

A silhouette loosened from the shadows of the corner and scampered to his bedside. "Nico Aganad?" it said.

From its size alone, he would have thought it was a boy with ears the size of dinner plates. But from the high-pitched squeak of its voice, he couldn't begin to guess the source.

"Who's there?" said Nico, swinging, grasping at the shadowed figure.

The figure stepped back, out of reach. "Mr. Aganad, you're a hard man to track down!"

With a snap of its fingers, cracks formed along the walls. They lengthened and widened until there was nothing left but snow, covering a landscape in a dazzling sheen of white. Once Nico's eyes adjusted to the brightness, he noticed a little man, naked but for a puffy, woolen hat. The lines of the little man's skin were deep etched, slick and brown as tooled leather. In his hands he held a flowing, silver beard, crimped near the end so that the tip pointed like an accusatory finger.

"What are you?" asked Nico.

"I'm the *duwende* of your grandparents' house. My ancestors and yours have lived together for centuries, but we lost sight of you shortly after your mother died."

"This has to be a—"

The *duwende* threw his hand aside, finger splayed. "No."

"You expect me to believe this is—"

"Yes."

"But that's not—"

"Maybe? Look, if we're going to have a conversation, you really need to finish your sentences."

The *duwende* sauntered off, his body sinking waist-deep into the snow. Nico followed, rubbing warmth into his arms, with nothing but a t-shirt and boxers to keep the biting cold away. A mile off, they came across an array of snowmen fashioned in tableaus, replete with bushes, flowers, and even trees all formed from snow.

"I made them while I waited for you," the *duwende* said.

"Was I expected?"

"Someone from your family always comes along, whenever you need us most."

"What could I possibly need you for?"

But the *duwende* only winked, as if he thought Nico already knew the answer.

Some of the snowmen wore ancient Filipino garb, topless with a hint of a loincloth or skirt carved into their lower halves. Others wore modern clothes, like jeans and t-shirts. They stood alone, or side by side, or circled around in groups as if engaged in lively conversations. One even sat beside an easel, a paintbrush poised over a plain white canvas—but whether it had finished its masterpiece or only just begun, Nico didn't know.

After they passed into the heart of the display, the *duwende* cupped his mouth and whispered, "Do you know how to tell the difference between snowmen and snowwomen?"

"Let me guess," said Nico. "Snow balls?"

Every snowman turned in their direction. The inside corners of their eyebrows furrowed and the pebbles of their mouths circled into O's. One snowman had collapsed onto its back, the coals of its eyes replaced by Xs shaped with twigs.

"No, by their *clothes*," the *duwende* said. "Careful about the words you say. Even words can sting."

The *duwende* shuffled away, too quick for Nico to follow. With each step the *duwende* took, the world faded. The dark-encrusted walls of a bedroom formed and, before Nico could even wonder about how to get back home, he found himself lying in bed beside his sleeping wife.

Nico shook Cathy awake and tried to tell her about the strange things that happened to him that morning. She just rolled out of bed and lurched from the room with a hand pressed against her stomach. To the incidental music of her peeing, his enthusiasm faltered and his mind wandered back to memories of when he and Cathy were young.

They were best friends before that one-off, drunken night when they shared each other's bed. As children, her compassion had drawn him to her. She was a shining light that led him through the worst of his loneliness and gloom. But somewhere along the way, life had melted him like wax, poured him into a mold and slipped him out as a warped and bitter version of himself. Now there was little left between them except the glue that leaked from their darling baby's skin.

Nico spent the majority of his day working on the docks with at least a dozen others, hustling through a sort line pulled from transportation trucks. A heavy wind swept in, tossing raindrops thick as bullets in their faces. No one dared speak. Not before every package, sack and envelope was unloaded. By the end of the shift, the muscles in Nico's arms burned, his hands had gone numb, and a kink in his hamstring made him hobble.

He insisted on making dinner that night, even though it was Cathy's turn again. The entire time he tried to ignore the state of the living room: clothes left unfolded, magazines spread across the floor, and the wrappers from her all-day snacks strewn around the couch like the litterfall of a junk food forest. He wanted to yell, to start another fight, but he bit his tongue for once.

"Words can sting," the *duwende* had said and he'd stung her long enough already.

Sometime in the unstirred morning, he felt his body shift, a sensation that called to mind liquid flowing through a metal strainer. He blinked, and when he opened his eyes he was hiking up a russet-colored hill. Snow covered the plains below, but moist, tepid air spilled from cracks and crevices, as if the hill were exhaling the first breath of spring.

When Nico reached the top, the ground plateaued, its surface smooth and flat as polished marble. Three enclosures made of wooden posts and chicken wire stood in the center of that summit. In the left-hand enclosure, a giant sat cross-legged on a small tree whose trunk and branches sagged almost to the ground beneath the creature's ample weight. A plaque fixed to the enclosure read: *A Light Kapre.*

"You don't look very light to me," said Nico.

"A common misunderstanding," said the *kapre*, the deep bass of its laughter pounding against Nico's ears. "I'm not light, but I could sure use one!"

It motioned to the unlit cigar dangling from its lips.

Nico made a show of patting his pockets before announcing, "Sorry."

He passed on to the next enclosure where what appeared to be a mermaid lay naked in a children's wading pool—except her lower half was sleek and tapered to a point, more like snakes than fish. She took no care to cover her breasts, not that they held any appeal for Nico. Absent nipples, they reminded him of the heads of two bald sailors bobbing beneath the water's surface. The plaque fixed to her enclosure read: *Mermaid of Moderate Rates.*

"Clean your house, mister?" she asked, before Nico could ponder the meaning of her plaque.

"Actually, I could use a cook. If you cook as well as clean, you're hired."

She scoffed, muttered under her breath. "For that you'd need a mercook, not a mermaid," she said and flipped around to face the other way.

In the last enclosure, a dragon lay stretched out on its side. It had two sets of wings, one rooted to its shoulders and the fragment of another sprouting from its lower back. Its scales were the rainbow sheen of an oil slick, and it snored in a way that called to mind a hundred knuckles cracking all at once. The plaque on its enclosure read: *Lazy Dragon.*

"What makes you so lazy, dragon?" Nico said, loud enough to wake it.

"His name isn't Dragon, it's *Bakunawa*," the Mermaid said. "You would know that if you had bothered asking."

"Sorry," Nico said. "What makes you so lazy, *Bakunawa*?"

Bakunawa stared at Nico through narrowed slits, the bags beneath its eyes big and round as plums. "I may be small, but I'm very heavy. Moving is a burden so I move as little as possible. Still, sometimes I must, and when I must I'm draggin'."

"You're... dragon?"

"Right." It gave a long and troubled sigh, as if the act of speaking strained it to its limits. "In the morning, I'm draggin' myself to the river to bathe. In the afternoon, I'm draggin' myself to the village to eat a few adults or a dozen children. In the evening, I'm draggin' myself into the heavens to swallow a moon or two and then, *Bathala* willing, it's back to bed for what little sleep I can muster. It's all so exhausting."

"You're awfully nosy," said the mermaid. "Don't you have better things to do than harass a sleeping animal? Why don't you focus on your own state of affairs? Lord knows your family needs it."

"I didn't mean to pry. I'm just curious."

"Ignore her," said *Bakunawa*, clamping its eyes shut. "She likes to nag; it's her way. In case you didn't know" —it yawned— "your people call her kind '*naga.*' It's a little on the nose, but it sure fits."

"A real man would have better things to do than waste our time. You should try to be one," said the mermaid.

"Look," said Nico, rounding on her. "Whatever I did to upset you, I'm sure it wasn't intentional."

"Don't take it so personally. I say and do only what's expected of me. No more, no less."

"What do you mean?"

"It's the way of the world. A muscle-bound oaf is expected to be stupid."

She threw a thumb in the direction of the *kapre* and it met Nico's eyes and shrugged.

"A monster is expected to be bestial."

She motioned to the dragon and, with its eyes still shut, it grinned and nodded.

"And a beautiful thing like me is expected to be—"

"A nag," said *Bakunawa*.

"Perfect!"

"But why not be yourselves? Who cares what other people think?" said Nico.

A chuckle from *Bakunawa*, a rumble of laughter from the *kapre*, and the mermaid tittered, covering her mouth.

"Think it's so easy? You have *no* idea."

In the morning, Dominique's screaming brought Nico to the nursery. Dominique wouldn't stop crying even after he was wiped and gleaming pink, so Nico brought him to window and bounced him in a beam of sunlight. He thought about his own mother, pictured her alone in their old apartment, cradling the screaming baby version of himself. She'd always found the time to care for him no matter how sad she was. She was stronger than Nico could have imagined, and he cursed the realization that he'd grown to be so little like her and so much like the memory of his father.

The smell of breakfast brought him downstairs. He found Cathy in the kitchen, sweat pooling on her forehead, her gaze somewhere far beyond the eggs and bacon sizzling on the stovetop. After they ate in their separate places, Nico sidled over to Cathy on the couch.

"Thanks," he said.

His tongue felt dry, a bloated thing too big for his mouth. He swallowed hard, gathering up the courage to continue, even as Cathy threw him an exasperated stare.

"I know I haven't been much help around the house, but maybe tonight we could tidy up together?"

She surprised him when her face softened. "Sure," she said—the first real word she'd spoken to him that week.

For the rest of the day, he emptied sacks from a dozen OTRs at work. Hours of manual labor ground his muscles into mush. When lunchtime came, he shuffled to his car and collapsed into the driver's seat, squirming from the aching of his limbs.

"Please," he said. "I'm ready again."

He concentrated on that other world, trying to pull himself back by the sheer force of his will. To his surprise, he heard a gentle rasp and felt something softer than the car's metal floor beneath his work boots. A second more and he was tramping through a meadow toward a cottage, monolithic in a landscape boasting only knee-high grass.

The cottage was made of stones painted rainbow colors. It had a soft white trim and a thatched roof that it wore like a bulbous summer bonnet. Beside the front door, an old woman stooped beside a raised flowerbed.

"Hello," Nico said as he approached.

He watched her spilling dust from a watering can upon a bed of flowers. The flowers had faces, all them scrunched and coughing, their wilted petals curling toward pallid stems. The woman didn't turn when he spoke; she just muttered insults, each one aimed at a particular flower.

"Ugly roses. Horrid peonies. Worthless Asters. Disgusting Gerber daisies."

With her silver curls, and the wrinkles of her skin sunk deep as trenches, he wondered if she might be deaf. "What are you doing?" he said, this time much louder than before.

"What's it look like?" she snapped. "I'm dusting my crops."

Once she emptied the dust can, Nico watched her traipse into the cottage. She returned carrying a digital camera and a small tin filled with paint.

"Smile, you fetid sacks of excrement," she said.

She proceeded to snap photos of the flowers' faces, their swollen eyes and puffy cheeks appearing stark and magnified upon the camera's LED screen. She then dipped her fingertips into the tin and flicked paint specks on every petal.

"What's that for?" he said, peering over her shoulder.

"Don't you know anything about plants? It's photosynthesis." To the flowers, she said, "Now thrive or, so help me, I'll pluck you all and throw you in the hearth!"

She scuffled inside again, still muttering curses, and slammed the door behind her. Nico let a few seconds pass before he crouched before the flowerbed, trying to evince an air of kindness.

"Are you okay?" he said.

The flowers shook their heads. "No sir," they said at once.

Their voices were small, delicate and hurting, a sound like someone making tiny rips in paper.

"You look starved. Do you need some water?"

"Yes sir," they said.

He circled around the cottage and found a bucket filled with water resting in the shade of a well's limestone wall. He returned to the flowerbed and slowly poured the water on soil so dry it had split into patchwork, leaf-shaped segments. The flowers closed their eyes and let out a contented moan. By the time the water absorbed into the earth, they stood erect. A darker hue bled into their petals, slow at first and then more and more until their corollas blushed with vibrancy.

"Thank you, sir," the flowers said. "The *mangkukulam* who takes care of us hasn't learned yet."

"Learned what?" said Nico.

"Malice withers."

Nico swung by a florist after work and picked up a dozen red roses. Then, at the grocery store, he purchased Cathy's favorite treats: chocolate covered nuts and chews. While he had no false notion that a modest box of sweets and a pretty floral arrangement would somehow spackle over all the cracks of their relationship, he knew it was a start.

At home, he handed the presents to his wife. She looked taken aback, didn't say a word, but he could tell she didn't hate them. He led her to the table. They sat down and he took her hand and cradled it in his own, realizing how much she meant to him and how long he'd craved the warmth of her skin touching his.

"I put you through a lot ever since the day we met," he said. "And I..."

He wanted to say more, to tally up the wrongs he'd done and wrap them in a soft quilt of his apologies. But shame pressed against his insides and that was all he could manage before he began to cry. A long silence passed between them: his nervous and imploring, hers quiet and aloof. For a while, he believed she would stand up and walk away.

Instead, she nodded and said, "Okay."

"Okay?"

A hint of the woman she once was peered from behind the sullen mask covering her face. "Yeah. Okay."

Nico wiped his eyes. He smiled, though he didn't know why. That little word had so much meaning packed inside it and he didn't have the wherewithal to decipher it completely. Still, it was a start, a shiny new path stretching out before them into a broadening horizon. And, for now, it was enough.

Nico stood on a cliffside overlooking a great expanse of grasslands, their leaves catching the sunlight and sparkling with the luster of emeralds. A herd of *tikbalangs* argued in the distance, the sound of their shouts and snorting punctuated by the stamping of their hooves. *Kapres* rested like black lumps on the trees of a balete forest lining the horizon. The slow bass of their snores—muffled by the distance—whispered in his ears, reminding him of an elegy or a prayer. Perfect for the task he had planned.

He spent hours collecting rocks. He gathered them together and then stacked them high as his shoulders, sealing up the gaps with mud and clay he'd scraped up from the ground. Once finished, he surveyed his creation. It was a cairn in the rough shape of a cone. He'd seen pictures of similar structures online, and though his version lacked the magnitude of Bronze Age artisans, he felt proud of his accomplishment nonetheless.

"I miss you, Mom," he said, shutting his eyes. "We haven't spoken for a while so I thought I would catch you up on what's been happening with me. I got a new job. It pays less than the last one, but it's not as stressful either. I have an amazing wife. You'd like her. She's far more forgiving than I ever deserved. We also had a beautiful child. He's two years old now and, one day, I hope to share this world with him the same way you wanted to share it with me."

He took the watermelon scarf from around his neck and draped it around the cairn.

"Thank you," he said. "Thank you for the love you planted deep inside me. It was slow to grow, but I think it's finally sprouted."

With that he kissed his fingers, pressed it to the cairn, and then willed himself back home. The other world vanished and, quicker than he could take another breath, he found himself standing in his driveway. Despite the somberness of the previous moment, he was giddy at the prospect of seeing his family again. They were waiting for him. They wanted him around. That realization made him grin and, for the first time in longer than he could remember, life didn't feel like a prison anymore.

ABOUT THE AUTHOR

Samuel Marzioli's work has appeared in numerous publications, including The Best of Apex Magazine (2016), InterGalactic Medicine Show, *and* Shock Totem. *His website is http://marzioli.blogspot.com/.*

BOIRDELEAU, WI
(POPULATION 3,017)

AIMEE OGDEN

T he town of Boirdeleau, Wisconsin, had a population of
three thousand and seventeen, three thousand and
sixteen of which were perfectly ordinary folk and
precisely one of which was an ancient mummy of questionable
provenance.

Boirdeleau, tucked in alongside the Mississippi River just a
few miles north of where it met up with the Chippewa, had a
nice winery and a few folksy shops on Main Street, but no
particular claim to fame other than the mummy, which resided
in a glass case in the local library. Miss Faulkman, the librarian
these past two years, took responsibility for the mummy's care
and upkeep. Right now, she could only hope that her charge
would not intervene on his own behalf with the young man
from the State Historical Society who had come to examine
him.

According to Mr. Brzycki, the mummy was a priceless historical artifact—a point which Miss Faulkman could not argue—and according to him, the State Historical Society in Madison had sent him to evaluate its condition. He flashed paperwork in Miss Faulkman's face, too quickly for her to catch more than the Historical Society seal at the top. "Specifically," said Mr. Brzycki, tucking the papers into the inside pocket of his rather threadbare sport-coat, "with regard to travel."

"I think he'll travel fine," said Miss Faulkman, who had enough experience of this to *know* rather than *think*, but who knew better than to tell Mr. Brzycki so. "Where do you mean to take him?" Another, more important question bubbled up behind that one. "And how long will he be gone?"

Mr. Brzycki smiled. It was a very nice smile, in a certain very well-practiced way. "Well, for good, of course! It needs to be sent back to where it came from."

"I see," said Miss Faulkman. "And where is that?"

They both turned to look at the glass case. The mummy rested in a seated position ("criss-cross applesauce" was the phrase as Miss Faulkman had learned it) with the top of his head against the back wall, in such a way that the outsides of his legs did not fully rest on the bottom of the case. He was wrapped in bands of brownish cloth, both arms individually sheathed and crossed across his chest. Based on the seated position he might very well have been a relic of the Inca or some other South American people; though based on the wrappings themselves he could also easily have been an ancient Egyptian mummy. Or then again, perhaps Chinese? He had no burial mask or jewelry or other ornamentation that would have helped in his identification. Miss Faulkman only referred to him as "him" at all because the mummy hadn't made any effort to correct this initial usage of hers—not because of any outward indication of his theoretical gender.

Miss Faulkman let the uncomfortable silence build between her and Mr. Brzycki, who had gone about pink about the edges. "Well, that is for the experts to assess," he said. "Knowing Captain Follett, it could have been just about anywhere."

Roger Follett was the individual responsible for the presence of the mummy in the library of Boirdeleau. Captain Follett had resided in the town some years before, insofar as his globetrotting permitted him to call any singular place his residence. Follett's expeditions had him described in some of the older town literature as an "adventurer", but Miss Faulkman thought that perhaps "marauder" might have been more accurate. Neither had the man been particularly forthcoming with the accounting of his travels. Fortunately, he'd brought relatively few such souvenirs back to Boirdeleau permanently.

She explained the situation to Mr. Brzycki as ably as she could: the mummy had been here nearly a hundred years, no one knew anything about it, there was no record of its origin. Like the mummy, she was one of the few residents of Boirdeleau who hadn't originated here, and she wasn't as familiar with the lore surrounding Follett as she might have been. In any case, she took care to avoid the words "adventurer" and "marauder" alike. "The only thing I can assure you," she finished, "is that the town will absolutely not part with their, er... " She wrinkled her nose at the placid mask of the mummy's face. "Very important relic."

Mr. Brzycki put one arm on a bookshelf and leaned toward her. He was very slightly taller than she was, and, in the lean, had grown a great deal more annoying as well. "Getting this thing back to its place of origin is simply the right thing to do. Surely someone like you, with an appreciation for the classics, can understand that."

Miss Faulkman withdrew a handkerchief from her pants pocket and dabbed at a smeary fingerprint that the overeager young man had left on the mummy's case. When she'd graduated the LIS program, she'd mailed out forty-two resumes. Only Boirdeleau had called her up for an interview, and she'd jumped at the offered job. She had never thought during that process to enquire about the side duties that might come attached to custodianship of a beloved local curiosity. "I'm sure that you can appreciate my position, too. I can hardly hand out priceless antiquities to the first person who comes along." She folded the handkerchief into tidy quarters before returning it to her pocket. "Even if you had a local library card, which I'm fairly sure is not the case."

"Trust me." Mr. Brzycki's perfect smile didn't flicker one whit as he straightened up out of his lean and adjusted his tie. "You don't want the Journal Sentinel here with a news crew, protests, bad press." Miss Faulkmann opened her mouth to say that the only *press* she might get in Boirdeleau was the Dollarclip Savings circular that came once a week on Thursdays, but he was still talking. "I'll be back with a moving van and get the whole mess out of your hair."

"You can't do that!" objected Miss Faulkman, as he brushed past her. On the off chance that he could indeed do exactly that, she called after him, "You'll have to go all the way down to La Crosse to rent a truck!"

But Mr. Brzycki didn't respond, other than to duck his head and mutter an excuse-me when he bumped into old John Goodbear on his way out the door. Mr. Goodbear stared after the man for a moment, holding the door open as he did, until Miss Faulkman scolded him over the cool wet draft off the river that he was letting in. "Is he in town to see our friend here?" he asked, wiping dirt off on the rug. Though no one in town did much to broadcast the mummy's presence, word did get out from time to time. "I thought I recognized him for a second, but… I suppose not. You just get to expecting familiar faces in a town like Boirdeleau."

"Yes, he was here about the mummy," said Miss Faulkman briskly. "But never mind about that." Her hands fluttered briefly at her sides, as if on their own accord they would just as soon have gathered up Mr. Goodbear into a firm embrace. That wasn't her place, though. He wouldn't care for a stranger fussing over him so. But she thought she knew why he was here, and pressed gently for the reason. It didn't serve her well to pry too much. The residents of Boirdeleau were an insular sort, with good reason. But library degrees didn't grow on trees—or in vineyards. "Your daughter was able to take you up to the Twin Cities yesterday, wasn't she, Mr. Goodbear? What did they say?"

"I keep telling you, just call me John. Everyone else does." Mr. Goodbear took off his hat, and spun it around between his big hands. "And, well, it's stomach cancer. That's what we expected. There's a program for treatment, one of those experimental groups, but there's a waiting list, and I was hoping our friend here—"

Of course the mummy was already moving, legs unfolding and straightening. Miss Faulkman hurried to open the glass case as he got all the way up and lumbered forward. "Let me get that for you," she cried, and swung the door out of the way just before he reached it. He didn't always seem to remember that the case front was there, and there wasn't any space in the library budget for a new case *again* this year.

The mummy stopped just in front of Mr. Goodbear, whose face had split in a smile even as tears rolled down his wrinkled cheeks. "Bless you," he said. "I don't know what we'd do without you."

The mummy's head inclined briefly. Then one bandaged hand shot forward, burying itself in John Goodbear's belly.

Mr. Goodbear's head pitched back, and Miss Faulkman looked away when a guttural moan ground out of his wide-open mouth. She would never get used to this, no matter how long she lived in Boirdeleau. She didn't think this was the sort of thing a person ought to get used to. But she stared down at the red tips of her shoes where they peeped out from under her pants, and counted breaths until the library grew quiet again.

She looked up just in time to see the mummy's hand pull back from Mr. Goodbear's belly, covered in gore well past the wrist. In the knotty brown fingers there was a handful of—best not to look too closely. Miss Faulkman had a degree in library science and not biology for several very good reasons. Instead she shooed Mr. Goodbear to a chair, while the mummy loomed in the background. She did not watch to see what he did with the handful of muck he'd dredged up from John's innards, but rather passed Mr. Goodbear a fresh handkerchief from her purse so that he could dry his brow.

Mr. Goodbear wound up blowing his nose into the handkerchief a few times before he was quite ready to stand up again; Miss Faulkman deftly declined his attempts to return it afterward. He asked for a moment alone with his "old friend", and she went to tidy up in the Young Adult section while Mr. Goodbear pressed the mummy's hand and spoke quietly to him. When the door jingled at last, she looked up again. The mummy stood alone, looking in her direction. Or at least with his head turned toward her; she had never been certain how much he saw or heard or simply knew.

She put both elbows up on the shelf of crime novels that abutted Young Adult to peer back at him. "Sometimes I wonder," she said, "what it is that you get out of this particular bargain."

The mummy shook his head at her. She ducked her head, feeling strangely admonished. "Yes, I know, we should get going. Let me find my car keys."

The mummy fit in the passenger side of Miss Faulkman's car, albeit with his lower legs crammed snugly under the dashboard. Miss Faulkman coaxed the engine to life, and they glided down out of the street-side space in front of the library and out along Main Street. Gaily-painted storefronts lined a two-block space on either side. Mrs. Lorson, who owned Ole and Lena's Handcrafted Norwegian Goods and Foods, waved from just inside her glinting window. Miss Faulkman hesitated, and then lifted the fingers of her left hand from the steering wheel in greeting. Her thumb stayed hooked behind.

It wasn't a long drive to Boirdeleau School, which took the town's children up to the seventh grade. After that they were bussed farther up the river to attend the junior high and then the high school in Pepin. But something drew Miss Faulkman farther northward on Main Street, up out of town and onto the highway that followed the Mississippi. You could see the water, sometimes just a distant glint on the far side of train tracks, sometimes a broad muddy bathtub between the two hillsides. If the mummy had any opinions on this jaunt, he kept them to himself, as ever.

Finally she pulled over in a shady overlook, just off the highway and up around a grassy hillside. She got out of the car, looking down on Boirdeleau to the southeast. She picked up her purse for a cigarette, and then remembered that she didn't smoke anymore.

The mummy rolled down the window.

Miss Faulkman came around the car to the passenger side. "Good thing they're automatic," she said. "I bet you'd have a devil of a time with a hand crank. Do you want to get out?"

A nod.

Soon enough he stood ramrod-straight beside her as she slouched against the hood, with a faded parasol in one bandaged hand to protect him from unwanted UV rays. "It's my job to take care of you," she said, and realized she was speaking as much to herself as to him. That wasn't right. She looked up at him, put a hand on his bony arm. "Do you—I mean, I should ask you, shouldn't I? Do you want to go home? Wherever that is?"

The mummy's arm lifted, stick-straight. Pointing back down the river to Boirdeleau.

"No," said Miss Faulkman. She squashed her annoyance. "Not your right-this-minute home. I mean, your real one. The one where you're supposed to be. Egypt? Mexico?" She let her arms fall by her sides. "Other-fill-in-the-blank?"

The mummy's arm didn't waver. But his head swiveled slowly around to her.

Miss Faulkman sagged. "Okay," she said. "We'll figure something out."

She parked at the school and hurried around the car to open the door for the mummy. He had offered her his arm so that she might assist him to a stand when the oddity of the situation struck her: as if they were a pair of junior high students themselves, on an awkward date in a parent's borrowed car. A laugh burst out of her before she could smother it—the town already must think their out-of-towner librarian was odd, no reason to give them additional fodder on that account—and the mummy's great head drifted in her direction.

"Sorry," she said, and gave another cautious yank. She wouldn't like to explain to the good people of Boirdeleau how she'd come to dismember their local mascot. "Just—look at the pair of us." Either of them as plainly from *out of town* as the other.

The mummy silently lumbered to his feet. She was just about to turn toward the school when a cold, well-wrapped hand tucked itself in the inside of her arm. When she turned to gape up at him, his head was canted to one side. "I didn't know mummies made jokes," she said, and a sound like sifting sand came out of his throat as he led her off toward the school's main doors.

"He's here!" someone squealed, as Miss Faulkman and the mummy edged their way into the back of the auditorium (which was really just the cafeteria with a row of risers dragged in). Several children ran up to wrap hugs around the mummy's knees, while their parents pressed him with firm handshakes. Miss Faulkman ducked out of the way, tucking herself into a seat at a ketchup-sticky lunch table, where shortly thereafter, the mummy joined her.

The concert, ostensibly to celebrate the end of the school year, proved to be a bit of a mummy-themed love fest. Aside from the usual songs devoted to academic achievement and the niftiness of the fifty United States, there were at least three lauding the local hero. Based on the liberal use of slant rhymes and awkward meter, these had been written by either the current crop of schoolchildren or a previous one. In any case, the mummy slowly bobbed his head in time to the beat.

Thirty-five increasingly sweaty minutes later (the school was not and probably never would be air-conditioned), Miss Faulkman finally unbent her cramped knees and stood. The mummy required some assistance untangling himself from the little bench, and by the time that task was accomplished, the cafeteria had half-emptied, as parents swarmed the risers to congratulate and collect their offspring. Miss Faulkman, of course, had no relations here; she carefully dodged eye contact as the room cleared out. Best if she made her way clear fast, before someone had to take pity on her with an attempt at small talk. They had their own friends and families already; no sense in her stealing that precious time with forced questions about the weather or the Packers or the cost of gasoline.

She glanced up and smiled only for Mr. Robinson, the retired librarian, as she guided the mummy back out to the waiting car. *How did you do this for fifty years?* she wanted to ask, but she certainly didn't know the man well enough to ask such a silly question, and so it went unsaid. Instead she offered only a solemn nod.

But Mr. Robinson caught her by the elbow. "Was that Gene Mitchell I saw going into the library this morning? How long is he in town for? Lori—that's Lori Mitchell who works for the postal service—didn't mention at Euchre Night that he'd be here to visit."

"I'm sorry," said Miss Faulkman. She glanced up at the mummy for reassurance, which was hardly forthcoming. "There was just the Ladies' Knitting Circle in this morning, and a gentleman from—from out of town." She swallowed the words "historical society." Best not to start a mummy-related panic in the middle of the elementary school cafeteria.

"Oh! Oh, well my eyes must be playing tricks." That would be no great surprise; Mr. Robinson's glasses must have been half an inch thick at the outsides. He gave Miss Faulkman's elbow one more kindly pat and released her. "That makes sense. The big Follett reunion isn't till August, anyway."

"Follett!" Miss Faulkman repeated. An electric jolt of she-wasn't-quite-sure-what shivered through her. "I thought you said Mitchell?"

"Lori Mitchell, nee Follett," Mr. Robinson explicated with the patience of a lifetime librarian. "Bill and Sandra Follett's middle girl." He smiled, and nudged those Coke-bottle glasses back up his nose. "There's not so many people in Boirdeleau, you'll learn them up in no time, dear."

"I'm sure I will," said Miss Faulkman. Her fingers tightened on the mummy's reed-thin arm. "Remind me. Gene is the one who went off to school in Madison?" She had no idea which, if any, of the expansive Follett clan might have gone to the University, but she waited for the side serving of small-town gossip that would come alongside the inevitable correction.

"No, no. Close, though! That was Sandra's sister's boy, Jonathan." Mr. Robinson tapped the side of his nose. "Gene's been in and out of some trouble, you know. Nice young man. Just made some bad decisions along the way." Miss Faulkman leaned away from the sudden gleam in Mr. Robinson's eyes. "Say, he's about the same age as you. When he comes around for the big get-together, I'll send him down by the library, I'm sure you two would hit it off something beautiful."

"I'm sure that won't be necessary! Thank you! Have a lovely day!" Miss Faulkman glued a smile to her face as she hustled the mummy outside. How much were those old bones worth to a collector, or in some Internet auction? How much more, if its seller knew exactly the value of what was on offer?

Money, she reckoned, was the best—or at least the most common—sort of solution to the kinds of trouble that a young man was likely to get himself into.

For the duration of the afternoon, the mummy puttered around toward the back of the library while Miss Faulkman answered questions, checked books in and out, and planned for the summer reading festival. Once, she caught him ducking out of her office, and broke her own library rule in shouting from the circulation desk to mind that he didn't mess up her carefully organized paperwork.

When she finally locked the front door and went to retrieve her purse and coat from the back, she found a rumpled piece of notebook paper lying atop her desk. In a wobbly scrawl, someone had drawn the outline of a knife, and the sort of sad face a child might draw, with two dots and a rainbow-shaped frown. She picked it up and held it at the full length of her arms, as if that would focus it into something like clarity. Finally, purse and coat in hand, she stopped at the mummy's case and held the drawing up to the glass. "You made this?" she asked.

The mummy's head canted slightly.

"An unwilling sacrifice." Her voice trembled.

But the mummy's head shook slowly, side to side. Miss Faulkman's brow creased, and so did the paper between her fingers. "Willing, then. But how is it any different here? You sacrifice for them every day, nurse them, give them nearly anything they ask. You live in a tiny glass box, for heaven's sake!" She leaned forward until her nose smudged the glass. "What do you want, *really* want, from life? Or, I mean—from undeath? Not to be somebody's collector item, I'm sure. But wouldn't you like to be helped, for once, instead of doing all the helping?"

She stepped back and pulled the case open, and thrust the paper and dull-pointed pencil into his featureless face. But in answer, he only laid one hand on his chest, over the spot his heart might have rested if he still had a desiccated organ of that variety. They stared at each other while Miss Faulkman drew another ragged breath. "Fine," she said. "Fine. I'll see you in the morning. Once I've got this whole thing figured out."

Miss Faulkman typically favored eight and a half hours of sleep, but that night she dipped down toward four and a quarter. Schemes, scribbled on notebook paper and increasingly elaborate, littered the floor of her little flat over the Chinese restaurant.

She woke up with a start at a quarter to eight, and the clarity of exhaustion blindsided her with most obvious idea of all: why not just hide the mummy in her own stupid apartment for the day, and keep hiding him until this ridiculous Follett scion simply ran out of patience or rental-truck money? But it might already be too late—she cursed her alarm clock as she floundered out of bed. Mr. Brzycki, or Gene, or whatever she should call him, might arrive at the library at any moment. If he had no qualms about returning to his hometown in disguise to abscond with the local mummy, he also might not object to forcing the rather shaky back door of a public building. She flung on the first clothes from the laundry pile and crashed out the door and into her car with an armful of supplies. She had never engaged in anything remotely resembling a heist or even an escapade before, but a roll of duct tape, a skein of twine (she didn't have any rope), and the baseball bat she usually kept by her bed seemed enough to cover all eventualities.

When she arrived, there was a U-Haul parked behind the library, and she found the back door open. She called out as she rushed through her office, but no one answered—she dropped the twine and duct tape, which bounced off her foot, to brandish the bat as she came out into the library proper.

The glass case was open, and the mummy was out of it. He stood in front of Gene Mitchell-Follett-Brzycki, who had crumbled to his knees. His head, though, listed sharply backward. The mummy's hand was wrist-deep in his cranium. "No!" cried Miss Faulkman, who certainly had not had jotted down *murder* on her list of potential outcomes for the day. "What are you doing? Stop!"

The mummy's empty face swiveled around to her, but his hand stayed where it was. A soft moan came out of Gene's mouth, as did a long tendril of saliva.

"I mean it!" Miss Faulkman said, and she realized she did. If she had to rough up Boirdeleau's oldest friend to save the life of one irritating man, she would do it. The loss of a job didn't amount to much next to that. She hefted the baseball bat and edged closer. Which joint might be more most vulnerable: a wrist? Possibly a shoulder? The anatomy shelves were two rows over and hopelessly out of reach. "Put him down!"

She braced herself for impact, and jabbed at the mummy's left elbow as hard as she could with the far end of the bat. He simply sidestepped. Miss Faulkman cursed her lack of Little League experience, and readied for another go.

But as the mummy moved, his hand pulled back from Gene's forehead. With it, there followed a slender trail of something like spider-webbing, but more delicate. It came free of Gene without a sound, and Miss Faulkman lost sight of it then. Gene staggered, but did not fall. Miss Faulkman clutched her bat and looked between the two. "What did you do?" she whispered. "What did you take from him?" Brain cells. Neurons? The spiderweb she'd seen had been spun out of secrets and memories.

"What did I take from who?" asked Gene Mitchell, and clambered to his feet with the mummy behind him. Miss Faulkman took a step back in spite of herself, and dropped the bat behind the display of newly arrived books. Gene looked around. "I'm... early for the family reunion, I think."

"Also for the library," said Miss Faulkman, cautiously feeling her way onto surer ground. Behind Gene's back, the mummy retreated quietly to his case and closed the door "We don't open till ten on Thursdays."

"Oh," said Gene. He looked down at his shoes, then around at the tidy shelves. "Sorry?"

"Quite all right," said Miss Faulkman, and mustered an absolute rictus of a smile. "As long as you're here, is there a book I can help you find?"

Gene Mitchell spent the next ten minutes browsing the paperback mysteries. When he'd finally selected a promising volume, Miss Faulkman checked him out, then unlocked the front door of the building to usher him on his way.

The very second the door shut behind him, she stormed across the library to the mummy. After a moment's hesitation, she flung open the door of his case to get in his face in the most satisfying way. "What the devil was that?"

The mummy held out both hands in a shrug. There was nothing to see on his fingers; whatever he had taken out of Gene Mitchell had disintegrated, or been absorbed into those many-stained bandages. "You can't just," Miss Faulkman said, and had to pause to decide what it was that the mummy couldn't just. "You can't just rewire a person to make them do what you want!"

The mummy's head craned over the New Arrivals bookstand to peep at the discarded bat, and Miss Faulkman's face flushed red. "Well, that's not the same thing at all!" she cried. "You just—you just fixed him, just like that! All this time you could do that, and you never... you never let me think I could *belong* here."

She was already moving toward him when he lifted one hand, his fingers right at head level. She walked into that outstretched hand without hesitation, and she choked as his fingers slipped inside.

A pounding at the front door slammed Miss Faulkman back into herself. She spun, stars bursting behind her eyes, to see Mrs. Lorson peering in through the blinds. Mrs. Lorson shook the door again, as if that might suddenly unlock it, and it rattled on its elderly hinges.

Miss Faulkman tossed her head to clear it, which didn't work. She looked back over her shoulder at the mummy, who stood just in front of his case. His fist was closed around a few sparse threads of absolutely the finest spidersilk she'd ever seen. When she peered closer, he opened his hand, and she lost the threads to a trick of the light. She grimaced. "Didn't the pages dust for cobwebs just two days ago?" she asked, and shook her head as she hurried down the central aisle to open the front door. "I'm sorry! I'll check their work more closely next week."

"Is everything all right in here?" Mrs. Lorson said, pink-faced and out of breath, as soon as she was inside. She waved across the stacks of books at the mummy, who lifted a hand in answer. "I just saw someone driving a moving van out of here like the devil was after him, and I thought you'd been mugged or robbed or something!"

"Oh," said Miss Faulkman, for the second time that day. "Oh! Patty! It was just Gene Mitchell back in town to steal our old friend."

"Gene Mitchell!" Mrs. Lorson gasped, delightedly scandalized. Miss Faulkman laughed. And Miss Faulkman, to her own great astonishment, flung an arm around Patty Lorson's shoulders.

"Don't worry! We took care of everything, our friend and I. Come on; I'll make you a cup of coffee in my office. It's quite a story."

Patty said she couldn't wait to hear it, but wouldn't it be better over some fresh lefsa? She'd left the oven on and didn't want to burn down Ole and Lena's, after all. Miss Faulkman agreed and locked up the library behind her. She paused with the key in the door, and stuck her head back inside to promise the mummy she'd be back in time to open the library at the proper hour. Then she followed Mrs. Lorson down the hill.

The mummy climbed back into his case, and shut the door carefully behind himself. He sat down on the floor, folded his arms across his chest and his legs in front of him. He leaned back, back, back, until his head touched the glass behind him and his stiff legs lifted ever so slightly off the ground.

ABOUT THE AUTHOR

Aimee Ogden's work has also appeared in Apex, Shimmer, *and* Escape Pod. *Her website is http://aimeeogdenwrites.wordpress.com/.*

THE GALLOWS MAIDEN

FRANCESCA FORREST

On some spring evenings, when the breeze feels soft on your face, when you can smell earth again, and even, here and there, see stiff, fresh, new green beginning to push aside last year's leaves, then you can skirt the base of the gallows hill and not even shudder. You can see the crows clustered in the high branches of the great sycamore there and maybe not turn your mind back to hangings. So John William Tracey thought to himself, but the very thinking of the thought called to mind the hanging of Joseph Hawes for housebreaking and assault last summer—and so he quickened his step, kept his eyes down, and was nearly past the hill when he stumbled upon a knot of boys with sticks and stones, tormenting a crow trapped on the ground by an injured wing.

"Here, leave off," he said, grabbing the wrist of the biggest boy. John William himself was no more than seventeen, but that gave him several years on the lad, and a stronger arm. "Drop that. Don't you know better than to tease crows? Look at her eye, see how she's staring at you? She'll remember your faces, all your faces, and tell her sisters and brothers, and they'll come after you. They have a taste for human flesh, you know. No doubt they'll go for your eyes first, and who knows what next, after that? But maybe, just maybe, if you beg her pardon most sweetly and run off home, she'll forgive you. Maybe."

The boy's endangered eyes were round as coins, his face pale as the moon, and when John William released his arm, the boy stammered out an apology, then fled away, the others at his heels.

John William looked at the crow and shivered, remembering last summer, how the crows had circled the body of the dead man, alighting on him in a black cluster by his limp head. But this crow was flying nowhere; the next dog or fox to pass by would make a meal of it. John William peered at it, trying to see which wing was hurt, but the bird hopped behind a briar bush, not yet in leaf but such a tangle of arching canes that it easily hid the crow. A few steps, and John William was behind the briar bush as well, and here before him was no crow, no; it was a girl with hair as black as crow's feathers, clutching a gray shawl tight around her with her left hand and her right arm limp. Her eyes were as black as her hair and seemed like chips of coal in her pale, pale face, no flush of pink on her cheeks, just bruising the color of a stormy sky along the line of her jaw.

John William's mouth went dry, and when he took a step backward, his legs were like water, and now the briars were grabbing at his coat. The crow girl just stared at him with her black eyes and didn't move, so a little of his fear left him.

"Have-have you hurt your… arm?" he ventured. She cocked her head to one side and continued to watch him, but still didn't speak.

"Do you understand my words?"

"I understand them," she replied, and her voice wasn't hoarse like a crow's; it was new and untried, a fresh-formed voice speaking into the air for the first time.

"Let me see it," he said. She raised an eyebrow, and there was a hint of a smile about her lips, and suddenly John William felt very foolish. But then she took a couple of steps toward him.

She let go her shawl, and he could see that her right sleeve was all torn, and yes, her upper arm was swollen and bruised, between the shoulder and the elbow.

"It looks like it could be broken; we should splint it. We'll need two sticks, and something to bind them round your arm with." He looked around on the ground, happy to drop his eyes from hers, and found some sticks the right size, and when he had picked them up, here she was, holding out the shawl to him.

"No, something else," he said. "I don't want to ruin it." But it seemed an old thing, really, frayed at the edges, and what else was there to use but last year's yellow grasses? So he tore a strip off the bottom, wrapped it round the splint, and bound it fast. Then he knotted the girl's shawl and slipped it over her head to make a sling for her arm to rest in.

"Now you just mustn't... mustn't use it. It'll knit itself back together."

She reached her good hand out and touched his hand, then his cheek. He jerked away.

"I'd better go now. Keep yourself safe."

But she was right in front of him, so close that he imagined he could sense her heart beating, fast like a bird's, and as he took a step forward, she stood on tiptoe and ever so lightly kissed him. Blood rushed to his face, and before he knew what he was doing, he had kissed her back, and he was once again staring into her black eyes, but what he fancied he saw there wasn't love but hunger. He broke away and ran the rest of the way home.

"You shouldn't have talked to her, or gone near her," said John William's oldest brother Michael, when John William told as much of the story as he dared. "She must have been some kind of witch." But his brother Robert, only two years' John William's senior, just laughed.

"Why can she not have been an ordinary girl?" he asked. "And John just not have marked where the crow had hid itself?

You should have walked her safely home, not run off like a terrified rabbit."

"I wish I had been the one to find her," said John William's little sister Joan. "I would have asked her what it's like to fly."

"That's foolishness," said their mother sharply, and Joan looked down at the table, running her finger along the edge of it.

"Michael's right, you know," their mother said, setting a bowl before him with more force than she needed to. "Crows live off the misfortune and death of other creatures. If one such as that takes an interest in you, you'll end up dead in a ditch, or of fever in your bed, or hanging from the gallows. You didn't touch her did you?"

"N-no... of course not," he said, looking away.

"Good. Keep clear of that hill for now. Take the longer way into town. Maybe she'll forget she saw you."

John William nodded, but pushed the bowl of soup away.

"Ah, poor Johnny; a witch girl's taken a fancy to him," said Robert. "Never mind, Anne Hallett still fancies you too. She'll dance with you next month—her sister told me so, just this morning. So don't look so pale and anxious." John William didn't even reply, just got up from the table and left the house.

It took him a moment to realize that Joan had followed him out.

"You did more than see her, didn't you, John William. You talked to her, didn't you," she said, catching up with him.

"Go away, Joan. Go back to the house."

"You did her a good turn! You saved her from those boys. It's good things she'll bring you, out of gratitude, not bad things."

"You think so?" It was darker now; the first stars were coming out, and all that was left of the sun was brightness on the western horizon. Birds passed overhead, and John William nearly jumped, but it was a cloud of starlings, not crows.

"Of course," Joan said.

"I set her arm for her," John William blurted out. "And then—and then, well… it doesn't matter. It's enough, isn't it. I surely touched her."

"It's why you're my favorite brother," said Joan, "Because you're tender-hearted."

Still, John William did avoid the gallows hill, those next few weeks, as all the trees began to put out their leaves and the hedges and meadows became cheerful once again. When Joan begged him to take her to the bluebell woods behind Sir Stephen Martyn's house, he willingly agreed, and it was just after they had passed the biggest of the old beech trees, and Joan was bending to pick still more of the flowers to add to her burgeoning bouquet, that John William caught sight of the crow girl again, walking toward them through the blue-purple haze of flowers, that same shawl, now much more ragged at the bottom, wrapped around her.

Joan stood up, saw John William standing stock still, saw this other one approaching, saw the look on John William's face, and knew who the other must be.

The crow girl was smiling. "All better now," she said, spreading both arms wide to demonstrate. "Thank you. I have a present for you."

"She brought you something," breathed Joan, and before John William could protest, Joan had dropped her bluebells and run to the crow girl's side. Just as it had those weeks before, John William's heart beat fast as a bird's as he followed his sister.

"Hold out your hands," the crow girl said to him, and into them she placed a golden locket on a golden chain. The chain and locket flashed in the dappled sunlight of the woods.

"It's fit for a princess," whispered Joan.

"How did it come to you?" asked John William, turning it over in his hand.

"I found it, of course," the crow girl said. "I like shiny things."

"It looks very precious—not something someone would care to lose."

The crow girl shrugged. "What do I know about what people care to lose and what they don't?" she replied.

"I wish I could have a present, too," said Joan wistfully, eyes still on the locket. The crow girl tilted her head, seemed to think a moment, and then said,

"Perhaps this would be to your liking? I've never found another of its kind so grand." She handed Joan a brass key that was bigger than Joan's own hand.

"Oh!" said Joan. "The key to a palace?"

"Or a tower. Or a dungeon," said the crow girl, smiling again. "You must find a safe hiding place for it."

"Off and find one now," said John William quickly. "And don't let mother see it." Joan looked from her brother to the crow girl, but both just waited expectantly. She sighed, put the key in her apron pocket, and went to retrieve her flowers. She turned back once, though, as she was leaving, and called,

"One day, will you tell me about flying?"

"One day," echoed the crow girl.

"Something like this," said John William, holding up the locket after his sister had disappeared from sight, "it's what a gentleman gives a lady, a lady he loves."

"And ladies never give gentlemen gifts, gentlemen they love?"

John William blushed.

"I'm not sure," he said.

"No lady has ever given you a gift?" she pressed, eyes obsidian bright.

"Oh, ladies and gentlemen," mumbled John William, "I don't know much about them and their habits. No girl ever gave me a present, nor did I ever give one."

"You did, you did give a present; you gave one to me," said the crow girl. "You gave me a kiss, and now I'd like another. I'll give you one back, or better still, let's give them together. But you must put your hands around me and hold me, because there's something fiery and shivery in me right now that wants to melt my legs and shake open my chest, and I think I might fall." She cupped his face in her hands, and of course he took her right in his arms, and yes, he could feel there was something fiery and shivery about her, and when they kissed, it passed between them and surrounded them, and the whole world seemed heated to a blue-white glow.

And then they were lying among the bluebells, the heat between them so great that the damp earth grew warm to the touch, beneath them, and the bluebells nearest them were dry as paper.

"I never have kissed such a one as you," said the crow girl, running her hand through his hair. "Always they're cold and pale, and they never kiss back."

John William sat up abruptly, knocking her hand away.

"Will I end up dead because of you?" he demanded. Where was the heat now? He could feel frost on his lips, and in his heart, too.

"How can I answer you? It's not I that determines who lives and dies; did you think it was?" She got to her feet, picked up her shawl and wrapped it back around her, tight.

"Go on; run back home, after your sister," she said, and there was frost on her breath, sure as in his heart, and maybe his heart banged against his ribs, for he felt it crack. He picked himself up slowly and began to walk away.

"But come back to me, later. Will you?" she said, voice all low and desolate, and that fissure in John William's heart deepened. But he didn't look back, and the last he heard, barely audible over the wind in the young leaves, was, "You will. You will come back to me."

For the next three days, John William stared out the door, lost in thought, brooded over his meals without eating them, and had to be asked questions twice before he heard them. It took Robert reminding him of how Anne Hallett wished to dance with him this Saturday, telling him how Anne Hallett had new ribbons for her hair, how she blushed when she spoke about John William, to finally summon a smile to his face and appetite to his stomach. Robert knew these things about Anne because Robert was courting Anne's sister Mary.

Anne had hair the color of honey, a smile that was always springtime, and laughter that was sweeter than birdsong. All the boys wanted to dance with Anne, and Anne wanted to dance with John William. Even the frostiest, most damaged heart had to thaw and heal a little, hearing that.

The dance was to be held at the hall in town, but everyone from the hamlets and farms in the hills around town was coming too, and Sir Stephen and his wife, and the mayor of the town and his wife, too, and all their servants and their guests— everyone.

"There will hardly be room to dance, for all the people," remarked Michael, but his brothers ignored him. Robert whistled and there was a bounce to his step; John William examined his jacket and wished it was smarter; as he dusted it off, the scent of earth and bluebells came to him, but he closed his eyes to the memories that the scent brought.

"What do you think of this?" Robert asked, showing his brothers and sister a pocket handkerchief of white linen, with lace all around it and roses embroidered in each corner. "It's a present for Mary," he said, looking pleased with himself. Joan nudged John William and said, "You should bring Anne something—a posy, maybe." John William grimaced, picturing himself in his dusty coat, a wilting posy in his hand, trailing his older brother. He put on the jacket and, feeling a lump in the pocket, put his hand in and discovered the locket that had lain there all these days. Joan saw what he did, and even though he didn't take his hand from the pocket, she knew what he had found there.

"You can't give her that," Joan whispered, glancing anxiously at their mother, whose back was turned to them. "You can't give one girl a gift you received from another." A number of retorts came into John Williams's mind but so also did the pale face and black eyes of the crow girl, and he lifted his hand from his pocket without saying anything.

"Are we ready to go?" asked Robert. "Let's step lively!"

The dance was as agreeable as ever a dance has been--not just Anne, but all the girls were lovely, and the musicians' instruments must somehow have been enchanted so that while they played, no one ever felt tired and everyone's foot was light. It was between dances that Anne, smiling and flushed, pointed to Robert and Mary, laughing at the far end of the hall.

"Did you know that your brother brought my sister a present?" she asked. "He has the most winning ways."

"Oh? Well, I have a better present, worlds better than what Robert gave to Mary. Something fit for a princess—for you." Anne giggled with embarrassment.

"What would that be, then?" she asked at last.

"Come a little closer; it's a secret just for you and me to know about." She came to stand right beside him, and he drew the locket from his pocket.

Her smile faded; it was a grave face she turned to him.

"How did you come to have such a thing, John William? In no good way, I think," she said.

"What? What do you mean? You think I—oh no, nothing like that! Anne, don't go!" But she gave a small shake of the head and stepped away, jostling the man behind her, who turned around in some annoyance and caught sight of the locket glinting in the candlelight.

"What's that?" he asked, and caught hold of it, and then his eyes widened.

"This is Lady Martyn's locket, that was stolen last year and never recovered." He turned it over. "See—here is an L, for Lucy, engraved on the back."

Sure enough, on the back of the locket was the letter L, engraved with loops and flourishes.

The man's eyes narrowed. "It's not the only thing that was never recovered," he said. "Maybe you know where the other jewels are, that Joseph Hawes' accomplice made off with. Maybe you're that accomplice. Somebody get Sir Stephen, and hold on to this one!" People pressed in close around, and through the crowd of faces, John William caught a glimpse of Joan, white faced.

When Lady Martyn decided that possibly it was John William who had been with Joseph Hawes that night last year, and when John William could not say exactly when and how he had come into possession of the locket, he found himself taken into custody and imprisoned in the jail beneath the town hall, to await the coming of a judge. He hunched his shoulders and didn't respond to the challenges and taunts of the others in the cell, though he couldn't ignore their cheerful assumption that here indeed was Joseph Hawes' confederate, who had been clever enough to avoid the law this long only to then foolishly show off his prize before his victims, and who would now surely pay for his crime. His mother's words rang in his ears, too, and it seemed to him that there must be no way for him to avoid death.

In the morning his brothers and sister came to him. Michael told him their mother was beside herself and pressed him with the same questions that others had already asked him and to which he had no good answer. He had found the locket in the woods behind the Martyn manor house, that was all, just the locket, just lying there, nothing more. Why had he said nothing and shown no one? He shrugged. No reason. He sensed his brothers' dismay and disbelief and turned away. Let them think what they must; there was no help for it, anyway.

When they were on the point of being escorted out, Joan put a hand on his arm.

"I have an idea of where to find help," she said.

"Don't try it!" he said. "Don't you dare! Do you understand? Michael, lock her in the house and don't let her go out anywhere, or she'll end up like me."

Michael looked alarmed, Robert troubled, and Joan resolute as they left the cell. John William closed his eyes and leaned against the wall.

Joan and her brothers took the quick way home, skirting the gallows hill, and sometime after they had passed it, Joan stopped suddenly.

"I dropped something; I know just when it must have happened—it must have been when I stumbled on a root back there. You go on ahead; I'll catch you up."

Michael frowned. "Hurry, then."

Joan raced back along the route they had taken, and when she came to the gallows hill, she looked up at the great sycamore tree, and her heart quickened its beat as she saw, even through the new leaves, the crows in its uppermost branches. She began to climb the hill, skirting the patches of briars.

"Who is it here who cares about my brother?" she called out. "One good turn deserves another; he didn't leave you to be eaten by foxes, and you mustn't leave him to be hanged for a crime he didn't commit."

The crows lifted from the sycamore, calling in their rough voices, and circled in the air directly over Joan's head, and she feared, as they came lower and lower, that they might fly directly at her—but then they rose again, higher into the sky, and settled back on the branches of the sycamore. The wind picked up and tugged at Joan's hair and set her skirts rippling and the canes of the briars bending. And there she was, over there by the briars, the crow girl.

Her black hair had lost its sheen and there was no brightness to her eyes. Joan could see her arms folded across her chest beneath her shawl. The crow girl met Joan's eye and lifted her chin. Joan swallowed, and took a breath.

"They think my brother stole that locket you gave him, and other things as well," she said. "They'll likely hang him as a thief, when the judge comes." She pressed her fists to her stomach to try to still the churning.

"Then that's the way he'll come to me," said the crow girl, the trace of a smile passing across her face.

Joan's blood ran cold at those words, and she felt faint.

"But... don't you love him... a little, even?"

"Oh I do. Very much. When the breath has left him, I'll shower his handsome face with kisses and then some." She looked out past Joan, down toward the town. "It's he that doesn't love me," she said, pulling the shawl tighter round her narrow shoulders. "He'd never come to me again, living. So lovely he was, alive and warm," she said, and for a moment there was some softness to those black eyes. But then they were hard and sharp as flint again. "But if I can't have him living, then I'll have him dead."

Joan licked her lips. "When you love someone," she said, voice quavering, "it's *you* would die for *them*, to keep them safe and whole. Not wish them harm."

"Oh is that how it is, among you? Even if your lover is faithless? Among my kind, a pledge of love is forever. Your kind are changeable as the weather."

Tears stung Joan's eyes. "Even if your lover is false, I think, so long as there is love in your own heart, then you, you..." but she couldn't continue. She wiped her sleeve across her eyes, but the tears kept streaming down.

"Poor John William," she whispered. The tears in Joan's eyes made the world swim; were there answering tears in the crow girl's eyes? Joan could not have seen, and when she wiped her own again and looked up, the crow girl was already walking away, up the hill. She turned back once, halfway to the top.

"You have a way of helping him, if you want," she called, a catch in her voice. "The key I gave you is the master for the cells below the town hall." Then she turned away again.

A wild surge of hope swept through Joan, and she would have rushed after the crow girl to thank her, but the girl had vanished. Joan let her powerful hope speed her down the hill and along the path to home.

It was several days later, after several evenings when John William's mother would come upon her remaining children huddled in tense conversation by the paddock gate, or at the kitchen table, conversation that ceased abruptly as she approached, that a fire broke out at dawn in the town hall. No one saw who first gave the cry of "fire!" but when the jailer and his men rushed to investigate, it was already blazing in strength, and they had to call up and down the street for others to come to their aid. It was only then that they remembered the prisoners down below, and when they made their way back down the stairs, holding their coats over their heads to shield them from the heat, they discovered the doors to the cells unlocked already, and all the prisoners gone.

John William ran to the stables of the White Hart and grabbed the first horse he came upon, for now he must flee as fast and far away as possible. As he led the horse, a nervous dapple gray mare, who tossed her head and balked as John William tried to get her quickly and quietly to the street, a crow landed before him, and when John William looked again, it was the crow girl who was standing there.

"Move aside and don't follow me," he said roughly.

"The key I gave your sister is the key that freed you from the jail, you know," she said, as he struggled to mount the horse.

"Yes, and the locket you gave me is what put me there to begin with, and now it has made a true outlaw of me," he responded bitterly, at last seated on the dancing horse and struggling to keep his balance.

"That horse is going to throw you, John William. Don't take it, or all the efforts of your sister and brothers will be in vain, and you'll be dead as surely as if you had been hanged on the gallows hill."

"Just spare me your tender concern," cried John William, and spurred the horse, who tore away up the cobbled street and from there onto a lane that led into the countryside. It didn't slow, and when John William tugged at the reins it turned abruptly and jumped straight over a hedge and pounded through the field on the other side, and over another hedge, and on, and all the while overhead the crow pursued them.

It was at the upper reaches of the mill river that it happened as the crow girl predicted: the mare shied rather than jump the stream, and John William went flying, landing hard among the rocks and pebbles over which the waters chattered, and now ribbons of red unfurled along the length of the clear shallows, more and more of them, until further down the stream, passersby might have thought some miracle had occurred, and the water turned to wine.

Up where John William had fallen, the crow girl knelt in the water and held his head in her lap and wept and wept, hoarse sobs like the a crow's call, and her tears and black feathers fell into the water, but he was gone, it was not she who could determine who lived or died; he was gone, and no powers could bring him back.

ABOUT THE AUTHOR

Francesca Forrest has lived in the United States, England, and Japan. When not working at her day job as a copy editor, she does volunteer writing tutoring and works on her own writing projects. She's had short stories and poems published both online and in print, along with one novel, Pen Pal. *She likes that Solzhenitsyn quote about the line between good and evil running through the human heart.*

The Boy Who Didn't Believe in Halloween

Tom Howard

J ack Pumpkinhead opened the door and looked down at the
boy standing on his porch. He was surprised he'd heard
the knock with the party in full swing. It was Halloween,
and all his friends were inside enjoying themselves.

"I'm sorry, little boy. We don't give out treats at this
house." His eyes flickered from the small candle he'd placed
inside the pumpkin he'd carved earlier. He'd tried not to make
the smile quite so wide as usual. Someone commented that it
made him look like a simpleton. With all the pumpkin seeds
rattling around in his brain, he was hardly simple.

The boy appeared to be around ten years old. He was
dressed in a black robe and wore taped up glasses. He looked
up at Jack Pumpkinhead with big brown eyes that regarded
Jack as if he was just another resident of the small town. The

fact Jack towered over him with wooden limbs and had a giant pumpkin head didn't seem to bother the child.

"I know," said the boy. "The older kids dared me to come up to the haunted house. They think I might see something horrible and run away."

"You're not afraid?" asked Jack.

"Never," said the boy. "That's why they always try to scare me. They know Mace Bigelow isn't afraid of anything."

Jack nodded, careful not to lean too far forward. He'd hate for his fresh head to fall off. "Shouldn't you be out collecting candy with your friends? This is a private party. We're celebrating having the night off."

"Monsters need a vacation?" asked Mace, peering around spindly Jack.

"Yes, from little monsters dressed up as us. We figure there's enough scary stuff going on for one night. So, we have our own Halloween party."

Mace shrugged. "I don't believe in Halloween."

"Would you like to come in?" asked Jack. He'd convince the boy otherwise. "It might be too scary for a little boy like you."

"I told you, I'm not afraid of nothing. My mom says that when they made me, they forgot to put in my fear bone."

Jack chuckled. "Fear bone, eh? Is that like a funny bone?" He opened the door and stood back.

Mace entered and stood inside the door. Jack expected him to run screaming from the dilapidated house when he saw the ghosts, skeletons, and goblins dancing around the room. Mr. Porter, a giant spider, worked behind the bar, a cocktail shaker in each of his arms. Two of the ghosts had decided the floor was too crowded for dancing and moved to the ceiling.

"Welcome to our Halloween party," said Jack. "We do know how to have a good time."

A green witch, hairy warts and all, stared down at Mace. "What is this, Jack? An hors d'oeuvre?"

"No children shall be eaten here tonight, Goodwife Gooch," said Jack. "Young Mr. Bigelow is my guest. He's come in search of his fear bone."

The old woman with gray hair bent to peer at Mace. "Fear bone, eh? I may have a potion for that." She dug into the pockets of her black robes and pulled out a cat, which she handed to Mace, a bedraggled bat, and a desiccated monkey's paw. "I must have left it in my other robe."

Mace stroked the black cat, and it purred in his arms.

Goodwife Gooch frowned and snatched the feline back. "If you let me put the boy in the oven for a few moments, I bet you that would put a yellow streak up his back."

Jack rested his hand on the boy's shoulder and guided him to the table and away from the muttering witch as she tried to stuff the complaining cat back into her pocket. "Cider?"

"No pumpkin juice?" asked Mace, staring at a zombie trying to retrieve his eye from the punch bowl.

"Indeed not," replied Jack, mortified at the thought. "We're not cannibals here." He looked down at the end of the table where a werewolf was chewing on a human leg. "Well, most of us aren't, anyway. Still not afraid?"

Mace shook his head. "It looks like the party at my parents' house but with fewer Kardashian costumes."

"Now that would be scary," said Jack. "If you're a lad looking to get in touch with his fear, you've come to the right—"

The front door flew open, and two large bats fluttered into the room. In a puff of smoke, the animals transformed into a man and a woman, pasty white and in fancy dress.

"The vampires always like to make a dramatic entrance," said Jack. "Don't worry about them. Mr. Porter keeps a fresh bottle behind the counter."

The vampires bowed to the scattered applause, and the man escorted the woman to the bar where Mr. Porter was already pouring.

"As I was saying, we have some of the scariest creatures in history in this room. If they can't scare you, nothing will."

231

Jack's chest swelled with pride at the thought of his ghoulish comrades.

Mace took a cup of cider from the mummy standing behind the table and carefully removed the soggy bandage hanging over the lip. "Where is the music coming from?"

"Look closer at the instruments, Mr. Bigelow."

Mace moved toward the fireplace where the bandstand was set up. Flames raced up and down the violins, oboes, and drums.

The tune was quite catchy, and Jack's head bobbed up and down in time to the music. "Fire demons. They love to play, and as you can tell, they can set the place on fire." He chuckled at his own joke, but Mace continued to watch the tiny men and women of flame as they flew around the instruments.

"Cool," the boy said.

"We've got zombies, witches, mummies, and skeletons," said Jack. "Don't any of them cause you the tiniest bit of apprehension?"

"I can give oral book reports on books I haven't read," said Mace. "I've seen worse on television."

"Scary movies?"

"Nightly news," replied Mace. "Where's Frankenstein? Shouldn't he be here?"

"Frankenstein's Monster, you mean. He married a plastic surgeon, and they live in California someplace. He has a prime-time police show. Too bad. I miss him. He had a wonderful singing voice."

As if on cue, a wispy woman flew through the wall of the room, screeching so loudly that several glasses shattered.

"Bavmorda the Banshee," explained Jack. "I really don't mind her screaming, but she drips water all over the place. As soon as she has a few cocktails in her and a kiddie pool to stand in, she'll be fine. Not scary?"

"No," said Mace, finishing his cider. "I guess I better be going. I didn't mean to interrupt your party." He sighed so deeply Jack expected the boy to break into tears.

Jack's calico heart swelled, and he feared his stitches might rip. "But you haven't found your fear bone yet. Let's talk to one of the skeletons. Maybe they know where it is and how to fix yours."

"No," said Mace. "I'll just have to go through life never knowing what it feels like to have my heart in my throat or break out in a cold sweat."

"You are an enigma, young man," said Jack. "If you have lost your fear, it could happen to other children. Without fear, we monsters have no reason to exist."

"I blame it on Hollywood," said a standing lamp nearby. "Kids today have no imagination. They don't need it. They can see all the blood and guts they want in a video game."

"Please, Mr. Wiggins," said Jack. "Have you been a lamp all night?"

The lamp wavered, growing wider and taller as it turned into a stiff-backed old man with a large nose. Of course, he kept the lampshade as a hat. "Yes. We shape-shifters aren't social creatures like you scarecrows."

"Spend your life talking to crows and ears of corn," said Jack, "and it makes you appreciate good conversation."

"What are you?" asked Mace.

"A changeling," said Mr. Wiggins. He removed the lampshade to reveal a shock of white hair and glittering green eyes. "Usually we change into living creatures, but some of us can become inanimate objects."

A waltzing creature from the black lagoon bumped into them as he swung his Medusian partner. "Sorry, mate," he said, gathering his giggling companion into his arms. "Nice costume."

Jack watched them go. "Mr. Bigelow is here in search of his fear bone, Mr. Wiggins. The lad is human but seems unafraid of anything."

"Yes, I heard," said the old man. "Radio was so much better. You could always imagine the most horrifying things. Now you don't have to. It's all presented to you. No imagination required."

"I have an imagination," insisted Mace.

"Really?" asked Mr. Wiggins. "When's the last time you piloted a spaceship from your desk? Went on an adventure in a cavern under your bed? Defended your treehouse from pirates?"

Mace grimaced. "I've never done any of those things."

"Used a stick for a ray gun? Tied a towel around your neck and jumped off the roof? Built a labyrinth out of books for your hamster?"

"I don't have a hamster."

Mr. Wiggins snorted. "I rest my case. Kids today sit in front of the television or on their phones and let their brains petrify."

"I bet they play their music too loud and won't stay off your lawn, too," said Jack with a chuckle. "Every generation says the same thing about their kids. If it's not television, it's books. If it's not books, it's newfangled jitterbug. You need to step into this generation, Mr. Wiggins, and help poor Mace out. Imagine what he's missing in life by never being afraid of anything."

Mr. Wiggins rubbed his chin and stared down at Mace. "I guess you're right. Without fear, there can't be the other side of the coin."

"Happiness?" asked Mace. "I'm happy."

"I'm sure you are." Jack patted him on the back. "I think Mr. Wiggins means escape from fear—security and safety. Without fear, you never feel the comfort of knowing you've faced it and come out the other side."

"Are you three going to stand here gabbing all night?" asked a goblin with green skin and orange hair. He limped over to join them. "We don't get a night off too often."

Mace stared at him. "Do I know you from somewhere?"

"Not unless you hang around with a lot of goblins, kid." He took an eyeball from the bowl he carried and popped it into his mouth. "You don't look like the kind to hang out in the lost woods reservation with the rest of us goblins and trolls."

"Please, Bixby," said Jack. "You know you were isolated for your own safety. Our guest is trying to discover where he lost his fear bone. He's come to us for help. Mr. Wiggins is afraid Mace is a symptom of something larger—a world where we aren't scary anymore."

"Kick him out or eat him," suggested Bixby. "Haven't these humans done enough damage to us?" He rubbed his thigh as if an old injury was bothering him.

Mace's eyes opened wide. "You were my boogeyman!"

Bixby frowned. "No way, kid. I'm a woods goblin through and through. You won't find me hanging out in a closet somewhere."

"Who said anything about a closet?" asked Mr. Wiggins.

Jack scratched his head. "And weren't there rumors a couple years back about boogeymen sub-contracting goblins to terrify children?"

"I think that pretty snake lady is trying to catch my eye," said Bixby. "I'll see you all later."

Jack snatched the squat green man by the collar and lifted him off his feet. "What did you do, Bixby?"

"He jumped out of my closet every night after my parents put me to bed," said Mace. "I thought it was just a nightmare."

"I never touched the kid," swore Bixby. "I just made creepy noises and scared him."

"Until I got fed up and stabbed him with something," said Mace. "I thought I'd either hurt him bad enough to leave me alone or else my folks would find him."

"You almost took my leg off!" Bixby wiggled in Jack's grasp, but the pumpkinhead's frame was made a seasoned hardwood and masterfully articulated by the farmer who had built him. "I barely made it out the window. My leg still hurts. Lousy kid. I say we eats him."

"I'll go look for the mad scientist," offered Mr. Wiggins. "We'll need him and his scalpel."

Mace looked worried. "Are you going to cut me up for stabbing Bixby in the leg?"

"No." Jack gave the squirming goblin another rough shake. "I think we've located your missing fear bone. I'm sure Bixby won't mind getting rid of it after all these years."

"No!" shouted Bixby. "You can't let the doc cut off my leg!"

A man in a dirty lab coat and glasses with soda bottle lenses appeared. "Whose leg am I cutting off?"

"I don't think that will be necessary, Doc," said Jack. "Mr. Bixby here was stabbed by a bone several years ago and needs it removed."

"Anesthesia?"

"I don't think that will be necessary either," said Jack. "Perhaps Mr. Bixby will think twice next time before posing as a boogeyman. Mr. Wiggins, if you'd get one of the skeletons to tell you where the fear bone should go, I think we can help young Mace."

The music continued, and the dancers and revelers ignored screaming Bixby as the doctor cut into his thigh. Jack held him down with help from Mr. Wiggins in the form of a set of wooden stocks. The incision was small and quickly patched with a dirty rag from the doctor's little black bag.

"I think we have it." The doc held a splinter of white bone in his bloody fingers.

Jack released Bixby, who was moaning dramatically and cursing them all for his rough handling. He swore he'd never attend another party at Jack's house. Jack only hoped it was true.

"Are you ready?" Jack asked Mace. "Are you sure you want it to be returned? You'll be afraid again."

"But I'll also feel safe and brave when I face my fear, right?" Mace glanced at the sliver of bone. "Will it hurt?"

"Yes," said Mr. Wiggins, returning to his old man form. "The skeletons said it rests right above your heart. They were surprised it had leaped out of your chest."

"Do you need to cut me open?" Mace stared down at Bixby, moaning and bloody on the floor.

"No," said the doc. "Easy out. Easy in." Without warning, he pulled the boy's robe aside and stabbed Mace below the collarbone so forcefully that the bone fragment completely disappeared. Only a single spot of blood spotted his white shirt.

Mace stood paralyzed and sweat broke out on his forehead. Jack moved toward the boy, but Mace's eyes opened wide in panic and fear.

"No!" Mace tore through the room, his black robes fluttering behind him. He rebounded off a one-eyed purple alien ingesting Jack's sideboard and continued wailing as he wrenched the door open and disappeared into the darkness.

"Well," said Mr. Wiggins, "you do give the best parties, Jack."

"Thank you," said Jack. Maybe he should carve a frown on the back of his head so he could spin it around to show he wasn't happy all the time. He'd miss Mace.

"Come on, Jack," said Mr. Wiggins. "Let's get you something strong to drink. You did a good thing here tonight."

"Yes." Jack watched the doc lift Bixby to his feet. "I think we helped the boy."

"But no humans next year, okay? They ruin Halloween for everyone."

Jack sighed and looked out the open door. Behind him, the party showed no signs of winding down anytime soon, and he really should see to his guests. He linked arms with Mr. Wiggins on the way to the bar. "You're right. They're all scary little monsters."

ABOUT THE AUTHOR

Tom Howard is a fantasy and science fiction short story writer who lives in Little Rock, Arkansas. His muses (or amuses) are his children, his friends, and the Central Arkansas Speculative Fiction Writers' Group.

Siphoning the Flames of Life

Kelly A. Harmon

B ranson Luc woke to the sound of water boiling over in the hearth—sizzling on the fire dogs—and pink smoke erupting from the communications cauldron. The smoke coalesced into a flat missive, then wafted back and forth in the air as it settled to the packed-dirt floor. Though the smoke was contained, it still filled the air with its burnt-paper smell.

He rubbed his eyes, then pulled on his prosthetic right leg—a stout oak branch padded out with sheep's wool—and eased out of bed. He lit a lamp with a brand from the fire, then retrieved the ragged-edged smoke-paper from where it had landed under the table. The message surprised him: *Tinker/Large Animal Doctor needed at Oakmoore Cauldron Factory. Well paid for services rendered. Come quick!*

Doctor and *tinker*, Bran thought, *something is wrong with the coke ovens.*

Lifting a cinnamon candy from the table's dish, he popped it into his mouth, hoping it would alleviate the smoky taste.

The candy bit into his tongue with a fire, softened by sugar, and left his mouth strangely cool, the lingering taste of cinnamon stinging the tip of his tongue.

He stood and limped to the window and looked up at the Great Oakmoore Mountain. Clear purple skies of early morning glowed in burgeoning sunlight, devoid of the usual cloud of smoke rising over the oak trees. The entire steel-making process had ceased.

So, was it mechanics, or dragons? He couldn't know unless he investigated.

But would they want him there?

He was a good mechanic, and a fine animal doctor. He couldn't be blamed for the accident. He'd told the abbey they needed to take more safety precautions—and when the worst happened they'd blamed him instead of owning up. And he was the one who'd lost a leg. It wasn't his fault—and yet, few seemed willing to trust him.

So would the witches want his help?

Well, the law was the law. They couldn't turn him away—unless the job was complete when he got there. And since he lived so close to the mountain, he might be able to arrive before anyone else—if he hurried.

If he could fix the ovens for the witches, maybe he could pull his reputation out of the cesspit.

Branson packed quickly, tinkering tools and doctor's bag—omitting the obvious items the witches should have on the premises—and including some things they probably would not. And just for good measure, he wrapped the rest of the cinnamon candies in a napkin and shoved them into his pocket.

Then, he saw to the horse and wagon.

It was always a challenge getting to the Oakmoore Mountains, even when the witches knew you were coming. Even when they invited you. You still had to cross the poisonous Shadow River, and make it up the slippery slope leading to the factory's front gate. But once you got directly on the path, things were usually all right.

Thank the one-eyed god it was springtime. He'd hate to have to do this in winter.

The trip was slower for him than it used to be, since he could no longer sit a horse. At least that allowed him to carry more equipment.

As he passed over the narrow, swinging bridge at Shadow River, he looked west to the docks where the cave-mouth opened over the water; the place where the witches loaded the cauldrons aboard ships for delivery. *Deserted.* This wasn't just the witches' problem. It affected nearly everyone in the area.

Branson slipped on the steep, gravel walk, catching his balance, the acute stabbing pain of the wooden prosthetic digging into his hip. He rubbed at the pain—sharper in the cooler air of the higher altitude—and approached bare, steel doors, built directly into the side of the mountain. He yanked on the overhead bell chain, with its tiny steel cauldron dangling from the end. Behind the doors, a bell-tone rang, *bah*-dah, *bah*-dah, *bah*-dah. Six beats of a ball-peen on three different-sized cauldrons, the pitches ringing higher every second beat.

A young witch answered the door, the pointed, green tabs on her collar announcing she was a novice.

Bran held out the pink-smoke missive. "I'm here to fix the ovens."

"Are you a tinker, or an animal doctor?" the witch asked.

"Both." Bran said it with pride. Not many tinker-doctors in the area.

Her smile died. "You must be Branson Luc."

He nodded, confirming her fears—and confirming his own suspicions about his reception.

The witch started closing the door. "Sorry—we've already someone working on the problem."

"I can wait."

"That won't be necessary—"

Branson stepped forward, leaning precariously on his prosthetic, keeping one booted foot on the threshold. "I believe the law says that you must let me try if your current help can't do the job."

The witch sighed—clearly having her orders if he'd pushed the issue—swung the door open wide and pointed to a bench. "Come in. You may wait right here." She started to walk away, but turned back to him. "Are you here in your capacity as a mechanic or a doctor?"

"Both," Branson said, knowing it would annoy her. It also gave him two chances to fix the problem. He lowered himself to the bench on his good leg, and waited.

A short time later the novice came back for him. "It's your turn. Please do not kill the dragons—or burn the place down."

The last crack was completely unnecessary. If anyone would burn the place down, it would be the dragons. But Bran didn't want trouble, not when he had this chance to clear his name.

"What's the problem?" he asked her.

"We can't keep the ovens hot enough to burn the coal," the witch said. "The temperatures keep going down."

She led him through a set of smaller, double doors into the factory.

Bran had never been inside before. It was larger than he thought it would be, stretching as far as he could see in both directions in the dim light, the walls carved out of natural rock. Coal wagons, heavy with ore and still as statues, lined one side of the factory. He'd bet his good leg they zoomed on their rails when everything was operational. Empty shelves lined the other side—*for finished cauldrons?*

This is where the magic happened—though not literally. Here, the witches forged the best steel cauldrons in the world—able to withstand a range of temperatures that no other cauldrons achieved. You could boil molten iron in them—if you needed to—then toss them into the snow to cool them off—no harm done. Neither would the cauldrons rust, due to the finishing spells the witches cast on them. They were a work of art.

But if the ovens weren't working, no cauldrons could be made.

The novice delivered Bran to the factory floor, to the foreman-witch in charge. Her long dark hair was pulled back and loosely braided. Her face was pale, like she'd never seen the outside of the factory. *Maybe she hadn't*, Branson thought. Behind her in the distance, loomed the three large coke ovens, like stone sentries, overlooking the entire process.

Bran approached the witch. "I'd like to see the dragons first, if I may."

"Why?" She looked irritated, brows furrowing, her lips turned down.

"If you can't get your ovens hot enough, the problem might be your heat source."

"Who said the ovens weren't hot enough?"

"The novice at the door."

The witch shook her head, and several strands of hair escaped her loose braid to curl around her face. "The heat source is fine—but it fluctuates. We shouldn't be seeing such large dips in temperature in the ovens, especially when we're trying to bake the coke. If things don't heat evenly we'll get volatility. Not good. There's definitely something wrong with the ovens."

"I'd still like to see the dragons first—just to rule them out."

She looked mutinous.

"If there's nothing wrong with the dragons, it's only a ten-minute check," Branson said. "Would you want me to spend hours on the ovens only to learn that one of your dragons is ill?"

"The dragons can't be sick," the witch said. "They're—"

"Why don't you let an animal doctor decide?" That silenced her. He knew the witch meant well, but she was just getting in his way.

The dragons rested in the caves below the coke ovens.

A small, rough-hewn passage circled downward at a gentle slope, but even the moderate angle aggravated Branson's hip. He'd regret this in the morning—and for days to come.

The dragon cave sparkled with iridescent flashes, torchlight bouncing off dragon scales—red, blue and green—of the three towering giants lounging on a great pile of gold. Branson wiped his arm across his brow, sweating in the warm, humid air of the cavern. He was glad he hadn't donned his protective gear.

Branson bowed to them—three separate bends at the waist—three separate pains in his hip. "Good morning, kind friends. I am Branson Luc, a doctor of animals. I have come to check your health."

It is not time for our annual check-up, thought the red giant. Branson heard the response in his head, deep and low, but obviously feminine.

He bowed to her again. "I know, grandmother, and I am sorry for the intrusion. May I take your temperature?"

The green interrupted with a shake of his beard, his voice booming in Branson's head. *WHY DO YOU WISH TO CHECK OUR HEALTH?*

Branson smiled, covering his confusion. Had the witches not informed them *why* they weren't working? He had to tread lightly here. One false remark and the great serpents would stand mutinous against him.

Branson bowed to the green dragon. "Grandfather, the coke ovens are not as hot as they should be. The witches are concerned for your well-being."

A scrabble of the gold coins they lounged upon heralded the entry of the blue dragon into the conversation. He rolled a gold coin over the knuckles of his claws and back again. Then he spoke. "The witches think we're taking a vacation, do they? Perhaps they should return to cutting down trees for their fires."

"Oh, no, Ancient One," Branson said, bowing lower than before. His hip would be purple before he finished this examination. "They make no such accusation." Would blame and groveling on his behalf soothe this beautiful, temperamental creature? He tried. "In fact, it was *my* suggestion. A quick test of your inner temperatures would quickly prove the problem resides in the oven mechanics. If you would be so kind to allow it, then I'll bother you no more."

The dragons looked to each other. There was nodding and shaking of heads, while tinkling coins rolled down the heap of gold and clattered to the cave floor. An unfurling of wings— just a quick shake—enough to wash a cool breeze over Branson as the red got to her feet. She turned to him, resigned. *Where's your thermometer? It must be warmed before you proceed.*

Branson smiled. Had that been the problem all along?

"Relax, grandmother." He pulled a band of treated, woven cotton from his bag—his own invention. "I need only touch it to your neck to take your temperature." He limped closer to the dragons. "It is difficult for me to climb the ladder. Would you do me the honor of bending?"

The red dragon stepped forward and bent, huffing moist breath the flavor of beef in Branson's face. Branson wrapped the cotton around the dragon's throat and watched as the thermochromic properties kicked in. The cotton warmed to blue, then deeper blue, to green, and finally a bright red, indicating that the red's temperature was perfect.

The blue and the green dragon were fine as well.

Branson bowed and thanked them, and made his way to the factory.

Before the witches employed the dragons to burn coal into coke, they'd used up most of the trees of the forest on Great Oakmoore Mountain. Employing the dragons changed everything.

It really was an ingenious system, Branson thought, while walking back to the factory floor. Shifting to dragon heat freed the witches from having to spell the wood to burn hotter and without oxygen—saving them both time and effort.

Now, the ovens were filled with coal and completely sealed. Dragons breathed flames into the ovens through special openings, burning the coal and creating the coke, a small amount of sulfur that the witches used for other things, and gas that they siphoned off the top.

The gas fueled the rail system above the ovens—opening and closing the oven doors and allowing coal to be dumped in or coke to be pushed out.

But the coke was the important thing. It was used as both a fuel and a reducing agent in the blast furnaces for smelting the iron ore. No smelted iron—*no steel*. No steel—*no cauldrons.*

Branson approached the three tall ovens, waiting for the heat to hit him. But he realized they hadn't worked for so long they were completely cool, making examination easier. He couldn't have asked for a better situation. Smiling, he pulled out his tools and started looking.

Three hours later, he leaned against the cavern wall, staring at the coke ovens. He hadn't found anything wrong.

He was doomed.

The witch-foreman came along, her braid now tidied. "What's the prognosis?"

"Not sure yet." Branson hated to admit that. "But I'll find it."

"There are others waiting."

Branson ran a hand through his already-disheveled hair. "I know why your temperatures are falling, I just can't figure out where it's happening. I need a few more minutes."

The foreman nodded and walked away. "Half an hour."

It was generous.

He'd checked the seals. He'd checked the gas pipes. He'd checked every port and opening that might allow air in and heat to leak out.

Where was the heat escaping?

Branson combed through the coke and ash and coal left remaining in the ovens, sweeping it away from the bottom edges, looking for something in the hardened steel of the ovens.

Could there be a minuscule crack? Maybe something that only showed up when the oven was hot?

He sighed, wondering if he'd have to heat up the ovens to find it. He didn't want to bother the dragons again.

"Time to go, Master Luc," the foreman witch said behind him. He startled, having been so engrossed he hadn't heard her arrive.

"Another moment." He had to see this through.

"Your time is up. You will be paid, of course, for looking over the dragons."

And then he saw it, the scat, the smooth, tiny ovals on the underside of the coal, so small he'd almost missed it. And if the ovens had been cool for a few days, *they* were starving.

"I know what's going on," he said, limping to his bag and retrieving a flask of lamp oil and a shallow dish, which he set just outside the oven door. The strong, varnish scent of the oil stung his nostrils as he poured a little into the dish and struck flint and steel together to light it. Purple flames licked across the surface of the oil. Branson waited.

"This better not be a trick." The foreman crossed her arms on her chest, looking as though she'd like nothing better than to turn him into a toad.

"It's not."

He limped away from the ovens, leaning on the rock wall near his tool bag, and pulled the napkin from his pocket. A cascade of cinnamon candy got loose and skidded across the floor to the ovens. He bent and stretched for the nearest, then stilled.

An orange nose, no bigger than one of the cinnamon candies peeped from inside the coke oven. The nose twitched.

As fluid as the flames in the dish, the neon-yellow lizard snaked out from behind the coal and raced to the nearest piece of candy.

Surprised, Branson grabbed another shallow dish from his bag, poured the remaining candies into it, and pushed it toward the salamander.

The salamander lifted his head, breathing in the cinnamon scent and scuttled to the dish. He lifted his head over the rim and plunged his blunt snout into the candy, the hard ridge above his nostrils clacking against the crisp, red, candies. He chomped on them one-by-one, crushing the spicy sweet to dust between flat teeth, saliva-turned-red dripping out of his maw like blood.

The creature looked at Branson and paused, lifting his head. A smile, Branson thought, smiling back. He bent and lay a hand against his booted prosthetic and waited.

The salamander went to the burning oil and sucked the flames from the top of the dish, leaving just enough fire to reignite the entire surface. Then it wheeled on its haunches and raced for Branson, leaping first to the wooden leg, then scampering across Branson's fingers and up his arm onto Branson's shoulder.

"You are quite the fine little fellow," Branson crooned, dusting a fingertip over the lizard's brow ridge and stroking down his back to his tail. Cat-like, the salamander closed its eyes and lowered its head as Branson continued to stroke the delicate, moist skin. The salamander purred, its tongue rasping slowly in and out of its mouth with each slow pant.

Suddenly, the creature sucked in a convulsive breath. Branson cupped it in his hands, thrusting it away from his body. He knew what was coming.

The salamander burped, expelling a cinnamon-scented fireball the size of a cantaloupe, singeing the hair on the back of Branson's fingers and very nearly his eyebrows.

"Salamanders?" the witch said, a sound of curious awe in her voice. "Eating the flames?"

Branson nodded, laying the creature on his forearm and stroking it again with his finger. "My guess is this is just one of a brood," he said. "A scout. We should be able to entice the others out fairly easily." He frowned. "Mama must have died. I don't think she would have allowed them to siphon off so much heat if she'd been around. Salamanders are rather crafty, and good at hiding their tracks."

"But you can remove them?"

He tickled the lizard under its chin and nodded. "It shouldn't be a problem to relocate them."

Branson was carrying his things through the great steel doors, ready to depart when the Head Witch came to greet him. She carried his payment in a small purse and she was smiling.

"Would you consider staying on?"

"As mechanic, or doctor?"

"Both, I think," the witch said. She handed over the purse. "The dragons say you have a pleasant touch."

Branson smiled—to have the respect of dragons—who could ask for more?

But he wasn't certain. He enjoyed tinkering around his cottage, helping the neighbors' animals—and he'd bet after this the villagers would call upon him for help again. To work for the witches would be an honor—and those dragons—beautiful creatures.

"What about the people in the neighborhood?"

"You could help them—as long as your official duties were taken care of."

He looked down the mountain to his cottage. The path was long and painful. And if he offered to help the villagers, he'd be making the trip often. It was tempting to stay, but...

"We could help with that leg of yours," the Head Witch said.

And yet, Branson still wasn't sure.

"Let me think about it."

He patted his horse and climbed into his cart, and headed for home. The yellow salamander climbed over his shoulder to watch. The red and the orange crawled out of his tool bag and played at his feet. They kept him company all the way down the mountain.

ABOUT THE AUTHOR

Kelly A. Harmon's short fiction has been published in Flame Tree Press's Swords and Steam; *Evil Jester Press's* Deep Cuts: Mayhem, Menace and Misery; *Parsec Ink's* Triangulation: Dark Glass, *and elsewhere. She is the author of the Charm City Darkness series, an urban fantasy that takes place in Baltimore, Maryland. Her website is kellyaharmon.com.*

Winter Horses and Other Unknowables

Leslie J. Anderson

The winter I learned the truth about Mary's deer was also the coldest on record since 1932. It was the kind of cold that made your lungs hurt and your skin prickle, but the horses still needed to eat, so I drove my hand-me-down hatchback through the woods to Black Star Stables, where Mary taught children to ride and rehabilitated horses other people would have sold for dog food. Some of them had already been sold for dog food, and we'd bought them for fifty dollars behind a rusting auction barn when lazy dealers didn't want to bother to load them onto their trucks.

One of the fifty-dollar horses raced my little car up the driveway that morning. He was young and had already put on enough weight that it didn't make me sick to look at him. I had no idea if he was trained at all, but we would find out when he was strong enough. With a happy flip of his head he disappeared around the corner of the barn, waiting for me to fetch him inside. *We might have to keep them all inside,* I thought. Horses can endure more than most mammals, but everything has its limits.

I didn't get out of the car right away. I let the heater run and hoped I could soak up some of its heat before I had to work, and I read the letter again.

Thank you for using GeneMatch Michigan™! Our goal is to map families across Michigan and eventually the Midwest! Your genetics matched 12 of our other participants! 3 of these matched as sibling! 1 matched as parent! 8 matched as cousin or other family relation. For full details on your genetic matches, see your Personal Genetic Relation Tree below. So far our results have been 99.8% reliable. If you believe we have made a mistake, please contact us. Thank you again for volunteering for our program. This information will contribute to genetic research for decades to come!

Below that was a detailed family tree, with participant numbers where the names should be. Over *father* was the number 087593 and below that were three sibling numbers, three more siblings than I'd had before I'd opened the envelope. Before I opened the envelope, there was only me.

There was a sharp tap on the window and I jumped, shoving the letter away as if it was something I should be ashamed of, though I'd done nothing wrong. I'd only been curious. I'd only let a sliver of a suspicion dig into my mind.

I don't trust your mother, Maria.

Mary stood beside the car, her hand raised in case she had to tap the glass again. Her sharp features were frozen in irritation, which could have easily looked like fury if you didn't know her. Mary was an old-school horse woman. She had a gun in her truck and dirt in her skin. I wasn't sure how old she was, maybe 65 or 92 or 300. She'd lost an eye in a riding accident before I could remember, and her white iris looked oddly opalescent, reflecting light almost like a cat's eye sometimes. A lot of people thought she was a mean woman. But even at 16, I could tell that wasn't true. She'd seen a lot of hurt in the world, and healed what she could of it. Mostly she was furious that the world rewarded her by sending her more hurt.

"There are more bones by the west gate," she said as we walked to the barn.

I hurried after her. The sunset threw strange light through the trees, reflected off the ice, lanced blue light through the forest. Somewhere ice cracked a branch, which crashed to the ground. I almost rolled my ankle on the way into the barn. The stones around the stable were oddly round, like ugly grey marbles, and I was always sliding over them and picking them out of the horses' hooves. It was just another strange thing, like all the other strange things about the place. Like the old dog who'd been hit by a car six months ago (the neighbor who hit him stopped to apologize, hat in hands, unable to look at Mary's white eye). The dog came hobbling home that evening and fell asleep in the tack room, like nothing happened. I told Mary we should take him to the vet, but she said he was fine, and he was.

We worked in silence for hours. Mary didn't talk much usually, and she almost never talked while she worked. It gave me a lot of time to think, and I had a lot to think about. I thought about my dad's head rolling across the pillow, his eyes focused on nothing. I tripped over the bottles beside the bed trying to catch him before he rolled to the floor. *I don't trust your mother, Maria. I know some things she did, and that's just the things I know! Merde, Maria, assiste-moi. Je suis glissais.* I realized I was falling behind when Mary came up behind me and punched me on the shoulder. I tried not to rub it, but it did hurt. I don't think Mary knew how strong she was, or maybe she did.

"You're dragging today," she said.

"Sorry."

"Don't say sorry. Do better."

I nodded. It was one of her sayings, something I'd heard again and again since I was six, like *heels down, eyes up* and *breathe at the halts* and *turn the water pump off when you're done with it.* I tried to put my head down and push through the haze in my brain. I checked the fifty-dollar gelding and found heat in one of his ankles. When horses are injured, their body produces heat, and the heat can kill infection, but heat can cause its own damage. It can cause the connective tissue to break down. I'd keep an eye on it. That's the best you can do sometimes. Keep an eye on it and wait. The cold was probably good for it today.

"What's wrong?" May asked, appearing over me like a phantom.

"I think he twisted his ankle."

"That's not what I meant."

"I found out my mom's cheating on my dad, or she did once."

Silence. I looked up at her and the gelding stepped away from me. He was one of those easily irritated souls. He had no time for whatever it was I was trying to do.

"So what are you going to do now that you know?"

"I don't know. It changes everything."

Her gaze didn't shift from me. If there was any movement in her face, it was the slightest deepening of her almost permanent frown.

"Doesn't it?"

"Maria, I want to show you something. But I'm trying to decide if you can handle it."

I didn't know how to answer that. For one, it was the longest string of consecutive words she'd said to me. Secondly, if Mary didn't think I could handle something, I almost certainly couldn't. I felt her goals for me were almost always just above my abilities. I was always failing by the skin of my teeth, and she endured me because I was the only one who didn't have a family emergency every time the thermometer dipped below 25.

I ran my hand along the gelding's neck until she finally nodded and shrugged one shoulder. When a horse follows you, they usually follow the motion of your shoulder because they can clearly see it. The best horsemen can control a horse just with that movement. Mary could, and she could move me with it too. We headed toward the Far Field, a pasture I'd never been to. There was a long, fenced path to it, through the woods. I assumed there was a paddock at the other end, but only Mary led horses out there. She said it was too far away and she wanted to keep an eye on us. Sometimes she wandered out there with a bucket and a loaf of old bread "to feed the deer."

That's what we did now. She went into her house, a tiny, battered white shotgun shack on the property. It had once been surrounded by flowerbeds, but she'd let the foals loose in her yard every once in awhile and they'd trampled or eaten all of it. There was a lawn jockey, half sunken into one of the beds. For some reason someone glued little mirrored tesserae over its eyes. They reflected the white snow and gray sky.

The ancient dog came out first, pushing the screen door open with his nose and leaning against my legs, heavier and heavier until I bent and scratched his eyes. Mary reappeared with a metal bucket and a loaf of bread. She handed me the bucket and I looked down at red—blood red, and meat— chunks of fatty meat. The bucket was heavy with it.

"Mary!"

"Keep your voice down and let's go."

"What are we doing?"

"Feeding the deer."

The ice was thick on the trail and cracked under our boots. The strange round stones rolled into the ditches and I could hear the ice breaking trees in the forest. There was no paddock at the end of the fence; it simply stopped at a metal gate that Mary unchained and kicked open. The old dog snuffled at my bucket, and I shooed him away without looking too closely at it. It made my stomach turn.

The path went on and on. I saw deer trails converge with it, the animals wandering from the forest to walk along the wide road. There were also tracks I didn't recognize, tiny bird tracks and little mammal hands, maybe a possum or a raccoon. There were larger tacks, four toed with little points of claws. My blood went cold as I thought of bears. Could there be bears in the woods? The ice beneath the tracks seemed almost blue, like antifreeze. I kept walking.

The path ended in a field with a lake in the center, or maybe a very deep puddle, as the tall, tan grass grew right through the ice. Standing on the ice, sniffing at the surface, were six or seven deer. As we walked closer I realized they were larger than deer. My mind corrected to elk, but elk didn't live around here. My mind corrected again, and again, as we walked toward them, flicking through mammals that made sense—that could possibly be standing in front of me, even if they had to escape from a zoo to be there.

But it was impossible. They were too huge, too lean. Their necks were too long. They were the wrong *color*, a tannish-green that reminded me of moss on the side of rocks. I kept walking, but my joints tightened. Blood roared in my head. My body reacted like an animal, afraid and unsure and afraid because I was unsure. Mary shrugged me forward.

The first one raised its head to look at us, and it wasn't a deer. Its eyes were centered in its face, huge and silvery, and its long face had no nose. It did have a mouth, and it opened to make a kind of rasping cry that the rest of the herd reacted to. Seven silver-eyed faces. Seven raspy cries. They came toward us, walking with a sliding step that stuttered at the end in a way that struck me as unearthly.

"Dump it there," Mary said, and I did.

The blood splashed across the snow and the things calmly bent their heads to eat. I wanted to look away from the tearing, slurping creatures, but something in my mind was certain they would attack if I did, chew and shred me to pieces and leave me in the snow with the rest of the meat. My breath came quickly, making tiny clouds in front of my nose.

"Calm down," Mary said.

She spoke coolly, as if we were discussing the gelding again. Her dog walked under the creatures, sniffing their green fur. One of them lazily pushed him aside with its foot—something that was both a paw and a hoof.

"Those are monsters, Mary! They were just out here the whole time?!"

"The whole time," Mary said, "long before you were here, I found one with a broken leg and helped it heal. I hid it in the shed for weeks. It was an interesting time."

I didn't know what to say. I watched the creatures finish their meal, lick each others' faces.

"They like bread too," She said, and started tossing bits of the loaf to them. They gobbled it up, long tongues as thin as shoelaces plucking the bread from the snow. In a way I felt betrayed, no matter that it made no sense.

"Why did you show me this?"

Mary looked disappointed, like I'd missed something obvious.

"Sometimes you learn something about how the world works, and it don't make anything clearer. It's just another thing."

The next morning was just as cold, but the wind died down. I pulled a hat on at the door and stood with my hand on my keys. Was everything the same, or was everything different? Did I know more about my world, or did the unknown simply recede slightly, giving nothing but a small sense of what I could never know?

"Maria, Maria, where are you going?"

"Work, dad."

"Do you know where your mother is?"

He was leaning on the kitchen wall with a bottle in his hand, but it was unopened. I walked over and put a hand around it. It was still cold. He must have just taken it out of the fridge.

"Come on, dad. Let me have it."

He looked at my hand around the bottle. I thought I saw his fingers tighten, but then he released it. I took it into the kitchen.

"I'm so sorry, Maria. I'm so sorry."

"It's okay, Dad. It's really okay."

When I arrived at the barn, the gelding was waiting for me and trotted along the fence beside my car. Mary was waiting for me inside, already leading a horse with nothing but a rope around her neck and a shoulder shrug.

"Go feed the deer, would you? The stuff's in the freezer, in the garage."

Her door was unlocked. The old dog perked up as soon as the door opened and woofed with something like confusion when she saw me. He heaved himself up onto his paws, and I could almost hear his old bones creak. I'd never been in Mary's house before. It was surprisingly feminine. Everything was pastel, including the pink carpet. There were doilies under the lamps and a cross-stitch on the wall that said *Bless This Home.*

I passed a photo on the kitchen counter in a white and silver frame that said "Family." The woman might have been Mary, a million years younger. There was a little girl in her arms, smiling and holding out her hands toward the camera. Sometimes you learn something about how the world works, and it doesn't make anything clearer. It's just another thing.

I found the freezer and the bucket and filled it. The dog followed me out to the field. The ice broke under my feet. There were the deer, standing on the pond, exactly where they were before, their strange long faces turned toward the ground. When they saw me they made their raspy calls and came over to eat. One of them kept coming, that slow shaky gait so unlike any other creature I'd seen. Was this the one Mary saved? Was it frightened by me?

I stood completely still, though it let the cold seep into me more deeply and I wanted nothing more than to thrust my hands into my pockets and hunch over—to try to shield myself. The creature leaned forward, its long neck stretching longer, until the tip of its nose brushed the top of my hand, the one I'd peeled a glove off, to better open the bread. Warmth spread across it, as if I'd brushed the top of a flame. Then it turned and went back to the herd.

I came back from college and decided to stay with Mary until I figured things out. I worry sometimes that I'm feeding off of her certainty, unable to make my own. My parents don't like it, but we don't talk much anyway. Mary sold the gelding to a little girl who uses him for 4H, his ankles clear as ice. There are still seven deer. There are always exactly seven deer, with metallic eyes and thin tongues and mouths full of teeth. The lawn jockey has sunk up to his neck and I think I'll let the ground take him. The old dog is still here. He sleeps at the foot of my bed. His eyes have gone silver.

ABOUT THE AUTHOR

Leslie J. Anderson was born and raised in Michigan, where she spent a lot of time falling off ponies and out of trees. She earned her M.A. in writing from Ohio University. Her writing has appeared in Asimov's, Daily Science Fiction, Andromeda Spaceways Inflight Magazine, *and* Strange Horizons. *Her poetry was nominated for the Pushcart Prize and a Rhysling Award in 2014.*

Last Knight and the Burning Sands

Chloe Garner

Ruggiero pushed aside a tent flap, taking off his sword belt and laying Gentleness, his long-suffering angel blade, aside.

"You summoned me?" he asked. The man at the small desk glanced at him, then resumed writing for several minutes before finally putting down his quill and turning to look directly at Ruggiero.

"You saw to your horse?" Ferrau asked. Ruggiero dipped his head.

"Of course," he said. Ferrau stood, smiling.

"Well met, friend," he said. "I had worried that your time on the continent would leave you little stomach for the desert."

"Frontino was certainly glad of your shelter," Ruggiero said, and Ferrau laughed.

"My servants will know better than to overload him with oats, but he can have as much hay as he likes, so long as he is here. Did you find the oasis of Ceylon?"

"Exactly where you described it," Ruggiero said. "But tell me, what have you found that drove you to such lengths?"

Ferrau indicated a cot, where Ruggiero sat as Ferrau regained his chair. The dark-skinned man rested his bearded chin on his fists and stared hard at Ruggiero.

"No. Even now, I cannot bring myself to do it."

Ruggiero pressed his lips.

"My friend, if you would send Hermus to me and ask me to come away from the war, all the way here, we both know that it is both important *and* that you will tell me. Now or in the morning, you will tell me."

Ferrau grinned.

"Exactly so," he said, standing. "So, for now, wine and stories. Tell me, how goes the war?"

Ruggiero allowed his friend to pull him back to his feet and they went out into the rapidly-cooling desert air where a man in a turban was kindling a fire. Ruggiero didn't like to talk of the war, because he had close friends on both sides of it. His own wife was fighting against his father, and eventually Ruggiero felt that he was going to have to choose a side once and for all.

"Land comes and goes between the sides," he said as Ferrau took a stool from another servant and set it out for Ruggiero to sit on, perching on the edge of his own stool and putting his elbows on his knees.

"Who will take it? Do you know?"

Ruggiero shook his head. Ferrau grinned.

"You don't even know who you *want* to win. Tell me, how is your beautiful wife?"

Ruggiero smiled, just watching the fire as the flames grew up through the dry kindling. There wasn't enough wood out here to burn, so they kept themselves warm at night with plenty of blankets and they cooked their food on dried animal dung.

Even now, as he watched, a man brought out a tripod with a kettle and fed it dried leaves. The southerners drank tea imported from places Ruggiero had never heard of; his father loved the drink.

Ruggiero accepted a small plate with a sweetened dessert on it, even warm, it had a cooling feel in his mouth, and a subtle spice put a heat in his veins.

"You haven't been sacrificing as much as I'd feared, out here," Ruggiero said.

"It's all trivialities, my friend," Ferrau said. "You know as well as I do that the token comforts are nothing compared to a real sense of home."

"Tell me, then," Ruggiero said. "What brings my friend Ferrau out to the middle of the sands, then to drag me out as well?"

Ferrau looked at the flames, settling a bit lower as a woman came to pour tea. Ruggiero shook his hands, declining, and a man offered him a skin of something; he smelled wine and he smiled a silent yes to this.

"There are stories that only the desert knows," Ferrau said quietly, sipping his tea and then setting it aside on a sturdy rug. "Secrets, perhaps, that only the wind here could keep. Whole cities that rose, climbing up above the sand for a time, only to be reclaimed and vanish, just the dunes." He looked at Ruggiero with a sharp expression of interest. "There is a rumor of a great, powerful city in these lands. Everyone knew where it was, everyone could find it, but when the queen died, the sand took it back, along with all of its treasures. How many men would be willing to dig through a mountain of sand to find it, but," he motioned with his arm, "which mountain? When the desert reclaims a place, it is well and truly lost."

Ruggiero sipped his wine. Ferrau didn't drink, but he kept good wine, anyway.

Ferrau looked away again, settled out over his knees.

"Djinn," he said. Ruggiero looked at him, but Ferrau didn't seem inclined to say more, immediately, and Ruggiero waited. He'd ridden a long way to get here; he didn't need answers immediately if they were going to cost Ferrau. He could be patient.

"Tell me of your wife," Ferrau said.

"She is strong," Ruggiero said. "Smart. As skilled with a sword as a lance. A capable rider, and a lovely singer."

Ferrau snorted.

"You describe a battle brother."

"She is that."

Ferrau shook his head.

"And what did she think of you coming to me, simply because I asked?"

Ruggiero looked away.

"The battle is never simple."

"She doesn't know?"

"I will tell her," Ruggiero said quickly. "It isn't a secret. It's simply…"

"Your worlds take you apart," Ferrau said. "And what of your father?"

"Margano hasn't come down from his tower in more than a year," Ruggiero said. "I don't know if I will see him again before he dies."

Ferrau stroked the edges of his beard with his thumb and the knuckle of his forefinger.

"Your father believes in his work."

"And very little else," Ruggiero answered. Ferrau gave him a dark look, and Ruggiero took another drink of his wine.

"You are my friend," he said after another moment. "I did not hesitate to come when you asked."

"That is the truth," Ferrau said. "What do you know of djinn?"

"A breath and whispers," Ruggiero said. "In truth, I don't even know what the word means."

Ferrau nodded.

"In the oldest of our stories, they are benevolent. They carry great wisdom and great insight, and like many creatures of age and wisdom, they are dangerous because they do not tolerate fools." The corner of his mouth twitched in a sneering anger. "I've found the truth to be less… flattering."

"Tell me," Ruggiero said.

"Demons," Ferrau said. "Taken to human form. With flashes of flame and light, they seduce men into worshiping them. They shift from flame to flesh and they consume anything around them."

Ruggiero shook his head.

"Demons don't shift forms."

"Ay, so I would have said, too, before I went down to them."

"You've seen them?" Ruggiero asked. Ferrau nodded.

"The very night I sent for you. The very night." He licked his lips and looked over at Ruggiero. "They found the entrance to a… a temple. I have no word for it, other than that. An awesome construction, buried deep in the sand."

"Your missing city?" Ruggiero asked.

"No," Ferrau said. "No. This place has only ever served one purpose. The walls, the floor… In the desert, there is nothing but sand to build with. The ancients knew the way of forming stone from it, and they constructed their buildings of great slabs, but down deep, it always remembers that it is sand. It always returns. And sand has no memory but that it is sand."

Ruggiero frowned as Ferrau held his hands out in front of himself. They trembled in the firelight. Ferrau closed them and tucked them back in against his sides.

"The sandstone in the temple, Ruggiero. It is *stained* with blood."

"New blood?" Ruggiero asked and Ferrau laughed darkly.

"Perhaps, but not enough new blood to begin to cover the old."

Ruggiero nodded.

"It is best you sent for me," he said. Ferrau nodded.

"I am a soldier and a merchant. I have seen great violence and I know a great many secrets, but I know when I am matched, and I know that there is more to you than there is the simple soldier."

Ruggiero nodded. He didn't talk about it very much, the things his father had taught him. He'd met his wife Aurora in battle, sword to sword, and it was the very first time he'd known someone with power like his own. They'd fought for days before they'd fallen, exhausted, next to each other, crawling to a nearby stream where they scooped water for each other as they spoke. He'd loved her from that moment, driving a division between himself and his father that he had no remedy for. The power remained.

Not many people knew about it. His father had friends—the type of friends who drove out the need for enemies—with a shared knowledge and power, and Aurora had a small group of men who had learned at the knee of a single elder, but Ruggiero himself had no peer.

Margano knew that. Aurora knew, but not with the same real *awareness* that Margano knew.

Ruggiero was the second most powerful man the world had ever seen, if Margano's system of measurement was trustworthy.

"I will look into it," he said. "If you will take me there and then promise to leave me on my own."

Ferrau laughed.

"I would not have it any other way."

They set out the next morning long before the sun had reached the horizon. The sky was colored enough to allow them to ride, and if they waited for dawn, the cool of the day would be lost to them. As it was, Ruggiero worried for his friend returning under the worst of the heat.

They stopped once to let the horses drink. Ferrau had camels who were better-suited to the desert, but both men preferred their fighting horses, for all the cost that came with tending them, simply because staying alive had justified those costs time and time again.

Frontino was as critical to Ruggiero as Gentleness herself. The horse had been with him since he was a child, and he had a mind that rivaled most men for tactics and commands. The two men agreed that Ferrau would take Frontino back to the camp and return in two days. Ruggiero would not be able to leave the temple in that time, but there was no place for the horse inside, and he would die of exposure, outside.

The dunes went on forever in every direction. There were no landmarks, no distinguishing features that Ruggiero might have used to make his way back here. The only reason that Ferrau knew where he was going was that it hadn't been long enough for the dunes to change shape since he'd last been here. Two weeks, three at the most, and the way would be lost.

"What are they doing out here?" Ruggiero wondered out loud. "Demons need people to amuse them."

Ferrau looked back at him but didn't answer. Ruggiero suspected that it was because there was no answer, with just what the two of them knew.

"Djinn," he breathed.

They rounded the arm of a dune and there at the bottom of the trough between dunes, like a siphon for all of the sand of the great desert, Ruggiero saw a gaping black door. To either side, he could see columns, and even at this distance he could see that they were carved with figures, but that was all. He dismounted, taking his supplies for the two days and a few other things, then he shook hands with Ferrau and his friend left, toting a skeptical Frontino behind him. Ruggiero gave Frontino a wave, then started across the slick sand, his feet sliding down into it deep enough that it covered the toes of his boots at each stride. It was a sucking exhaustion, walking in sand such as this, and he hoped that Frontino was able to recover well during his rest. Ruggiero only had some hundred yards to cover; Frontino had traversed a sea of the stuff.

He reached the stone floor outside of the door and looked up at the columns. Three times his height, they bore figures of men and animals, many of which he knew, but many more that he didn't. Strange limbs and faces, they seemed fantastic, but standing next to dogs and camels and horses, he had to wonder if they weren't real. The men hunted them, fled from them, consumed and were consumed by them. Making nothing of importance from this, but noting as much of it as he could in case it did prove relevant, Ruggiero approached the door.

The sun cut a hard line into the dark, a wedge of searing light against blind darkness, and Ruggiero stood to cast his own shadow across it, listening for anything but the ever-present wind and the sound of shifting sand.

There was nothing.

He took a step forward, holding up his hand and blowing across his flat palm to spark a white flame into existence. Rather than scorching, like the sun outside, the white flame glowed with a cool purity that lit the space without blinding him.

A shadow moved and Ruggiero drew Gentleness from his hip, the angel blade resonating with the power of the angel flame in his palm.

Ruggiero took another step forward, wanting to be out of the unkind sunlight, but not wanting to advance further than he was sure he should go.

Patience.

Patience won as many battles as swords did.

Gentleness was perhaps less willing to wait for him to become aware of his surroundings; he didn't need anything more than the indignant flow of magic off of the sword to know that there were demons about.

There was a roll of flame some distance in front of him and a man appeared. He had a solid build and smooth skin the color of the sand, and he wore an ornate outfit of the same color, loose in the style that Ferrau wore and decorated everywhere with bits of bronze. Smoky orange flame rolled away from his feet as he stood.

"Who are you and why do you disturb us?" he asked.

"I am Ruggiero, son of Margano," Ruggiero answered. "How many are you?"

He could see, in the white light from his palm and from the orange flame around the djinn that Ferrau hadn't exaggerated the extent of stain on the orange sandstone. There were streaks on top of streaks, staining two rows of columns that went the length of the great room, and the floor was almost black. Even so, the air smelled of nothing but stale and dry. It was old blood.

"We are many," the djinn answered. "And you are few."

"I am one," Ruggiero said. "Why do you hide in the darkness?"

"We choose darkness or light as it suits us," the djinn said. "You will bow before us."

Ruggiero looked up at the ceiling, at the way the stone was worked and carved. It would have been beautiful, in the right light. The time that men had put into creating this place was extraordinary.

"I've never known a powerful demon to hide out this far away from men," Ruggiero finally said. "I'm more inclined to believe that you are here out of fear, that you have come here to hide."

The djinn tipped his head back at the ceiling and roared, a howl that sounded like the wind in a sandstorm, and he flexed his arms in, up over his head, then spread his hands.

"We will tear you into pieces and feast on your flesh," he said, bringing his head back down. "But not before you worship me."

He closed his hands and the temple vanished, as did he.

Ruggiero found himself standing on a grassy hillside overlooking a shallow pool. The rocks on the bottom were a cheery color of green, like the hill just continued down into the crystal water. A great tree spread branches over his head, and everything twinkled with a sense of new, of fresh, of clean. Without indulging in it, he could smell the damp of the air, the smell of new life and healthy earth. He checked his grip on Gentleness, who was still on an angry alert at the darkness of the magic around him, then he extinguished the angel flame in his palm. What he saw was not with his eyes, and the angel flame was a dangerous thing to control when he was in possession of *all* of his wits.

Aurora drifted down out of the forest shade behind him wearing a gauzy blue gown, walking to the water's edge in bare feet and looking back at him. She smiled, a simple, devastating smile, and held a hand out to him. He shook his head.

"I'm sorry, my love," he told her. "I can't."

She tipped her head to the side.

"We work," she said softly. "And we fight. And sometimes I feel we do very little else. Is there never a time for us?"

"There will be," he answered. "When the work is done."

"Do you never fear that perhaps I won't be here, when the work is done?" she asked.

She had a lovely face. Not as wan and willowy as was fashionable in some of the places Ruggiero had lived, nor as ample and round as was popular in other places, but firm and featured, with a scar over her eye where someone had landed a fist during a fight, and another down the side of her face where the tip of a lance had flung off her helmet. It was her eyes, though, that he'd admired, laying on the ground next to her, exhausted like his body might never recover, Gentleness in his hand and Frontino walking a cautious circle, snorting at Aurora's horse.

The ground had been heavily trod from their fight, that day, but it had been ground like this. Clean-smelling and earthy, full of green life.

He felt the longing in his body to take that still-offered hand, to pull his feet out of his boots and stand next to her ankle-deep in the water, and he shook his head.

"I cannot stay," he said.

"We will miss each other entirely, if we aren't careful," she said to him, and he pulled his mouth into a tight line.

"Such is the cost of power, beloved."

She dropped her eyes, then looked at him with intensity.

"I miss you."

"And I miss you," he answered, turning his head away. "This place will not keep me."

He took a step and the brilliant color of the place twisted and spun, dissolving into flat, dank gray.

A dungeon.

It smelled of must and human waste, and Ruggiero found himself face to face with himself. He did not recognize his own body, but he knew his visage, and he knew that the other self recognized him.

The scrawny, ill-dressed man sat on the floor, his arms held in shackles over his head.

"What's happened to you?" Ruggiero asked.

"The inevitable," the other Ruggiero answered. "What did you think would happen?"

Ruggiero looked around the cell. Two walls were square, one with a door, but the rest was an arc, a subset of a round wall. This was no ordinary prison.

"Who?" he asked, looking back at himself. "Who put you here?"

The other man spat on the floor.

"You think you're so free and so powerful that no one will ever force you to take a side. They conspired against you, you fool. Both sides wanted you gone, because neither could trust you."

"What of Aurora?" Ruggiero asked.

"Dead," the other man growled. "Died trying to defend you. Last thing she saw was her own failure."

Ruggiero went to the door, looking out.

"Whose prison is this?"

"Who do you think?" the other man asked. "Don't tell me you don't know the place."

He did.

He didn't want to admit it, but he did know this building.

Only from the outside, but the size and shape of it was unmistakable.

"Margano would never allow it," he said.

"He wears the key around his throat," the other Ruggiero said. Ruggiero came and squatted in front of himself, looking into his own eyes.

"I will not fear," he said. "My future is not known, and I will not be swayed away from my path by what may be."

The other Ruggiero blinked at him.

"You will suffer as no other man has suffered," he said. "You will lose everything at the hands of men you trusted."

Ruggiero stood.

"And yet I will not despair," he said, turning his face away and taking a step. The gray blurred and melted, and he found himself in a room constructed of wood and plaster. There was a tapestry on the wall, and he stood next to the solid post of a canopy bed. He turned his head and smiled once more as he saw Aurora curled there against a pile of pillows. He tipped his head, frowning, and took a step forward.

Yes.

Cradled there in her arms, swaddled tight, there was an infant.

Aurora sighed, seeming to be unable to see him, this time, and a man walked into the room. It was a friend, a man that both Aurora and Ruggiero had fought alongside in the war, as need arose, and Ruggiero recognized the home he was in, as he saw Montalban.

Aurora looked up at Montalban with a friendly smile, then looked down at her child again.

"Any word?" she asked.

"No," Montalban said. "The king does not know where he is."

Ruggiero frowned, and Aurora put her hand to her mouth, blinking quickly as she put on a pained smile.

"I know that he is where he should be," she said. "I just wish..."

"Of course," Montalban said. "He should have been here for the birth of his son."

Aurora shook her head.

"He will come."

"No one has heard from him in months," Montalban said. "I think perhaps..."

"Do not speak to me of this," Aurora said. "Not today."

Montalban lowered his head in a slight bow and then stood straight, looking directly at Ruggiero.

"You are, of course, welcome to stay here for as long as you need," his friend said. "I will send someone down into town to hire you a nurse."

"I am fine with my own two arms," Aurora said. "Thank you."

"You need rest," Montalban said, his attention still fixed on Ruggiero. "Especially with Ruggiero not here, you must take extra care that you keep yourself healthy and give yourself time to recover."

"He is out there," Aurora said. "And he will come."

"God willing," Montalban said, the corner of his mouth twitching up. He turned and knelt next to the bed. "But you will remain as my guest, either way, until you are fit to travel. I will not hear of anything else."

"Of course," Aurora said. "And we will be grateful of your hospitality."

Ruggiero closed his eyes.

He felt it.

Unwonted and unbidden, he felt it.

Jealousy. Mistrust. Anger.

He took a long, slow breath.

"This is not real," he said. "And even if it were to happen, I trust my wife and I trust my friend. Even if something were to kindle between them in my absence, I forgive them."

The words were freeing, though not magic. He opened his eyes again and found that he was still in the room, but now the child was to the side in a bassinet and Montalban lay in bed next to Aurora, his arm supporting her shoulders.

"They confirmed it today," Montalban said, watching Ruggiero. "He died in a fight."

Aurora nodded.

"I've suspected it," she said. "He would have come, if he had been able. At least..." She paused. "At least he died doing what he felt he was meant to do."

Montalban nodded, kissing her hair as he watched Ruggiero out of the corner of his eye.

"Yes. You must keep that in your mind."

Ruggiero steeled himself.

"That man is my friend," he said, meeting Montalban's eye. "I trust him, even if he *would* do something like this, because my trust is about me and not about him."

He turned his face away and the vision vanished like cut ribbons. He was once more in a forest, dark, with trees so old and so tall that he couldn't see any branches. It was just the great trunks of the aged trees and the dim forest floor. In front of him, in a slanted shaft of light, he saw himself, once more, fighting sword-on-sword with a man in black armor. The Ruggiero of his vision was helmetless, but otherwise fully armored, and his shoulder-length hair flew in the air behind him as he attacked. Light glinted off of his armor, and the other knight fell back, step by step.

There was no sound but that of steel against steel in the muted forest, and the fight seemed to go on for forever, Ruggiero handsome and powerful against the black knight, always winning, always pursuing. Finally, he slew the black knight and another man with a blue pendant stepped forward, shoving his standard into the soft earth and unsheathing a sword.

This fight lasted perhaps longer than the first, with more give-and-take, but without Ruggiero ever seeming to have to give ground. He was fast and powerful, and it was only a matter of time and waiting for the other man to make a mistake before he won again.

Yet another man stepped forward with a red flag on a standard and once more Ruggiero fought. He did not sweat and he did not fade.

He was matchless.

Even Ruggiero, standing off to the side, could see that that was what was going on. The man in the shaft of light was invincible, the most powerful man alive with a sword or with magic.

He beat the red knight and a fourth man stepped forward, a man in robes, who spread his arms and threw a fireball at the Ruggiero in the glinting armor. That Ruggiero crossed his arms and braced as the fireball crashed into him, then he roared and spoke words of magic - words that Ruggiero recognized and would have used, himself, if he'd been up on the sunlit knoll instead of the vision of himself. The mage fell back, spreading his arms again and throwing a glass bottle at Ruggiero. The exchange was complicated, and at the highest level of skill in magic, but the Ruggiero in the light never flinched, never failed. When the time came, he vanquished the mage.

Ruggiero took a step back, away from the vision of himself, and he shook his head.

"I am a man," he said. "I am not invincible, and I will die when it is time for me to die. I will not count on my own strength to give me victory."

Trees from overhead crumbled and fell onto him like fine ash, and when he opened his eyes again, he was standing in sand.

There was no shelter anywhere. No water, no other person.

He was alone.

The sun overhead was unbearable, and there was no landmark anywhere to give him a sense of direction.

He was lost.

He was hopeless.

He peered up at the sun through slitted fingers, then he squatted down, covering his head with his arms, and he pointed himself at his shadow.

"The sun travels east to west," he said out loud. "In an hour I will know which way is north, and I will go that way. If I do not find settlement, I will continue on until I perish, and I accept it."

The intensity of the sun went away, and Ruggiero blinked, standing and holding out Gentleness at the sudden darkness.

"I will not sacrifice my duty for my desires," he said to the echoing space. "I will not succumb to despair or greed or jealousy. I will not feed you."

"Very well," a dark voice said. "If you will not come willingly, we will devour you as you stand."

He opened his palm, blowing across it and letting the white angel flame grow higher, burning his very self, an oil sourced from deep within him, but one that he tended and kept at reserve for moments like this one.

The circle of demons drew back, throwing up their arms at the sudden, pure light, and Ruggiero held out Gentleness, the angel blade impatient to be involved.

Once more, Ruggiero looked around the space, bending time to let himself really look at it as he drew on long-practiced spells that bound the demons to their own space. They could not glitch from one place to another, while his magic was active, and he felt the way the temple reacted to his light magic.

This was a place of great, great darkness.

The deep-rooted dark magic flexed around him, unaccustomed to the intrusion of light, and he pushed harder, changing the shape of his cast to address the room as much as the djinn. They flamed around him, one by one kicking on the roll of orange flame about their feet until their legs disappeared into the fires.

The walls were bloody shoulder high and above, and the floor under Ruggiero's feet had lost its sanded texture.

"Where do you find the men to bring here?" Ruggiero asked.

"They are *drawn*," one of the djinn said. "They hear the promises of what we can give them and they come to us."

"The *desire*," another djinn breathed. "They *season* themselves."

"How many die, trying to find you?" Ruggiero asked. "And how would they know to search?"

There was a dark chuckle behind him, and Ruggiero turned, just a simple foot-over-foot motion, to face a djinn who had slid ahead of the rest.

"Because, once in a while, we let one go," he said. "All it takes is a wish, and men will feed themselves to us for the rest of time."

The demon raised his arms over his head, spinning a ball of flame there, orange and black, murky with smoke, and Ruggiero counted the djinn he'd seen.

There were at least a dozen of them.

Conjurers of fantasy, demons who fed on lust and anger and greed, and ultimately on blood.

"No," Ruggiero said, looking at the walls, at the signs of lives wasted. "No. You will not have *one more*."

There was a laugh, but he spun, casting strong, light fields of protection, ones that spread until they hit the walls and kept going. The temple trembled and the djinn moved to throw the great fireball at him, but Ruggiero breathed in at a break in his spell and blew across the angelflame in his palm, the white flame lengthening and stretching to take in the demon's fire and suffocating it.

Silently.

Angel flame was breathlessly silent, and as Ruggiero put his hand out, letting the white crystalline flame seek out the rest of the demon fire, the room grew quieter and quieter.

The walls shook and sandy dust drifted down from the ceiling as Ruggiero continued to cast. The demons hesitated, Gentleness keeping them out at arms' length.

Only when he was ready, as he felt the dark magic rumbling through the temple beginning to crack and shatter, did Ruggiero let the angelflame touch the floor.

It took to the human blood there like its native fuel, burning ruby red. The demons screamed and tried to flee, but they could not glitch, and the flame burnt, spreading through the temple out of Ruggiero's control, racing across the bloodied surfaces. It still had a hook into him; it was the only way he could hope to extinguish it when it had run its course, but it left him on his own at the center of a red inferno, weakening as the powerful angelflame sucked at him. He felt the last of the djinn ash, returning to the fiery plane they came from, and he felt the walls of the temple turn back the angelflame, finally. He had underestimated how large the place might be, and he had no idea where the door was. What he did know was that he didn't expect to find a second door.

He sheathed Gentleness and held his arms out to either side, allowing angelflame to sprout from the other hand and join the rest of the fire, pushing it out of his way as he walked.

The walls of the temple creaked and groaned, and somewhere they partially collapsed, pouring an ocean of sand in on the fire, but it yet burned. It didn't need air like earth-bound flames. It would burn until its fuel was consumed - until the human blood in the temple was purged. Ruggiero let it go, taking another step and another step, only the vaguest sense of the shape of the building around him guiding a guess at where to go.

He was tiring.

If he fell, the flame would burn until his body was gone, and then it would go out, but it would burn everything else, first.

The temple would go.

He thought of Aurora, hoped that, if he didn't make it, she would find happiness with a man who cherished her as Ruggiero did.

Thought of Ferrau, and hoped that his friend would feel no guilt at sending Ruggiero into the temple on his own. Ferrau would have been no aid, and Ruggiero was glad he didn't have to worry about rescuing other victims as he trudged, struggling not to fall to his knees.

He couldn't see anything. The crimson, fluid-surfaced flames were higher than his head, and they climbed the walls around him.

He walked on.

Another wing of the temple collapsed, and bits of sandy gravel rained down on Ruggiero's head.

He thought of soft, green forest and of water that covered mossy stones.

The roof behind him gave and he looked over his shoulder to see sand spilling down in a waterfall around the sandstone.

He was almost empty.

And he could not see.

He would die here, but he had done what he needed to do.

Sand splashed against the walls, and the angelflame extinguished in a great collapse as the blood ran out through most of the temple.

It was only here, in the room with him, keeping him company and finishing the job he'd been here to do.

There was little dark magic left; it collapsed with the stone.

More sand clouded his vision as he walked through a sheet of it coming down between stones, and he blinked, shaking sand out of his hair.

There.

That was a cut in the stone that looked like a doorway.

And there was no angelflame beyond it.

He kept going, his legs no longer supporting his body. Something else was, some primordial desire for survival, some magic he didn't know, perhaps something else. Another pocket of flame went out.

Ruggiero was through the doorway.

The entire room collapsed behind him and the deluge of sand knocked him forward, buried him.

He crawled, pushing himself through the sun-scorched sand.

He was close.

Only the top layer of sand could be this hot.

A hand grabbed his, pulling him loose, and the last of the flames went out.

Ferrau dusted Ruggiero off with firm hands, then held his shoulders.

"I am to take it that they are gone now, yes?" he asked.

Ruggiero flinched against the intense sunlight.

"Why are you here?"

"It is the agreed time," Ferrau said. "Two days."

Ruggiero shook his head, sand falling down the back of his neck. Ferrau grinned.

"It was an epic battle then," he said. "You must tell me everything. Come. Come."

Ruggiero looked up at the top of the sand dune, relieved beyond measure to see Frontino standing with Ferrau's horse.

"You must tell me everything," Ferrau said again with a happy grin. "Your stories are always the best."

ABOUT THE AUTHOR

Chloe Garner acts as the conduit between her dreaming self and the paper (or keyboard, since we live in the future). She writes paranormal, sci-fi, fantasy, and whatever else goes bump in the night. When she's not writing she steeplechases miniature horses and participates in ice cream eating contests. Not really, but she does tend to make things up for a living. Find her on Twitter as BlenderFiction, on Goodreads and Facebook, or at blenderfiction.wordpress.com.

Necessary Threads

Lora Gray

On your last day of solitude, you find the straw man in the gully, that deep gash between the cornfield and the trailer park where Lucy's Husband Casey chucks old tires. A creek, thin and murky, hiccups through the sallow muck there. Water? Sewage? In this corner of Ohio, it's difficult to tell.

The straw man is crumpled on the bank. He wears human clothes, plaid, denim, bright orange cotton, but he doesn't smell like skin.

You breathe deep and creep forward, one broad foot in front of the other. Mud squelches. Your arm fur snags a blackberry bush. A songbird flickers between the trees. But the straw man doesn't move and so you crouch beside him.

His torso is puckered at the seams, his legs and arms tied to stumps at the ends. His head is a sphere of newspaper and paste (you taste to be sure), and rain has softened the left side until it's slumped and pulpy where the cheek and eye should be. Clods of straw surround him and you can see yellow peeking from the tears in his clothes.

You reach out, fur dragging through the water-maybe-sewage and touch him with the tip of your finger.

He does not pull away and so you gather him into your arms.

You take him home, into the deeper woods, far from where humans call you Bigfoot or Grassman, where oak trees give way to evergreens and the air is full of sour earth and rotting leaves. You shoulder into your copse, the sunlight distant and pale above you. The only musk you smell is your own.

It's been so long since you've had another someone in your home. Your kind have wandered off or withered away, and the humans are so terrified of you that you don't dare approach. The scent of you is enough to frighten them, the sight of you enough to make them scream.

The straw man doesn't seem to mind.

You lift the stone beside your bed of pine and moss. You choose a needle, the one Lucy abandoned last week, and a piece of thread and you begin to mend the holes in the straw man's body. There is a delicacy to it your big hands can't quite master, but you understand the mechanics.

You've watched Lucy do this so many times before.

Lucy mends her ragdoll daily.

Every morning you watch her from the edge of the gully as she escapes the trailer at the end of the road, the one with the rusted siding and broken rocking chairs huddled against the outside wall. The one with the ragdoll in the bedroom window. Lucy eases the screen door open, clicks it closed, toes her way down the cinderblock stairs. Quiet. Careful. Her legs and arms are thin. Some days, they are bandaged. Some days, welts wind up her thighs and bruises spread across her cheek and lower lip, blue-black and raucous as crows mid-flight.

At first, she moves as if a fist is chasing her, arms crossed over her breasts, eyes wide and darting, head drawn back, but as soon as she clears those trailer steps, Lucy swaggers. She juts her chin. She laughs too loud. She crows.

"You kiss your momma with that mouth?" she says to the boys draped over the picnic tables three trailers down. The ones who call her 'crazy' and 'honey.' The ones who take her into their pickup trucks for twenty minutes each when Husband Casey is at work.

"This place ain't so bad. Just gotta know how to play your cards is all," she says to the women at the beehive mailboxes. The ones with puckered eyes and cigarettes clamped between their lips. The ones who cackle when they think she's out of ear shot and call her 'slut' and 'dirty whore.'

"I didn't do nothing! I'll be good. I swear, I'll be good," she says to Husband Casey at dusk when the trailer is dark except for T.V. flicker blue. You watch the shadow play, Husband Casey's swift hands, the tangle, the struggle. You hear the muffled blows. A beer bottle collides with a window, makes the frame shudder. A thump. A dangerous thud.

Every night, Lucy reemerges when the sun is setting, her ragdoll in hand. She marches away from the trailer park, strides along the edge of the gully.

And she rips her ragdoll apart.

Sometimes it's the arms, jerked off one after the other mid-stride. Sometimes it's the hair, fat chunks of yarn yanked out in short, furious bursts after she's dropped herself onto the dry earth. Sometimes it's the whole body, wrenched in two, her hands clawing and digging through the cotton like there are answers buried in the poly-fil.

When Lucy finally stops, red faced and panting, she raises her head.

Sometimes she looks directly at you.

You are downwind and so deep in gully shadow that she can't possibly see you, but something about her narrow focus pins you. Her eyes climb over your height, wind around your breadth. They grapple with the darkness you have hidden in for so long and you imagine emerging, soft and quiet as morning fog, through the evergreens to settle beside her, but

281

you don't dare move. Eventually Lucy's eyes wander, listless with the impossibility of you, back to the mangled doll in her lap.

Slowly, she fishes a needle and thread from her pocket and, as the dark folds over her, she stiches her ragdoll back together again.

Sometimes she pockets the needles.

Sometimes she lets them fall.

You don't anticipate the crows.

You have taken your straw man to the edge of the abandoned field south of the trailer park, so he can dry in the sun. He's been through so much already. So many days rotting and alone. So many nights in the damp belly of that creek with no one to talk to, nobody to touch or hold. He deserves to be warm and dry, especially now that you've mended him so carefully.

But when you return from foraging, the crows are there, ripping and tearing your straw man apart, a swarm of blue black feathers and raucous voices. Orange cotton and plaid are flayed open between them. A chaos of straw. A wide, churning circle of it. The crows stab into him with beaks and claws, launch themselves off the ravaged lump of his head, wing toward their nests with his insides clutched in their mouths.

You chase them.

Full of anger, rage, *hurt*, you chase them. They have ruined everything. You thunder through the field, startling rabbits and sparrows and a covey of quail. They have ruined everything! You charge into the woods. You shake them from trees. You barrel through the gully.

They have ruined everything.

You burst into the open, crows and straw scattering in the air above you and there, standing near the edge of the trailer park, is Lucy. Her hair is gnarled. Her lower lip is bitten through. A fresh bruise purples the hollow of her jaw. A severed arm is clutched tightly between her fingers, the rest of the doll torn apart around her. A breeze teases shredded cotton over Lucy's bare feet. Yarn clings to her ankles and the naked curve of her shin.

You cringe and wait for the fear, the scream, but Lucy only looks at you, eyes wide and dark. She inhales slowly. She uncurls her fingers and drops the remains of her ragdoll.

The sun is setting.

The air is heavy.

The crows have winged silent before either of you gathers the courage to move. When you finally do, it is hesitant and hopeful. It is soft and quiet as morning fog. It is with fingers outstretched like fractured stitches and whispered promises to mend.

ABOUT THE AUTHOR

Lora Gray's writing has appeared in various publications including Shimmer, Strange Horizons, The Dark, *and* Flash Fiction Online. *A graduate of Clarion West, Lora currently lives in Northeast Ohio with a handsome husband and a freakishly smart cat named Cecil. When they aren't writing, Lora also works as an illustrator and dance instructor. You can find them online at loragray.weebly.com.*

PINECONES

C.A. BARRETT

E lida told no one when she first saw the water's heartbeat, a thrum of bright points piercing the still surface of the pool with their light. When the adults found out, she would sit at the table beside the other students. She would be watched, and she wouldn't be allowed to dawdle at the dryad's pool.

Elida loved the dryad. She was a flicker of blushing flowers among the dark conifer trees, softness and light in a hard, dark forest. When Elida lay very still and pretended to sleep in the summer sun, the woman-shaped flowers came so close that Elida could smell white trumpet-honey blossoms and freshly trampled mint. She always ran when Elida turned her head, making great speed look effortless as her branch-like legs grew to touch the ground and then snapped off as she ran. Each afternoon, Elida filled her bucket at the pool and then held still a little longer than the day before. Each afternoon, the scent of flowers was a little stronger when she could no longer resist opening her eyes.

The dryad's water sparkled more than any water that Elida had seen since waking to the heartbeat. She tried to catch as many of the motes as she could, so that Racker would keep choosing her to fetch water. Today she had brought a tight pinecone from the forest as bait to trap them. Racker said that the pinecones opened when there was a fire, but the forest had not burned since before Elida was born. She knew them as tight green eggs, knobby and scaled like a lizard's back.

She knelt and held the pinecone out over the sparkling water. Elida felt the water's attention as lights gathered under her hand, forming a luminous shadow. She placed the pinecone on the water's surface, and the bright motes touched it.

"Lift it," she whispered.

The pinecone did not sink. As soft ripples echoed its shape across the pond, more motes gathered to reinforce the net of light.

Elida raised her iron-bound bucket and started a smooth and careful movement toward the water. At the instant that the rim touched the water's surface, the lights recoiled, clustering on the other side of the pinecone. "Get in," said Elida, shoving without words in the way that raised the water, sometimes. She felt a very small tingle run up her neck.

She felt the water's will push back, like gentle hands on her shoulders that nudged her away from the pool.

"Get in," she said. She shoved harder, leaning forward. "You have to do what I say. You're little." The bright specks scattered and the pinecone dropped, sinking.

Elida whined and threw down her bucket. She threw herself backward after it, landing in the grass beside the pond. She'd pretend to nap until the lights came back. Maybe she'd see the dryad, too.

She pretended so well that she actually slept for a while.

Loud sniffing woke her. The feet beside her were large cloven hooves, and Elida looked up to see a mean little face. The man's nose was smashed flat, and his red eyes were close and piggy. Wide animal ears jutted from either side of his head, under two ridged and curling horns. Thick hair circled his entire head, and a dark short beard flowed seamlessly into the fur of his muscled chest. He was squatting, hunched over Elida, scowling and sniffing.

"You stink, little milk-drinker." His breath was hot and fetid. He stood and tugged the ash-blackened cloth around his body back into place. A horse's tail emerged from the base, and he draped it over one arm. He carried a stick in his opposite hand, wrapped with ribbons, and on the end was a pinecone like no pinecone Elida had ever seen, its scales open to dark little caverns.

"Well, you smell like a goat that's rolled in burned fish," replied Elida, sitting up.

He hissed with laughter, grimacing widely over closed teeth. "This is not your water," he said. "It smells of sweeter visitors. I have been following her scent for six long days, since I caught it on the wind. So tell me, milk-drinker child, where is she?"

"Which she?" asked Elida, her throat thick. "Our whole village comes to this pond."

"Don't play-act a simpleton." The goat-man reached out and gripped Elida's jaw in his fleshy palm. "I can see your power and I will have your dryad *now*, little water-wizard."

"I don't know what any of that is," said Elida. He squeezed, and she yelped in pain. Then he stopped, his eyes looking over her head, and released her face.

She turned and looked across the water. The dryad stood at the edge of the trees, white in the dappled shade. Elida could see the fear on her open, pink-blooming face even from this distance.

The dryad ran, and the hairy creature sprinted around the pool, his cloven hooves packing the dirt at its edge. Both figures disappeared into the trees before Elida got her feet under her. She stared into the dark forest, already closed over the figures, and then balled her tunic in her fists and hiked it up to run up the steep hill home.

She went straight to the long wooden table where the learners hunched over their gilded bowls, and she shouted. Racker turned from his pacing as he supervised the line of students. Their faces lifted, every tendril that had been laboriously coaxed from the water splashing back down into golden bowls.

"Hush," Racker said as he caught Elida by the shoulders. "Where's our water?"

"There's a goaty-man by the pool," said Elida. "A monster."

"A satyr has finally come," said Racker. He released Elida and nodded to the others. "No more practice, today. We'll tell the Elders and then we can help them protect the village."

"What about the dryad? Who will protect her?" asked Elida.

"We don't interfere with wild magic," said Racker.

"But what is he going to do to her?" demanded Elida.

Racker exchanged a glance with the oldest boy at the table, and both their mouths quirked to one side in a leer. "Nothing you need to worry about, little one," he said.

"She looked afraid," Elida pressed.

"I bet she is." Racker picked up a bundle of sticks and handed each student a thin switch. "That's how things go, out there in the wild. Change is brutal and scary and tough. We stay away from it and protect our own."

"We know her. She's part of our village too," said Elida. "She's not wild."

"We've seen her, but she's not one of us," Racker said. "We don't owe her anything. Besides, it's a satyr. Even the Elders can't call enough water to fight a satyr. Go inside the longhouse, and wait."

"I'm not a baby and I will not hide with the mothers," said Elida.

"Everyone will be in the longhouse except for us chosen by the water," said Racker, with a proud lift of his head. One hand went to the silver brooch on his homespun tunic, a thin boat with a dragon's-head prow. It was a badge for the strongest student, given as a reminder to break the water to his will so thoroughly that, like the ship, he would not only float but dare to taunt it with a symbol of fire. The brooch was also a sign of his authority over the other children, because he was the tasked with teaching them what came naturally to him. "We will go with the Elders and keep the village from burning, and then you can all thank us."

"I'm chosen too," said Elida.

"I don't believe you," said Racker. "You're lying. Go inside."

"No," said Elida. "I'm going to go help her, even if you won't."

"You have to do what I say," he said. "You're little."

Elida turned and ran down the slope, back to the pond. She could see only the top of the dark green mass of trees, and as she ran toward them and dropped away from the village she heard Racker's voice shouting, then adult voices. She ignored the shouts and looked past the pond toward the trees where the smoke was thickest.

Elida ran to her abandoned bucket where it lay beside the water. She crashed into the ankle-deep shallows, ignoring the twinkling motes. She felt their fear as they scattered, but they were thinking of the burning woods now, not her vessel. Elida scooped water in a single huge motion, using all of her strength. She hurried between the trees, pursuing the fire with the heavy bucket hitting her kneecaps.

She smelled crushed petals before she saw the two creatures. The satyr had run the dryad to ground in a dark bed of conifer needles, not far from the tree line. He crouched over her still, pale form, stroking a nearby seedling tree with his black fingernails. As he pulled his fingers along its length, the green wood began to smolder and flame. Trees behind him already burned, and the pinecone on his staff was aflame like a bright torch. He reached for the dryad's back, a thin rib of stick with the petals ripped away, and caught one of her branches between his fingers.

Elida planted her feet and lifted her bucket.

The satyr raised his face to her in a grotesque smile, and she poured the entire bucket of water over him before he could speak. His staff was extinguished.

With a roar, the satyr launched himself at her. His two ram-horns caught Elida in the belly, tossing her into the air, and his curly hair hung wet and straight and whipped her as she flew. She hit the ground hard, breathless.

The wet satyr stepped toward her and ripped the bucket handle from her grasp. "No water wizard needs a bucket," he said, sparking quick flame on his fingers and igniting the wood. He threw her bucket aside, new kindling for his fires, and seized Elida in his burning hands.

She screamed as the flames caught her shirt and hair. Smoke stung her eyes, and she struggled against the grip that held her as her flesh began to scald and broil. His hooves drummed at the dirt.

He stopped abruptly, jarring Elida, who he still held aloft in her burning clothes. The heat was drying his hair even as it consumed Elida's. Stinking like any wet mammal, it began to curl around his red eyes. "You are untrained. You are nothing," he said. "Let's see if you are so pathetic that you drown."

The satyr threw Elida backward into the pool.

She heard his laugh start before the water closed over her ears. She sank, limbs struggling, the hot burns on her chest eased but still raw. She called to the lights. *Lift me*, she thought. *Lift me! Lift me!*

The motes gathered around her, trailing her sinking body like the bubbles that escaped her tunic. They didn't understand the urgency. "Lift me," she said aloud, angry at their curiosity, and her air escaped with the command.

She felt them push back, a wordless *no*.

Elida's next breath was water. Her chest spasmed inward trying to throw it out, but her flaring nostrils and frantic mouth only took in more water. The motes pushed her down. Her rump touched the bottom of the pond, and Elida saw a cloud of sand rise up after the bubbles and motes, dimming her vision.

All she could see were the sparkling lights, and they were beautiful and wild and free.

"Do what you want to, then," whispered Elida, her lips moving around the water.

The lights came crashing down on her. She felt the shiver start in her fingertips and collide over her heart as they drew something out. She was not commanding the motes. They were drawing something out of her for their own purpose.

The pond's water surged up, and the light around Elida grew brighter for a breathless heartbeat as she approached the surface. The water dropped her on the shore and then all of it rushed into the woods, flying together in a great clear mass, even flowing out of her lungs. She took in sweet air, on her knees and palms, and stared at the empty bowl of wet sand that had been the pond. Then she turned her head in the direction of the water's roaring.

The wave surged back, still flying over the land, with the satyr suspended inside. His mouth gaped when he met Elida's eyes, but whatever insult he tried to shout cost him his last breath. The water parted over Elida, whisking the goat-man to one side, and flowed back into its pool.

She stood, and turned to the pond. The light-spangled surface was perfectly smooth, although Elida could see a brown form struggling in the depths, chained in golden lights.

She could hear adults shouting her name, and she looked to the hill. A perfect line of rain clouds waited at the top of the ridge, dazzling with spots of white light in their dark depths. A thick fence of rain was coming down. The Elders, all wearing blue cloaks, were spaced evenly underneath it with their thick staffs held high. She saw one distant figure gesture to someone behind to stay back, and then they all stepped as one, moving the rain and the clouds closer to the burning forest. A crowd pressed forward just behind the rain.

They were coming for her. The village was braving the satyr to come for their child, but they were only coming for her, and they were too slow to help the dryad.

Elida turned away and plunged into the fiery trees. She followed the water's path over wet, extinguished logs back to the clearing. The flames here had been extinguished by the living pond, but the dryad was no more than wet ash outlined by skeletal sticks. Her petals, and her lively magic, were gone from the corpse.

Elida fell heavily to the ground with a sob. She reached out to touch one burned rib, and the thin charcoal crumbled beneath her fingers. Her fingers followed it down until she hit something firm, and she sat up and brushed ash away.

A pinecone as large as her head was at the center of the burned dryad, its scales fully open. Bright lights glowed within. She lifted it and saw a newborn baby curled in one of its crevices, and then another, and another. Each would fit in the palm of her hand, and had a greenish inner glow. The tiny dryads slept, folded tightly in their niches.

Elida lifted the pinecone reverently, cradling it in her arms.

She walked back toward the pond, her burned skin aching. She could hear adults shouting. Her father's voice was loudest above the others, calling her name. She emerged from the trees to see the line of rain more than halfway down the grassy hill, advancing slowly, with the adults of the village gathered behind it.

When he saw Elida, her father ran forward through the barrier of water, ignoring the Elders. He lifted her, and she folded herself up against him, curling limply around the pinecone. She smelled sweat in the bend of his neck. Others followed him, running forward to surround Elida and her father, then spreading out to roam curiously. The Elders on the hillside lowered their arms, and the clouds cleared.

After a long quiet, her father spoke. "Elida," he said. His voice was thick with fear but already getting hard and scolding by the end of her name. "You—"

"Did you see the water?" a soft voice interrupted him.

Her father lowered Elida from his face and turned to the speaker.

The oldest of the wizards, his thin hair soaking wet, stood before them. "Did you see the water? Don't scold the child," he said. He looked deeply into Elida's eyes and then down to the pinecone she held. He nodded at her slightly.

The Elder took off his own damp cloak. He lifted the blue mantle and placed it around her shoulders, and then he tucked it over the pinecone. The wizard held out his hand. "Racker," he called.

The older boy stepped out of the crowd. "She's the youngest," he protested.

Elida gently squeezed her small charges.

"That's a satyr," said the Elder, "dead at the hands of an untrained child. She has discovered something that she needs to teach us all." He beckoned with his fingers, never taking his dark eyes from Elida.

Racker stepped forward and gave up the ship-shaped brooch.

Elida put her cheek back down on her father's shoulder. "I don't want to stand by the table," she said, looking over the water at the blackened tree trunks. Her childhood freedom had burned today. She saw the friendly sparkles in the pool, and she felt the tip of the pinecone bite into the soft flesh under her jaw. "The wild little ones are part of our village too. That's all."

The Elder gently plucked a fold of blue cloth away from Elida's chest. "Then your only work is to remind us of that lesson while you go about your business." He pinned the ship to her robe with a soft touch.

The pond winked to Elida as she was carried home.

ABOUT THE AUTHOR

C.A. Barrett is a lifelong reader and writer. This is her first fiction publication.

The Pooka's Day

Darrell J. Pursiful

D anny stopped cold as the end of the woman's walking stick poked him in the chest.

"We don't want any trouble," she whispered. "You can just move along."

He should have heard them coming—five of them all told, but he hadn't been paying attention. Too much on his mind. He just charged across the cow path on his way back to the creek, and there they were.

As it was, he barely had time to throw on a decent husk. He was pretty sure they didn't notice, though, when his ears and nose shortened to more human proportions and the glow faded from his amber eyes.

Whoever these people were, their leader meant business. One of the others sucked in a labored breath. Two more, children, whimpered in the dark.

"M-miss Claudia?" a different woman whispered, "Lige... he ain't looking so good." This woman was helping the only man in the group to stand. Danny sniffed the air. Amid the soil and grass and growing things was the unmistakable iron scent of blood. He spied a ripped and bloody trouser leg.

The first woman's eyes blazed. She and her friends were dressed in dingy, patched clothes barely fit for a brownie. That and their dark skin was all he could make out.

He raised his hands. "Whatever you say, ma'am." He wasn't in a mood for any mischief. Well, that wasn't entirely true. He still had three more farms to case before daybreak. But he didn't have time for anybody else's mischief. Not tonight. Not with *him* liable to show up at any minute.

"And not one word, you hear?" The rumble in her voice demanded Danny's full cooperation.

He was about to say something when he caught the sound of dogs barking.

"Lord have mercy!" the other woman gasped. The younger child, no more than four years old, started to cry, but his big sister slapped a hand across his mouth.

The first woman spun and raised her stick horizontal to the ground.

"Head for the woods," she ordered. "Go!"

Four shadows stumbled past.

"Those are my woods!" Danny's throat went dry. Something settled in the pit of his stomach. He was *fairly* sure he shut the door…

"You want to make something of it, mister?"

"You don't understand. You ain't got no business poking around over there. It could be… dangerous."

"It's about to be dangerous right here, now that those slave catchers have caught up with us."

Slave catchers! It suddenly made sense. He'd stumbled upon a group of runaways. Seems he'd overheard something about a new law the deathlings had passed. Folks at the Crawford farm were talking about it. Even in a free state like Indiana, runaway slaves could be rounded up and sent back down south.

There was no way they were going without a fight.

Two hound dogs burst into view. The woman, Claudia, held out her walking stick with her right hand and angled her body away from them. She let a worn leather satchel slip off her shoulder to the ground. Danny dropped to a crouch.

"If you know what's good for you, mister, you'll stay nice and still till I say differently."

"But—"

"Shh!"

The dogs bounded forward.

The woman uttered a word. The nearest dog flew backward with a yelp.

Magic! Danny stood mystified as the woman trained her walking stick on the second dog. She blasted it just as she had the first one.

"You're a witch?"

"Later," she said. She held her walking stick upright. "They're coming."

Claudia was right; Danny heard the sound of approaching footsteps.

She began to chant a singsong tune.

"You find 'em, boys?" a man said. He lumbered into view on the edge of the corn field—big and swaggering, with a shotgun in one hand and a lantern in the other. "Chief? Banjo? Here, boys!"

Something told Danny Chief and Banjo were taking the rest of the night off.

Two more shadows joined the first. The woman kept chanting. Her voice was barely audible beneath the cold autumn breeze.

The three men trudged forward a few more steps, but slowly. The closer they came, the slower they got.

The first man toppled to his knees by the time he came even with the first of the unconscious dogs. The second brought his shotgun to his shoulder... but wobbled backward with the effort. A minute later, all three lay on the grass, mumbling and snoring.

"That was some mighty slick conjuring," Danny said.

"Not now," the woman hissed. She had spun around to see where her friends had gone. She gave an exasperated sigh. "They were right there!" she said.

"Uh oh!" Danny said. The others were nowhere to be seen—and Danny had a sinking feeling he knew where they had gone.

"Now, you gotta admit this ain't my fault!" he said. He looked about frantically. Surely they didn't...

"What?"

"I warned you those was my woods." He started toward the tree line at an easy lope. The woman reclaimed her satchel, hitched her skirts, and followed.

"I would think you'd understand why my passengers needed a place to hide!"

"Yeah, it's just... Well, maybe you'd better see for yourself." Danny came to a stop. He wiped his sweaty hands on his trousers.

"See what?"

"Um..." Danny held up his right hand. With an effort of will, he produced an orb of golden flame and held it like a ball.

The woman's eyes flashed as she jabbed her walking stick once more into Danny's chest.

"You're a witch, too?" she said, astonished.

"Not exactly." Danny looked down. The woman followed his gaze to the ring of mushrooms spread out in a circle eight feet across. A subtle wisp of sparkling dust rose from it like gold and silver fireflies.

When the woman raised her eyes to Danny once more, he had dropped the illusion of a human appearance. He stood before her with his eyes glowing yellow and the points of his ears peaking over the brim of his flat woolen cap.

"You're one of the Fair Folk." She said it without fear or amazement.

"A pooka," he said. "Danny's the name."

"And you just... left this portal open? What were you thinking?"

"It's Hallowe'en!" he protested. "You know how hard it is to shut a portal down proper on Hallowe'en? Plus, I was in a hurry! I still got three farms to visit! But if your friends stepped into the ring, we'd better—"

The witch didn't let him finish. She just barged into the mushroom ring and vanished.

Danny followed. With his first step, there was a brief shimmer of light and the feel of a gentle breeze on his face. Then everything was back to normal. He had crossed into the Wonder.

The witch was already ten yards ahead of him. She had cast some kind of light spell on the tip of her walking stick—not faery fire, but close enough—and was holding it over her head as she inched along the forest path.

"Susanna!" she called. "Elijah!"

No one answered.

Danny caught up with her. "Miss Claudia, is it?" he whispered. "My cabin is up ahead. Maybe they headed that way."

Her icy silence was all the answer Danny got.

"And keep it down, if you don't mind. See, I'm kind of expecting somebody… and…"

She walked away. Danny followed. A minute later, she offered, "Elijah's injured. He had a run-in with one of those catchers' dogs. And now this!"

"Look, I tried to tell you to stay out of the woods…"

"Now you listen here," the witch said, spinning back and drilling a finger into Danny's chest. Her voice was low but seething with anger. "Those people are my passengers. They're my responsibility, understand? If anything has happened to them… Well, sir, I wouldn't want to be in your shoes." Once again, the rumble in her voice got Danny's full attention.

"Yes, ma'am."

She continued down the path.

They inched forward. "Elijah!" Claudia softly called, looking this way and that. "Betsy! Timothy!"

"Turn left here, Miss Claudia. That'll take you to my place."

"Susanna! Can you hear me?"

There was a rustle in the trees. Claudia aimed her stick at something she thought she saw.

"Probably just little folk," Danny whispered. "They come around sometimes to bum tobacco or some such. They ain't gonna hurt nobody."

Claudia merely grumbled.

Just then a tiny man appeared out of nowhere on the path in front of them. He was barely two feet tall, dressed in buckskins, with his hair held back in a beaded headband. Claudia trained the glowing tip of her walking stick at him, and he let out a stifled peep of fright.

"Shh!" the little man hissed—even though he was the only one to make a sound. Danny reached for Claudia's hand. She yanked herself free and backed away from both men.

"We got trouble, Danny," the little man whispered.

Danny gestured for Claudia to hold her fire as he dropped to one knee.

"What's up, Littleberry?"

"Somebody's at your cabin."

"Well, good," Danny said. "We was looking for 'em. Four big folks?"

"Not good!" Littleberry said. "Those big folks showed up maybe five, ten minutes ago. But that's not what I'm talking about." He leaned in closer. "Greycoat's here."

Littleberry shuddered, and his whole body shook. If Greycoat gave Danny the willies, there was no telling what he did to Littleberry.

Danny swallowed. "About time."

"He just now showed up. I got out the back way and came to find you."

"Who?" Claudia said.

"By oak, ash, and thorn, don't he know I can't pay him tonight?"

"Who?"

"We had a deal. I can't do him no favors this close to November first! It's my busiest time of year!" Danny cursed under his breath. "Where are the four big folks now?"

"Me and the boys got 'em inside at your place. We just come by looking for you. We wanted to give you a present, tomorrow being your birthday and all. One of them's hurt. One of the big folks, I mean."

"I know."

"We glamoured 'em all up as best we could. I don't think Greycoat saw them."

"Well, at least that's something."

"Hey." Claudia snapped her fingers in front of Danny's face. "You want to tell me what's going on?"

"Let's just say I got some trouble with the landlord," Danny said. "And I'm sorry to say it, Miss Claudia, but it looks like your passengers are stuck in the middle of it."

"Show me."

If Danny never had another visit from Egil Greycoat, he wouldn't have shed a tear. But there he was, standing outside Danny's cabin with his arms folded, tapping his toes. His pale skin was only slightly darker than his long, platinum hair. His clothing, however, was dusky gray—topcoat, trousers, riding boots, sheathed cavalry sword at his side.

Above his head floated two blue-white will-o'-the-wisps. They flitted and flickered like living things, casting dim shadows on the ground.

The trunk of the Virginia pine at the edge of the clearing gave Danny, Claudia, and Littleberry a hiding place while they took it all in.

"Underhill!" the elf shouted. His accent was vaguely Germanic. "I would have words with thee."

When Greycoat was born, people still said "thee." Apparently, he never saw the need to change.

Danny gestured for Claudia to stay put. It surprised him when she obeyed.

He took a breath. There were four deathlings in his cabin with two or three little folk. One of those deathlings was injured, maybe badly. Danny figured Claudia could do something about his wound if she could get to him, but that was going to be the hard part.

The way he saw it, he had two advantages. One, the runaways were protected behind the threshold of his cabin. It wasn't much of a threshold: it wasn't much of a cabin! But every home generates a barrier against magical intruders. And unlike his little folk friends, Danny had never invited Greycoat in. If things went bad—and Danny didn't see how they wouldn't—his cabin would give everybody at least a little bit of protection.

Two, Greycoat didn't know about Claudia. Danny didn't know how much magic she could pull off, but she was a sight to see against those slave catchers. He'd have to keep her presence a secret if he could.

By contrast, Egil Greycoat only had one advantage: he was Egil Greycoat. He may not have been the match of a powerful sídhe, but Danny wouldn't have bet against him. He knew too well the elf was powerful, fast, and tricky. Furthermore, he was close to the Erlking of Twear—close enough there'd be the devil to pay if anything unfortunate ever happened to him.

More magic. Better connections. And Danny owed him a favor.

He didn't want to give away Claudia and Littleberry's position, so instead of just walking out of the woods, he blinked—disappearing and then reappearing half a second later in a flash of superheated dust. He chose a landing spot to Greycoat's left, in clear view of the cabin door.

"Evening, Mr. Greycoat," he said. He worked hard to keep his voice calm and light. Nope. Nothing odd going on. Not a thing.

The elf spun gracefully in his direction. His hand found a resting place on the hilt of his sword.

"Ah, Mr. Underhill," he said. He stared at Danny with his pale blue eyes. "I feared thou hadst forgotten our appointment."

"I ain't forgot," Danny said. "I been busy."

"Of course. I trust thou hast had a pleasant All Hallow's Eve? Oh, and happy birthday."

Danny risked a glance toward his cabin's door. No signs of movement. Good.

"It ain't my birthday till tomorrow, Mr. Greycoat. And if I might say, after the last dozen years, I'd have thought you'd figure out I can't pay the rent right now."

Greycoat made a slashing gesture, and Danny felt a stabbing pain at his temple. He gasped and fell to one knee as the world spun around him.

"I'll thank thee to keep a respectful tone, pooka," the elf said.

Danny looked up at him and wiped the sweat from his forehead with his sleeve. In the cabin, he heard the shuffling of feet, a stifled groan. His pointed ears instinctively pivoted toward the sound. If Greycoat heard, he didn't give it away.

"Do not forget, child," the elf said. "Thou wert the one who bargained with me for seisin of this valley and the mortal world beyond it. Thou wert the one who agreed to my terms: one non-negotiable favor, paid every year *on or before* the thirty-first of October. Thou art too young to be so forgetful."

Yeah, I really should have thought that one through, Danny thought.

He tried again. "Be that as it may, I'm busy. Tomorrow's November first, you understand? The Pooka's Day. Anything the deathlings leave in their fields after tonight is rightfully mine, but it won't last forever. If I don't take it now, I don't eat this winter."

"So you keep telling me."

There was another stifled groan from the cabin, followed by a sharp shushing noise. Another trickle of sweat snaked down Danny's neck.

"Why can't you come earlier?" the pooka said. "Why do you always gotta wait until the very last minute?"

"Because I can," the elf said, and smiled.

"Yeah, that's what I figured," Danny muttered.

"Now, down to business," Greycoat said. "I propose—" He stopped abruptly and whipped around.

Danny gazed at his cabin door. His heart sank.

There was the little boy, halfway outside, one of Littleberry's friends tugging at his arm, trying to hold him in.

"Thou hast guests," Greycoat said. His thin lips pulled back into a grin. "Thou didst not tell me."

"That's 'cause it weren't none of your business," Danny said.

Greycoat either didn't hear him or wasn't paying attention. Instead, he addressed the boy.

"Hello there!" he said, his voice dripping sugar.

The little person, eyes wide with fright, kept pulling on the boy's arm. The girl, maybe nine or ten, appeared in the doorway and set her hands on her brother's shoulders. Neither seemed able to pull their eyes away from the elf. The will-o'-the-wisps bobbing above his head had them mesmerized.

"Betsy!" their mother called from inside.

Greycoat dropped to one knee.

"I had meant to demand of thee a mortal child," Greycoat said. "What sayest thou, Underhill? I would forgive thy yearly debt for two fine changelings."

"No!" Danny blurted.

"Be sensible," Greycoat said. "'Twould spare thee time and effort to give me these. Thou couldst spend tomorrow collecting thy bounty in peace."

"Well, yeah, but—"

"'Twould be to their advantage as well, yes? They're slaves: that much is clear. What have they to hold them to human earth? I could give them their hearts' desires. Make them great. Powerful. Thou knowest this, Underhill."

Their mother came to the door. Danny tried to read her tear-stained expression: bewilderment, fear, awe. She'd heard everything the elf had said. She looked over her shoulder. Somewhere in there, her husband lay dying. What could she do for her kids alone in the world?

If Danny had kids, he couldn't imagine giving them up. But if he thought it would give them a better life?

What was going on inside that head of hers?

Greycoat reached into his topcoat pocket.

"What beautiful children," he gushed. "I have some chestnuts. Do you like chestnuts?"

He produced a paper sack and poured some nuts into his hand. Faery food. One bite, and keeping those children out of Greycoat's claws would be a hundred times harder.

The little person grunted, but the boy was too much for him. He pulled free and stumbled onto the grass. His sister shuffled after him.

A second little person appeared in the doorway. "Danny!" he squeaked.

"Now wait right there!" Danny shouted. "Those kids are under my hospitality. You can't just—"

Greycoat gestured again. Danny bent over and grabbed the sides of his head. Visions of torment passed before his consciousness: sheets of frigid water pouring over him, blinding lights, cold iron spikes piercing his flesh.

"Tone, Mr. Underhill," he said coolly. "Besides, they are mere deathlings. The Law of Hospitality doth not apply to them."

"Well, I say it does!" Danny grunted.

"Then what sayest thou to two years' relief instead of one? Two years for two changelings. 'Tis only fair." His eyes never left the children.

"What is thy name, young man?" he whispered.

"T-Timofy."

The little boy reached tentatively toward the treat in Greycoat's outstretched hand.

"What sayest *thou*, Madam?" Greycoat asked the mother. "Shall I make thy children free? Shall I take them to a place no slaver can ever reach?"

"Don't say anything!" A voice called from the edge of the woods.

Claudia appeared.

Greycoat was on his feet in half a second.

"He doesn't care about your children, Susanna," Claudia said.

She nursed a block of wood in her hands, no bigger than a brick. It had been carved into a vaguely human form, but stooped and snarling and angry like a wolf. A tiny mirror, flashing in the moonlight, was fixed to the figure's belly.

What kind of magic is that? Danny wondered.

The mother hesitated. She opened her mouth to say something, but her words couldn't find their way out.

"Thou dost these deathlings no service, young lady," Greycoat said as his eyes trained on Claudia. He flexed the fingers of his right hand. His will-o'-the-wisps grew brighter and bluer.

"M-miss Claudia," the mother whimpered, "Lige…"

She raised a hand, and the mother held her peace. "I've no quarrel with you, sir," she said. "But those children are my responsibility, not his." She gestured toward Danny with her chin. "And I mean to get them to Salem before daybreak."

Greycoat smirked.

"Thou wouldst be wise to leave them be," he said.

"I was about to say the same thing to you." She began to chant.

"Thou art loyal, no doubt, and brave. Be thou not stupid. Thou canst not—"

Claudia raised her voice. A mist began to swirl around her wooden figurine.

Greycoat whipped forward his hand to unleash a faery blast.

At the same time, something shot from the figurine—a glowing white ball of mist, but it was as fast as a cannonball.

Greycoat flinched. His blast struck harmlessly high in the trees.

Danny rolled out of the way. The mist had taken form: mostly human, but stooped over like something half-bestial and with an angry scowl. It sported a shield of animal hide on its left arm, and in its right hand it held a war club. It was on Greycoat in a heartbeat, pounding at the elf and driving him back from the cabin door.

Timothy stood stunned. Danny leaped forward and scooped the boy up in his arms.

"This way!" he called to the big sister. He grabbed her by the collar and hauled her to the cabin door.

Littleberry just beat him inside. The little person had Claudia's satchel. He spied where the injured man lay on the floor and hurried to his side. Three other little folk were already gathered around him.

"Tend to your brother," Danny told the girl. In a second, he was back outside.

By oak, ash, and thorn, he thought. *What next?*

Greycoat was fending off the mist-man with his sword. The side of his head was swollen and bloody, and he held his left arm close to his body.

Danny couldn't help but enjoy the beating this strange woman was giving his landlord. Then realization set in.

I am in so much trouble!

He had no love for his landlord, but he sure didn't need Greycoat's buddy the Erlking as an enemy.

"Whoa, whoa, whoa!" he called. "There's no need for—"

"Out of my way, pooka!" Claudia thundered. She advanced on Greycoat with steely determination in her eyes, which never left the mist-man she was controlling.

Greycoat fell to one knee.

"C-can't we just talk about all this?"

Claudia intoned another command. The mist-man hoisted Greycoat like a sack of potatoes and caught him in a headlock. Claudia smacked him on the hand with her walking stick. He dropped his sword, and she kicked it away.

She walked around the elf and the mist-man, tracing a circle in the ground with the tip of her stick, chanting as she went. Then she reached into a pocket on her skirt, pulled out a small pouch, and strewed a fine, silvery powder around the perimeter.

As she finished her chant, the air shimmered: her magic circle came to life. The mist-man dissolved into fog and blew away. Greycoat's orbs of faery fire vanished just as quickly.

Greycoat surged forward, but hit an invisible barrier where Claudia had drawn her circle. He recoiled as if from a hot stovetop.

"Underhill!" he spat.

"N-now... Now, Mr. Greycoat..." Danny started. "This lady, sh-she ain't... I mean, I ain't never seen her before... and—"

"Get me out of here!"

"Do it and face my hunter." Claudia held up her figurine. Danny jumped back.

"She's bluffing!" Greycoat insisted. "No deathling witch can throw that much magic. She's spent."

"You're welcome to test the man's theory, Mr. Underhill," she said. The rumble in her voice shook Danny to the core. "I wouldn't recommend it."

Claudia glanced toward the cabin. "I need to see about Elijah. Invite me in."

Danny's eyes bounced between Claudia and Greycoat. Even injured, the elf was seething with anger. "M-miss Claudia, I—"

"Now."

Claudia rummaged through her satchel and set a jumble of tiny packets and bottles on the floor beside Elijah on a handkerchief of homespun cotton. The little folk had cut away the leg of his trousers, exposing a cleaned but very nasty bite wound.

The figurine Claudia had used to summon that "hunter" thing lay at her side.

The mother knelt beside her husband.

Littleberry and his friends huddled in the corner, trying to distract or entertain the two children. They shot Danny worried glances.

Claudia set a short, thick candle at the wounded man's head.

"Light that candle," she commanded.

Outside, Egil Greycoat cursed in his native tongue.

One of Littleberry's friends squeaked with fright.

Danny pinched his brow. As if it weren't bad enough he was caught in this mess...

"What am I gonna do?" he muttered. "I am in so much trouble!"

"Underhill!" Greycoat barked.

"I said light that candle!" Claudia rumbled. "I don't have all day!"

Danny stooped over and produced a spark of fire in his fingers—not faery fire, but a real fire that ignited the candle's wick when he touched it.

"He's right," Danny whispered. "You ain't got much magic left."

"Plenty to deal with the likes of you," Claudia said. She began mixing ingredients in a wooden bowl. "Fire magic isn't exactly my specialty—but that doesn't mean I can't turn you into something tasty if the mood strikes me. Understand?"

"Now listen here!" Danny said.

Claudia turned away. She stirred her mixture into a pungent salve while chanting under her breath.

"I ain't done nothing to you!" Danny continued. "You're the one trapping my landlord in a magic circle, barging into my house..."

She started rubbing the salve into the wound on Elijah's leg.

"By oak, ash, and thorn, woman! Egil Greycoat is a pretty important fae in these parts! Sure, I don't like him, but I'm stuck with him, ain't I? I figure you and your passengers will be moving out as soon as he's able to walk." He gestured toward the wounded man. "But what about me?"

"Underhill!" Greycoat called from outside. "Get me out of here this instant!"

"You see?" Danny said. He shook his head and leaned back against the wall.

Elijah expelled a breath. Claudia caught his wife's eyes and nodded. She smiled and started to weep.

"Now you listen, Mr. Underhill," Claudia said. She rose to her feet. "You left open a portal into the Wonder. My passengers knew nothing of this world or its dangers—until now. If it wasn't Greycoat, it might have been any number of things: ogres, water panthers... I'll bet there are even horned serpents around here. Am I right?"

"Now, wait—"

"I've already told you these people are my responsibility. I promised to see them through to Canada, and I mean to do it."

"Underhill!"

Danny sighed. The throbbing pain that had been creeping into his head finally exploded. "Miss Claudia, I understand about keeping promises. I really do. But... Egil Greycoat!"

"Underhill, come thou forth at once, or thou art a dead man!"

Danny crumbled to the floor, his head in his hands.

"What are we gonna do, Danny?" Littleberry asked. "Without you to look after us..."

"I know, buddy. Don't worry. I'll figure something out."

He opened his eyes. Claudia was looking at him. Her expression had softened.

"Don't you have passengers to look after?"

She glanced over her shoulder. Elijah had drifted off to sleep with his head in his wife's lap.

"Underhill!" Greycoat shouted, and followed up with a string of curse words.

"I didn't mean to be rude earlier, Mr. Underhill," Claudia said. "I'm... rather passionate about my job."

"Yeah," Danny said. "I guess I can't blame you for that. I take it you're a runaway, too?"

She shook her head. "My mother was a slave. I was born free."

"Your ma, she escaped up north?"

"She... escaped."

Danny quirked an eyebrow. "You mean into the Wonder."

She nodded. "Soon after she met my father. But that's a story for another day." Her gaze drifted to Littleberry, who still cowered over Danny's shoulder.

"These little folk are your responsibility."

"You might say that," Danny agreed. "We look after each other. That's what happens in farm country—you probably know something about that. Neighbors help each other out."

"You rally together," Claudia offered.

Danny nodded. "Anybody has a barn to raise or tobacco to cut or hogs to butcher, people are proud to chip in. It's a point of honor."

"We're family," Littleberry said, puffing out his chest.

"The little folks are the best neighbors you'd ever want, but when it comes to dealing with the likes of Greycoat—"

"You protect them," Claudia said. "And by putting you in danger, it appears I've put them in danger as well. I assure you, Mr. Underhill, that was never my intention."

"Underhill!"

Danny sighed. "You got a long hike ahead if you plan to make Salem tonight."

Claudia stole another glance at her sleeping passenger.

"Elijah needs his rest," she said. "And it seems I need to help you find a way out of this mess I've put you in."

Claudia's hunter hoisted Danny by his belt and collar and flung him through the cabin door. He flew a good ten feet, hit the ground with a crunch, and rolled two or three times before stopping flat on his back.

"Underhill!" Greycoat called.

The hunter bounded after Danny. Claudia stood defiantly in the doorway.

The mist-man scooped Danny up and slammed him against a tree.

"Oof!" Danny gasped. *Take it easy, you misty oaf!*

"And never trouble my passengers again!" Claudia rumbled. She held her figurine aloft. The hunter dissolved into fog and wafted away.

Danny slumped to the ground.

Claudia disappeared inside the cabin. Seconds later, a parade of figures departed: Claudia, Elijah limping beside her, Betsy, and Susanna taking up the rear with a sleeping Timothy in her arms.

They made for the mushroom ring and passed out of sight.

"Underhill, dost thou hear me?"

"I hear you, Mr. Greycoat," Danny muttered. He summoned an orb of faery fire into his hand. "That witch was… just too much for me."

He struggled to his feet and stumbled toward his landlord, still trapped inside Claudia's magic circle.

"So it appeareth," Greycoat said. "Alas, those youngsters would have completed thy yearly charge. I fear thou must find me another deathling child, Underhill."

"Another one, sir?"

"Aye. That was the favor I bespoke. Or hath the witch's enchantments addled thy brain?"

"No, sir," Danny said. He kept his eyes down. "It's just—"

"Just what, Mr. Underhill? The terms of our agreement haven't changed this past hour."

"Of course not, sir. It's just…"

"Yes?"

"Well, I sort of figured you'd ask me to set you free from that circle."

Greycoat's mouth dropped open.

Then his eyes grew wide.

"Thou meanest to keep me trapped here?" Greycoat's cheeks, usually pale as chalk, turned rosy pink.

"No, sir! Not at all, sir!" Danny protested, still limping forward. "I overheard the witch talking about how she... uh... inconvenienced you like she did. I'm pretty sure I can reverse it. In fact, I know I can."

"Good!"

"Of course, if you'd rather have a mortal child, I can run out and find you one right quick. It shouldn't take more than a couple days. A week at most." Danny gestured dismissively. "There ain't no way that spell's gonna last that long, d'you think?"

"Underhill!"

"But it's all up to you, Mr. Greycoat. Whatever you want. You're the boss, after all. You want a deathling kid? You got it! I'll get on it right away."

"Get me out of here!"

Danny paused. He dared to look up into Greycoat's eyes.

"Well, sir," he began. He took a breath. "If that's the favor you're asking of me, I'm oath-bound to deliver."

Greycoat growled.

"And that makes us even, right? I done everything you asked." He chuckled. "'Cause everybody knows a fellow as close as you are with the Erlking would never go back on his word." He laughed out loud. "Could you imagine what the Erlking would do if one of his biggest buddies made a bonehead move like that?"

Greycoat clenched and unclenched his fists, helpless behind Claudia's magic circle.

"So... if you'd like me to set you free... and that settles our accounts... you just say the word... Sir."

"Free me," Greycoat whispered. "Now."

"I'll be right back," Danny said. He disappeared into his cabin long enough to retrieve a pouch of powdered herbs Claudia had left for him.

He tossed a handful of the powder into the air in front of Greycoat, and the magic circle collapsed at once.

Greycoat took a step forward. Danny backed away.

"If you're still interested in those deathling kids, I think they went that way," Danny said.

"This is not over," Greycoat said.

"Actually, sir," Danny said, "I'm pretty sure you gave me your word that it was."

Greycoat huffed. He retrieved his sword and returned it to his sheath. He stalked into the woods.

Danny sighed.

He shook his head.

He hobbled through the front door of his cabin.

"How was that?" he whispered.

"Perfect!" Claudia gushed. She held Susanna's hand. Elijah was sitting up at Danny's table with his arms around his children.

"But you sent Greycoat after your little friends," she pondered. She led Danny to the table and sat him down. His back was stiff. He ached all over.

"I sent him after *you*—Ooo!" Claudia began massaging his shoulders. It hurt like fire at first, but the cool touch of her hands soon eased his aching muscles. "Little folks are tops when it comes to glamour tricks like that. But I expect they took off those husks as soon as they were out of sight. Even if he runs into them in the woods, he'll never suspect *they* were the runaway slaves he saw leaving the cabin."

"You've got a devious mind, Mr. Underhill," Claudia said with a smile.

"I know another way back to human earth. When you're ready to move, I'll show you. It comes out by the Crawfords' place. They're Quakers, so they won't give you no grief if they catch you sneaking around. They might even put you up for the night. And it's Danny, if you please."

She came around in front of him and offered her hand. "You're too kind."

Then she turned serious. "There's no telling what Greycoat will ask of you next year."

"Well, that gives me a year to make other plans. See a little bit of the world. Maybe do a favor or two for the Erlking myself—just to be on the safe side."

"Something tells me you'll come out on top," Claudia said. "I'd like to think you'll be here next time I pass through, though. We got off on the wrong foot, I know. I'd like the opportunity to show you I'm sorry."

"It wasn't your fault I left the blamed door open."

"No," Claudia agreed. "It wasn't."

"Seems to me I owe you something for all your trouble," Danny said. "So if you do ever pass this way again, come on by. I'll show you and your passengers a fine time, and that's a promise."

"Perhaps I'll take you up on that, Mr. Un—Danny."

"I'd be honored if you did, Miss Claudia."

ABOUT THE AUTHOR

Darrell J. Pursiful is the author of the five-part Into the Wonder series of YA fantasy novels. He lives in Macon, Georgia, where he works both as a professional editor and a part-time college professor. You can find him online at intothewonder.wordpress.com.

Road Trip

Aaron DaMommio

E ven through the silver bars of his cage, bolted down behind the partition that separated the front and back of their panel van, Kane could see that Leann was stressed. Two hours of driving the icy interstate up from Oklahoma City would wear on anyone. He couldn't help her drive, so he was glad he could make her laugh.

"You're telling me Mikael Behrens showed up to one of your parties?" Leann said. "No joke, *the* Mikael Behrens? Did he sing, too?"

She'd opened the window between the compartments as soon as they got on the highway, away from the judgmental eyes of their teammates. Now it was just the two of them, on a mission Leann had engineered.

"He said he had a cold," Kane replied. "Didn't hurt his appetite any. I made a white gazpacho, sautéed summer squash, a chateaubriand with béarnaise, and a sorbet." What kind of sorbet, though? He frowned, trying to remember. Then he sighed. You couldn't get food like that now. The Calamity had cities turning in on themselves.

But that was what their mission was about. When no one else would lend Kansas City a hand, it was Leann's idea to send just one wolf—Kane—to stem the tide.

"There's your trouble, then," Leann said. "Shoulda stuck with sandwiches." Leann wasn't much of a cook, but she was constantly trying to get Kane to give her recipes for sandwiches. "A sandwich doesn't need a recipe," he'd say. Then he'd give her sandwich advice anyway. In the post-Calamity world, a sandwich was something attainable.

Kane couldn't see Leann's eyes, but he could imagine their small dark points, dancing to the rhythm of the laugh in her voice. He hugged his arms tighter around his midsection. The interstate around them was the kind of vast featureless expanse that only three days of snow could create, a white ribbon speeding toward them, barely visible through unfogged patches of windshield.

Leann started to say something, but he didn't hear what, because that was when they hit the ice patch. Leann slammed on the brakes and the van skidded. They cleared the guard rails in time to slide right into the ditch. There was a thump, and Kane blacked out.

Kane woke with a sharp pain in his right arm. His stirring arm. He tried to move it and almost threw up where he sat. The wrist hung at a sickening angle.

"Leann?" he called. Nothing. He couldn't see her from where he was sprawled.

He must've broken his arm hitting it against the silver-plated bars of the cage. The cage door was busted now, the structure bent so that it wouldn't latch. He could leave at any time.

But what about Leann?

Back in Oklahoma, Appleton almost never let him leave the cage. The head of Crisis Team Five liked to say that "safety first" was his watchword. It was clear he judged Kane to be anything but safe.

At first, Kane agreed with Appleton. After all, Kane had turned himself in. When he woke up in the alley behind the restaurant with blood on his hands, he knew it wasn't safe for him to walk around free. But he'd thought it would be different, working with a crisis team. Homeland Security was always on TV talking about how changelings like Kane were going to turn the tide of the Calamity. They were saviors, an antibody response to the walking dead.

Heroes.

As far as Kane could tell, though, Appleton valued Kane for exactly one trait: when he was a wolf, he'd eat absolutely anything. Which was why he and Leann were on their way to Kansas City. Leann's analysis showed that sending just one wolf to the beleaguered city could double its chances of holding out until real help could arrive.

Leann. Kane pushed himself to his feet with his good arm, keeping the broken one pressed against his body. He couldn't help moving it a little and a twinge of pain raced through him. He looked through the compartment window. Leann was slumped head down against the steering wheel. He called her name again but she didn't answer. That made it urgent.

He grabbed at the handle of the van's back door. It took him a second to figure out how to get the leverage to raise the roll-up door with one hand. Every move jostled his broken arm. When he lifted the door high enough for the springs to take hold, he stumbled out into the biting wind. His boots disappeared into the snow. Everything was white until he painted it orange by throwing up.

When the heaving stopped, he ate some snow, then loped to the front of the van. Another door to fight with, long seconds as he yanked at the handle and finally jerked it open and slid into the passenger seat, shutting the door against the wind.

"Leann, honey, you're gonna be all right." He lifted her head carefully. She seemed to be breathing okay but she didn't respond when he moved her. She was bleeding a little from a cut on her forehead. The metallic tang of the blood in the air reminded Kane how hungry he was.

But he couldn't think of that now. He opened the glove compartment, found a first-aid kit, and started fumbling with the bandages. It was awkward trying to move in the cab without jostling his arm, but he persevered, using his elbow to pinch the kit against his body.

Now he sniffed. There was something in the air he hadn't noticed before. Brown mustard. A bit of basil and olive oil. He looked down. A small cooler had slid out from under the passenger seat and spilled open in the crash. He'd almost stepped on them: a pair of sandwiches, each wrapped separately in wax paper. Real food.

His mouth watered. It had sat there in the cooler for hours and he didn't care. When he was a sous chef in Dallas, he'd thrown out better food. Now he'd have cheerfully killed for it. He reached down for them. With his right arm.

The pain drove the smell out of his mind. He yowled, then he took a deep breath, swapped hands, and grabbed one of the sandwiches. Roast beef, balsamic vinaigrette and parmesan cheese. Had Leann made these? He'd said something to her about basil with roast beef once. He unwrapped one and took a bite. It was heavenly. He gulped the rest of it down.

How long had it been? Just bread and meat, but all of it cooked for once, none of it spoiled. He slipped the other sandwich into his shirt as his mind raced ahead. He was still hungry. But he needed to plan. He was going to need some kind of a sling for his arm. And he needed to get into a coat. The jacket he'd been wearing in the cage wasn't going to cut it with the engine off.

But they were going to need help in any case. Leann's purse was on the floor of the passenger side. He found her phone, and when the screen lit up he sighed with relief. He dialed the Oklahoma office. But when he heard the voice that answered, he knew his luck was running true to form.

"Hey, Leann, how's the trip? That wolf give you any problems?"

Appleton was the last person Kane wanted to talk to, but as he'd come to expect since the Calamity, he didn't have any good options. "This is Kane. We hit ice about two hours out of town. We're in the ditch in the middle of nowhere, and Leann's unconscious. Can you find a militia group or someone to come pick us up?"

Appleton swore. "I knew I shouldn't have sent her out there alone. What happened, Kane? Is Leann all right?" He didn't ask how Kane was. Appleton had thought the one-wolf expedition was a great idea until Leann volunteered to drive.

"She's okay, best I can tell," Kane said. "Just knocked out. She's breathing fine, anyway. More than that, you'd need a doc to check her over. But it's cold here and getting colder."

Appleton swore again. "I'm picking up your GPS now. Database says we don't have anybody who can get to you before we can." He shouted something to someone on the other side of the line.

Kane knew the small towns along the highways were either deserted or hunkered down for the duration. He looked at the time on the phone. Only a couple of hours till moonrise. "It's getting dark," he said. They both knew the walking dead were more likely to stroll in the nighttime.

"I've already got a squad gearing up. But I'm assuming you're out of the cage?" Appleton said. When Kane didn't respond, Appleton swore a third time. Then his voice became oddly measured. "Can you lock yourself back in?"

"No, the cage is all bent. Anyway, I have to keep watch over Leann."

He could picture the frown on Appleton's face as he composed his next words. "Think about it, Kane. Think about what brought you to us in the first place. Your priority has to be getting far away from her before the moon rises. You know that, right?"

Bereft of its usual sneers, Kane almost didn't recognize Appleton's voice. "I can't leave her alone." They didn't know what the crash might have attracted.

"It's not what might be coming that worries me, Kane," Appleton said. "If you head south now, you can let the wolf out as soon as the urge hits you. Follow the highway, and we can pick you up on our way in."

A squad wasn't going to take the time to stop and net a feral Kane when they were on their way to save Leann. The best he could hope for from them was a silver bullet. "I leave her now, and we're both dead," he muttered.

"Kane, so help me, if you hurt her, I'll hunt you down if it takes the rest of my life."

Kane thought he'd never heard Appleton sound so sincere.

If Appleton had his way, Kane would never eat something as simple as a proper sandwich again. When he was a wolf, Kane only cared about finding his next meal. He wasn't picky about where it came from. Friend or foe were all the same when he was under the influence of the moon. And wolf-Kane was happy to scavenge.

The slow shamble of zombies made them easy prey, the rank taste was no deterrent, and his wolf-body healed their infectious bites in seconds. But a zombie whose brain he ate couldn't recover.

The last time Kane had eaten his fill was in Norman. Team Five rode into the city's stadium to rescue evacuees from an army of the dead, and Kane plowed through the hordes with abandon. But that was days ago. He'd had precisely one sandwich to eat in the time since. Appleton liked to keep his weapons sharp.

He stepped out into the cold. The front end of the van was in bad shape. He didn't see any hope of getting the van moving again. He headed for the cargo door.

He grabbed a shirt from his bag and started tying it into a sling, using his teeth to substitute for his damaged arm. The movements brought pain so strong he felt a fresh bout of nausea, and had to pause and gasp for breath. The urge to change into the wolf was strong. The pain would disappear, bone and flesh knitting together before his eyes, if he only allowed himself to change. But he couldn't risk doing that, not with both Leann and the moon so near.

The arm still ached after that but at least every movement wasn't agonizing. He put his coat on over that, then he stuffed his clothes back into the bag and carried them back to the cab, where he started piling them over Leann. Then he got the rifle from the rack in back of the cab and set it next to her.

Kane felt it like an itch between his shoulder blades. The moon was coming up fast. He had a decision to make.

He'd been happy to take this trip. Happy that Leann was willing to solo with him, and happy to get away from Appleton, even if it was only for a week. Plus he knew with only one person guarding him, there was a chance he could make his escape. He'd planned to spend his thirties yelling at sous chefs of his own, not being launched from a cage at shambling horrors, one monster aimed at the others.

But Leann had never treated him as anything other than a person. When she asked how his missions went, Kane put aside how much he hated to revisit the time he spent as a wolf, and told her how it felt to be a watcher in his own body, eating his way through the hordes, with Appleton egging him on.

He'd been working on control. He felt like it had eluded him from that first night when the moon spoke to him, waking a new hunger. Appleton hadn't noticed, but Kane knew he'd been making progress.

Still. He couldn't risk Leann's life. He pulled the remaining sandwich out of his shirt and set it on the upholstery in case Leann woke up hungry. Then he zipped up his jacket and headed out into the snow.

He heard the moans when he was a hundred yards from the van. He glanced at the sky. He shouldn't be anywhere near Leann. But when he looked back, he saw movement at the tree line.

If he loosed the wolf now, his arm would be made whole. He'd grow taller and stronger and win a fur coat. He could lope effortlessly toward the zombies with the speed of a hunter, and savage them with his long canines.

He could feast on their brains.

His stomach churned, but he wasn't letting that roast beef go so easily. Instead, he breathed in the cold air, turned back toward the van, and broke into a jog. The moon was rising, but it was still maybe twenty minutes from its zenith.

He should have taken the rifle. But he'd expected to wolf out as soon as he was far enough from the van. And with a broken arm, he could hardly use it.

Still, he'd watched ordinary folk fight zombies plenty of times. He kept his eyes open as he ran and grabbed the first large branch he found near the road.

When he reached the van there were three of them crawling all over it, looking for a way into the cab. They didn't even look up as he rushed among them swinging. He howled in pain and exultation as he laid about him with the branch.

He gritted his teeth as one of the dead shoved at him, jostling his broken arm. He whacked it with the branch, and it reeled back, but another one came at him.

This wasn't working. He couldn't do enough damage with a tree branch. He ran toward the hood of the car. It was low enough that he could jump onto the hood and then onto the roof.

Now he could play king of the hill with the zombies while he caught his breath.

The zombies, though, could climb up as easily as he could. He found he had to keep defending the front end while watching for the grasping hands of others around the edges.

That's when he heard it. The moaning was getting louder. He looked toward the tree line. Dozens of zombies, pouring out of the trees and running toward the road, fifty yards away from him.

"Change of plan," he muttered.

He leapt off the roof and started running toward the mob near the trees. He glanced back: his pals from the van had joined the chase. Up ahead, the mob was joyfully converging on him. He felt like a slow quarterback who'd unwisely decided to make a run for it.

But as the dead became a wall around him, he let go of everything he was holding back. His muscles expanded and his blood boiled. He let the sling fall as his bones fused together. His jaw stretched and his teeth grew. He threw his head back and howled.

His prey lacked the sense to run. They didn't understand that this was no longer a fight, but a feast. He struck with tooth and claw and his prey fell. The moon rose higher and he grew stronger. He smashed their skulls and tasted their brains. What had disgusted him before seemed like poetic justice, and not merely the best way to ensure they didn't get back up again.

Finally he stood in a circle of the fallen, breathing hard. Out of the corner of his eye he saw it. Movement, fifty yards away.

He bounded towards them, two body lengths at a stride. His teeth closed around the neck of one that was trying to scale the van. He leapt to the top of it, a metal hill he could now defend against all comers. It was familiar. It felt right.

When a hand reached for him, he grasped it as if to shake hands, pulled its owner up to the top, then slashed its head off.

At last there was only stillness around him. He gnawed on an arm while he listened. Nothing moved. But there was still something that bothered him. An enticing smell, and right below his feet.

He jumped down and stood next to the door. He found his paws knew what to do to open it.

The smell that had brought him here... he wanted it and didn't want it. It was something he shouldn't have. But the wolf didn't care about that. The wolf smelled fresh meat.

Then he smelled something else he'd missed.

The shouting brought him back to full alert. It was so cold on top of the van, he was on the verge of dozing off. As soon as he heard the shouts, he looked up and saw the two SUVs heading their way. The SUVs stopped a couple of car lengths away and eight men jumped out, fanning out around the van with weapons drawn.

Kane saw that Appleton was with them, looking awkward in his tactical vest, though his sidearm seemed to fit his hand okay.

When there was a break in the shouting, Kane spoke. "I'm putting the gun down." He set it on the roof. Then he stood up, slowly, counting off each movement, until he was standing tall with his hands high in the air. He put his hands behind his head.

The team checked the zombies in pairs, one member covering another as they poked at the bodies with rifles. Then they checked the cab and found Leann.

"She's okay," came the call, and everyone relaxed.

When it seemed safe, Kane jumped down. He let them lead him to the silver cage in the back of one of the SUVs.

They made it to Kansas City in time to take the wind out of the outbreak there. Appleton was hailed as a hero. Kane got all the brains he could eat.

A week later he was back in the cage. Leann came to see him. She seemed shy.

"How'd you do it?" she said. "No one's ever held back from the change during a full moon."

"Oh," he said. "No, I didn't hold back."

"You changed and then you sat on top of that van and left me alone, fighting off zombies? Quite the hero."

"Not exactly," he said.

He'd crouched there in the cab on the moonlight-dappled seats, listening to her breathing for a whole minute. At that range he could hear the blood rushing through her veins. Then he smelled it again. Basil and vinaigrette. The wax paper package was on the seat next to her, with his name written on it in magic marker. "I changed back. I'm sorry, though," he said.

She stared at him. "You changed back, during a full moon." She shook her head. "What on earth are you sorry for?"

"I ate your sandwich," he said. He still had the wax paper in his jacket pockets. Two pieces. One with his name, and one with hers.

"You remembered the basil," he said. "I could hardly eat you after that."

ABOUT THE AUTHOR

Aaron DaMommio has had stories published in Daily Science Fiction, Stupefying Stories Showcase, *and* Mirror Dance.

The Dove of Assisi

Troy Tang

Once upon a time there lived a young dragon, whose cave lay nestled within a great deep forest in the lush green land of Italy. The nearest village was many miles away—quite a way on foot, and only a little less by wing—and its inhabitants enjoyed a life of the finest quality. Plump, woolly sheep dotted the hills around the forest, accompanied by fat, sleek cows. In summer, the wheat-fields hummed with flies and farmers and the rhythmic swish of the scythe. It should have been a wonderful village for a young dragon like ours—after all, there were lots of good things to eat, and no dragon-hunters to bother him.

But it wasn't.

Perhaps an example will suffice. As we all know, dragons are meant to do three things: steal, hoard, and breathe fire. One day, in the woods near the old dragon's hunting grounds, a particularly plump cow presented itself for the taking. The new dragon crept out, the trapper sounded his bugle, and the villagers came a-whooping, waving pitchforks and scythes and torches and even the odd sword. But instead of baring his huge teeth or beating the air with his wings or even snarling, the dragon scrabbled around and flew off as fast as his wings could carry him, leaving some very disappointed villagers.

"For shame," said the baker, tucking his rolling pin back into his belt. "What a coward."

"Such a thin one, too," said the threshers. "We're going back to the fields."

"He's not a very good dragon," said rosy-cheeked Gianna, the most beautiful girl in the village, who had come to watch the fun.

"No, he isn't," agreed everyone, and they followed her all the way back home.

Our dragon went home, too. There was nothing in his cave save bones and a single coin of ancient gold. The coin had a hawkish man with leaves on his head on one side, surrounded by letters, and a woman with a sword and a sheaf on the other. On rainy days, he liked to pry the coin out and tap it with his biggest claw, which was as long as your left hand's index finger and thick as the last two. Dragons like the sound of metal. The bones were piled very high, mouse-bones and wishbones and the odd old dog's, but they were not the type of bones that any respectable dragon would be seen lounging over.

Our dragon had two squirrels and a thrush for dinner, and then he went to sleep. While he was snoring, little Pietro crept into his cave, squeaked, and ran out laughing. And that was how the whole village learned that their dragon was not just a terrible thief, but only hoarded bones.

"Our very own dragon," groaned the blacksmith over his dinner of rye bread, ham and lentils. "How will we face those louts from the city? They have one that's a field long, and bright purple to boot, and every month it eats twenty cows and ten sheep. And ours is whiter than my bottom."

"Just terrible," agreed his wife amiably. "More water, Gianna dear."

"Well," said beautiful Gianna, passing the jug with the cultivated air of a rural dilettante, "I think you're all being quite horrid. Think of it from the poor dragon's point of view. Why, if he could talk, I'd bet he'd tell you that he didn't like the way you looked, either."

The blacksmith snorted, rolled his eyes to heaven, then ripped his slice of bread asunder. Gianna gave her most offended huff. It was the blacksmith's wife who made to reconcile them, having, as mothers tend to do, a brighter brain than her daughter's and a damper fuse than her husband's.

"Now, now, dears," said the good woman, "you both know very well that dragons can't talk—although I do suppose it would be rather interesting. Imagine that, Father, a talking dragon! Why, they'd come to us from miles around. Even the city doesn't have one of those."

Father Adorno, who was seated at the table with them, wiped his mouth and looked solemn. He was a stern silvery man, not given to sentiment, and knew, among other things, that the village's old dragon had only been kept at bay because he was nearly toothless, that every week the city paid their dragon-hunters fifty silver pieces, and that young worms could grow older.

"I would beseech the help of San Giorgio," he said, and nothing more.

And so the months passed. There was one thing left for our dragon to do, which was breathe fire. He did breathe fire, or at least he tried. But it was more smoke than anything, a very weak and spindly fire, speckled quite often with dragon-spit. Sometimes, the village boys would sneak into his cave, holding sticks stabbed through with bits of raw meat, and see how many they could roast without getting singed. And as they scrambled out of the cave, laughing, with blue meat sagging from their wilting sticks, the dragon would curl up and look vaguely befuddled.

"I am meant to be a big and scary dragon," he told himself, "but instead I am small and weak. And the boys look very tender, but I cannot get at them. I cannot even breathe fire properly."

Now, dragons are smart, especially the weak ones. Unlike his little brother, the komodo dragon, who turns sluggish and lazy in the cold, the real dragon has a fire deep inside him, which keeps him cozy and alert even in the bitterest winter night. And because our dragon was small and weak, he had to think and plot and plan more than the big dragons, who roar and gnash and shake the world, spit a few blinding gouts of flame, and then swoop in amongst the panicked crowd and eat the stragglers. They are used to getting their way, the big dragons, but big our dragon was not.

So there he lay in his little cave, thinking, tapping his one coin, and munching the miller's housecat.

"I need a name," he decided. "All the great dragons have names."

It was not his intention to take a name like the one your parents gave you. Dragons have their own dragon names, but no one can pronounce them. No human can understand what a dragon is saying without a lifetime of practice, and as a rule, dragons do not come out to chat very often. No, what our dragon wanted was more like a nickname.

"I will eat my first person," he decided, "and then I will drag him out into the middle of the village. They will be so afraid that they will give me a name."

He did not know why he wanted to be feared, only that it felt very proper for a dragon.

At that moment, he heard a soft braying, and the dull pad of hooves on the forest floor. It was a donkey, he realized, and donkeys were smaller than horses, if a bit more ornery. He spat out the last fluffy bit of cat's-tail, crawled to the mouth of his cave, and watched.

The man on the donkey was very thin, with scabs and bruises all across his face. There was a large bald patch on the crown of his head, shaved around his pate so that his hair hung out like the crust of a hollowed pie. He wore a strange brown tunic, as rough as the sacks the miller kept his flour in, tied at the waist with a length of rope. His beard was thin and wispy. And as the donkey plodded along, the thin man sang a cheerful song. The song was in French, but even if you know French you would have a hard time understanding it. This was a very long time ago, after all. It went something like this:

Most High, all-powerful, good Lord,
Yours are the praises, the glory, the honor,
and all blessing.

To You alone, Most High, do they belong,
and no man is worthy to mention Your name.

Be praised, my Lord, through all your creatures,
especially through my lord Brother Sun,
who brings the day; and you give light through him.
And he is beautiful and radiant in all his splendor!
Of you, Most High, he bears the likeness.

Now, that is what we have from the Italian, as it was written down later—or rather, Umbrian, which is a type of Italian they spoke back then. But our dragon did not need any Italian or Umbrian or even French to understand it. Dragons can understand all the languages of the world, though they cannot speak them. And so our dragon decided that while this thin man might be stringy and lean and therefore bad eating, he was not very likely to put up a fight, especially if he sang songs like that in the middle of an unknown wood. Our dragon drew himself up to his full height, blew a great hacking puff of smoke, and flapped through the trees and down in front of the man like a big white pigeon.

The donkey gave a *hee* of surprise, and then a terrified *haw*. The thin man looked up, surprised; but it was the surprise of having an unexpected friend show up at your doorstep, and not the surprise of having a plow-horse–sized dragon land three feet in front of your face.

"I am going to eat you, thin man," said the dragon a little sheepishly, "and there is nothing you can do about it."

The thin man put a hand on his donkey's quivering neck, lowering himself slowly to the ground. The donkey stamped its hind hoof and grunted nervously.

"Go hence, Brother Donkey," said the thin man in Umbrian, "and may God be with you. Thank you for bearing me thus far."

The donkey bolted. Our dragon began to feel rather excited. This might actually work.

"Yes," he said, "that's right. Now, I've never actually eaten anyone before, so you'll have to forgive me if I'm a bit slow with the chewing. I really don't want to hurt you that much— oh, but you can't understand me, can you?"

The thin man looked up at him and smiled. It was a very gentle smile, and though the man's lips were cracked and parched with the sun and his teeth were all crooked it was much nicer than any of the sneers that the villagers gave him, even beautiful Gianna's.

"But I can," he said in perfect Dragon.

To say that our dragon was shocked would be an understatement. You might as well call the sea slightly wet.

"How?" he squeaked, accidentally sending a plume of smoke into the thin man's face.

"It is the gift of God, Brother Dragon," replied the man, wiping the soot politely off his face. "I have been sent with the blessings of my Lord Pope to the village up ahead. I have come to preach penance and sacred poverty, and to do mercy unto their poor and sick."

His hands, black and grubby, moved like flickering flames as he talked. Despite himself, our dragon was intrigued.

"What's your name, thin man?"

"I was born Giovanni di Pietro di Bernardone. But now I am Francesco, your brother."

Our dragon blinked. It was a kind of shuttering of his pale chalky eyes.

"But that doesn't make any sense. You can't be the brother of the sun and that donkey and me. You're just a man. You should be scared right now, or running for your life."

"On the contrary, Brother Dragon, we are all sons and daughters of the Most High. How can I be afraid, when my lady Sister Oak is right beside me, and my lord Brother Wind is fanning my face, and my blessed mother, Sister Earth, holds me like the hands of Our Father? How can I be afraid of Little Sister Death, when I own nothing, and will pass to my true abode at her demure touch? I am the least of my brothers and the poorest of servants, but my family—ah! how great it is!"

Francesco spread his hands, and his eyes danced in the dragon's way.

"You may eat me now," he said, with perfect sincerity. "Perhaps it is ordained."

But our dragon was beginning to have second thoughts about eating this Francesco. He seemed a bit addled, with all his talk of mud mothers who were also soil sisters and looked like big men's arms—but he could also speak Dragon.

"I'm sorry if I scared you," said the dragon, curling his long thin tail around his front feet and wrapping his veiny wings around them. "I haven't really had a chance to talk to anyone at all. I didn't actually want to eat you—well, I did, but not because I was hungry or anything—well, I am, but..."

He stopped, sounding quite miserable. Francesco looked at him with something strange in his eyes. Not hard like anger or watery like fear, but soft and sweet like dew.

Kindness?

"You need a name, do you not, Brother Dragon?"

"How... how did you know?"

"A little bird told me," smiled Francesco. "Come, stay still."

The man moved closer, then, as if seized by a sudden impulse reached out and placed his hands on our dragon's snout.

"Your scales are very beautiful," he said wonderingly. "White as snow."

Our dragon, who had never been called beautiful once in his life, looked terribly embarrassed. Francesco closed his eyes.

"You are Colombano, the Dove. Praise God, and do His will."

Now, what our dragon felt on becoming Colombano was a bit like what you feel after jumping into a hot bath on a rainy day, when you let the warmth sneak straight into your bones. He felt right all the way through, as if he had always been Colombano but only just realized it.

"Thin man?"

"Yes, Brother Colombano?"

"Wait here. I have something for you."

Dragons don't smile, because when they try they look horrendous. But as Colombano flew back up through the trees, scattering leaves like feathers from a burst pillow, there was a lightness in his wings that made him feel like a sunbeam. He whipped into his cave, nosing and clawing through the scattered white bones. To his surprise, when he came back Francesco was still waiting for him.

"Here you go, thin man," mumbled Colombano, proffering the glinting coin between his teeth. "You may take this."

It was like he had charbroiled Francesco's hair. The man stepped back, an expression of well-mannered pain on his face.

"No, no. I cannot accept this, Brother Colombano."

Colombano was confused.

"But aren't these what you trade in? You men do not hunt and refuse to live in caves. You need these bits to get food and shelter. Don't you?"

Francesco shook his head, poise returning to one of whippet-like grace.

"I have sworn to my Lady Poverty that I will forever abide by her sacred rule," he said with the air of a gallant knight, "and a man does not break his oaths. I shall never take from another what I have not earned with the work of my hands, and even then, I shall never carry more than I need to buy my daily bread. I have no purse, you see."

"Can't I pay you for your kindness?" pleaded Colombano.

"It was not I who named you, but God," said the thin man. "Shall I take from my Father His rightful due? Nay, Brother; the Almighty has no need of gold or silver. I feasted on a sop of bread this morning, with a sip of wine to grace my throat, and tomorrow I fast in thanksgiving. Give your coin to someone who truly needs it."

Colombano mulled this over.

"But the villagers are all stout and healthy," he said. "I have never seen anyone as thin as you. I do not think they would find much use for this coin."

"You have not seen," smiled Francesco, "because you do not seek them. But the widow and the fatherless and the leper are known to God, who hears their every cry, and it is to them that I am sent. If they are not in your village, you will find them elsewhere."

The thin man gave his blackened robe a final dusting, before bouncing jauntily on the balls of his feet.

"Fare thee well, Brother Colombano! Perhaps we shall meet again on the way back."

Colombano watched him until he looked like a little brown cocoon of cloth between the oak trees. Then:

"WAIT!"

The birds scattered and the dust ran. The trees trembled, shedding their leaves for fear, and the spiderwebs snapped for miles around. It was the dragon-roar, that incredible sound that nothing on this earth can ignore, the many-layered shout that shoots through every part of you and leaves your teeth a-quiver, like at any point they might start dropping from your mouth.

Colombano was a very small dragon, but he had roared just like any city's bane. And as he flew towards the cocoon he saw it grow larger and larger, until at last it was Brother Francesco again, with a bright spark in his eyes and a stray leaf in his hair.

"Did you forget something, Brother Colombano?"

Our dragon wheezed. He did not think he had ever flown so far so fast, even when running away.

"I scared off your donkey," he said, "and it is a long way to the village. Please, let me take you there."

He panted, smoke jetting from his nostrils, a desperate light in his scale-ringed eyes. Francesco peered at him.

"It would be an honor, Brother Dragon," said the thin man at last, and bowed deep.

Now, Colombano had never carried anyone before. You may not think this a big deal, particularly for someone as thin and bony as Francesco—but the fact is that flying with someone on your back is very different, and much harder, than giving your little brother a piggyback ride.

For one thing, anything that flies by flapping its wings has a very hard time of it. Their bodies have to be very light and their wings have to be very fast, and they end up using most of their strength in the air alone. The old winged horses flew only because of their godly blood, passed down their pedigree like drops of red in sea-foam; in other words, with something very close to magic. Dragons are much the same, but like all other things they have to keep a close eye on the laws of physics. Otherwise they would be prone to falling up and living backwards and all other sorts of chicanery, which is usually much more trouble than it is worth.

And so poor Brother Francesco, clinging with all his might to the scaly white neck, had his thighs and arms horribly battered from all the bucking and swaying, and poor Brother Colombano found himself pitching and swerving like a dizzy pigeon, trying with all his might not to drop the holy man.

"I'm terribly sorry about this," panted Colombano. "I never knew I was quite this bumpy."

"Even if I fall," said Francesco, "I shall meet our Mother Earth with praises. Or perhaps an angel shall catch me. Fly on, Brother Dragon."

"I'd rather not," said Colombano, and started to descend. At last, in jerks and spurts, they reached the forest floor. The sun was setting, and the shadows of the trees danced across the travellers' exhausted forms like fire. Francesco slid off the dragon's back, pulling his robe back over his hairy legs and tightening his cord-belt. Then he sat, sinking into a tree-root as if it were a cushioned chair.

"You are weary, Brother Colombano. It would do you good to take some rest, and fill your stomach."

"If you can go without food tomorrow," said Colombano resolutely, "then so can I."

Francesco stretched out a gentle hand and placed it on his flank.

"Fasting is a long study, my brother. It takes many years to learn how to conquer the pangs of the flesh and to learn to live without any luxury."

Colombano's stomach was growling, but the roar was still tingling in his bones. Now that his feet were on the ground he felt like he could do anything.

"I'm sure I can do it," he said.

"By no means!" cried Francesco, once again in the grasp of that curious animation. "If you fast to set your mind on our Father, please, heap that pile of leaves on my head. But if you fast merely in empty imitation of me, thinking that you cannot be second to a human, a mere bag of skin and bones and pious platitudes—why, then you commit the mortal sin of pride, which was ever the dragon's curse, and all your thrift will turn to avarice! Do not yield to it!"

The man's reedy voice stuck Colombano in the heart like a flashing rapier. Our dragon stared at him, stunned. Even his roar seemed like nothing now, a storm of vast empty bluster with no substance.

"I'm sorry," he said. "I'm not acting like a dragon should."

He raised his head and bared his neck, which is how growing dragons apologize. The older ones don't even think of it.

"On the contrary," said Francesco, all gentleness once more, "you were acting exactly like a dragon. But God has given you a name, and you must live up to it. It is no longer a question of your nature."

"Must I always be different?" asked Colombano wistfully.

The thin man reached into his robe with his spindly hands, rummaged for a while, and came out with a dry loaf of bread. There was only a small pinched-off hole in the side. It was very flat.

"I am a simple man," he said, "and barely lettered. But the auctors say that the Lord God created the dragons on the last hour of the Fifth Day, the mightiest things in all Eden; and that because of their pre-eminence He gave them many gifts. Wings to awe the beasts of the field and bid them worship, glittering scales to dazzle the eyes of the birds and all the things of the sea — and greatest of all, fire, to light the night for Man and keep him warm."

Francesco proffered the loaf in both hands, falling to his scabby knees. Colombano stared.

"Do not be misled, Brother Dragon! The cunning of your kin is naught but the shadow of their fallen wit, the gutted dregs of what once made Adam roar and Eve rejoice; for the whole of Creation was cast down when we sinned. But if you will humble yourself, as I am humbling myself before you, and serve, as I am serving you, then what your brethren have lost will be restored to you, and you will be whole again. For it is a great and glorious thing to be abased before men."

Colombano sniffed the loaf. It smelt homely, like nest-straw, and a little dry. It looked very nice.

"If I went and knelt before the villagers," he said, "I'm sure they would come and chase me away with their sticks and scythes."

"God knows," said Francesco evenly, the bruises shining on his face.

"I'm not sure I can eat that," said Colombano. "I've only ever had meat."

"God knows," was the response again. "Try it."

Colombano took the loaf in his jaws and chewed; slowly at first, but then ravenously. It was the nicest thing he had ever eaten, including the housecat. As it sank into his stomach and the weakness subsided, he tingled with warm bliss, just like he had on receiving his name.

And as our dragon swallowed and chewed and swallowed again, Francesco made a cross in the air above his head, and blessed him.

It was on the strength of that loaf that Colombano soared through the air the next morning, leaving the forest far behind. Not only that, he was getting the hang of flying with Francesco. The trees gave way to rolling hills and fields, speckled with sheep and cows that Colombano nearly shaved with his claws in passing. He dipped low for the sheer joy of it, for the smell of the summer flowers and the rush of the wind in his face. And as they flew, the thin man sang his song, bright as an uncaged bird.

Be praised, my Lord, through Sister Moon and the stars;
in the heavens You have made them bright, precious and beautiful.

Be praised, my Lord, through Brothers Wind and Air,
and clouds and storms, and all the weather,
through which You give Your creatures sustenance.

Be praised, my Lord, through Sister Water;
she is very useful, and humble, and precious, and pure.

Be praised, my Lord, through Brother Fire,
through whom You brighten the night.
He is beautiful and cheerful, and powerful and strong.

Be praised, my Lord, through our sister Mother Earth,
who feeds us and rules us,
and produces various fruits with colored flowers and herbs.

Be praised, my Lord, through those who forgive for love of You;

through those who endure sickness and trial.
Happy those who endure in peace,
for by You, Most High, they will be crowned.

The villagers had difficulty believing their ears.

"Did you hear?" asked the blacksmith's wife. "Our little dragon is winging it right towards us."

"The threshers say there's a man on his back," said the baker, filling her basket with sweetbreads and hearty loaves. "He's going right for the mill, they say."

The loaves were so crisp you could hear them crackle as she laughed. She pinched off a thumbful of bread and sniffed it.

"A bit dry today, don't you think?"

"It's your copper," shrugged the baker. "Take it or leave it."

"A man?" asked beautiful Gianna back at home, as her mother passed her the loaf. "Oh, I do so hope he's handsome."

She spread a thick slice of bread with white butter and tossed it on her father's plate. The blacksmith scowled. He normally regarded their dragon with a sort of vague contempt—after all, it'd never done anything save run away and steal the miller's housecat—but things were different when the brute was heading right for you. Even a stray ember could burn down a house.

"You get that thought right out your head, you stupid girl. Dragons don't bring anything good, not to your doorstep. And if that man so much as looks at you askance, I'll knock his head in."

"I think you're horrible," said Gianna, and tossed her hair. "Soon I'll be married to the dashing dragon-man, and I'll go to a big city where they mint their own coins and you'll never see me again."

"And the sooner the better, you ungrateful wench!"

But all in all, the idea of their dragon's arrival stirred enough of the villagers' interest to merit a small welcoming party at the mill. The scythes were cleaned and polished. The clubs had a few more nails hammered into them. The swords were oiled and whetted. The baker brought three rolling pins, in case he needed to throw one or two. The women (all excepting beautiful Gianna, who was right at the front with her hands clutched to her bosom) brought pots, pans, butcher's knives, and buckets in case anything burnt. The trapper dusted off his best bear-trap, set it right at the end of the bridge, and scattered his most expensive caltrops all around it. The hunters got together and pooled all their heaviest arrows, hiding in the balcony and windows of the mill. And the blacksmith stood amidst the crowded heads like a shark in a shallow pool, clutching his terrible forge-hammer and bristling like old Vulcan himself.

The only unarmed man among the lot was Father Adorno, but only because his vows forbade it. He was not particularly angry at the dragon, but neither was he against the mob. After all, it was better that the worm should die now, when the villagers were still capable of killing it, than for it to grow strong and sleek and impossible for swords to even scratch. Stewardship was all very well and good, but this was a fallen world; one still had to be practical. He was more concerned about the man. Little Pietro had said that he looked like a reed in a sack, with a rope around his waist. To Father Adorno, this sounded suspiciously like one of those crazy poor men who had nothing better to do than wander through villages, towns, and even cities, hectoring the good inhabitants for enjoying even the slightest bit of comfort. What were their names... Fryers Manure?

Father Adorno shook his head and frowned. He would not go so far as to see the man be hurt, but nonetheless he would have to be careful. No matter how weak the dragon, a mendicant would always be weaker; particularly a self-professed one. And the people were seething.

"What will you do in the village, thin man?" asked Colombano. They were nearing the mill now, a large wooden hut with a great wooden wheel on its side that turned and turned in the rushing river.

"Why, Brother Dragon, I shall do to them exactly what I told you before. Preach penance and sacred poverty, and do mercy unto their poor and sick."

"Well, there certainly are a lot of them," said Colombano nervously, "and they don't look very sick. They seem to be carrying some very sharp things."

"Even so, Brother Dragon."

"Why do you want to help them? They're not like you. They tried to hurt me, and laughed when I ran away, even though I had never done them any wrong. I only ate that cat because I was hungry, and could not live on squirrels for much longer."

"Yes," said Francesco sadly, "we are cruel and venal wretches. If all of us were like you, my dear Brother Colombano, and just as willing to repent, then my Sister Moon would not have to hide her face from all this suffering. But even so..."

"Even so?" asked Colombano.

"You were made in the image of fowl and fish and beast. Your wings and scales and teeth and claws tell you as much. You are at the apex of all things. Do you think yourself weak, simply for being a stripling? Look down there at the benign babe in its mother's arms, or the boy clinging to her skirts. See how weak the young of humans are."

"Yes, they are very small and pink, and have no scales. If I wanted, I could make a mouthful of any two of them. I think I feel better about myself now."

"You must do no such thing," said Francesco sternly, "or you will answer for it. Man is made in the Image of God. His immortal soul is not yours to take."

They touched down on the river's other bank, to a chorus of *ooh*'s and *aah*'s from the crowd, and more than a few scattered grumblings.

"Welcome, stranger!" cried a beautiful girl in a florid dress, fluttering her eyes across the bridge.

"Hah!" laughed the huge man with the hammer. "I think you should get your eyes checked, daughter dearest—just look at him! He's a bleeding-heart religious!"

"Well," pouted Gianna, "you don't know that. He hasn't even taken off his hood yet, and have you ever seen a habit quite like that? Personally, I think it's just one of those new city fashions."

"*Personally,*" yelled a rotund man in a flour-stained apron, "I'm more concerned about the dragon!" And he brandished his rolling pins in menacing glee, to a wave of general agreement.

"They sound very eager to use their weapons," whispered Colombano worriedly.

"Don't fret, Brother Dragon," murmured Francesco. "Are you resolved to do as you said?"

"I am," said Colombano.

"Then do it, and God be with you."

And Francesco took off his hood, showing his pie-crust hair, gaunt face, and crooked smile.

"Do not fear me, good people. I am your most humble servant."

"So he *is* a religious," squinted a little old man.

"Oh, the poor dear," clucked a bevy of matrons. "Look how thin and pale he is. He needs to be fattened up."

Gianna wilted visibly. It was Father Adorno who stepped through the crowd, a serious look on his stern face.

"Don't take a step further, young man," he warned. "The ground at your feet is strewn with caltrops, and our hunters are quite ready to poke a few holes in your dragon's wings should he so much as flap them. Where did you get that tonsure?"

Francesco gave a deep and theatrical bow.

"I am at your service, Father," he said, voice filled with deep and genuine feeling, "but my Brother Colombano is his own dragon."

"What did he call him?" choked the blacksmith.

"Beats me," said the baker. "He's off his rocker, he is."

"Know that I took the tonsure in Eternal Rome, after kissing the ring of our Lord Pope and obtaining his blessing. I am Francesco of the Friars Minor."

There was a general ripple of disbelief at this. Could this scruffy man possibly have seen the Holy Father — nay, even been to Rome herself? Never mind that, what was a Fryer?

"If you have truly obtained the blessing of our Lord Pope," said Father Adorno in measured tones, "then surely you must have his seal in writing. Where is it?"

"Alas," said Francesco, "it never occurred to me that I could ask. You see, I am not very wise. But I was assured that my Lord Innocent's word was his bond, and that all Christendom would know it."

"Yes," said Father Adorno. "I think I do see. Thank you."

"Now look here," roared the blacksmith as he shoved his way to the front of the crowd, "what exactly did you bring that dragon here for? I know you've come here to beg, but you don't need that worm here with you — unless you want to use his mouth as an almsbowl!"

The big man opened his mouth to laugh, glanced around at the other villagers in the hopes of some mirthful accompaniment, got none, and then laughed anyway, which sounded a bit like a nervous shark gargling sand. Francesco did not stir. He looked straight across the river into the blacksmith's eyes, a strange fire flickering about his countenance, until at last the burly man flushed and jerked his head away.

"If you please, Brother Dragon."

The crowd gasped. The women blanched. A few men staggered. For the noise that came from the thin man's throat was not the voice of any man, but a guttural growl, deep and beautiful, full of the sound of mountains melting in a hidden furnace that no mortal eye could see. And Colombano bowed his head and knelt, eyes closed, his white nose touching the grey silt in the grass by the river.

"Friend Miller?" asked Francesco in Umbrian.

"Yes?" The miller was a stocky man, dusted with flour like the baker; but unlike the latter he looked rather bored with the whole business.

"Brother Colombano asks forgiveness for stealing your cat, and eating her. He wishes to make restitution." And Francesco produced the old gold coin from inside his robe, tossing it up and catching it in the other hand like a juggler's ball.

"*See?*" howled the blacksmith. "He has money!"

"Is that real gold?" baulked one of the threshers. "That's a month's wages, at least!"

But the miller grunted.

"Ah, I had a feeling that old puss was going to end up eaten one day or another. She barely earned her keep, neither—lazy as a sack, she was. Mice all over. Keep your coin, young'un, and God bless you."

"It isn't mine," said Francesco, with a twinkle in his eye.

Colombano raised his head from the grass and blinked.

"Hold it!" yelled the blacksmith again, face red. And he jumped straight into the river, fording it with barely a stumble. He came up with his breeches and apron soaked, staring down at Francesco like a thundercloud.

"You think you can worm your way out of this with a few fancy words?" he hissed. "I know your type. You'll wait until the night comes, and then get that pet salamander of yours to burn this whole village down!"

"If that was what I wished, my Brother Blacksmith, would I not have done it already? You are all out here, and your houses are unguarded."

"That's... I..."

Uncharacteristically, the blacksmith actually thought about this — the sheer effort of introspection made him sputter and spit like a quenched poker, and his hands, quite confused, clenched and unclenched on the hilt of his hammer. From the middle of the bridge, Father Adorno spoke again.

"If you truly are a holy man, and not a magician in league with the Devil," said the practical priest, "then show us a sign."

"I have asked nothing from you," smiled Francesco, "save absolution for my Brother Dragon, and offered you nothing save his indulgence. I came to you in broad daylight, and before me the birds sang of my coming. Which of you have I tempted or led astray?"

"There is more than one way to tame a serpent's tongue," replied Father Adorno, eyes clear. "I charge you to do this in the name of Christ."

Francesco nodded, then bowed low to the priest of God. He laid a spindly hand on the blacksmith's shoulder, who with a furtive start made way for him. Francesco raised his hands and closed his eyes, and the sun seemed, for a moment, to bend his radiant head, kneeling in honour of the sorry shabby man with the sores and sackcloth.

"Brother Colombano, in the name of Christ, speak to your masters and beg pardon."

The dragon raised his head from the bank, looking quite confused.

"Well," said Colombano in a thin reedy voice, "if they don't mind hearing any more Dragon, then I guess I will. I really am terribly sorry about all this trouble. I didn't..."

And then he stopped short, because he realized that he was speaking perfect Umbrian, and that everyone except Francesco was staring at him with their jaws on the ground and their eyes six feet out in the air.

"A miracle," whispered Father Adorno, and crossed himself.

"A miracle?" balked the baker, shoving his rolling pins back into his apron-strings with some haste. The third pin fought back, wiggled, and burst them with aplomb.

"A MIRACLE!" bellowed the blacksmith, before sweeping Francesco onto his hulking shoulders, running pell-mell back across the river, and tossing the hapless mendicant into the arms of the rejoicing crowd. The trapper swept the caltrops off the bridge. The hunters dropped their bows and tussled to be the first out the mill. Beautiful Gianna led the women in a hymn of thanksgiving, fluttering her eyelashes violently, and warbling completely off-key. The miller raised not one, but two eyebrows.

"Oh dear," said Colombano, and at this everyone cheered even louder.

"A feast!" cried the threshers. "A feast for our talking dragon!"

"A feast for the holy man!" echoed the crowd, the blacksmith loudest of all.

"If it's all the same to you," said Francesco serenely, bouncing up and down on the wave of heaving hands, "I'd rather have some water."

But Colombano sat at the other end of the river, feeling completely addled, a little overwhelmed, and ridiculously, impossibly happy. There was a shifting by his snout, and a nervous cough. It was Father Adorno, who, uncertain how exactly to address a dragon, was looking somewhere in the vicinity of his left nostril.

"I have wronged you, dragon," said the priest, "in both word and thought. I blinded myself to the hand of God, and let my pride unman me. Forgive me."

"Well," said Colombano, still somewhat surprised at his own new-found power of human speech, "I don't see how you could've done any different. And I did steal that poor cat, so, ah, well..."

The dragon thought for a few moments, leaving the anxious priest with bated breath.

"Would you like to fly?" asked Colombano at last.

If you had been at the feast that night, or indeed for many nights to come, you would have seen a small but noble dragon, in bright and beautiful white, sitting at the table of honor in the center of the village square. And you would have seen children scrabbling up and down his tail, and a garland of flowers on his neck, and a beautiful new-forged harness on his back; limned with copper, gleaming in the firelight, and bathed in the fragrance of roast lamb and the sound of laughter from the tables all around him. And every few minutes some reveler would yell out a wine-sodden question, and the dragon, terribly embarrassed, would have to answer, and everyone would hoot and applaud and stamp their feet.

(There was a priest, too, with stray feathers in his cassock and honey in his hair, but his legs were still too weak to stamp on anything.)

And if you stared hard enough at the dragon's side, you would have seen a poor mendicant with a trencher of bread and a wooden cup of water, holding up the dragon's whole left wing like a bale of precious fabric, and singing. And the song he sang went something like this:

Be praised, my Lord, through Brother Dragon;
He is bright and noble, and fiery, and great beyond compare.
His speech is the laugh of mountains, and his wings are the envy of birds.
His flame is warm and tender, and awful and strong; and of all your creatures he is first.

Be praised, my Lord, through our sister Bodily Death,
from whose embrace no living person can escape.
Woe to those who die in mortal sin!
Happy those she finds doing Your most holy will.
The second death can do no harm to them.

Praise and bless my Lord, and give thanks, and serve Him with great humility.

ABOUT THE AUTHOR

Troy Tang hails from sunny Singapore, but currently resides in Auckland, New Zealand. He has been previously published in Apex Magazine. *You can find more of his serial fiction, articles and assorted musings at https://steemit.com/@t2tang, with a static directory at troytang.wordpress.com/works/.*

THE UNANSWERED RIDDLE

TOM JOLLY

L amatia handed Dr. Hamilton a clipboard as they walked down the sterile white hallway. "It's down on the receiving dock. Too big to get into one of the exam rooms."

Hamilton glanced down at the giant fairy. "Big, huh? Human intelligence?"

Lamatia waggled his head. "Sort of. Can't hardly get it to shut up with its stupid riddles, and its handler is being careful not to leave it alone so it doesn't kill anyone. He has to keep reminding the thing that it's not at home, guarding the family jewels."

Hamilton flipped through the charts. "This is really supposed to be a medical problem?"

"So they say."

"'They' being…"

"The handler is some sort of pharaoh prince. The sphinx is bound to him somehow and does what he tells it to. It's his coffers the thing apparently guards. Been in the family for three thousand years, he says."

Hamilton whistled. "Good rejuvenation mechanisms, I guess. Vamps do that well. I wonder if the sphinx is using a similar process."

Lamatia winced at the use of the diminutive 'vamps', even though he knew Hamilton used to date one, off and on, and so might be excused for the familiar usage. "I don't think so," he said. "It clanks when it moves."

"Hmm." Hamilton perused the clipboard as they walked down the hallway. "Riddles are out of sync? What do you think that means?"

The fairy shrugged, a motion amplified by the lumpy wings concealed under its coat, giving him a hunchbacked appearance. "I didn't ask a lot of questions. Every time I asked a question, the sphinx asks one back, and won't answer anything else until I come up with an answer to his stupid riddle. Which I haven't done successfully, I might add. Really exasperating."

They walked through the double doors onto the receiving dock together. Off to the left was an enclosed storage area with a roll-up door, and a personnel door to the side. "Over there," Lamatia said.

There was a small crowd on the dock looking expectantly at the roll-up door, as though the sphinx might explode out of it at any moment. Piles of boxes were stacked outside the roll-up door to make room for the sphinx inside. Hamilton nodded to Medjine at the admittance desk facing the rear of the building. At Backside Clinic, all the supernatural customers entered via the alley door, which was carefully glyphed by a local witch so normals would ignore it. Medjine nodded back, her eyes showing narrowly through wrapped layers of cloth, an affectation that conveniently hid all of the decaying bits of her body. A sandalwood incense stick burned nearby to help cover the odor. Ventilation fans carried away the worst of it. Even the undead needed work, and how many businesses dealt with this segment of society?

Hamilton entered the large room with Lamatia in tow.

The sphinx was large, filling a good portion of the storage area. Standing next to him was the prince, dressed casually in loose-fitting slacks, penny loafers, and a silk shirt. "Doctor Hamilton?" he asked. Next to him was the sphinx, who looked down at Hamilton and Lamatia, and snorted. The smell of oil and burned wire filled the room. Hamilton raised an eyebrow as he took in the sphinx. The sphinx was mostly brown, with reddish-amber eyes. Its skin looked like a cross between sandstone, brown fur, and rust, while its claws appeared to be no more than an extension of the rest of its hard body. It slid its tail across the floor, making a sound like a jeep driving down a dry gravel creek bed.

He approached the prince. "Hi. I'm Dr. Hamilton. This is my nurse, Lamatia."

The prince nodded. "I am Prince Abdul al-Debaran. And this is my sphinx."

Hamilton glanced at his clipboard. "And he has a problem… with his memory?"

"Yes, he…"

"I do speak, you know," said the sphinx. Its voice rumbled like a bass drum.

The prince glared at the sphinx. "And he interrupts me constantly. If you have a medical treatment for that…"

"So you can just ask me what the problem is," continued the sphinx. "Please. I'm all ears."

Hamilton cleared his throat. Lamatia waved his hand to get his attention. Hamilton bent over while Lamatia whispered urgently in his ear. "Oh yes… asking questions is a bit of an issue here, isn't it?" Hamilton said.

The sphinx's ears twitched forward, stone appearing to flex like candle wax. "Was that a question?"

"No, no, just a rhetorical comment." He looked at the clipboard. "It says here your riddles are out-of-sync. Can you explain—or rather—please tell me what that means."

The prince nodded respectfully at the artful twist of a question into a command. The sphinx raised the corner of one rocky lip. "It began nearly four hundred years ago. You understand I don't get a lot of visitors, so it took a while before I or my master figured out that there was a problem. The prince observed me consuming a man even though he answered the riddle correctly..."

"A servant," the prince interrupted, dismissively waving a hand.

Hamilton glanced between Prince Abdul and the sphinx. "Ah, well, *that's* all right, then." Neither of them noticed his sarcasm. He tapped his clipboard and frowned. "You mentioned that your sphinx is 'out of sync'?"

"Yes. A few more riddles established that the answers he wants are for two riddles later than the riddle he asked. They are mismatched—staggered, offset. If they were offset in the *other* direction, this would not be much of an issue. The servants could just record the answers it gives two riddles ahead of time and provide those answers to get past it during their duties, and the thieves... well, it would just provide an extra level of inconvenience for them. But as it stands, the sphinx asks a riddle now, but in response, expects the answer to a riddle it will ask two riddles from now, which is inconvenient for everyone."

"And if the person gets a riddle wrong..."

"The sphinx eats them, assuming I am not there to control its base impulses."

Hamilton looked up at the sphinx, who smiled a toothy quartz smile at him. Turning back to Prince Abdul, he said, "This doesn't exactly strike me as a medical issue. Why did you think I could cure it of this malady?"

"You have quite a reputation in the supernatural community. There are stories about you that are frankly unbelievable, I admit, but this is certainly worth a try. I am quite fond of my sphinx."

Matthew Hamilton tapped his clipboard with a pen, a tiny rhythm that he ended with a snap of the clip. He prided himself on weeding out the supernatural mumbo-jumbo of each case and digging down to the roots of the natural causes. He was a cynic surrounded by the supernatural, mechanistically devolving each bizarre illness into its mundane natural elements with the thorough insight of a scientist, pulling the sense from the nonsense. The things he couldn't explain, well, those were the things he just hadn't looked at closely enough yet. Everything had an explanation.

"You understand, I hope, that we have a policy here about patients not being in the business of killing people. Things that go bump in the night have to forego their bumping-off tendencies before we cure them of their ailments. If we heal a werewolf, we have to be sure that it isn't going to run out and snack on a bunch of locals on his way out of town. In your case, you have to swear that your sphinx isn't going to be consuming any more humans, and that you will take measures to remedy your creature's diet."

The prince frowned, cleared his throat and swallowed. "Swear how?"

"We have some documents to sign." *Written by our onsite contract demon, who has some expertise in the matter,* Hamilton thought.

"Ah, well. I can certainly do that." He smiled again dismissively, his voice full of disdain.

Hamilton stared at him for a moment before saying anything else, just to make the man nervous. "I'll hold you to that." The prince's smile became somewhat strained. "Do you know how the Sphinx was created or spawned originally?" he asked the prince.

"How? Not in any detail. A magician working under Khafre created this one, some 4500 years ago. His techniques have been lost or hidden away in Khafre's tomb. Either way, they are long gone."

"Too bad." Hamilton walked around the sphinx, who tracked him with its crimson eyes. There were no openings or panels in the beast besides its mouth, no joints where stones connected. When the sphinx rolled a shoulder, the apparent stone surface stretched and compressed like taffy. He reached out and touched the skin. It was cool and hard, and gritty like sandstone. He turned to the prince. "When it... eats... does it excrete?"

The prince looked startled and pulled at his short beard. "You know, I am not certain. There has never been a need to, well, clean anything up. So perhaps not. Perhaps those that he eats become part of him."

"Hmm." Hamilton continued to circle the sphinx, inspecting it. He came to a stop in front of it, the sphinx staring down at him impassively. "Do you mind if I spend a bit of time alone with it?"

The prince frowned. "It's quite dangerous. Unless I'm here to override its natural tendencies, I'm afraid it will trick you into asking it a question, and then..."

"Please trust me in this. It will not be a concern."

Prince Abdul looked doubtful, but shrugged. "Very well. If half the stories about you are true, then perhaps you will survive."

Hamilton bowed slightly to the prince and said, "Thank you. I will call you in when I'm done. Lamatia, you leave too. I don't need any casualties today."

Lamatia nodded and left with the prince.

"Corwin?" Hamilton called to the air.

A ghost materialized in the room. It wore a rakishly tilted fedora and a light-blue suit. "Yes, boss?"

"I need to see inside this creature and I don't think x-rays are going to cut it."

Corwin glanced at the sphinx, who stared back at the ghost, unperturbed. "What am I looking for?"

"I think this creature is an ancient computer, like a Babbage machine, but with an artificial intelligence. I would like to know what mechanism inside is out of whack. Perhaps a tiny gear or pulley, some damaged mechanism that should be whole, but isn't. Probably not a printed circuit board."

Corwin stuck his head through the side of the sphinx, then pulled back out. "What am I getting paid this time?"

"Isn't haunting the hospital payment enough?"

"How about some more audio books?" Corwin suggested.

"I'll see what I can do." Hamilton said.

Corwin entered the side of the sphinx, then came back out a few seconds later. "It's dark, and there are lots of mechanical noises, like the inside of a large watch."

Hamilton rubbed his forehead. "And?"

"And I can't really see in the dark."

"Can't you glow or something?"

"I'm a ghost, Doctor, not a candle."

Hamilton pulled a small exam-flashlight out of his shirt pocket and turned it on. He sighed. They weren't cheap. He held it up to the sphinx and said, "Eat this."

"Not without a riddle. And you attached to it."

"Do I need to call the Prince back in just to order you to do it?"

The sphinx rolled its eyes. It snapped the flashlight out of his hand, tilted its head back and swallowed.

"Now, Corwin?"

Corwin reentered the sphinx, returning in a few moments, a look of surprise and wonder on its face. "It's... quite unusual. It's much larger on the inside than the outside. A vast room, I think. I'd look around a bit more, but I can't pick up your flashlight, you know. There's at least one corpse in there that I could see."

"A room I could stand in?"

"Oh, easily, Doctor Hamilton."

He looked up at the sphinx's mouth. One way in. He clutched at the pendant hidden under his shirt, the gift from his vampire girlfriend that kept him from getting torn apart more than once. This would certainly be a test for it. It was the one thing that let him function safely as a doctor to the supernatural community.

"I'm afraid I need to ask you a riddle, sphinx."

The sphinx jumped up like a puppy, swinging its stone tail back and forth, flipping over pallets and tables.

"Once I'm inside you, how can I get back out again?" Hamilton asked.

The sphinx frowned, leaning over him threateningly. "It must rhyme, human. Else I get to ask the first riddle. You have one more chance."

What rhymes with escape? Crepe? Gape? Tape? Or with eaten? Beaten, neaten, Wil Wheaton? Hamilton thought hard. He didn't know how much time he had to compose his poem before the sphinx tried to eat him. *Out again, big fat hen.*

He smiled and held up a finger. "If you consume me like a grape, what are the means for my escape?"

The sphinx winced. He sat back on his haunches and said, "That's not a riddle, it's just a question that rhymes. But I'll give you points for the iambic tetrameter. Here is my answer; A reversal of fortune will come if you but say it."

"Wait a second. You answered my question with another riddle?"

The sphinx shrugged, accompanied by the sound of crunching gravel. "You gave me a riddle that was not a riddle. I gave you an answer that was not an answer. It seems fair, does it not? Now, my riddle for you. You have but a minute to ponder it, or I will consume you;

"An answer to all questions,
This proper response we condone.
The truth is undeniable
If the answer is unknown."

Hamilton already knew the sphinx would try to eat him; in fact, he depended on it; but he was a little disconcerted that he didn't know how to escape from its innards. A reversal of fortune would come if he said it? What did that mean? If he wanted to continue his medical practice, he'd need to do it from the outside of the sphinx.

"Do you chew a bit before you swallow?" he asked.

The sphinx scraped stone claws against the cement floor, gouging it. Hamilton thought about adding that to the bill. "Is that your answer?" asked the sphinx.

"Just a question. You're out of sync, anyway, so it's somewhat irrelevant what answer I give you, isn't it?"

With that, the sphinx gleefully snapped up Hamilton, tilted its head back, and swallowed him whole. Hamilton held onto his pendant as he slid down a marble-slick gullet, landing on his back on a stack of old clothing. The clothing crunched as he hit it. His previously consumed flashlight, jostled from his impact, rolled around until it swept across the empty eye sockets of a desiccated corpse. He quickly pushed off the dried body and picked himself up, dusting the flakes of bone and skin from his clothes, trying not to breath until the dust settled, and once again grateful for the pendant that Clare had given him. Otherwise, the sphinx would have broken his back when it grabbed him. He pushed his black hair back from his eyes and looked around.

It was, indeed, much bigger on the inside than the outside. His flashlight swept across a blue vest that moved toward him. "Hello!" said the apparition.

Hamilton fell backwards, dropping his flashlight and cursing, then rummaged around on the floor for it. He glared at Corwin. "I really wish you wouldn't do that."

"My goals as a ghost today are fulfilled."

"Ha, ha." Hamilton retrieved the flashlight and swept its beam around the floor. It was littered with corpses. Most of them appeared to have broken necks or backs. A few of them were piled together near the end of the sphinx's gullet. Two metal cables were strung up along the inside of the sphinx's throat, which led back to a diaphragm attached to a large mass of gears. "Voicebox, maybe," he muttered. "Wow. Prince Abdul really needs a mechanic, not a doctor." The ghost hovered next to him as he walked around the room examining the mechanisms surrounding him. The machine had layer upon layer of densely packed gears, levers, and springs, the deep complexity of the assembly blocking the flashlight's penetration after a dozen feet or so. Each wall of the huge room was merely the first layer of a mechanical computing device, fifty feet wide on each side and thirty feet high. A narrow passage at the back beckoned to him.

Treading quietly down the passage, he came to a smaller chamber. Inside was a table with scraps of paper, hieroglyphs and mechanical sketches scribbled upon them, scattered dry remnants littering the floor. A dried inkwell and quills rested in grooved recesses on the table. To the right was a mummified man holding on to the handle of a pickaxe. Above him was a meshed set of metal gears. One of the gears was missing a tooth. He looked around the corpse, and saw the sheared metal tooth lying near the head of the pickaxe. How did he get the pickaxe inside the sphinx? Or was the sphinx just too dumb to realize that eating a man with a pickaxe would give it indigestion?

So, maybe the gear skipped an answer one time, then a hundred years later, it missed another answer, and ended up two behind. That would mean that eventually, given another full rotation of the gear, it'd be off by another answer. The dead man with the pickaxe couldn't have known what he was doing, angry and confused, swinging in the dark.

Hamilton bent over the corpse. It looked like he had a broken back, too, like many of the other corpses. Dried-out blisters covered his face and skin like small craters. What had caused that? It must have been a brutal struggle to crawl this far into the machine. Why? He stood up, looking around. "Corwin, any idea why this guy crawled all the way back here instead of whacking the first wall he came to?"

The ghost shrugged. "Try turning off your flashlight. If the man saw something in the dark, perhaps you will, too."

Hamilton smiled. "That's why I only hire the smartest ghosts."

"I'm getting paid?"

Hamilton switched off his flashlight. About five feet beyond the damaged gear, he could make out a dim blue glow. He let his eyes adjust to the darkness. The glow was at the core of a web of glass and metal. Steel tubes led away from it to other parts of the machine. "Oh, that's not good."

"What?"

"It's probably the power source. My guess is that it's something with a half-life." He looked down at the corpse near him with the blistered face. "And without much shielding. We've got to get out of here." Unless the pendant could protect him from radiation, too, but he suspected not.

"Are these the riddles?" Corwin asked from behind him.

Hamilton glanced back at the opposite wall of the chamber where Corwin was hovering. A series of fifty disks were slotted into metal slots, a large disk above and smaller disk below. Hieroglyphs were written next to each one. "Could be. And these little marks look like they could be numbers." He pulled out a copper disk. It was covered with small Braille-like dimples. "If I just move the small disks over by two, it might be back in sync. For a number of years, anyway. Then, the sphinx can go back to...hmm. Eating people properly." He started moving all the smaller disks over two spaces in their slots, verifying from the numbering that he was shifting everything the right direction. He stepped back, pulled out his cell-phone, and took a dozen quick pictures of the hieroglyphs.

"What are you doing?" asked Corwin.

"I've got an idea. Help me find the freshest corpse in here."

"You have the only flashlight."

Hamilton took a breath and let it out slowly.

"Alright. Then take that riddle about 'reversal of fortune' up to the Oracle and ask her what it means. We, or rather I, still need to get out of here."

Corwin disappeared.

Hamilton rummaged through the pockets of the man with the pickaxe, finding a wallet with documents and currency nearly two hundred years old. He left the room and kept searching for the least mummified body. One of them seemed a bit less desiccated than the others, the dried rind of his eyes staring like little prunes from the sockets. He searched the man's pockets. A small hand-drawn map was in one pocket, along with a letter with an address and a postmark only fifty years old. A rope was tangled with one shoulder bone and a knife rested in a thin leather sheath. This might work, Hamilton thought. If the little map and rope were any indication, the man could have been a thief looking to plunder whatever tomb or treasure the sphinx guarded. If he could track down the guy's family, they'd probably be ecstatic to be handed the answer sheet for the sphinx's riddles. And after that, the sphinx wouldn't be guarding much of anything, would it? No more killing required.

Corwin hadn't come back yet. Hamilton sniffed at the air and grabbed at the nearest wall as dizziness turned the room around him. He shook his head and looked down at his pendant, realizing he didn't have a really good grasp on its limitations. Getting chomped on by a sphinx, no prob. Radiation poisoning and oxygen deprivation, not so sure. So, what did the riddle mean, 'reversal of fortune will come if you say it'? Well, literally, that would mean saying either 'it' or 'enutrof', wouldn't it? It couldn't be that simple, could it? Would he have to say it in Egyptian, or was the meaning adequate? Swaying in the toxic air, he shouted "Enutrof!"

A door suddenly appeared in the side of room. Of course. The designer of this space-time discontinuity would need some way of getting in and out during the design process. Or a way of sneaking out once he was disposed of by the pharaoh of that time, consumed by the very sphinx he created. It was curious that the door opened via a backwards English word, but it could be that the machine had somehow learned to ad-lib in new languages over the centuries, making it an even more amazing mechanical contrivance.

Perhaps the creator died of radiation poisoning afterward, but Hamilton guessed that anyone who could provide power for something as complicated as the Sphinx would have a pretty good understanding of radioactive materials, too.

He ran for the door and flung it open, finding that Prince Abdul and Lamatia were anxiously fretting in the storage room, Abdul wailing that the doctor had foolishly not heeded his warnings. Hamilton stepped out of the dark innards of the sphinx, switched off his flashlight, and closed the door, finding himself exiting at the rear end of the sphinx. *At least the designer had a sense of humor,* he thought. The seam around the perimeter of the door disappeared.

The sphinx was glaring down at him. Hamilton waved a hand dismissively. "Pfft. Easy riddle."

Lamatia ran up to the doctor, grabbing his sleeves with both hands. "You're alive!"

"So it seems. And prince, I believe your sphinx will be able to function normally, now." *And I'll be long dead by the time it trips up again.*

"My family gives you its undying gratitude. Sphinx, give me a riddle."

The sphinx duly delivered one of its riddles, and when directed by the prince, grudgingly provided the answer. Hamilton breathed a sign of relief; the answer made sense.

His gratitude won't last long, Hamilton thought. *Not when the thief's family gets the answer sheet to the riddles, unless he keeps his promise to keep the sphinx from eating anyone else. If the sphinx isn't guarding a vault, it won't need to eat anyone. And if it is guarding a vault and the prince lied, then he'll just be out a treasure when the next thief successfully answers all the riddles. One way or the other, he'll be keeping his promise. Either way, better for him than violating the hospital demon's contract.*

"It was a pleasure, Prince. Lamatia will see you to the receptionist." He bowed slightly as he shook the prince's hand, then left the room. Corwin suddenly appeared next to him. "I see you escaped without my help, after all."

"I figured out the riddle."

"Fortune, backwards? The Oracle did a web search and found the old riddle in about a minute."

Hamilton laughed. "Makes you wonder what good an Oracle is."

"Don't say that in front of her. She did say something about helping you track down the address in your pocket." He disappeared into the ceiling.

Medjine, at the receptionist's desk, held up a folder for him. "Doctor Hamilton, you have a new patient waiting for you in exam room 4."

"The fun never stops. What is it? Please tell me it's something I've seen before."

"A variable shapechanger, stuck in one shape," she said.

"Dare I ask?"

"Think of it as a surprise," she said, chuckling.

ABOUT THE AUTHOR

Tom Jolly's stories have previously appeared in Analog, Daily Science Fiction, Perihelion, Something Wicked, *and elsewhere. His website is silcom.com/~tomjolly/tomjolly2.htm.*

The Lady and the Unicorn

Terri Bruce

T he motorcycles thundered by, heading north to the annual Motorcycle Week rally in Laconia, a cavalcade of flashing chrome and dark leather in the bright June sunshine. Tam gripped the table's hard Formica edge as she leaned on it with one hand, the other holding aloft a coffee pot, to look out the diner's window. This was a large—and loud—pack, the pastoral small-town quiet rent by the blare of straight pipes. The shrieks and growls of the engines tore at her, and she wanted to clap her hands over her ears.

Ten.

Fifteen.

Twenty.

Twenty-five.

They flashed by in a seemingly endless parade, the noise drowning out everything else—the whisper of the trees outside, the crunch of tires on gravel as cars entered and exited the parking lot, the burble of conversation inside the diner, the sizzle of the grill where Marge, large and humorless, swiped back the iron grey hair from her eyes as she pressed every last inch of life from the burgers, and the rattle of silverware and plates dumped into a plastic tub by slim-as-a-boy Suzie, the sixteen-year-old busser.

The roar went on and on and on and just when Tam thought she would scream from the noise the last one rolled by.

And caboose, she thought, the Philip Booth poem inexplicably running through her head.

She turned away from the window with its frame of blue gingham curtains and found she was shaking. She tried to shrug off the nameless unease. Large groups of motorcycles were a common enough occurrence this time of year as hundreds of thousands of enthusiasts from all over thronged New Hampshire's roadways, streaming north to the rally. However, the tension was in the air, and now she had picked it up, too.

A loud crash sent Tam whipping around into a defensive stance, fists raised, knees soft, as her rudimentary mixed martial arts training kicked in.

Suzie had dropped a tub of dishes.

Across the diner, Jen, lifted green eyes tired beyond their twenty-nine years from an order pad and locked gazes with Tam. She was as white as one of the sheets of parchment paper they used to wrap to-go sandwiches.

The customers at the next table stared at Tam as if she'd sprouted a second head—she was, after all, standing in the middle of the diner absent-mindedly holding a coffee pot in the air. She smoothed down her apron and pasted back on the pert smile that made her face ache.

"Refill on the coffee?" she asked, hoisting the coffee pot higher.

Mutely, the couple shook their heads in unison.

She tucked a stray brown curl back behind her ear and hurried past rows of large, comfortable booths with their antiseptically white tables and faux-leather seats of cheery yellow as she headed to the kitchen to pull herself together.

The other women were there, a wall of wide-eyed stares that greeted Tam when she entered. A moment later Jen arrived, pale and trembling—as she had many times throughout the day. Tam frowned, unsure of the source of the anxiety. She didn't know these women well—she'd only started at the diner a month earlier when college classes had ended for the year—but their fear was palpable and it was catching. When Jen shook her head and the other women visibly relaxed, Tam found herself releasing the breath she'd inexplicably been holding.

A Fryolater timer went off and the women started. Lori, tall, blonde, and tan, laughed and the tension broke. Everyone scattered back to their stations. Lori's perfect, white teeth flashed in a grin and Suzie's humming hung in the air as they both disappeared through the door back to the dining room. Sizzling overrode the beeping as Marge leaned hard on the burgers.

"Get that, will ya?" Marge said as she rubbed a meaty paw across her glistening forehead.

Tam lurched to life. She yanked the basket out of the bubbling oil and hung it to drain. She tried to get hold of herself, to ignore whatever it was that was going on around her—it was nothing to do with her, after all. She crossed back into the dining room, intent on coffee and club sandwiches.

And then she heard it.

They all heard it.

Approaching engines that dulled not in Doppler but in the easing off of the gas as they coasted to a stop.

Tam looked around, feeling like a mouse caught in a trap. The frightened gazes of Lori and Jen looked back.

There was the sputter of engines cutting off and the squeak of kickstands and the creak of leather seats suddenly relieved of a heavy load. There were loud voices and boots on gravel.

The air in the diner grew thick with worry. Tam's pulse fluttered. She and the other staff drifted to the window one by one to stand shoulder-to-shoulder to gaze out at the men in the parking lot—diners, burgers, and Fryolators all forgotten.

FELL BEASTS AND FAIR

"What's wrong?" Tam asked, her voice hardly more than a whisper, first to the waitress on her right and then to the dishwasher to her left. Neither woman answered. "Are they *Hell's Angels* or something?" she asked a little more forcefully, though she scoffed at the idea that some outlaw biker gang was roaming the scenic byways of New Hampshire. The men were rough looking, to be sure—beefy and unkempt, the wiry bristles of their bushy beards disappearing into their jackets— but that didn't make them dangerous. She knew better than to buy into stereotypes. Most bikers were never any trouble, even if they did come pouring out of places with a certain rough, backwoods flavor, like Webster, Loudon, Henniker, and Northwood. They were mostly quiet men who just wanted to be left alone. They drank their coffee quickly and silently and paid their bill with no fuss. The rest were usually weekend warriors—reclaiming freedom and lost youth in the all too short breaks between their nine-to-five days. Heck, Tam's uncle rode a motorcycle, a bandana tied to his head and aviator shades covering his eyes, like he was Jack Nicholson in *Easy Rider*, and he was an accountant.

Still, a nameless fear prickled at the back of her neck.

"Worse," Marge 'The Barge', who'd marched out from the kitchen, answered in a flat voice, never taking her eyes from the bikers.

What could be worse than Hell's Angels? Tam wondered.

There was a silence, just long enough to be noticed, and then Marge said, "Unicorns."

Not joking. Not as an aside. Not apropos of anything. Just flat and monotone, as if providing some unfortunate but necessary news. *The car has a flat tire. It's going to rain tomorrow. There are bats nesting in the attic.*

Tam waited for the punch line to the joke, but it never came. In fact, Marge said nothing further.

Marge has lost her mind, Tam thought just as flatly and matter-of-factly as Marge had said the word "unicorns." *She's scared; so scared, in fact, that she's gone crazy.*

Tam had a sudden flashback to a junior high math class. Heather Baxton, a plain, solidly-built tom-boy with a physique for rugby, had, one day, inexplicably turned to Tam and stated in that same matter-of-fact tone that she was tired because she'd been up all night, waiting in the woods for a unicorn.

Tam had blinked in surprised confusion and returned no answer. Unicorns were not something she had ever thought much about, and she was unprepared for the sudden introduction of them into any conversation, let alone in math class of all places. Math and unicorns just didn't mix. Reality and unicorns didn't mix. Tom-boys built for rugby and unicorns didn't mix. Tam's brain had rebelled at all facets of the statement. It was odd enough that a girl of fourteen, long past the age of fairy tales, should believe in unicorns, and a little crazy that she would actually stay up all night waiting for one to appear to her as if they were real and there was any possibility that it might happen. Crazy as that all might be, it was outright insane that plain, solid, *staid* Heather Baxton, of all people, should believe one would come to *her*, of all people. Unicorns were for pretty, slim-waisted, sweet-faced storybook princesses with long, flowing hair and girls who liked glitter and high heels and things that sparkled and the aggressively pink artwork of Lisa Frank. Heather was neither.

Marge was still staring out the window, unblinking, transfixed by the bikers. A tremble of fear ran through Tam, chilling her worse than if she'd been locked in the big walk-in freezer. Marge's bizarre—no, strike that, absolutely nuts—statement frightened Tam as nothing else all day had—not the pack of burly bikers milling on the hard packed gravel of the parking lot, not the strange, unnerving fear and silence that had descended over the diner's staff, not the ritualized gathering at the window to stare out at the bikers as if they were the fabled Horseman of the Apocalypse. The most frightening part of the statement hadn't been the weirdness of it; no, the most frightening part was that Marge was serious. Marge, large and fearless, was going to pieces.

That morning's cup of coffee soured in Tam's stomach and threatened to come back up. She looked around for help—help making sense of Marge's words, help getting Marge to pull herself together, help in understanding what was happening. It was then that she noticed there weren't any men working in the diner. Not Matt the owner, not floppy-haired, pimple-faced Joe who was working two summer jobs to save up for his first car, not Joe-Joe, the silent and surly sixty-year-old busboy who was on work release as part of his probation.

Unease slithered down Tam's spine, replacing generalized dread with a warning bell of alarm. Where were all the guys? Why today, of all days, were none of them working? The motorcycle rally happened the same time every year. Motorcycle Weekend. Fourth of July fireworks. The State Fair on Labor Day Weekend. These were foundational events— fixed and unchanging—that meant big crowds, busy staff. The guys should be here today of all days, if for no other reason than the fact that the diner would be busier than usual. It was, after all, the first stop anyone coming east on 101 would make.

"Where are all the guys today? Why aren't they here?" Tam asked, starting to panic. Even Joe-Joe, who was always staring at her chest, would be a welcome sight at the moment.

"Men just make them worse," Leyla, the dishwasher, said softly. "It's up to a woman."

In response to Tam's questioning frown, Lori, who had gone pale despite her tan, nodded at the bikers. "Look," she said. "Really look."

Tam looked and she didn't have to ask what Lori meant. Outside, in the parking lot, the sun glinted off the wiry beards and bushy hair and leather jackets and chrome tailpipes and Tam could see the tossing heads and spiral horns and pawing hooves, flashing in and out of the sunlight. She gasped and clapped a hand to her mouth, terrified they'd hear, while her eyes strained and her brain spasmed as they tried to make sense of the impossible, crazy, unbelievable thing before her.

Unicorns weren't supposed to be like this. The fairytales her mother had read to her as a child described unicorns as delicate, slim-legged, graceful creatures of pure white, ethereal and fragile. However, Tam could see the evidence of this untruth with her own eyes. The unicorns were big and beefy and wild-eyed, more Clydesdale than Lusitano, but unlikely to be mistaken for horses anyway—they were too fierce, too feral, too ferocious for that.

The unicorns were whooping now, making as much noise as they could, and one leaped onto the hood of a nearby car, jumping up and down on it with unrestrained glee, while his fellows hooted and hollered and kicked up their hind legs, striking out at anything in their path.

Tam looked down the line of women, looking for fear that mirrored her own. There wasn't any. Instead, the anxiety that had been present all day had flattened and dulled into stoicism and resolve, the line of women transformed from a gaggle of weak and frightened girl-children to a line of warriors.

Without a word Marge grabbed the broom from Suzie's limp-wristed grip and, hollow-eyed and stiff-legged, headed out the door to the parking lot. By the time she reached the gang of bikers, she wielded the broom like a quarterstaff.

One of the unicorns stepped forward. The trees, the sun, the whirring, chirping insects that made the landscape so pastoral all faded away, leaving only the dark, sparkling glint of quartz-encrusted gravel and a ring of burly, frenzied spectators in Tam's view. The quarterstaff arced through the air as the unicorn lowered its head and charged. Marge wasn't fast, but she was strong and solid. The horn and the staff thudded against each other with a bone-jarring force so visceral that Tam could feel it vibrating down the length of her own arm.

The other unicorns gathered around the two combatants, fists pumping, hooves pawing, their shouts and squeals as deafening now as their tailpipes had been earlier. Tam gritted her teeth against the sound that grated its way down her spine like nails on a chalkboard.

Marge and the unicorn crashed together and then sprang apart, circling each other, thrusting and retreating, dodging and parrying, testing each other's strengths and weaknesses.

"What happens if she loses?" Tam asked breathlessly.

"It'll be a bad year," Jen said, in that way farmers talk about a killing frost or a drought or a hard winter. Dire. Calamitous. Heart-breaking.

Tam could well imagine what she meant. Seeing the unicorns so wild and lawless, she knew that unless they could be settled down, they'd run rampant over the countryside like an outlaw biker gang, wreaking mayhem wherever they went, until the winter snows drove them back into the forests.

"Why doesn't someone do something?" Tam asked wildly. "Shoot them or something?"

"Kill them?" Leyla echoed as if Tam were crazy. "They're unicorns." She said it not in a 'they're really tough to kill' kind of way but instead in a 'they're too special to kill.'

"They're kind of beautiful, in their own way," Suzie added wistfully, and Tam knew what she meant as she watched, mesmerized, the knife-like horn and flint-hard hooves jab at her friend.

"We just need to tame them a bit. Make them respect human settlements. They come out of the woods after the winter a bit wild." Jen turned away to fill a diner's coffee cup. Tam had forgotten the customers. She turned to survey the diner, expecting angry customers, wondering why all the wait-staff were gazing out the window. Instead, the diners calmly sipped their coffee and continued to eat, as if nothing strange was happening.

"Does she have to fight them all?" Tam asked turning back to the fight outside. The unicorn sliced the air a hair's breadth from Marge's face.

"No, just the leader. They're herd animals. They'll follow Marge and do what she says if she can subdue the leader."

"What do you mean, 'subdue'?" she asked.

The unicorns could never be tamed, that much was abundantly apparent to Tam. In the stories, only a woman could capture a unicorn, never a man, and a woman's power over the unicorn lay in her softness, her gentleness, her biddable nature. Only the purest, sweetest, most innocent of young maidens could attract and capture a unicorn, her docility luring it to place its head in her lap so she could take hold of its horn. This, however, like the slim legs and white coat, seemed to be utter crap.

Parry, dodge, thrust, retreat.

The unicorn and Marge clashed together over and over as Tam watched balanced on the knife-edge between fear and fascination. The unicorn wasn't going to bow down to sweetness; strength is what it would respect. Not raw, brute power—it would never allow itself to be dominated—but strength, which was something different altogether—as she was just now realizing as she watched Marge match the unicorn blow for blow.

The unicorn reared, towering over Marge, its hooves mere inches from her head, and pawed the air. The women gave a collective gasp. Marge held her ground. Tam's heart leapt into her throat, and she pressed the heel of her hand to her mouth to keep from crying out.

The quarterstaff swept in under the unicorn's pawing hooves, thudding into its unprotected mid-section with an audible crack so loud Tam swore the windows rattled. The unicorn screeched in pain and fell heavily to all fours and then crumpled forward on its front knees. The throng surrounding the combatants grew silent. Marge lowered her arms, letting the tip of the broom rest against the ground. The unicorn raised its head, and Tam saw what Marge did not: defiance flashing in its eyes. Too late, Marge tried to raise her arms, but the horn was already plunging deep in her belly.

There was a collective gasp from the women and then a sickening silence. Marge knelt on the ground, her hand pressed to her guts as the unicorn towered over her, triumphant.

"Someone go!" Jen shouted. "Before they get away!"

"Screw them!" Tam cried, horrified at Jen's callousness. "What about Marge?"

And eight pairs of eyes answered the question: *what happens if she loses?*

Dire. Calamitous. Heart-breaking.

Things started to go a bit fuzzy and Tam's legs were about to give out as she bit her palm to keep the sobs at bay, but it was going to be okay because tall, blonde, and good-in-a-crisis Lori had pulled out a cell phone and was dialing 911, and then it wasn't so okay after all because beanpole Suzie was saying, "Tam knows martial arts" and eight pair of eyes had swiveled back to Tam again.

"Mixed martial arts," Tam corrected reflexively, nearly babbling. "I'm not very good. I'm just a beginner. It's a beginner class."

Eight pairs of eyes stared back, expectantly.

Time stopped. In the parking lot, Marge held her guts in with one hand, the blood seeping between her fingers, life ebbing away in rhythm to the ticking of the clock above their heads, while the unicorns squealed and pawed and shouted and thumped each other on the back.

Tam's eyes met the anxious yet steady gaze of the other women and something sparked between them, strength telegraphing across the cheery yellow faux-leather seats and white Formica tabletops. *This is a ritual, a sacred duty*, the women's eyes said. *We are the guardians of something great and terrible. And you're a part of that now.*

Tam's thudding heart beat slowed until it, too, matched the ticking of the clock. Everything beat in rhythm. Slowly, Tam nodded. She was a part of it. Or perhaps more true to say it was a part of her.

She turned and headed for the door, and time was moving again, only it wasn't really, and she was in the world, but she was out of it, now, too.

She pushed the door open, the bell above it jangling merrily, and stepped out into the bright June sunshine.

The unicorns stood before her, snorting, pawing, belching, scratching, and at last, Tam understood why it had been—why it had had to be—staid, stolid, built-for-Rugby Heather Baxton, of all people, who had waited for a unicorn in the woods all those years ago.

Tam raised her fists.

ABOUT THE AUTHOR

Terri Bruce has been making up adventure stories for as long as she can remember and won her first writing award when she was twelve. Like Anne Shirley, she prefers to make people cry rather than laugh, but is happy if she can do either. She produces fantasy and adventure stories from a haunted house in New England where she lives with her husband and three cats. Her website is terribruce.net.

Like Sand in Your Teeth

April Steenburgh

The first time I saw the boy I laughed. There is nothing elegant about hiking pants up past knees in order to scrabble around in the sand and surf on gangly limbs. His skin was browned, legs obviously used to being exposed to the sun. The look of concentration on his young face, furrowed forehead and intent eyes all crinkled at the corners, was endearing enough that I did not continue to snicker. I floated out past the break of the waves, head just above water, and watched as he scavenged for things I could not fathom. There was no food to be found where he searched and scrounged, no treasure I could remember being buried. I had no idea what he could possibly be doing, bouncing around the shore like a willet.

I have always been cursed with far more than my share of curiosity. I rode a wave in, slipping out of my skin after being deposited gently on shore and stood, hands crossed behind my back in an imitation of posture I had observed over the years, and leaned close. "What are you looking for?"

I gave him a bit of a fright, stepping up to look over his shoulder without any prior announcement of my presence. After he recovered from his half-choked shout and clumsy leap to the side, his eyebrows drew tight over his forehead as he took a look, and then did his very best to look anywhere but my direction.

"Who are you? What are you doing? Where..." He gestured at me, a flush rising to his cheeks to color them as if they had been kissed by the sun.

"I couldn't very well swim in my clothing, now could I? I left it on the beach." It was not a lie—my sealskin was settled neatly between some stones a few paces down the shore. "My name is Coira. What are you looking for? Can I help?"

He frowned, ever so slightly, but his stiff and startled posture eased a bit as he fixed his gaze over my left shoulder. "I am looking for shells."

Shells. Of all the little, silly things in the sea. Of course he was looking for shells. He had a few settled in a piece of cloth he held out for me to see, posture losing some of its stiff embarrassment as his attention focused on his collection. Some colorful, some bearing the marks of rough treatment, all meticulously selected as no two were the same. This was a fair place for shells. He knew his task well.

"I am Dylan." He offered me his name with the same stoic dignity with which he chose to ignore my nudity. "I suppose you could help."

"I am very good at finding shells." I smiled, but stopped short of showing teeth. No need to scare him off.

It was enjoyable, mucking around in the sand, skipping past waves as they came pounding down around us, hauling the tide in as time passed. Dylan relaxed a bit as we worked. I took credit for that, as I am more than a fair singer and added my own tune to the symphony of wind and wave and gull as his shell collection grew.

The tide was fully in when Dylan drew back from the water, let his pants down in relatively dry safety, and tilted his head as he regarded me. His eyes were very green, like the eel grass that danced sinuously with the current. "I am going to go home now."

"I should as well."

I will never tire of it, the way shock twists and tickles through human expressions. I took far too much delight in the way Dylan gasped, almost dropping his shells, as I retrieved my sealskin, wrapped it about myself, and slipped back into the sea. Dylan took a few steps towards the surf, curiosity blooming where surprise had been only heartbeats earlier. It had been a fun game, playing at being a human girl, learning the nuances of *excited* and *interested*, enjoying the company of someone too young to worry about strangers on the shore and the dangers they could present. I was dangerous—all selkies were—and he had caught my attention with his smile.

I did not expect to see him again the following day, walking that same bit of shoreline as if the tide had left him there, gathering shells as before but this time casting regular glances out towards the sea, his forehead furrowed with what might have been consternation, might have been determination. He returned again the day after, his game of gathering shells obviously disrupted by wondering whether I was there, watching from just beyond the breaking waves. It was one thing to tease and taunt a human, quite another to appear after revealing my nature. I have seen too many of my sisters taken as seal wives—their skins snatched and hidden, binding them to the shore as they slowly pined. I had no desire to suffer that unsavory fate.

"Coira?"

He called my name every now and then, inquiry pulling the vowels long and high. It was unsettling, his persistence, and I dove down deep in response, where the wind and his voice could not reach me.

But I always came back. Drawn to the shoreline and the boy, and then young man, who walked along it. I don't know how long we played this game of staying just out of reach, he and I—time is strange to those of us who have no use for aging. One day I noticed he was taller, broader in the chest, face darkened with a splotchy start of a beard, voice deeper and stronger—no longer my little shell-waif, and lovely.

And not alone. I did not like the fact he brought another male to our beach. It felt like a breach of some unspoken contract. It was a danger for a selkie maid, being outnumbered by human males. He should have known that. He must have known that.

I suppose I should not have chosen to ignore him for as long as I had, granting only a flash of my spotted skin or splash of my departure. I could not blame him, but I did.

I came out of the surf and arranged myself atop the rocks where I liked to set my sealskin, sprawled so that the sun caught the pale skin of my long legs, of back and breast. I smiled the way seal maidens do when they want to lure a lover into the surf. A smile filled with the knowledge only one of us would return to the surface. I wanted this strange male gone, wanted his hair to tangle with the plants on the deep sea bed as they danced. He saw me. How could he not? And he started to come to me. It was how this scene always played out. I raised a hand, beckoning, fixed him with the full power of my attention.

"Coira?" Dylan's voice ruined it, the abrasive curl of betrayal in each syllable urged my shoulders to hunch defensively. I bared my teeth, showing every sharp edge my enticing smile had concealed. They cut through glamour as well as flesh and the stranger stumbled back, face a tangle of confusion and fear.

I just wanted them off my shore, if it was no longer to be a thing Dylan and I shared between us, if Dylan wasn't mine.

"Coira... please. This is my brother Benneit. I wanted him to see you, to meet you." Dylan's voice grew quiet. "To see why I come here day after day."

"Why do you?" My voice was hard as old, dead coral, tone just as sharp. I had my sealskin secure in one fist, should I need—no, want—to leave.

"To see you. I keep hoping you will come ashore to look for shells with me. To walk with me." His voice was quiet, uncertain, nothing like the blunt child I had been so enamored of. But it slipped through my fury, warming my desire to remain hard and cold.

"We are fickle, those who are fey. You should not wait on us."

"But he did." Benneit interrupted, with a voice rough as the tides, but so quiet.

My hand convulsed around my sealskin, reflexively making sure it was still there. Human male. Thief. Prey. Dylan's kin. I flashed my teeth again, covering my confusion with ferocity. "I did not ask him to."

"You did not send him away."

Introspection does not come naturally to a selkie. I did not like this, did not like Benneit. He stirred up the waters until they were too murky to make sense of. Of course I did not send Dylan away. The quiet song of his voice when he thought no one was listening, the way he stepped just so as he moved across the beach, the wind-teased mess of his hair brushing a muscular back—these things caught my attention. Held it. I did not want him to go away, to turn his bright eyes elsewhere. "I want him here." It was an unwelcome admission, one that made me vulnerable. I did not want to be vulnerable, especially in front of Benneit, a stranger. I started to pull my sealskin over me, covering as if I were cold.

"I do not want your skin, selkie. I wanted to meet the seal maiden my stubborn brother has been so excited about." Benneit stood very close to Dylan a moment, speaking quietly, and then slowly began to walk away.

"Coira, may I come sit with you?"

This was all backwards. I should not be the one nodding slowly, as if enthralled, and watching every step he took to get to my side. I should not notice how the muscles in his calves worked with every step though wet sand, the way his toes flattened and grasped for purchase. I should not be dreaming of the touch of his skin, the patches that promised to be warm as they were a sun-touched red.

He should be dreaming of me.

Perhaps he had been. He lowered himself to sit with a caution that spoke of discomfort, a bit of nervousness. I could clearly see the way his pulse pressed against the skin of his throat now that he was beside me, the way his jaw clenched and worked with nerves. He was brave, my shell-waif. Brave and perhaps just as stubborn as me. I wanted to run sharp teeth along that stretch of skin at his throat, feel his pulse quicken.

Instinct can be hard to manage, especially when the warm human smells of sweat, grass and dirt tickled at me with every breath. He gasped slightly, delightfully, as I nipped at his neck, ran my cheek along the curve of his chin. He tasted of things I had no name for—I only knew they fascinated and excited me. So different from the sea.

"Coira?" His voice was a rumbling vibration against my cheek as I pressed it against his. There was a note, the way he turned my name up at the end with inquiry, which pleased me.

"Hello," I murmured, greeting him as I had not before. "Hello, Dylan."

I wanted to touch him, taste him, keep him. But I did not want to drag him into the depths, wrapped in my embrace, did not want to steal his last breath or dine on his flesh. Possessive, yes, but not in a way I had wanted to possess a human before. I rolled the realization around in my mouth, getting a sense of the sandy grit of it, trying to get the taste of it, the taste of him. I pulled back from him. "What do you want?"

"What?" He seemed startled, awkwardly unfamiliar with the question.

"What do you want? Why do you come here, reliably as the tides? Why do you risk bringing your kin to me?"

"I wanted to see you again. I want to see you again." He was not struggling against me, even with my sharp angles and sharp teeth visible, so close. "I wanted to talk with you, get to know you."

"I am here." He did not fear me. It pulled my mouth into a wide smile. "I gathered treasure for you." I pulled him to his feet, my sealskin falling forgotten from my lap to lay atop the rocks we had been sitting on. "Come. Come with me."

Those were not words uttered by a selkie that humans generally survive. But he came with me without hesitation, curiosity instead of trepidation in his eyes.

I set a fierce pace and we ran down the beach, leaving behind widely spaced tracks for the waves to sweep out of existence. We startled some gulls as I pulled him up to the small cave I had found years ago, splashing in and out during high tide, slipping in dry during low. The tide was coming high now and there was no avoiding dampening his pants as I coaxed him to duck through the low entrance.

The rocky shoreline held many such secret places close— this was the first I had shared. It was not a large cave, but we could stand without brushing against the ceiling. It was not deep enough to swallow its contents in gloom, and I could step back enough to watch Dylan take it in. He brushed a finger against the ancient barnacle shells on his left, wriggled his toes in a patch of optimistic sea vegetation, and then drop both hands to hang limp at his sides in surprise as he finally looked forward.

Shells. I had been gathering them for him through the years, pulled from the deep places where they rested quietly. I had polished fan mussels until they gleamed, piled periwinkles, constructed a collection of whelks beside a stack of cockles. All for the boy who had been collecting what the sea left behind.

Dylan turned towards me, eyes wide. "Coira...?"

"For you."

His lips were rough as he leaned in, textured in a way that was new to me—dried out by sun and wind. They tasted ever so slightly of salt, just before they parted and his tongue touched mine. Then he tasted like nothing I had ever experienced before. And was warm, so very warm. Everything about this human was warm. He had pulled the chill from my bones, from my magic, years ago. And I was just now noticing.

I had expected Dylan to take shells home with him, and he did—but it was such a select few. I could not understand his fascination with leaving the bulk of them in the cave, but I was pleased as he puttered about in the salty dimness, holding a shielded lantern up to this and that, to examine them better without moving them out into the sun. I offered to help him carry them, as I assumed there were simply too many for him to move alone.

He rounded on me, fierce as I had never seen him before, and I took a breath to appreciate the adult my shell-waif had grown into. There were lines to his face that had been previously obscured by smiles and wanting, a tightening of the lips that pulled them thin and stern. There were new angles to his cheekbones and chin to be enthralled by, a sharpness to his beautiful eyes that caught my attention. "No. These are ours. They stay here." And so they did. Who was I to try and combat Dylan's ferocity? Shells were settled and rearranged to meet Dylan's mysterious standards. Not since I had been a pup drifting and playing in the tides had I taken orders from anyone, but I was developing a taste for the steel in Dylan's voice and face as he directed me to and fro, arms full of oceanic treasures.

He kissed me before he left that evening, eyes warm with something not quite gratitude. Something far more tangled, entangling. He nipped lightly at my lower lip, wanting to make a mark, make a point, to claim. There was definitely a bit of bite to my mortal. I brushed a hand through his tangled hair, breathing deeply to catch as much of him as I could before he was gone. I was not content with our parting, wanting him to come with me. Wanting to follow him. But his death lay in my embrace in the sea, and mine would follow me up that shoreline unless I surrendered my sealskin.

My sealskin.

I raced back to the rocks by the surf where my skin lay crumpled but unfound. My magic and my freedom. I could not give it to him. I would make a feral, terrible seal wife.

I wrapped it tight around me, slipped back into the sea and down deep. To chase tiny silver fish through long branching vegetation and skeletal coral. To clear my mind.

My family waited, flashes of speckled sealskin through the forest of lazily waving sea vegetation. I tried not to meet their eyes, eyes that had gone hard with disgust and distrust. My brothers bumped against me, accusing. My sisters slid across my skin, trying to wipe the scent of the shore and of Dylan off of me. Humans were for liaisons, languid slips into the deep. They were not to be returned to.

Accusations are thick to swim through, so I turned from my family and slipped off into the dark waters.

I was already remembering how Dylan tasted. The scent of him.

His voice called me up each day, summoning me from wherever the sea had taken me the night before. I always came ashore a woman, and slipped my sealskin some place safe when I felt he was not looking. It was not that I was afraid he would steal it, bind me. Not Dylan. Each day I hid it to fend off a twisty desire to hand it to him and let him pull me to his home.

I learned the curve of his neck, the feel of his pulse, the little sounds he made when surprised and especially pleased. I traced the back of his knees, learning that he was ticklish and enjoying how he twisted like a caught fish when I touched him there. I learned the strength of his arms when he tired of tickles and moved to gain the upper hand. I learned that he was warm in every way I could make the word be. His eyes were deep with it, his voice rich with it, his body infused with it. And I craved it. Craved him. They said selkies were the dangerous ones—Dylan's warmth was far more treacherous.

I learned that Benneit had a quick sense of humor, visible even as it took his eyes some time to soften to me, to trust me. I cannot blame him—selkies are not known for being safe and staid. The ocean is a lively mistress, and her children are adept at shifting to meet the demands of her tides. He was a sailor, one of the men who clambered and shouted as they rode the waves, and they knew the dangers of the watery fey. But he was kind, and he loved his brother very much. Their affection danced through their smiles as they chattered, in the jokes and verbal jabs they launched at each other with a warrior's precision. Slowly, that affection extended like a warm blanket to engulf me as well.

I ignored my family where they floated just past the break of the waves, as they sunned on quiet beaches or dove to hunt and play. I was not interested in sitting with my sisters and brushing my hair out in the moonlight. I pulled no mortal victims down with me, beneath the waves. I was a selkie tamed, and I was doing my best to ignore that fact.

"Benneit is off to sea."

We were laying on our backs on the beach, letting the morning sun dry the sweat from our skin.

"Oh?" I rolled over, pillowed my head on his chest to better listen to the beat of his heart, noting it was quick, unsteady, and not from my attentions.

"He left with some other men from the village. They are going to work the fish run." His hand raised to draw fingers through my hair, rub against my scalp. "I always worry when he is at sea."

"I am of the sea—and I would not harm him. He will return to you, safe and smiling." His fingers were brushing across my forehead, soothing and distracting. Beneath my ear his heart had slowed a bit, but I could still taste his unease in the air. I wanted him happy, my warm human.

I pulled myself up and over Dylan, pressed my nose to his before nipping at it lightly. "I will watch over him." I kissed him, all tooth and tongue and pressure. I set my promise deep into Dylan, marking him to show my sincerity, caressing him to express affection and something uncomfortably close to love. We broke patterns and rules, my Dylan and I. We disrupted the established order of things just as soundly as we disturbed the sand beneath us.

He gave me a necklace before he left, as the sun was creeping towards the horizon. Carefully strung together, bits of shell and stone. This is what he did with the treasures he gathered, had been gathering since he was small and wandered onto my beach. Dylan slipped it over my head and I smiled before curling my sealskin close. I stayed for a moment, not slipping back into the sea as swiftly as I had in the past. Dylan knelt down close and ran a hand across my head, brushed against the jewelry still secure around my seal-form's neck. Nothing was said, but I could taste *goodbye*, harsh as I inhaled.

I nudged against him, once, and then slipped into the surf, following the sloping sand out until I could dive deep.

I knew next to nothing about ships and sailing, but fish runs were familiar. I followed warm currents and flashes of scale until I met up with sprawling schools of fish darting and feeding. Breaking the surface with a huff I glanced about.

There, past a pair of resting pelicans, a small group of boats bobbed atop the water. I could just make out bits of speech, the splashes of their work. There I would find Benneit. I startled the pelicans with a happy little bark before starting to swim.

The sea was thick with my family as I grew close to the working ships. They filled the sea with their displeasure, disgust, until even the fish sensed it and started to flee. An elder brother hit me as I swam, the impact of his larger body against mine knocking me to the side.

Why? Pleading, confused.

You are of the sea. It was a snarl, a shout, and my family battered me with their bodies and their magic, keeping me from my beloved Dylan's kin.

I felt it rising, the storm that was my brothers' fury. I felt the magic seethe up from the depths, pulling unpredictable currents and impossible waves in its wake. I could sense it spiraling through the sky, stringing together clouds. I struggled against my family as I felt the storm break all around me.

The creak and moan of ships breaking apart filled my ears, and I was not sure who my family was punishing—their errant daughter or the human that had tamed me.

They left me to flounder and recover in the storm—humans had been thrown to the sea, their point had been made. Not a sympathetic eye was to be found amidst my siblings and cousins, not a friendly brush of fin or head. I was left to pull myself together as best I could, and to follow like a good daughter. A good selkie.

I pulled myself together, and swam towards the wreckage.

Never had I directly opposed my family so. I dove again and again, trying to find Benneit amidst the seething and unsettled water. I wriggled as well as I could through crest and froth, making progress where things not fey would surely be swamped. A bit of red caught my eye—Benneit's fox hair limp against his face as he clung desperately to a small bit of board, all that remained of the ship I had felt, heard, splinter and start to sink.

He was so pale, so cold, and barely breathing. I had no way of pulling him to shore—there was not enough strength left to me. My family had made sure of that. I was not sure he would have had the capacity to cling to a seal even if I had the strength to ferry him to safety.

Dylan loved him so.

It seemed I was going to give him my sealskin to keep after all. I removed it, gasping briefly at the sensation of arms and legs in the angry waters, missing webbing and insulating fur. I had to be quick—swimming like this was not natural, not easy. I curled my sealskin around Benneit's cold, still form, wrapping him in magic freely given, giving him my seal shape. A seal slipped awkwardly off the bit of wood he had been clinging to and stared at me with wide dark eyes. I wanted to laugh, tried to, but choked on water as a wave hit me in the face. I scrabbled onto the wood Benneit had so recently abandoned.

So strange—fingers and toes and skin in the ocean. I hated the feel of water in my ears. I hated how very cold I was becoming. I hated feeling helpless.

Selkie-Benneit nudged me with his nose, eyes a mix of concern and confusion. "It's okay." I coughed to try and clear water out of places I did not think it had any business being. "Be safe. Go home. Go to Dylan."

It was very cold in the ocean without a sealskin. And I was very tired. I had given away my magic. I thought of Dylan's warm eyes as I closed my own.

I did not expect to wake up, but when I did it was with a choking cough that turned inappropriately quickly into a rough laugh. Dylan was asleep beside me, head pillowed on his arms as he rested up against the bed.

Bed. Dry and warm and still. This was very new, and I was still too raw to sort out whether or not I was interested and excited about new sensations.

"Coira?"

My waking, barking laugh, and slight shift had woken Dylan, and he rubbed at his eyes as he spoke my name.

I suppose I was still Coira, but the name curled differently through my ears now, carried a different meaning. Coira the girl. Coira without magic to let her sink beneath the sea as safely as a babe curling into its mother's arms. Coira who had passed on her freedom. The realization, in the quiet that follows decisions made amidst conflict and confusion, was like sand in my teeth. Abrasive, bitter—I could not work through each individual granule, they were all too adept at getting into and under my skin.

"Hey, Coira. Talk to me." Dylan wrapped his arms around me as if trying to hold me together, hold me in. "Benneit brought you. He told me."

He smelled the same, dirt and dust and human sweat, a hint of something fresh from the oven. His voice was warm, heavy with concern and something close to that human entanglement known as love.

He was my selkie lord, beckoning me to come to him, to turn from everything I knew. I had been beaten at my own game. He was warm, and pressed tight against me so I could feel his breath, hear the rhythm of his heart.

"Thank you, Coira. Thank you for my brother."

That was not what I wanted to be thanked for, all things considered. I wanted to be thanked for not-so-soft kisses and little piles of gathered treasure. I wanted to be thanked for crooked smiles and runs across the beaches laughing in the moonlight. I did not want to be thanked for being human.

"Will you stay?" There was a note of nervousness amidst Dylan's relieved gratitude, as if he still expected me, at any time, to try and slip away to somewhere he could not follow. Cautious with his hope—something I had taught him along the way, buried amidst the laughing and the loving.

"Yes." My voice was rough, all of its pleasantness burned away by the ocean. Of course I would stay. How could I not? I had been mesmerized by this man since he showed me a handful of sea shells, so long ago. This thing we had, it had grown from whimsical interest into something I had no power to control.

We would learn secrets, Benneit and I. He would learn just what hid down in the darkest parts of the ocean, would learn how a seal laughed and how it felt to coax a pretty lass out into the waves. He would learn the art of slipping his skin into hidden places when he wanted to curl his arms around his brother in a hug. I would learn how Dylan looked on horseback, how dirt felt beneath my feet and what grass smelled like when it was rolled in. I would learn what to do with burning, abrasive love, to become familiar with the way it felt, like I had a mouthful of sand the first time I tried to shape the word with my voice.

"I will stay."

⫸◦〰◦⫷

ABOUT THE AUTHOR

April Steenburgh is an author and freelance eBook formatter living in the Finger Lakes Region of New York. She shares her small homestead with a lively band of animals and a very understanding husband. Her stories appear in The Modern Fae's Guide to Surviving Humanity *and* Were-, *and she edited the anthologies* Fight Like a Girl *and* What Follows. *When not writing, she can be found working as a librarian at a local community college. Online, you can find April at https://aprilsteenburgh.com/.*

WHEN GRACIE'S FATHER FOUGHT

ANTHONY EICHENLAUB

That baby girl wasn't mine, and I knew it soon as I saw her pale skin, luminescent green eyes, and seaweed hair.

My wife, Anna, looked up at me, sweaty from the effort of childbirth. "Don't you say one word, Walter." The little girl latched onto her breast.

I didn't say a word. What was there to say? A shoe factory worker like me didn't have much place to complain about a kid that wasn't his. My high school championship wrestling trophy wasn't doing me many favors ten years out. It made sense that she'd been with another guy. Lucky she came back to me at all.

Anna glowed with that little baby clutched to her breast. There's a certain shine a woman gets after childbirth. Dark bags hung under bright, luminescent eyes.

"Grace," Anna said. "Grace Nicole Jones."

I stroked the little girl's seaweed hair. Gracie was beautiful.

Sure, I was upset. What decent man wouldn't be? But Gracie was as good a daughter as I could ever expect to have. Did it matter who the father really was?

I swore then that I wouldn't say one word about it. Not ever.

I nearly said a word.

Three months of Gracie crying, fussing, and not a bit of sleep wore at my nerves. Anna stopped breastfeeding when the baby's wicked sharp tooth cut her a bloody mess.

An old trail ran from our house along the banks of the Mississippi. Anna said there was magic there. Sometimes she took Gracie down there. Once, she took me.

Gracie's seaweed green hair had faded to a golden blonde. The green only showed as a wispy halo of emerald in the sunrise or sunset. Her green eyes still sparkled. Skin, pale at birth, had transformed to a nearly translucent white. She was like a porcelain doll when she held still. Not that she did. Stay still. Ever.

Gracie fussed in that special place, so I picked her up out of her stroller and carried her. Anna was to go back to work the next day. We needed the money. Anna would work third shift at the casino, so that we could avoid having to pay much for daycare. I wanted to assure Anna that her baby was in good hands.

"I love you like my own," I said as I patted Gracie's back.

Anna scowled. "Don't you say that," she said. "Not now, not ever."

Frustrated, I sputtered. then did what I always did—I shut up. That evening, Anna was cold to me. Colder than she'd ever been.

Gracie was a brilliant, beautiful two-year-old girl. She never really learned to sleep through the night, transitioning from midnight feedings to regular night terrors. Her teeth came in all sharp, but straight, and her green eyes glowed in the moonlight.

I'd wrestle with her every day. Getting an elbow lock on me thrilled her every time. She'd giggle and laugh. Anna would frown and shake her head.

Gracie and I were home together when she fell down the steps in front of our house. She cried and cried. The little girl didn't know many words, but "ow" and "hurts" were two of them, and she used them plenty.

But she cried so much. It tore my heart out to hear her cry so hard. She wouldn't listen to my voice. That was the first time I noticed how she wouldn't look me in the eyes.

"I love you, Gracie," I said. "It's going to be okay."

It wasn't okay. When Anna arrived home that night she blamed me for what happened. She didn't say it, but it was in her eyes when she glared down at me.

"We need to take her to the hospital," Anna said.

Her arm needed a cast. As she healed, Gracie would shoot distrustful looks my direction. It pierced my heart, seeing in her in pain, but seeing her distrust was far worse. Anna wasn't much better. It seemed neither of them were going to give me much respect. So I got a dog.

After that Gracie would never make eye contact. It was hard for me to remember if she had ever done it before.

By the time she was four, Gracie's doctors were using words like "autism spectrum" and "attention deficit." All I knew was that Gracie was more difficult than any other kid I knew. She had a rigid adherence to strange rules that only she understood.

Rufus, my dog, took a liking to the girl. He was a Lab mix, and his energy was nearly enough to keep up with her.

One psychiatrist went on and on about obsessive behavior being a sign for autism. "Your daughter certainly loves fish," the doctor said. "This is just one sign."

Gracie loved eating fish, catching fish, drawing fish, sculpting fish. She drew the most beautiful fish using all sixty-four crayons from her box, and I only wish it hadn't been on the dining room wall.

She would sit still with a fishing rod in her hands for hours. How could this girl have attention deficit problems? Any time either of us caught a fish she talked to it, called it beautiful, and asked it where it had been and what it had seen. She learned from them about the man under the water.

"Who is the man under the water?" she asked me.

I didn't have an answer for her.

She loved eating the fish she caught, though it's not good to always eat fish from the mighty Mississippi. When I explained how dirty the river was, she looked very sad and thoughtful.

"But why?" she asked.

Again, I had no answer.

Once, when we fished the Mississippi near Anna's magical place, the water went placid, despite a stiff wind. The area around our boat became like a mirror, reflecting the bluffs.

Gracie leaned over the edge. She smiled. Waved. By the time I got up next to her, the stillness had dissipated.

"What did you see?" I asked.

She smiled. "It was the man under the water. He waved at me."

Gracie's first day of Kindergarten did not go well. Halfway through the day I got a call and had to leave the factory.

"She bit one of the other students," said the principal. "We don't stand for that behavior here." Her voice was stern, as if she were scolding me for the transgression. As if I should have raised a better little girl who wouldn't do such things.

Gracie grinned sheepishly from her seat across the room. Her smile was jagged with her wicked teeth. I wondered if her behavior was due to her real father or just some aspect of being a little girl who didn't fit in. I still didn't say a word.

The principal sighed. "She can come back tomorrow, but I think it's best if you take her home today."

It wasn't best, but I didn't argue. I wondered if Gracie had drawn blood with those teeth of hers. Probably.

Missing work was bad, but they could afford to go without me for the afternoon. Explaining to my boss would be easy, but having to explain to Anna terrified me.

Gracie spent the rest of the day wrestling playfully with Rufus, and I spent that night curled up on the sofa, head in my hands. Weeping.

It was Valentine's Day and Gracie was eight.

Used to be that Anna and I didn't involve ourselves in traditional Valentine's Day gift-giving. For that day, and every day, she would have my love. My whole self. Everything and all of it.

That year I only gave Anna flowers. I was too exhausted to give anything else. Anna smiled sadly at the arrangement of lavender and roses as she placed them near the window.

When I looked later, they were in the garbage.

I asked Gracie why they were there.

"They're not good flowers," she said. "They're stinky."

I sighed. Gracie's rules, again. It wasn't an allergy, but rather a sensitivity to certain smells. Lavender was, apparently, offensive.

She stuck out her chin, her whole body tense and ready for a fight. I didn't give it to her. Rescuing the flowers wouldn't make anything better.

She was ten when I said those words.

Gracie was terrible at school. She barely tolerated it. Most days went without injury, but even the special arrangements we had for her didn't alleviate her wild nature. Every day could be the day they finally kicked her out. The day something happened that made them give up.

But I would never give up. How stubborn I had become.

Then, one day, she wanted to participate in the Science Fair. She came up with her own project, varying how she fed some otherwise identical fish and measuring their outcomes in size and color.

Anna didn't help at all. Due to her working second shift, I hardly ever saw her. Even on weekends we were like passing barges. This had gone on for years, so it hardly seemed strange. It almost didn't seem bad.

The experiment worked perfectly. Gracie worked so hard on it. It wasn't the prettiest project, but her numbers were good.

It was fine.

I was so proud.

On the way to the Science Fair, Gracie sat quietly with the folded project board on her lap. She had pulled her blonde hair back into a long braid and she had long ago learned to smile with her mouth shut. The girl almost looked normal.

"Are you excited?" I asked.

She didn't respond for a long time, and I wondered if she heard.

"No," she said.

Gracie was an honest girl.

Soon after we set up her display, the boy assigned to the next spot set up his. His experiment involved watering mint plants with various substances.

Gracie reacted the second he came close. He lined up his tiny flowerpots, each with a fresh, abhorrent plant. She shook her head, silent at first.

"It's okay, Gracie." I put my hands on her shoulders to steady her. I tried to meet her eyes, but she wouldn't do it. "I'll talk to the people in charge. We'll move our display."

"No, no, no." She vigorously shook her head. "Move him."

"I'll see what I can do." I gave an apologetic look to the boy's mother. I wished so much that Anna had come. But, no, I could leave Gracie for a few minutes, couldn't I?

It took time to track down someone in charge, and the results were less than helpful. No, we couldn't move. Why would anyone want to move? Her voice said, "I'm afraid I can't change the rules." Her eyes said, "That's not a good reason, and you're a bad parent for asking."

But Gracie's special, I wanted to say. *She's different! She's not like the other kids and she's so smart and wonderful and you'll never get it because you only see me as a bad parent and her as a bad kid.*

I didn't say those things. I should have.

Gracie shoved the boy, her face red with anger. I pulled her off. Tried to help pick up the project. Gracie flailed, out of control. Without a word, I hauled her out of the fair and to the car. Some random parent trailed behind us with her project. I don't even know who it was.

It mortified me. Ashamed me. Devastated me.

Anna woke when we burst into the house. Gracie went to the back yard and started tearing apart her project in a fit of rage.

"Oh," Anna said. Nothing more.

"What?" I snapped. "What could I do? I didn't see you helping and she sure tried her best."

Outside, the red-faced little girl cried huge tears and tore her cardboard in half. She ripped at it with her pointy teeth. Rufus watched from a safe distance.

Anna said nothing.

I slumped, energy gone out of me. "I wonder sometimes if she gets this from her real father."

Gracie's shouts ceased. Had she heard? No, she wasn't in the back yard anymore.

She was gone.

Anna broke into tears. "No," she sobbed. "You said it. I told you not to." She thumped her fists into my chest. "Why? I thought you understood."

Then, I knew then what I had done. The unspoken thing between us shattered. A weight lifted.

My little girl was gone.

Anna touched my shoulder, as if she didn't know how to comfort someone in so much pain. I buried my face in my hands. Sitting next to me, she pulled me close.

"Why?" I asked.

After a time, Anna answered. "I was so lonely back then. He was there. He came from the river. He said if we ever spoke of it, she would go live with her true father."

"He said it, so that makes it true?"

"He's magical, Walter." She put a hand up to stop me from commenting. "He lives in the river. It's his river."

"And now he has our daughter."

"There's nothing we can do. She's *his* daughter."

But I was done doing nothing.

Anna followed me to that magic place on the shore of the Mississippi. The melting ice was open, and a ripple of waves lapped at slush.

I felt a sealed plastic bag from my pocket. I must have pocketed it at the Science Fair. It contained a few sprigs of mint. "She probably gets her dislike of this plant from her father. I'll cram it down his throat."

Anna blinked. "Give that to me."

I did.

"If you have it," she said, "Gracie won't come to you. I'll hold it. She wouldn't come to me, anyway."

"This is what you've always done, isn't it?" I asked her as we walked down to the shore. "You kept me from saying anything by driving me away."

She didn't answer.

As the sun peeked over the treetops of the Wisconsin shore, the river became unnaturally calm.

"Walter," she said. There was fear in her voice. "What do we do? What if he won't come out?"

"I don't know," I said. Then, shouted, "Gracie!"

A minute passed, with nothing to show for my hollering. The river sat eerily calm, and the man; Anna's lover; didn't emerge.

"This is the place?" I asked.

Anna nodded.

"All right, then."

I shed off my coat; threw my hat and gloves to the ground. My boots I kept until the mirror water lapped at my toes. Then, I slipped out of those, too.

Maybe if Gracie had been an easy kid, I wouldn't have done it. If every day hadn't been an exhausting struggle for sanity, maybe I'd have let her live with her father. As the water numbed my toes, I realized that this was the first time I had fought for her, but I had *always* fought for her.

I was her father.

The cold of just-melted river is not the cold of ice. It did not bite like ice—it penetrated. The frigid grip sank so deep, so fast that I stumbled as muscles seized.

But I kept going.

"I'm coming for her," I shouted to the river. "I'm her father, and I'm taking my daughter back."

The slope was steep. My legs sank deep into the muck. Breath burst from my lungs as my middle went under. I stopped. Pulled in another breath. Went under.

Time did not pass in such cold.

A fish passed in front of me, silver and quick. A Northern. Its emerald eyes flashed. It swam around me, nipped at my face.

Green rays streaked through the ice, giving everything a dull glow. Mud sucked at my feet as I struggled forward. My arms—sluggish and slow—propelled me forward.

Then, he appeared out of the murky depths.

His seaweed hair drifted around his sleek body. His eyes were piercing green, sharp, even through the blur of murky waters. The man was muscled. Strong. He was fast. Much faster than me.

I could not speak to him, but he knew what I wanted.

The fish swam between us, then the man and I wrestled. Our arms locked. He was strong and lean, but I had weight.

Not that weight would do me much good underwater.

I ceded his strength, sank low and twisted to gut-wrench him. He slipped loose, avoiding an elbow lock. We separated.

He looked at me, his green eyes dancing across me, sizing me up. My lungs tore at my chest. I needed a home run move.

I would get my daughter back or I would die trying.

We closed again. His hands shot through the water almost faster than I could see, but I grabbed a wrist. He snapped with sharp teeth, but I was too quick. We parted.

Again, we locked together. My fingers, stiff from cold, barely held as he squirmed and fought, but I had him. I twisted his arm and locked his elbow.

Our eyes met. The green in his eyes flashed anger. Frustration. Hatred. Fear.

Then, he stopped. He looked away.

I let go, and the man under the water swam away, defeated.

My vision darkened, and the cold took me. Air bubbled from my lungs.

Slender arms wrapped around my body and clutched me tight. The last thing I remember was Anna coming to meet us in the water. They pulled me out.

Gracie and I still fish the Mississippi. Whenever we do, the man under the water greets us. He never tries to take Gracie. He knows who her true father is.

So do we.

ABOUT THE AUTHOR

Anthony Eichenlaub's short fiction has appeared in Kzine, Asymmetry Fiction, *and* Kobold Quarterly. *He has two novels in the Metal and Men series, and he spends his time in Rochester,*

Minnesota, teaching writing classes and gardening. His website is anthonyeichenlaub.com.

AFTERWORD

Thank you for reading! We hope noblebright fantasy has captured your imagination as it has ours. You can find more noblebright fantasy at springsongpress.com and at noblebright.org.

C. J. Brightley
Spring Song Press